IRON

(Book 1 of the Kalima Chronicles)

By Aiki Flinthart

2018

To all the creative people out there, ignore the inner doubt-ridden voices. Do what you love and do it to the best of your ability. Then it's always good enough. You're always good enough.

Thank you to the readers who loved the 80AD series enough to let me know. Because of you, I kept writing and didn't give up.
And...as always...thanks to my husband for his patience and encouragement.

IRON

Cover artwork by Croco Design

Copyright © 2015 (2018 2nd Edition) Aiki Flinthart

A Cataloging-in-Publications entry for this title is available from the National Library of Australia.

ISBN-13: 978-0-6482878-6-5 (Trade Paperback)
ISBN-13: 978-0-6482878-5-8 (e-book)
Computing Advantages & Training P/L
PO Box 3388, Darra
QLD 4076, Australia

Discover other titles by Aiki Flinthart
at: **www.aikiflinthart.com**
Including:

The Ruadhan Sidhe Novels (YA Urban Fantasy)
Shadows Wake (#1)
Shadows Bane (#2)
Shadows Fate (#3)

The 80AD series (YA Adventure/Fantasy)
80AD Book 1: *The Jewel of Asgard*
80AD Book 2: *The Hammer of Thor*
80AD Book 3: *The Tekhen of Anuket*
80AD Book 4: *The Sudarshana*
80AD Book 5: *The Yu Dragon*

The Kalima Chronicles (YA Adventure/Fantasy)
IRON (#1)
FIRE (#2)
STEEL (#3)

Sold! (Contemporary Romance/Adventure)

Short Story Anthologies
Return
Like a Woman

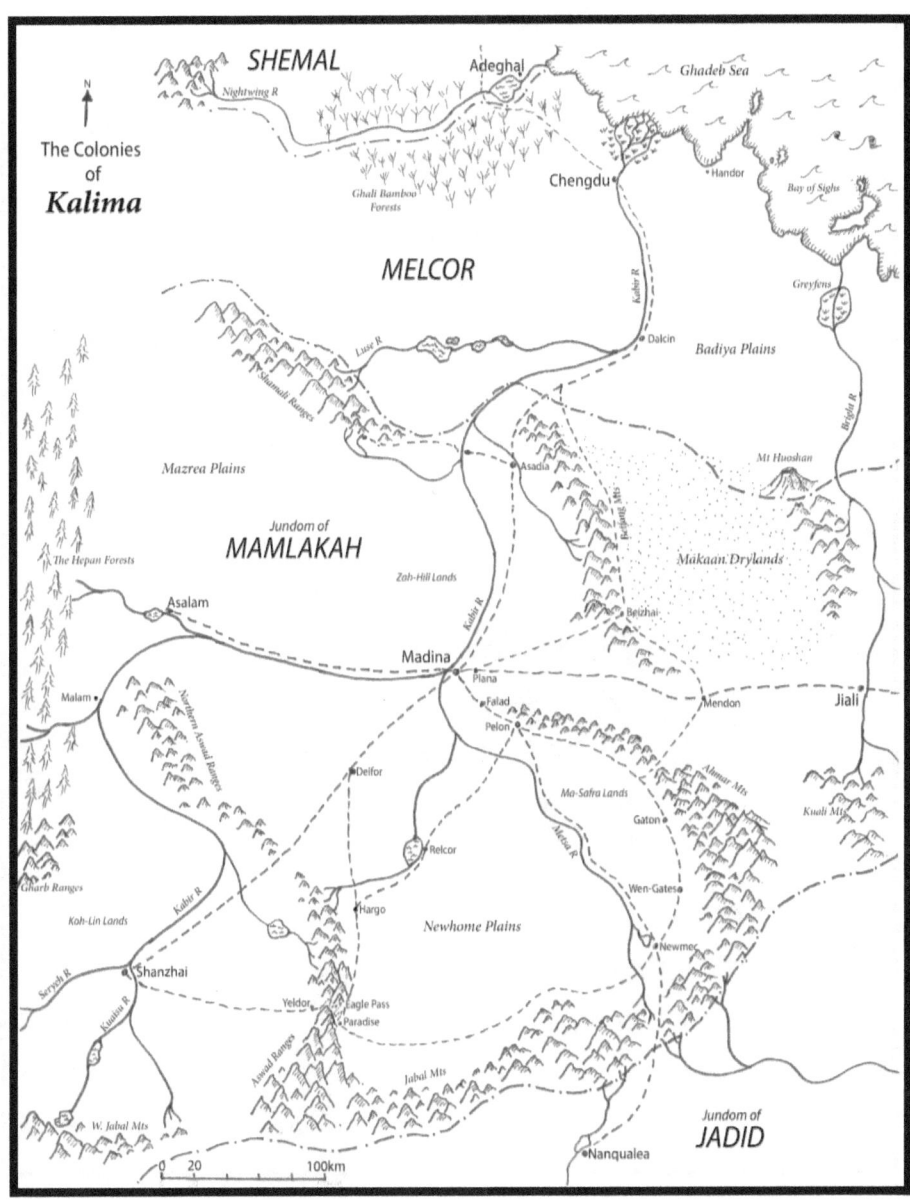

The Colonies
of
Kalima

SHEMAL

Nightwing R

Adeghal

Ghadeb Sea

Ghali Bamboo
Forests

Chengdu

Handor

Bay of Sighs

MELCOR

Kahir R

Dakin

Badiya Plains

Greyfens

Luse R

Sharmali Ranges

Mazrea Plains

Asadia

Mt Huashan

Bejuni Mts

Brjela R

Jundom of
MAMLAKAH

The Hepan Forests

Zah-Hili Lands

Makaan Drylands

Asalam

Kahir R

Beizhai

Madina

Plana

Malam

Northern Aswad Ranges

Falad

Pelon

Mendon

Jiali

Delfor

Ma-Safra Lands

Ahmar Mts

Gaton

Kuali Mts

Relcor

Mesa R

Wen-Gates

Gharb Ranges

Hargo

Newhome Plains

Newmer

Koh-Lin Lands

Kahir R

Serugh R

Kunina R

Shanzhai

Yeldor

Eagle Pass

Paradise

Aswad Ranges

Jabal Mts

Jundom of
JADID

W. Jabal Mts

Nanqualea

0   20   100km

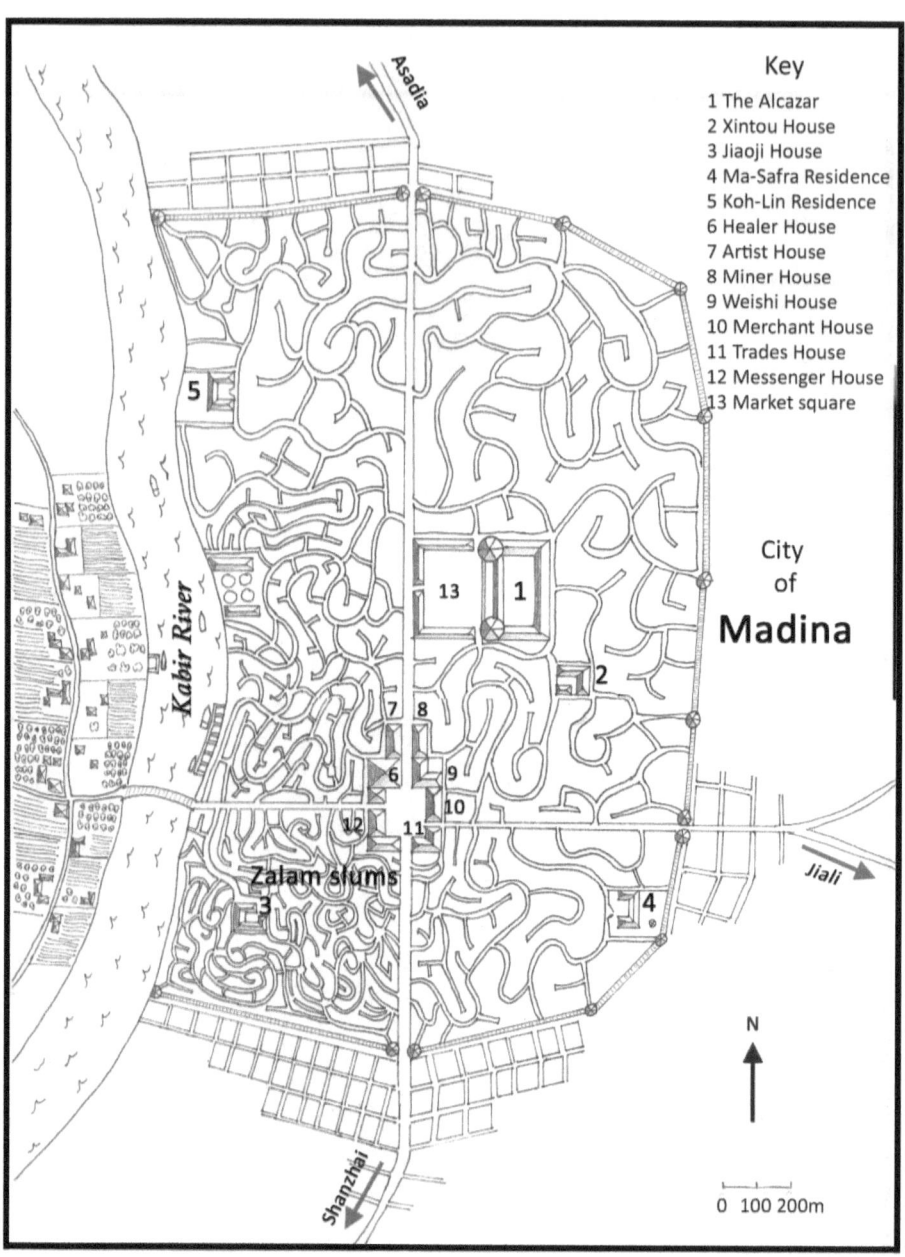

Key

1 The Alcazar
2 Xintou House
3 Jiaoji House
4 Ma-Safra Residence
5 Koh-Lin Residence
6 Healer House
7 Artist House
8 Miner House
9 Weishi House
10 Merchant House
11 Trades House
12 Messenger House
13 Market square

City
of
Madina

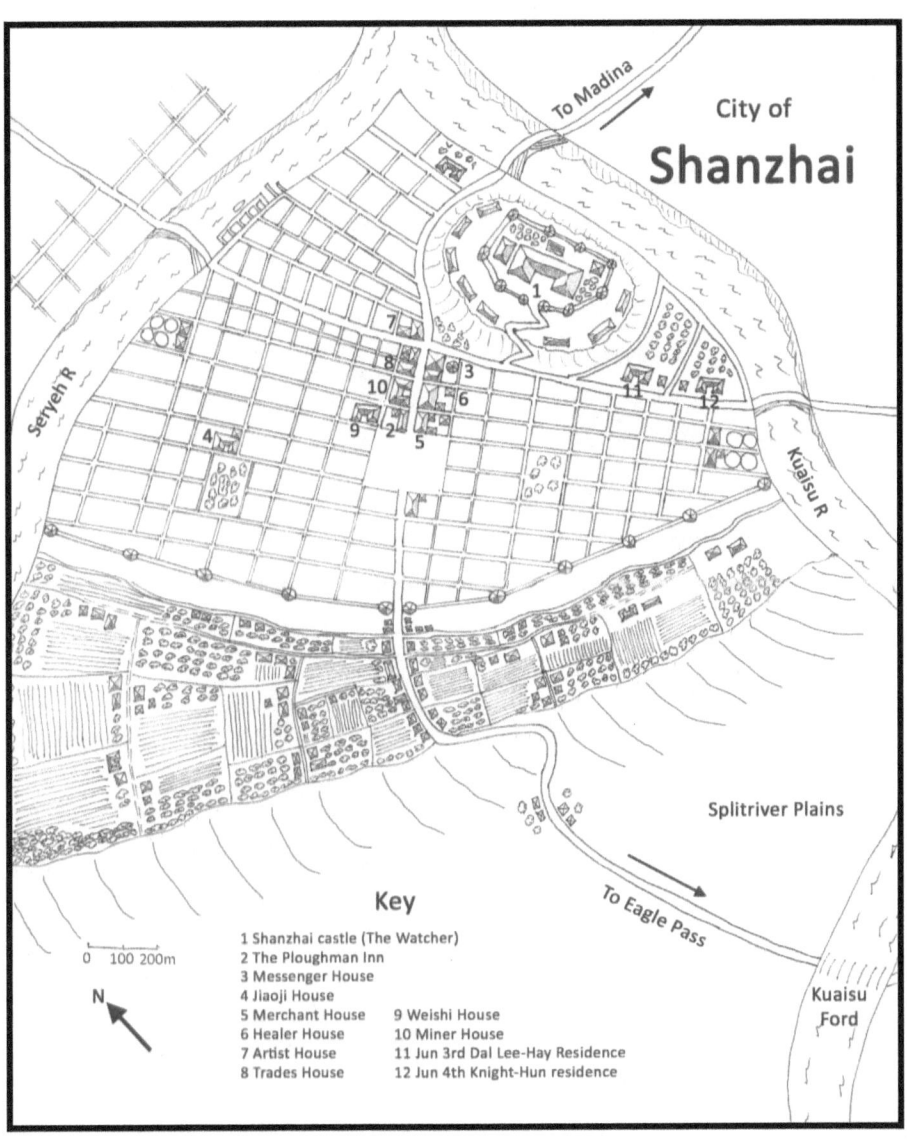

City of

Shanzhai

To Madina

Serveh R

Kuaisu R

Splitriver Plains

To Eagle Pass

Kuaisu Ford

Key

0 100 200m

N

1 Shanzhai castle (The Watcher)
2 The Ploughman Inn
3 Messenger House
4 Jiaoji House
5 Merchant House   9 Weishi House
6 Healer House   10 Miner House
7 Artist House   11 Jun 3rd Dal Lee-Hay Residence
8 Trades House   12 Jun 4th Knight-Hun residence

IRON

Aiki Flinthart 2018

Part I

CHAPTER ONE

ALERE

Freedom, however imaginary and brief, should be savoured.

Alere danced a few steps along the cobbles. Each moment in the blood-orange sunlight was a gift to be treasured; hoarded against days to come. She raised her face to the warmth. But the veil, though it softened the grey cityscape into dusty shades of gold, clouded her vision; a cage and a reminder. She shoved the gossamer silk up onto her forehead. Then, with arms flung wide, she embraced the jewel-mirage of free will; perfect and unattainable as a yanstone. The long sleeves of her gold silk Xintou-House robe fluttered like a jin-bird's wing.

She smiled and strolled on through the Zalam slums of Madina. Her steps slowed, even though she was already late returning to

Xintou House. With the veil lifted, reality's sharp edges cut into her pleasant delusion.

Overhead, drunken houses – held up by washing lines and hope – crowded the narrow street and threw shadows the colour of day-old bruises. Mud and dung mired her embroidered shoes, and it took effort to ignore the stench of rotting food and human waste. A small child, filthy hands upraised in supplication, watched with hollow eyes as Alere and her weishi-guards passed.

Alere hesitated, but her purse was empty and the child was one of thousands in the slums these days. Regretfully, she turned aside and concentrated on the sky, visible as fragments of pale peridot between the uneven rooftops. The people here were poor, but they were also free to choose their own path. She envied them that. Tomorrow she would lose even this small independence of walking home from Jiaoji House. For now—

She bumped into Kett's back and the illusion shattered, as it had to.

'What is it?' Alere peered around him.

Ahead, five people had someone cornered in the mouth of an alley that reeked of urine and vomit. Coarse laughter rattled off the surrounding patchwork of violet bamboo and mudbrick walls. Window shutters closed as tenants hid from the future.

'Looks like another brawl,' Kett said. 'Blocking our route back to Xintou House. And before you ask, no, you can't help.'

With work and food scarcer every day, fights were rife in the Zalam. Annoyingly, Kett never interfered lest his actions endanger Alere.

'Fine. We can try a different way.' Alere pointed over her shoulder. 'This place is a maze. I've never been down that street two blocks back. Could be interesting.'

'Interesting is what I'm trying to avoid,' Kett replied. 'Which would be easier if you didn't insist on coming this way every week.' He continued to frown at the group ahead. 'But there's something…'

What made him hesitate? Kett was the senior weishi-bodyguard of Xintou House, calm and fearful of nothing. Were there threats he'd seen and she'd missed? The motley assemblage blocking the path was nothing unusual: four men and a woman, all in shabby versions of various trades-House uniforms. They clustered around a figure curled on the cobbles. Nearby, the bodies of three Madina city junren-guards lay sprawled on the road, their black and gold uniforms spattered with blood. The junren must have been protecting someone important for they usually avoided the Zalam.

The biggest of the five aggressors, a blond xiao-bear of a man, drew a dagger and prodded the figure huddled at his feet. His companions egged him on. Their victim whimpered.

Alere bared her teeth; half a grin, half a grimace of anticipation. This was her last day. Her last chance. Kett had to allow her some experience. She pushed past him, one hand on her short-sword.

'I said no, Shunu Alere.' Kett gripped her shoulder.

She glared at him. 'And I told you not to call me that. I don't deserve the title.'

Kett's grey eyes gleamed with amusement. 'Take it up with Mistress Li. She pays my wages.' He nodded towards the altercation ahead. 'Remember your training? Observe first, act second.'

Alere tried to shake free, but his fingers bit deep into her shoulder. She didn't protest, though she rarely allowed such familiarity. But Kett was her personal weishi, shifu-master, and friend. He had earned the right. He gestured to Bren and Tamir, and the two black-uniformed weishi boxed Alere in. She fumed in silence.

Kett paid no attention so she let irritation slide away.

'Please, don't,' sobbed a female voice.

Kett stiffened and released Alere's shoulder. His hand dropped to his sword. He scanned the surrounding buildings.

'Now?' Alere slid her ceramic blade from its sheath. 'It's a woman, Kett. A healer, I think. Looks like a grey robe she's wearing. We have to help. It's the weishi credo to protect those in need. There's only five of them and four of us.'

'*I* have to help. You're not weishi. It could be a trap. You keep giving money away every time we pass through. People notice.'

'It's the only thing I can do. You won't let me fight. I've trained for ten years, Kett. I'll just—'

'Killing those who prey on the weaker isn't always the answer.'

'This, from you?' She lifted her brows. 'After all those talks about how wrong the kin-child murders were? How much the junren who carried out those orders deserve to die?'

'That's different,' he replied, his eyes narrowing. 'These men are just desperate, they're not choosing to act on orders they know are wrong. Besides, your training was for self-defence, not murder. And you're due at the Alcazar tomorrow. Mistress Li would have my head if something happened to you.'

'*We're* due at the Alcazar, you mean.'

Kett said nothing, only continued to watch the alley.

'Besides,' Alere muttered, 'I'd be better off dead than in the Alcazar as jiaoji to the Jun.'

'You don't mean that. Stay here.' Kett swept a swift look around. 'They've killed three city junren. It's not safe.'

'But you said the city guard's hiring complete shazis these days. I can—'

'You'll stay here with Tamir.' His face was stone; an expression she knew well. She glowered, but sheathed her sword with a snap of ceramic against wood. At this rate she'd never get to test her skills in a real fight.

'And cover your face,' he added.

She yanked the gold veil down and scraped long strands of dark hair back out of the way. Kett didn't normally object to her lifting it. He knew Alere felt like a fraud wearing the veil. But he was right: the scrap of silk was a symbol of Xintou House and should provide some protection in this neighbourhood.

Kett and Bren drew their weapons and strode into the alley. Carmine afternoon light glinted bloody off Kett's steel sword blade. The weapon attracted furtive stares from onlookers scurrying past. Unlike Bren's ceramic blade, steel swords were rare; worth more than a year's wages.

Alere held her breath, waiting for her weishi to engage. It wasn't often she got to see Kett in action.

One of the thugs yelled a warning and turned. He stabbed a bronze dagger at Kett, who struck it aside. Steel cleaved the soft metal in half. Kett's blade continued its arc and sliced through brown leather, into a thin chest. The tradesman slumped to the ground. Bren lunged and skewered a man wearing tattered merchant-green. Blood dripped from the protruding tip of his blade. Alere resisted the urge to shout encouragement, lest she distract her weishi.

The female in the group screamed a curse and slashed a chipped ceramic knife at Kett's head. Kett caught the strike with his dagger. The clash of ceramic split the cool air. The woman struck again. Kett sidestepped and thrust his blade into her chest. Her shriek lanced through the scuff of Kett's boots and Bren's grunt of effort.

Only two men still stood against them. The giant blond bared yellowed teeth and snarled something in old Mandrin. Alere caught only *selb* and *erheyi*. The words meant nothing to her, but Bren paled. Kett replied in the same tongue, low and calm, too quiet for Alere to hear. She frowned, straining to catch their interchange.

'Farran.' The blond grinned at his companion, a stocky bald man in grey, and switched to the common tongue. 'Seems these weishi are interfering in our business.' He spat into the dirt at Kett's feet.

'Finish it, Dennat.' Farran wiped a hand over his sweat-slicked pate. 'We've got no time for this.'

Dennat chortled. His teeth showed brown, darkened by chewing the narcotic blackweed favoured in the Zalam slums. 'But these Xintou House tunnel-pigs think they have us beat.'

'Then they'd be wrong.' Farran yanked their female captive off the ground and held a bronze knife to her throat.

Kett raised his dagger-hand, palm out. 'She's a healer. Are you mad? Let her go.'

'Interfere again and she's a dead healer.' Farran backed away and dug the knife point into the woman's honey skin. Blood trickled down her neck and stained scarlet the high collar of her grey and white healer's robe.

Alere peered closer. A fluttering white veil hid the upper half of the healer's face. But something about the sharp jawline and the shape of her full lips seemed familiar. The only healers Alere knew were two dignified old men who attended her House-sisters.

The woman whimpered. Her nails tore at Farran's arm, leaving long, red welts.

'Stop it, chouhuo,' he snarled, laying the blade along her cheek. 'Slavers won't pay as much if you're cut up.'

Alere growled and gripped the hilt of her weapon. This had gone too far.

Kett took a half-step forward, bloody sword raised.

'Don't do it, weishi.' Farran slipped the dagger under the healer's collar and slit open her robe to the shoulder. A thin line of blood welled on her skin. Farran's fingers whitened on her arm and the girl's cry of pain became a sob.

'Please!' She gasped as Farran pressed the knife edge to her throat again.

Kett shifted his feet, hands flexing on dagger and sword.

Alere half-drew her blade.

A footfall scuffed on the cobbles behind her.

'Shunu Alere! Watch—' Tamir yelped.

Alere spun, weapon drawn, slicing before she knew why. Her blade clashed with another. The sharp clang of ceramic on bronze ricocheted in the street's narrow confines. A sixth man had snuck up from behind. He struck again, a vicious overhead blow. Alere froze, her mind numb. Her arms hung heavy and limp at her sides.

The bronze edge cut at her head in slow motion. She watched, detached as her arm jerked up reflexively. But the sword-grip felt clumsy and thick in her hand. She forced her feet to move though she couldn't feel the ground. Her blade caught his and she spun aside. Her attacker stumbled past. Alere sucked quick, panting breaths and faced him.

He ran at her again, at full speed, his lips twisting into a snarl as he swung the sword. Alere deflected. She struck at his stomach; thrust the blade deep into flesh until it jarred on bone. His mouth and eyes widened in a silent scream. With shaking hands, Alere yanked the sword free. He collapsed, twitching, movements slowing as he scrabbled on the stones.

Blood roared in her ears. Alere gritted her teeth against an urge to throw up. There was no time for that. Where was Tamir? She turned. Tamir lay huddled on the ground, curled into the foetal position.

An arm snaked around her throat. She drove an elbow backwards. A hand seized hers and wrenched the sword loose. The world faded to sepia. Alere gasped for air and clawed at the forearm across her neck. Seven seconds. Kett's teaching rang in her head. She had seven seconds before unconsciousness. Panic swelled from high in her chest, strangling thought. Three seconds. No! The blind urge to scream and lash out in panic lodged in her throat. She quelled it and dug her thumb into his elbow pressure-point.

The choke relaxed and blood rushed back to her brain. She jabbed an elbow into her assailant's ribs. He grunted, but instead of loosening, his grip tightened again. A knifeblade touched her throat.

'Now, shunu,' a gravelly voice muttered in her ear, 'you and me are gonna have a chat with your weishi friends.' The sick stench of rotten teeth and jiu-alcohol made her gag. How had she let yet another of these hmari scum sneak up on her?

Her captor half-dragged her to the alley where Kett and Bren still faced off against the men holding the healer.

'Alere!' Kett took a half-step but stopped when Alere's captor dug the knife in, under her jaw.

Pain sleeted across her skin and she sucked a quick breath. With her head tilted back she could barely keep balance, let alone free herself. Anger flared, deep in her stomach. She was better than this.

Farran, still holding the healer, chortled. 'Nicely done, Yeno. Well, we've got a fine haul for the slavers today, don't we lads?'

'Let them go,' Kett growled.

With a cool smile for Kett, Farran studied Alere. 'No mind-tricks, xintou? Seen you come this way before, throwing coin around like it'll fix what ails people. You got no idea what we need, chouhuo. Didn't think you were a real gold-robe, either. Seems I was right, huh? High and mighty xintou'd never come here. Well, that'll change soon.' He jerked his head at Yeno. 'Take 'em to the docks and put 'em on the ship to Melcor. Dennat and I'll take care of these weishi and join you later.'

'No!' The healer struggled in his arms. 'No, don't. You can't take her. Please. Let them all go and I'll come with you peacefully, I promise.'

'Awww,' Farran said, 'how gouri noble. Sorry, girlie. Slaves are valuable and a few less weishi's a good thing. And I fancy that steel sword.'

'Shunu Alere?' Kett's attention was fixed on Farran.

Alere tensed. The wrong choice would end everything. But did it matter? Her life was worthless, no longer her own. And life in the Alcazar was little more than slavery, anyway: duty-bound, without choices. The blade dug deeper into her skin. Warm liquid trickled down her chest.

But at least, in the Alcazar, there was a chance of freedom – once her duty was complete. And the healer woman deserved better than slavery, too. Alere shifted her feet, trying to get better purchase on the blood-slippery cobbles.

'Don't do anything stupid, little shunu,' Yeno whispered in her ear.

Fury blossomed, obliterating despair.

'Do it, Kett,' she commanded.

CHAPTER TWO

Kett leapt. He grabbed Farran's dagger and wrenched it away from the healer's throat. Bren sliced open Dennat's neck in one stroke. Alere seized Yeno's hand and twisted it away from her collar. His wrist dislocated in a series of sickening pops. She smashed her elbow into his cheekbone. Something crunched. Perfect. Yeno screamed and staggered backwards, clutching his face. The bronze knife dropped to the cobbles, clanging a death-knell. Alere snatched up the dagger and rounded on her attacker with rage in her heart. She shortened her arm for the strike.

A length of steel stabbed through Yeno's barrel chest from behind. Alere jumped back and choked off a cry. Yeno gaped at the red-slicked sword. The blade vanished. He crumpled at her feet, eyes rolling into his head. Blood flowered across his shirt.

Kett flicked gore from his steel and scanned the surrounds. Scarlet drops glistened on the cobbles and spattered Alere's robe. Only Bren, the healer, Alere, and Kett remained alive. The whole fight had taken less than five minutes but it felt like an hour. Her memory of the action was blurred and warped as though seen through the bottom of a dirty glass.

'Bren,' Kett said, 'check for survivors.'

The ground steadied beneath Alere's feet and she followed Bren's movements, morbidly fascinated. Asu-flies already buzzed around the bodies sprawled on the ground. The skinny beggar-child Alere had seen before scurried from the doorway and rummaged through the corpses' pockets. The healer-woman lay crumpled on the cobbles, sobbing. Alere looked away lest the woman's distress eat into her own artificial calm.

'You alright?' Kett pointed at Alere's neck.

She touched her skin and her fingers came away bloodstained. Was she alright? She opened her mouth to deny it, but the calm expectation in Kett's eyes silenced her. Instead, she nodded, swallowing down fear and adrenalin. The bronze dagger lay heavy in her hand. She hurled it aside.

Behind her, Tamir groaned. 'Master Kett.'

'Tamir...' she managed.

'You see to him,' Kett said. 'I'll help Bren make sure the rest of these lowlife hmari are not a threat, and check the city guardsmen.' Kett strode away, stained sword ready in his hand.

Tamir lay on the road, curled around an oozing wound in his side. Gasping pleas for help stretched his mouth wide and his life snaked away, crimson, between the cobblestones. Alere gathered her wits. Tamir needed her and focusing on him gave her purpose. She pushed the gold veil up so she could see clearly. With fingers made clumsy by fear, she tore two long strips from her under-robe, folded one and used the other to tie it in place against the ugly wound.

'Don't you die on me, Tamir. Kett would never forgive us. Besides, you and Kett are supposed to escort me to the Alcazar tomorrow. Not going to let me down, are you?'

'No, Shunu Alere,' he whispered. His head sagged to one side, eyes closed.

'Tamir?' She slapped his cheek lightly. He couldn't die. Kett had made her responsible. 'Stay awake. That's an order. Kett?'

In the alley, Bren helped the healer rise, his arm around her waist. The girl buried her face in his neck. Kett broke away from them and strode to Alere's side. He pulled the gold veil down to cover her eyes again. Alere was too rattled to object. The veils should have made her, and the healer, both, unassailable. The telepaths of Xintou House and the healers of Healer House were revered throughout the land.

'Tamir is...' She waved a helpless hand. She should have been watching for threats with him, not focussing on Kett and Bren.

'We need to get him back to Xintou House.' Kett's voice was strained.

'No. Healer House is closer.' The healer stepped away from Bren. She smoothed the front of her stained robe with trembling hands. She crouched beside Tamir, lifted the reddened bandage and inspected his wound. Then she turned to the man Alere had stabbed. 'This one lives, too. Bring both to the Master surgeons in Healer House. Quickly.' She pointed up the street. 'It's only three blocks away.'

'Him?' Alere scowled. 'He tried to kill me.'

'Healer House is for everyone.' There was no mistaking the gentle rebuke in the healer's tone. 'Do you want his death on your conscience? Look. He's just a child.'

Alere tried to ignore the lurch in her stomach at the sight of the ragged hole in the boy's body. He was scrawny and young; dressed in patched rags, his skin filthy and darkened by old bruises. Hardly a worthy opponent. Kett was right: the healer's attackers were just as desperate as anyone else in the Zalam slums. Alere turned away, sickened by her handiwork.

'Master Kett.' Bren knelt beside Tamir. 'Tamir's unconscious. There's so much blood. He'll—'

Kett waved Bren to silence. Doubt clouded Kett's eyes as he glanced first at Tamir, then back and forth between the healer and Alere. He ran a hand over his head, smoothing a stray dark hair back into the mawei tied low at his collar. His gaze lingered on the healer.

'Very well.' Kett crouched and, with a grunt of effort, scooped Tamir into his arms. Tamir's blood smeared on his hands. Kett nodded to the healer. 'Lead us. Your name?'

'Mina,' she replied.

'Why did they attack you?' Kett frowned at her exposed shoulder. 'Did they hurt you before we arrived?'

Mina clutched together the torn pieces of her dress. A flush crept up her slender neck. Below the white veil, her lips pressed together. 'They didn't hurt me. They wanted the city junren who escorted me.' She glanced at the bodies lying in the alley and shivered. 'They called themselves the *selb*. Said something about the city junren persecuting them. I think I just got in the way.'

'You were brave,' Kett replied. 'You're safe now. Lead us, please.'

'The House is this way.' She flushed and pointed.

Bren gathered the injured boy into his arms.

'Shunu.' Kett jerked his chin at Alere. 'You next, where I can keep an eye on you. Keep that blade sheathed. I'll have enough explanations to make to the city guard Shangwei as it is. Bren,' he called. 'When we get to Healer House, report to the city guardhouse. Advise the Shangwei what's happened. Then go to Xintou House and bring two men to escort Shunu Alere home. And send a message to Weishi House-Master Anh. He can advise Tamir's family. I'll wait to hear about Tamir.'

'Bai, shifu,' Bren acknowledged.

'Don't you think we should—' Alere began, but the look in Kett's eye stopped the hot words on her tongue. She'd never seen him so troubled. If only she possessed the telepathic skills the Xintou House veil implied and could read his Outer thoughts. He switched his gaze back to Mina and the tension in his jaw deepened.

Silenced, Alere studied Mina as they walked. But the white and gold veils obscured all but a suggestion of dark eyes. A few strands of black hair escaped Mina's white coif. But something about the healer obviously unnerved Alere's stoic weishi. Had he seen beneath Mina's veil, perhaps? Did he know her?

An unwelcome suspicion formed. Had Kett fallen for a pretty face? Surely not. He wasn't so impulsive or shallow. She quashed the glimmer of unease in her stomach. For the last decade Kett had been not only her weishi and training master, but also surrogate brother and best friend. He was pledged to come with her to the Alcazar on the morrow. He wouldn't abandon his duty for a girl he'd just met, would he?

Alere slowed her steps to walk beside Kett. She eyed the healer's straight back as Mina picked her way along the muck-strewn street.

'Do you know her? Is she someone important? If she's not, why on Kalima would someone attack a healer?' Alere looked sidelong at her weishi, trying to judge Kett's reaction. Knowing Mina's first name wasn't helpful. Her last name was the key to her heritage. Did she have a family name extending back to the First Ships? Or was she a kin-child – the offspring of unwed parents? No, that was unlikely. The laws that had made kin-children illegal for the Juns and other nobility twenty years before, meant there were fewer such children these days, even amongst common folk.

'No idea.'

'She seems ordinary enough,' Alere said. 'Maybe from a Trade family? They apprentice their children to the Houses. Isn't that how you came to be in Weishi House?' He never mentioned his family and she'd long-since stopped asking.

Kett said nothing, but cradled Tamir's limp body closer against his broad chest.

'Obviously, she's not the daughter of a Jun family,' Alere continued. The twenty-one ruling Juns traced their names back to the original Funding families, financiers of Kalima's colonisation. 'No daughter of a Jun would ever be allowed to serve in a House. So maybe Mina's right and it was the Madina city junren they were after. What do you think?'

'I think,' Kett said, 'you should be worrying about Tamir.'

'Bai, shifu,' Alere responded, flushing. He was right. Mina's family was none of her business.

Mina turned a corner and vanished into a cramped passage between a food market and a hostelry. Alere lifted her robe to avoid a pile of decomposing wedi leaves and gidfruit scraps. The stench of urine and decaying fruit thickened the cool autumn air. She screwed up her nose and half-ran to keep up as Mina hurried through the narrow alley.

The lane opened onto a broader street, with rutted stone paving and leaf-clogged, broken gutters. A huoche, stacked high with baskets of black jilla-fruit, rolled past. Its bronze-strapped timber wheels rattled on the road. One wheel dropped into the hole left by a missing paving stone. The che-ma towing the huoche shook its stiff, red-striped mane and nickered in protest, straining against the load. The driver swore and cracked a whip over the animal's long ears.

'Only a few years ago this area was one of the best in Madina,' Kett said, scanning the houses on the opposite side of the street.

Alere studied the once-regal sandstone and sulcrete dwellings and shivered. Jagged glass made empty windows into gaping mouths and despairing eyes. Formal gardens were withered and weed choked. She looked away from a pot-bellied boy in filthy rags who crouched in front of a door half-ripped off its bronze hinges.

Mina cast a pitying glance at the toddler. 'Every day more of Madina feels the bite of poverty. At Healer House we try to feed those we can, but our resources are small. The Alcazar withholds tithes that are rightfully ours.'

'Why won't the Jun First come and see what's happening to his city?' Alere asked. 'He never leaves the Alcazar these days.'

'It's not Jun Radan causing this,' Kett replied, his tone bitter. 'He's been unwell for months. It's his wife, Shunu Hanna, who's behind this. She—'

'Here.' Mina ushered them through the side entrance to a massive sandstone building, into a stark, windowless room that smelled of cleaning fluid. Lights glared and Alere jumped, squinting against the aching brilliance. So few buildings had electricity any more, but she should have expected it in Healer House.

Mina gestured to a pair of alzin tables and gathered bandages as Kett placed Tamir gently on the polished metal. Bren dropped his burden unceremoniously onto the other table. Mina pressed a button by the door then lifted the bandage on Tamir's wound. Blood oozed from the torn skin and she pressed the cloth hard again.

Kett touched her arm. She flinched, her lips falling open in a gasp.

'I didn't mean to frighten you,' Kett said. 'I just wanted to ask if he'll be alright.'

'Yes, you need not wait. I believe they'll both recover.' Her warm smile held professional assurance. 'I'll send a runner to Xintou House when I have news.'

Alere's guilt eased. The boy wouldn't die at her hand, nor Tamir through her neglect.

'I'm lucky you came along,' the healer added, still addressing Kett. 'But why were you in the Zalam area? It's nowhere near Xintou House.'

'We escort the shunu to Jiaoji House three times a week for lessons,' Kett said. 'She insists on walking and it's quicker to go through the Zalam.'

Mina's brows rose. 'Jiaoji House? Lessons in seduction for a xintou? I didn't think—'

'And music and dancing,' Alere said stiffly, irritated that they spoke as though she was absent. 'Kett, we have to get back. I'll be late for dinner.'

He bowed. 'Of course. Bren and I will escort you and he can report to the city guard Shangwei after.'

'I'm sorry to detain you, shunu,' Mina said, bowing. She rose on tiptoes and brushed her lips across Kett's cheek. 'And thank you.' She smiled gently and returned to her patients.

Alere spun on her heel and marched from the room. After a brief silence, Kett and Bren's steady footsteps followed close behind. Relief swept through her. She stalked in the direction of Xintou House, unwilling to speak until she had mastered herself.

When Alere arrived at the House, thoughts of tomorrow crowded back, supplanting all other worries. She stared at the steel-studded door that proclaimed the House's wealth and power. Above the door, carved in Old Anglish, Rabic and Mandrin, was the House motto:

Clarity, stability, responsibility, and compassion.

The House had been her home for the past ten years; those tenets reinforced every day. After tonight that part of her life would be over – yet inescapable.

The Jun First's palace, the Alcazar, stood a bowshot away in the city centre, dominating the blood-lit skyline. To the people of Madina, the Alcazar's twin steel towers were a monument to freedom and hope; the last remnants of the first colony ship. Seven hundred years ago, twenty thousand idealistic people had escaped war and oppression by fleeing from Earth to Kalima. Now the blunt-nosed towers loomed over a city of a hundred thousand miserable souls, mired in poverty.

Alere blinked back angry tears as she studied the gleaming spires that would be her home. Most people believed the Alcazar to be steel – rarest of all metals. But the Jun's towers were an aluminium alloy; as hollow and false as the Jun who lived inside.

The Alcazar embodied not hope, but the end of her dreams. Tomorrow she would become jiaoji to the Jun First. No matter what her true role in the Alcazar, to the world she would be just another contracted courtesan. Jun First Radan Zah-Hill already had four jiaoji. Why had he asked for her? Alere's shoulders sagged under the weight of duty and resignation. Why not? Jiaoji was her only real option. Mistress Li seemed to think Alere was fit for nothing else.

The sun dipped behind the Alcazar, casting purple shadows across the empty street. An evening breeze picked snow-cold off the distant mountains and threw the chill over the city. Alere shivered.

She steeled herself and headed to the stable to clean her sword. To meet the House mother with a bloodied blade in hand would be unforgivable. For a xintou to even carry a weapon was frowned upon by most in the House. A true telepath had no need of weapons. Her lips twisted into a bitter smile.

'Shunu Alere.' Kett's deep voice halted her as they entered the yard. He dismissed Bren.

She lifted her veil. 'Don't call me that.'

'That girl, the healer—'

'What about her? You seemed quite impressed.' Alere regretted the sarcastic words as soon as they left her mouth; more so when Kett responded with an admonitory look. He was her shifu-master and she had no right to question him. Her cheeks burned.

'She was you,' he said.

'What?' His words made no sense, so she waited.

'I saw her for a moment,' Kett continued. 'She wears your face, Alli.'

That got her attention. He'd used her familiar name, not the formal adult name she'd chosen at her Threshold ceremony two years before. Kett only called her Alli when they were alone and he was off duty.

'What do you mean? She looks like me?'

'Exactly like you.'

'She wore the veil, Kett. You couldn't have seen her clearly. I'm sure it was just a similarity.'

A gong sounded inside the House, calling her house sisters to dinner. The conversation would have to wait until the morrow. Tonight's dinner was her last in the House and she couldn't be late. She was to be honoured with a ceremonial leave-taking. To arrive splashed with blood and her robe torn would be an insult to Mistress Li.

'We'll discuss it later. I must change for dinner.' Alere unbuckled her belt and held out her scabbard. 'Clean this for me, please?'

He hesitated but took the weapon.

'Your first blood. Well done too. I'll bring it to your room.'

She rubbed at a spot of blood on her wrist. 'It wasn't well done. I almost killed a child, Kett. Younger than me. And so…I should have done better.' She bit back self-disgust.

'He was young, but he would've slain you without hesitation. But I am glad you didn't kill him.' Kett grimaced. 'Once you cross that line, there's no going back. I don't want that for you.'

'But I let two of them sneak up on me. I should have been watching, with Tamir. And I froze.' She dropped her head, unable to meet his eyes. As her shifu he had every right to be angry that she'd failed Tamir. 'I panicked, shifu. When I did fight back, I wasn't calm. I was so angry I could hardly think straight. I feel like I've disgraced my sword.'

Kett lifted her chin with a knuckle. His grey eyes searched hers. 'Don't be hard on yourself. It was your first real fight. Freezing is normal, but you overcame it and did your training proud. Anger's just another face of fear. You'll overcome that, too.' He hesitated and frowned. 'But when that knife was at your throat, what were you thinking then?'

Alere glanced at the Alcazar. 'That I was already a slave. That no-one really cares what happens to me. That I have no choice; no chance to be free. Maybe ever.'

'*I* care. As does your mother, Elmira.' He laid both hands on her shoulders. 'There are always choices, Alli. You could run away again, but you've chosen to do your duty by the House and there's nothing wrong with that.'

She smiled bleakly. 'I haven't run away since I was fourteen. It never did me any good. I always knew you'd be sent to find me. Besides, duty isn't a choice. Mistress Li needs my help in the Alcazar.' She shoved his hands off. 'In my position I have to do what people expect.' Her eyes blurred with tears. 'And as everyone here keeps telling me: I'll never be xintou. I'm a disappointment to Elmira. I'm nothing. What option do I have but to do my duty?'

Kett opened his mouth then sighed. 'You're wrong, Alli, but I know you don't believe me. Duty and responsibility doesn't have to be a cage. But I agree that you need to stop letting others choose your path for you. Freedom isn't out there.' He indicated the high, sandstone walls surrounding the House, then tapped his temple. 'It's in here. You are free to think whatever you like. To do whatever you like.'

Alere gave a sardonic laugh. 'Think what I like in a House full of telepaths? I'm a non-telepath so I can't tell if they've breached my wards. I watch every thought, Kett. You know that.'

He grimaced. 'Imagine how the rest of the world feels, then. They don't get trained to ward at all so they have no hope of keeping their thoughts private. You are free, Alli, you've just chosen to believe you're not.' He sighed again. 'One of these days, you'll start choosing to live, instead of just waiting for life to be handed to you. I'm looking forward to that.' With another bow, he vanished into the guardhouse.

Alere stared after him as darkness slipped across the city. He was wrong. So wrong. She had no choice and her life was over before it had even begun.

She hurried to her room, stripped off the torn robe, washed her hands and face, and dabbed healing cream on her neck. If only she could wash away the memory of blood as easily. Putting the attack out of mind was simpler for Kett, perhaps, than for her.

The bell rang again as Alere dragged the plain yellow house-robe of a student xintou over her shoulders. She fumbled with the toggles and her mind drifted to tomorrow. No, she shouldn't torture herself. She need only focus on getting through dinner. Morning would come, regardless of how much she worried. She would handle whatever happened.

With face and mind schooled to serenity, she hurried through whitewashed halls to the dining room. A servant slid open the black, lacquered door. Silence swept the room. Thirty-three women turned towards her. Alere held her head high and strode to the main table to make her bow.

Mistress Li, as leader of Xintou House, sat enthroned at the head of the hall, flanked by her assistant, Renna, and the House-mistress,

Mara. Mistress Li acknowledged Alere with an inclination of her smoothly-coiffured head. She indicated the vacant seat at the end of the main table. Alere hesitated. That position was an honour reserved for girls on their last evening before telepathic Bonding with one of the twenty-one Jun-families.

If only that were her fate: to be a Bonded Xintou. Alere sank into the seat. She hid the ache in her chest and endured the tedious dinner, tasting nothing, hearing none of the conversations, either spoken or telepathic. Her last night in the House. Her last night deluding herself with the hope that she could ever be xintou.

When the meal was over, she stood before the high table. In a corner, a servant beat a heart-rhythm on a drum twice his height. The heavy thudding silenced the room. Three senior xintou stripped off Alere's plain yellow house-robe. Traditionally, the xintou dressed their departing sister in a Bonded Xintou's fine gold formal robe.

The audience gasped when, instead, Mistress Renna draped a jiaoji's ornate red robe over Alere's shoulders. Humiliation and anger churned in Alere's stomach. Why must Mistress Li demean her before her sisters? This red-robing might be a pretence for others, but that thought failed to bring comfort. Jiaoji were respected, but not revered in the same way xintou were.

The jiaoji veil fell over Alere's eyes and washed the room red, wiping away her dreams.

She lifted her chin. The tears built in her throat, but she refused to let them fall before her peers. No, not her peers. Her superiors now.

The drumming ceased. Heavy silence held the room in thrall.

Alere avoided every eye and, unbowed, stalked from the room. She strengthened her mental wards. The last thing she wanted was her Outer thoughts to be Read, for she was in no mood for sympathy or derision.

In the safety of her shielded room, Alere finally relaxed her wards. With a sob, she ripped the veil off, flung it into a corner and collapsed onto the plank-bed. She let the tears fall at last, not caring if they stained the blood-red silk of her robe.

CHAPTER THREE

A knock on the door sent Alere scrabbling for a cloth to wipe her face.

'Come in.' Her voice cracked. She scrubbed the tears from her cheeks and stood.

The door slid open and Mistress Li entered. With a wave of an elegant, parchment hand, she motioned for Alere to close the door. Mistress Li eased herself onto the bed and nodded for Alere to sit.

'You're frightened, child, and angry.' Mistress Li cocked her head like a small, grey bird. It was a statement, not a question. 'Control yourself, and we shall speak.'

Alere avoided the Xintou's eyes and dropped back onto the bed, studying instead at the bare, windowless walls and scuffed bamboo floorboards. Xintou were meant to be above fear and anger. One more way in which she failed. She didn't question how the Mistress knew. After all, the woman had been a xintou for at least a hundred years and had led the House for sixty. Her telepathic skills were legendary.

'I do understand.' Mistress Li's lined mouth cracked into a rare, sympathetic smile. 'But remember: you're special and in a unique position.'

'What, Elmira's genetic mistake? And in a horizontal position in the Alcazar?' The words spilled from Alere's mouth. 'Such a comfort when the Jun-First—' She snapped her teeth shut.

'You are not Elmira's mista...' Mistress Li pursed her lips. 'That is a conversation for later, when you're older.'

Not a mistake? Was that a deliberate slip of the tongue? If so, it made no sense. Everyone knew the great Elmira Connor, Bonded Xintou to the Jun Second Ma-Safra family, had created a flawed gene-daughter in Alere. A daughter without xintou powers. Useless.

'For now, child,' Mistress Li continued, 'you must remember your job in the Alcazar.'

'Oh yes, I know.' Alere folded her arms. 'Contracted to a man more than twice my age so I can spy for you. What I don't know is *who* to watch and *why*?'

Mistress Li patted Alere's knee. 'I'm here to tell you.'

'And why can't I be weishi instead of jiaoji?' Tears stung Alere's eyes. 'I've trained with Kett as weishi for ten years and only three with Mistress Houlia at Jiaoji House. I won't need jiaoji skills to seduce Jun Radan. Being female is enough, from what I hear. So why? It makes no sense.'

'It makes perfect sense,' Mistress Li replied, 'if you take a moment to think calmly, child.'

Alere glowered and bit down on a hot retort.

'As a jiaoji to the Jun First,' Mistress Li continued, 'you'll have more freedom to move about in the Alcazar.' She smiled thinly. 'If you were weishi, you would be under orders from the Shangwei, Master Penon, and his most-distasteful second, Khaler. Believe me, jiaoji is better.'

Alere opened her mouth to argue, but Mistress Li raised a finger. Years of obedience held Alere's tongue.

'Trust me. It is for your own protection. More important,' Mistress Li said, 'is who you must watch: the Jun-Heir, Ven, and his mother, First Shunu Hanna.'

Alere suppressed the fear fluttering in her stomach and waited.

Mistress Li's small eyes rested shrewdly on Alere. 'Madina – no, the whole Jundom of Mamlakah – has descended into poverty over the last decade. The Jun First is a weak-willed man. For years, the First Shunu has manipulated him; bent him to her wishes. In her insecurity and desire for power, she has drained the people, but still she seeks more. Until recently, her reach has been limited.' With twisted fingers, she smoothed the gold silk over her knees. 'Now, Jun First Radan's illness has worsened and he has lost what little control he had over Hanna. She's planning something.' Mistress Li frowned.

'And you want me to find out what?' Sweat prickled on Alere's back. Her heart stuttered, thudding against her ribs. Madness. Everyone knew what happened to people who crossed the First Shunu. Their bodies swung from the top of the walls for weeks, their families with them. This must be serious if Mistress Li was willing to endanger not only Alere, but Elmira and the House as well.

'It's crucial for the Jundom that we stop her.' Mistress Li drew herself up. 'Radan's weakness creeps through the country like a disease. Melcori slavers make forays into our realm. The trade Houses rebel against the Juns, demanding changes that can only harm us. A Jun-Bonded Xintou was allowed to conceive twins. It's only a matter of time before a boy-xintou is birthed.'

'But twins and boys are forbidden to xintou in the Teachings of Lei.' Alere shuddered. 'It's dangerous. Even commoners fear twin-births. How could a Bonded Xintou do such a thing?'

Li clutched at the heavy gold chain tucked into the front of her robe. Whatever hung at the end of the chain lay concealed beneath the gold silk, but the gesture seemed to calm her.

'That's not an issue for you to worry about.' Mistress Li's fingers crushed the silk tighter, balling the cloth and hidden pendant in her fist. 'You must find out what the First Shunu is planning.'

'But what about Jun Radan's Bonded Xintou? Isn't that her job?'

'Celia Edwards has recently replaced her mother as the Xintou in the Alcazar. But she has closed her mind to me. I fear she's joined the First Shunu and Turned against the House.'

'That's impossible!'

'There have been others, in the past,' Mistress Li said. 'Xintou, Bonded to lesser Jun, have succumbed to the life of luxury in a Jun family. Or gone to their Jun for support. Usually when the House demanded the death of a boy-child or twins. But this is something else.' For the first time, Mistress Li's eyes glittered with fear. Her hands trembled in her lap. 'You must find out what Celia and Hanna are planning.'

Alere shrank away. Mistress Li was never afraid. She was the rock that anchored the Jundom of Mamlakah in stability. Her wisdom guided the incorruptible Xintou, who worked for a higher good and kept the twenty-one Jun families from tearing each other apart. Mamlakah's peace rested in her hands. In the hands of all xintou. Yet now the Xintou to the First had betrayed her House. How could that be?

Alere smoothed a curl of dark hair behind her ear. She wasn't the right person for such an important task. She was nothing – not a xintou, not a jiaoji, not a weishi – a crude, half-done mix of all three and mistress of none.

Mistress Li rose, graceful even in age though her silk robe draped heavily from her thin frame. She stroked Alere's cheek.

'You underestimate yourself, child. You always have. You must overcome that – and your regrettable tendency to be impulsive. You may not be a telepath, but you've learned all the skills you'll need. Self-defence from Kett. Seduction and control from Jiaoji House. And Xintou House has taught you politics. Use these to your advantage in the Alcazar.'

'But Mistress—'

'None of your instructors, I notice, have curbed your impatience,' Mistress Li said. 'In the Alcazar, you must think before you act. Then act with the knowledge that I have confidence in you.'

'But Mistress, I don't *want* to be jiaoji to the First.' Alere seized the red-robe in both fists and shook it. 'I thought I'd be free when my time here was done. I'm not xintou and I'm not jiaoji. Let me find my true path in life.'

Power and superiority slipped like a veil over Mistress Li's face. 'Have you not yet learnt, child? What you *desire* and what's *important* is not always the same thing. Xintou or not, you will obey. You will do your duty, as we all must. Your path is what I deem it to be.'

She hobbled to the door and paused. 'One more thing. While at the Alcazar, you'll wear your veil at all times. Understood?'

Etiquette in the Alcazar court was stricter than elsewhere in Madina, but the fashion for the veil was dying out. Alere hated the thing, as Mistress Li well knew.

'Jiche! Is *that* why I must be jiaoji and not weishi? Because you want me to hide my face?'

'Yes.' Mistress Li ignored Alere's expletive. 'It is necessary. One day you'll thank me for insisting. Do not fail.' She indicated the bed. 'Sleep now. Morning will bring light into darkness. I'll give you further instructions before you leave. Tonight, let the austerity of this room remind you of the truth and certainty you've learned here. Tomorrow you'll need it when you're surrounded by luxury and corruption.'

But Alere slept little that night. No matter how Mistress Li dressed the situation up, Alere was being sold to a man she'd never met, her dreams of freedom and a meaningful life gone. Jiaoji skills were respected and in high demand. Most jiaoji had full control over their contract and choice of partner, but Alere was denied even that.

She was Mistress Li's pawn on a qi game board, being moved for unfathomable reasons. And duty to Xintou House was a cold comfort to take to the Jun First's bed.

Alere rose drained and haggard. Dressed in the hateful red robe, she endured her twentieth nameday ceremony; her mind elsewhere and the day forgotten before it ended. Not until she stood in her room for the last time, with a small, wooden trunk of belongings under one arm, did Alere return to the present. She paused in the door of the bare cell that had been her home for ten years and bit back tears of despair and loss. The walls were scratched and dented by her childish anger. The ceiling had never been repaired from her third attempt to run away. But the room represented a secure haven from a tumultuous world she comprehended only in theory.

She pulled back her shoulders and held down sorrow. She would find some way to make her time in the Alcazar bearable. Somehow.

In the hall, her sisters formed an honour guard. From each, she received a word, a touch, a kiss, a kind glance, which buoyed her flagging will. As a non-xintou, Alere had always been set apart, unable to form strong connections with her house sisters. They lived in a world beyond the physical. A world of the mind, which she could not enter. Thoughtful as the farewell was, the xintou wouldn't miss her.

As Alere neared the door a senior student, with dark troubled eyes, pressed her cheek to Alere's.

'Be careful,' the girl murmured. 'My mother, Celia, the Xintou to the Jun First, she is—'

'Tali Edwards.' Mistress Li's command cut through the silent hall. Tali stepped back into line, silken black hair falling forward to hide her flushed face.

What had that been about?

Alere emerged into the sunlight. She smiled as Kett and his men snapped to attention as they lined the steps from the front door to the cobbled road. The six weishi bowed formally, both hands pressed flat to their chests. Alere cast a final look at the House's imposing facade. The great steel-studded doors clanged shut with resounding finality. Would it be the last time she ever saw the inside? It seemed impossible to believe; frightening, but somehow…liberating.

But what if she wasn't up to the task set for her? Would she be caught and hang from the wall?

Kett handed her up the step, into the huoche. With a word to the driver, Kett climbed in and closed the door. When the huoche was in motion and the House behind, Alere lifted the red veil and covered her face with her hands.

'Shunu…Alere.' Kett's hesitant words pulled her from behind the protection of her fingers.

'Kett.' She grasped his hand. She fought to keep tears from falling. 'How would I cope without you? I'm glad Mistress Li's allowing you to attend me in the Alcazar.'

He studied their linked fingers and grimaced. 'There's no need to be frightened, Alli. The Alcazar's not the monstrous bed of iniquity Mistress Li makes it out to be. They're people, just like you and me. No better, that's certain. Keep that in mind. Just stay out of Ven and Hanna's way.'

'You sound as though you know them.' Alere smiled to ward off the doubt creeping into her heart.

He shrugged. The huoche turned into the Alcazar's back gate. 'I know people and I've known you since you were ten.' The corner of his mouth lifted. 'It's hard to believe a decade has passed. Remember that first day you came to Xintou House?'

'Of course. I was dressed in my finest. Terrified; clinging onto Elmira's arm. And you were a newly-made full weishi. So proud of your uniform and tattoo. And what, seventeen? Barely old enough to tie your hair into a man's mawei.' She touched the throwing-star tattoo, blue with age, on the inside of his wrist.

'And I recognised trouble the minute you walked in,' he said, smiling.

'I know I haven't been your best student—'

Kett chuckled. 'Stop fishing for compliments. You're my best student – and the one I've lost the most sleep over. Especially every time you ran away.'

'Be serious.' Alere brought his hand to her cheek. 'I'm trying to thank you. And apologise for being rude yesterday. You've been a brother to me, Kett. Guarding and guiding me. Even when I didn't want it.'

He sobered and stroked her cheek, then pulled his hand away and gazed out the window, frowning.

The huoche halted at the servants' entrance. Kett paused in the act of reaching for the door. 'Alere. I've dreaded this moment and put it off far too long. I'm sorry. Hopefully you will, in time, forgive me.'

Dismay snaked through her stomach. 'You're scaring me, Kett. Put what off?'

'I can't come with you. I'm... It's impossible for me to enter the Alcazar.' He looked away. 'Believe me, I want to protect you. I can't.'

'No. Kett!' The cry spilled from her. She clutched at his sleeve.

He tore his arm free. The black silk ripped. Without another word, he opened the door and climbed down. He stood rigid outside the huoche, his face blank.

A slap across the cheek would have been less shocking. Alere's breathing faltered. She caressed the scrap of silk like a talisman. Kett would not come. *Could* not come? The concept made no sense. He was honour-bound. She stared at the black cloth then closed her eyes.

He'd deliberately waited until they reached the Alcazar's door. Four black-and-silver-clad servants, two weishi and one of the Jun's red-robed jiaoji waited to receive her. She could hardly cling to Kett like a frightened child, or draw back from her duty to the House.

She pulled back her shoulders and raised her chin. Her throat and chest tight with unshed tears, she stepped from the huoche and swept past Kett without another word or look.

***

'Jiaoji!'

Alere froze at the sound of Ven Zah-Hill's light voice. The Jun-Heir couldn't see her, could he? She held still, hidden behind the tapestry. Any movement might disturb the cloth and draw his attention. She'd ducked into the alcove to avoid drawing Nahlia's eye. The senior Jiaoji enjoyed giving the newest girl the most demeaning jobs. Alere had found this niche on her second day in the Alcazar and the hiding place had saved her several times in the last two weeks.

'Shenshi Ven,' Nahlia's sultry contralto replied. 'How may I serve you?' Her heavy, dew-flower perfume saturated the air. Little brass bells tinkled on her ankle as she walked.

'You know exactly how you can serve me, jiaoji.'

'Shenshi.' Nahlia's voice was breathless, pitched a little higher than normal. 'I don't—'

'Silence,' Ven snapped. 'You know I don't like you to speak.'

Alere peered between the tapestry and wall.

Nahlia's flame-red head hit the wooden panelling with a thump that echoed in the Alcazar's empty Great Hall. Ven's long fingers encircled her throat, holding her in place as he ripped at the red-robe and squeezed the soft flesh of her breast. Nahlia whimpered. Ven's fingertips whitened on her neck and her strangled breaths rasped, harsh in the vast hall.

'You're hurting me. Please!' Nahlia cried, but he silenced her protest with a slap. Ven laughed and tore at her clothing, exposing her, stripping away her arrogance. He towered over the petite jiaoji, one lean arm effortlessly holding her in place as his grip on her neck tightened. Her blood-red nails sliced matching tears in his skin. Ven only smiled wider.

Alere pressed her forehead to the wall. She fought the instinct to interfere, glad her weapons had been confiscated on arrival at the Alcazar. This was neither the time nor place to stand up to the Jun-Heir.

She disliked Nahlia, but no-one deserved such treatment and, if rumours were true, Nahlia and the other girls endured far worse from Ven behind closed doors. Jiaoji were free to break a contract in abusive situations. Jiaoji House protected their own and retribution against the abuser was swift and often fatal. Nahlia stayed, too ambitious for her own good. The security of a life contract and the luxury of the Alcazar were not worth this pain and humiliation.

With Jun First Radan confined to bed, Ven's attentions to his father's jiaoji went unchecked. If the Jun died, Alere had no intention of staying to suffer at Ven's hands. As the newest jiaoji, she was untouchable – until Radan had seen her. Once that happened, or if Radan died, Ven would seek her out.

Ven was five years older than herself. He was not unattractive, though he wore his straight black hair in a mawei longer than a woman's. His ugliness shone through his narrow, gold-brown eyes.

Another slap cracked the silence. Alere winced in sympathy.

Ven chuckled, low in his throat, as he squeezed Nahlia's neck. Nahlia's face darkened to purple.

'Ven, enough!' First Shunu Hanna strode across the Hall's basalt floor towards her son.

Alere breathed a sigh of relief.

Hanna's pale blue eyes swept, with sneering disdain, over Nahlia's disorder. 'Get to your quarters, *jiaoji*. Neither my son nor my husband need your services.' Her eyelids drooped. 'When the Jun dies, your contract will be cancelled. Pack now. You'll be out the second the bell tolls for him.'

Nahlia coughed and rubbed at her throat. She clutched the torn red-robe to her breasts and fled, bells jingling. Ven laughed. Hanna flipped back the cowl of her ruffled pink robe.

'Mother dearest,' Ven said, brushing at his tunic, 'you shouldn't deny a man his pleasures.' He habitually wore severely-cut black and silver clothing, making him an arresting figure in the Alcazar's maze of gilded halls.

'Your pleasures, as you call them,' Hanna replied, 'are expensive. Every time you treat Radan's jiaoji like that their contract demands compensation. And do you know how much we owe Shah Jahil and his revolting SlaveMaster, Hallon, for your…interests?' She shifted a sparkling yanstone pin in her curled blonde hair.

Ven yawned. 'No, and I don't care.'

'You should. The vaults are almost empty. We cannot afford to keep paying Jahil not to harry our borders. We must fight back, but training the army of junren has drained us. Then there's the extra city guards to keep these selb fanatics under control. It all costs a fortune.' Her blue eyes narrowed. 'And now I have to pay off that disgusting, hairy mountain man.'

'Oh?' Ven leaned against the wall and Alere forced herself to stand still. Only an armslength separated them. 'You've had some success there? Good. Now we need confirmation of where it is and we can move.'

'Don't you think I'm trying?' Hanna glared. 'Radan is stronger than I anticipated. Celia assured me the poison would weaken his wards.'

Alere pressed a palm over her mouth to stifle a gasp. They were poisoning the Jun? How? The security around his food and drink was extreme.

'I assume your charming demeanor this afternoon means darling Celia's again had no success.' Ven inspected his nails.

'Radan's concealing the location deep in his Inner thoughts.' Hanna flipped a dismissive hand at her son. 'Celia can't breach his Inner wards without risking Fusion and death for them both. Why can't Radan see it's our only hope for the future? The Shah of Melcor has too much power over our economy. Radan must tell us where it is.'

Location of what? Alere held her breath. Whatever the Jun First hid from his wife, he must think it worth dying for. And Mistress Li was right: Celia conspired with the First Shunu. A Bonded Xintou was meant to remain just and bipartisan in the Jun world of political intrigue. What was Celia thinking?

Ven levelled a disinterested look at his mother. 'Find another way to get the information. Men will do anything for sex and my father has a weakness for women. What about that new jiaoji? I hear he's been asking for her.'

'That wisix chouhuo!' The ugly oath distorted Hanna's painted-pink lips.

'You're a hypocrite, mother. You keep two male jiaoji of your own. But, if you don't want to talk to the jiaoji, send Celia with an offer to pay the girl.' His smile became predatory. 'Or give her to me. I'll convince her to help us.'

There was a long pause and, for a few moments, Alere could see neither mother nor son. Her heart thudded so loudly they must be able to hear it. She froze, trapped, awaiting discovery.

'Khaler did say she was quite lovely,' Hanna's tone held a hint of bitterness. Alere sagged against the wall, her legs trembling.

'Ah.' Ven chuckled. 'The deplorable Khaler has exercised his right to see her face, has he? I might have guessed.'

'Of course. He's second in command of our weishi and responsible for our security. She had to raise her veil. He was, however, obliged to discipline her.'

'Now you intrigue me. Discipline her how?'

Hanna's mouth curled in contempt as she moved back into Alere's line of vision. 'The girl had the presumption to tell Khaler and Penon their security was lax. Khaler gave her a well-deserved backhand. She may not be so pretty any more.'

Alere touched the faded yellow bruise on her cheek and grimaced. The division of weishi loyalties between Radan, Ven and Hanna led to gaping holes in the Alcazar security. But pointing that out to the Shangwei and his second in command had been stupid.

'Now you instill me with a deep desire to meet this girl. And if she's that naïve she would be a perfect tool to use against my father.'

'You might be right,' Hanna said. 'Have the girl taken to Celia's quarters. She'll trust Celia as her House senior. Yes, that could work.' She raked Ven with an impatient glare. 'Well?'

'How long do you think Mistress Li will let you play this little game, Mother?'

'That old woman's had a stranglehold on the Jundom for too long. She'll see. I'm not afraid of her.' Hanna's eyes narrowed. 'Find that jiaoji.'

Ven bowed with a flourish and strode away, his booted heels tapping on the basalt floor. Hanna watched him go, then mounted the broad stairs and vanished into her room.

CHAPTER FOUR

Hurried footsteps slapped on the flagstones outside Alere's hiding place. Voices, lifted in irritation, called her name. The Alcazar weishi and servants searched for her. She hesitated. Mistress Li had ordered her to spy on Celia and find out what was happening in the Alcazar. Was her duty to report what she'd heard to Xintou House, or should she meet with Celia and the Jun First to learn more?

Celia was a skilled telepath. There was a chance she could Read more than Alere wanted her to know. As a non-xintou, Alere wouldn't be aware if Celia breached her wards. Every moment spent in the Xintou's company was a risk of exposure. On the other hand, there was no proof of the conspiracy, or what Hanna wanted from Radan. As arbiters of the law on Madina, xintou required evidence, not hearsay. And, if the Jun died tomorrow, Celia and Hanna would destroy any evidence before the Xintou House Law-Mistress could mount an investigation.

The only way to find out what Hanna wanted was to meet with Celia.

Alere inspected her clothing for dust, wiped her sweat-slicked palms and emerged from behind the tapestry.

Moments later, a servant ushered her into Celia's chamber. The Xintou rose from behind a plain wooden desk. She was delicate and sharp-featured, her dark hair worn in a single, long plait. Her robe was simple; her translucent skin bare of makeup or jewelry. In her early forties, she looked a decade younger.

'My dear girl, come in.' Celia raised her gold veil and gestured to a couch below a small window. 'Sit with me.'

Alere studied her. Most people would see Celia's humble smile as genuine. Yet, for all her severity of style, Celia wore her status like a ball gown. Not only was she Bonded to the most powerful Jun family, she was also a direct descendant of the Edwards sisters, founders of Xintou House five hundred years earlier. Awareness of her value showed in the lift of Celia's chin, the coolness of her gaze, the disparaging slide of her eyes over Alere's red-robe.

She had a right to be confident. Celia had two gene-daughters in Xintou House. Her gene-daughter succession and control of the First family was assured – unless Mistress Li could stop her.

Alere held her wards firm and bowed. 'Mistress Celia,' she murmured as she perched on the gold-embroidered couch.

Xintou House was visible through the east-facing window. Sunset burnished Xintou House's sandstone walls to deep, jin-bird gold, and bloodied the peaked red roof. Had Celia chosen this room deliberately or was it the Alcazar Xintou's hereditary quarters?

The curved wall meant this room was inside one of the metal towers and therefore one of the oldest in the Alcazar. The furnishings and wall hangings, although few, reflected the original settlers' ethnic mix. The desk and bed were simple and made of pale timber, but the ceiling was painted with red-and-gold geometric patterns, dragons and phoenixes. Underfoot, a frayed rug rioted with strange leaf-and-plant patterns in greens, black and gold.

'Now,' Celia said, 'we haven't had time to meet, have we? You may raise your veil, child. You're safe here. How has your first two weeks with us been? Is Nahlia making you welcome?'

A jiaoji raised her veil only to her contracted partner so Alere ignored the insult and left the silk in place. Besides, she had secrets to keep and it would not help to give Ceclia any advantage. Celia's question about Nahlia had to be rhetorical. If the Xintou was half the Reader the stories proclaimed, she'd know Nahlia's thoughts about the newest jiaoji. Alere firmed her wards, allowing only superficial nervousness and worry to show in her Outers.

'Yes, Mistress Celia.' She kept her eyes downcast, hands still in her lap.

'I'm so pleased.' Celia handed over a glass of water.

Alere made a pretence of drinking and buried all thoughts of poison deep.

'And you're Elmira's daughter,' Celia continued. 'That makes you Nasra Connor's granddaughter. I was close with Nasra many years ago. She was good friends with my mother, Zarra, who was Bonded to the First before I.' She smiled condescendingly. 'Nasra was a remarkable woman. Very kind to me. I miss her still.'

'I've heard, Mistress. She died before I was born.'

'Ye-es.' Celia's agreement was oddly lilted. She patted Alere's leg. 'Enough. Now, I have wonderful news. The Jun First has asked for you.' She held up a palm. 'No. Not for reasons of pleasure. The Jun is far too unwell for that. But you have the chance to do the Jundom a great service.'

'Oh, yes Mistress?' Alere parted her lips in an eager half-smile and leaned forward. Could a Xintou be fooled by a mere jiaoji who'd taken acting lessons? She had to try.

'You may not be aware,' Celia said, her tone condescending, 'that Mamlakah's northern borders are often violated by Melcor slavers. They raid our towns and take our people for slaves.'

Alere opened her mouth in feigned astonishment. She was, in fact, perfectly aware. She and Kett had held many discussions on the subject of slavery and its economics. And her encounter in the Zalam proved how bold the slavers had become.

'It's worse than you know. Not just slavers.' Celia fiddled with the wooden toggles at the neck of her gold robe and her gaze slid away from Alere's. 'The Shah of Melcor is building an army. He intends to invade our Jundom, our sovereign Mamlakah. We need your help to prevent him.'

Alere had no need to fake her gasp. Was the Shah's intent true or just part of the tale Celia had been told to spin? She pushed the doubts deep down and strengthened her Outer wards.

'But what has that to do with me, Mistress?'

'There is…' Celia shifted in her seat. 'A treasure. It will help us stop the Shah. The Jun knows its whereabouts.'

'Treasure?'

'Yes.' Celia cleared her throat and straightened her robe. 'The Jun has become paranoid, in his illness. He won't reveal its location to his beloved wife. We need you to gain his trust and find out where it is.'

'But what sort of treasure, Mistress?' Alere widened her eyes, affecting naivety. 'Surely the Jun has no need of more riches?' Recent tithe increases ordered by Hanna had tightened the noose of despair throughout the Jundom. Would Celia defend Hanna's extortion?

'I don't know what sort of treasure, child. That's not our business.' The Xintou lifted haughty brows and scratched at the side of her nose. 'Your task is simply to find out where it is, so the First Shunu can ensure the safety of our people and our land.'

Alere bowed her head. If the situation weren't so disturbing, she would have laughed aloud at the pitiful explanation. Celia might be skilled at her craft, but she had not learned to control her body language. She betrayed herself with every movement. Jiaoji training showed Alere the truth in the body over the lies on the tongue.

What was this charade really about? What did they need from the Jun?

When Celia escorted her to the Jun's bedroom, Alere hesitated, trying to settle the sudden unease in her stomach. She tugged at the veil and smoothed the front of her red-robe. Celia, with a warning look and an admonishment not to be nervous, left her at the door. Alere lifted her chin and nodded to the weishi outside the Jun's room.

He patted her down for weapons, his attention more on her breasts than his job. Alere hid a sneer, glad for the distraction. He was one of Hanna's men. He rapped on the Jun's door. A black-and-silver-clad servant ushered her into the room then bowed himself discreetly out.

Alere snicked the lock and leaned against the door. Heavy furniture of burgundy zitan-wood and blackened iron dominated the massive room. Overhead, a geometric chandelier of interlocking, open iron cubes held twenty or more bulbs. But only half a dozen worked, their feeble light doing nothing to dispel shadows clustered in the corners. Bare, basalt floors and polished-metal walls radiated cold into the desolate space. She shivered. Sunset's last, bloody rays slipped between thick curtains and transformed airborne dust into dancing lights in the darkness. The room was a mausoleum, not a comfortable place for a loved one in his last hours.

Dwarfed and trembling, Alere bit back fear, threw her shoulders back and trod silently to the bed. The Jun First lay there, weighed down by ebon bedlinen. His pale mouth stretched into a thin smile and he raised skeletal fingers, gesturing her closer.

On the wall behind the bed hung the ancient, black silk flag of the Earth colonists: a silver dragon entwined around a gold lion and a white, spread-winged eagle. The flag symbolised unity and tolerance. How ironic that the original colony leader's descendant was being poisoned by people intent on war.

Radan patted the mattress. Alere perched on the edge of the bed, an acre away from the emaciated figure caged between the four iron bedposts. In the oppressive stillness, Radan's panting breaths were those of a dying animal; shallow and harsh with pain.

'Come closer, child. Let me see your lovely face.' The whisper from his thin lips scratched the silence. He struggled to sit up, scrabbling against the heavy quilt that pinioned his legs. 'Come, come. I must see you. I must be certain.'

She lifted the red veil.

'Ah.' He sighed the relieved exclamation and waved her closer. 'Yes.'

Alere slid across until she sat, legs folded, next to the old man. No, he couldn't be more than fifty. Not so old, just aged by those conspiring against him. A little knot of fear dissolved in her stomach.

That Radan still lived spoke of surprising determination. There must be something keeping him alive beyond his murderer's expectations. Was that the reason he'd requested to see her? The least she could do was hear him out. Alere leaned closer, ignoring the sweet-sour miasma of decay tainting his breath.

'Shenshi,' she whispered, 'Celia will be Reading you. Please ward if you're strong enough.'

The Jun First raised his rheumy gold-brown eyes, so much kinder than his son's. 'Of course. But there is little time.' He grasped her sleeve and tugged like a child.

She shifted closer. His lips brushed her ear.

'Hanna and Ven want to know where the ore is. But they must not find the iron deposit. Understand?' He waited for her nod, breath wheezing in his chest. 'They wish to make weapons of war. Reclaim the technology our ancestors deliberately left behind on Earth. They defy Mistress Li's advice.'

An iron deposit? Weapons? Impossible. Alere twisted the black bedlinen into a knot between her fingers. Iron was one of the scarcest metals on the planet. A mineable deposit could change the fate of jundoms. The manufacture of iron weapons had been unachievable on Kalima for over five hundred years.

'What do you want me to do, shenshi?' she whispered.

'If they find the deposit before winter…' He coughed and bloody spittle frothed on his lips. 'They'll be ready to march on Melcor by summer. War would ruin both Jundoms. Hanna must listen to Xintou House.' His feeble fingers gripped Alere's wrist. 'They'll destroy the House. The Jundom. Everything we've worked for since coming to this world. You must stop them.'

'How?' Alere quashed a flare of panic. 'I'm nobody. What can I do?'

The Jun refocussed on her, his eyes glittering with fever. 'Under the bed. In the drawer, there's a box. A gift. Find your real mother. Take the box to her. She and Nasra will help you. Take the box, and what you learn from your mother, and go to your father. What's in the box is crucial. And he needs you, now.' His attention slid away and he frowned, plucking at the cloth over his knees. 'Did he understand what he'd created? Surely not. It could change everything. Can he be trusted?'

'My real mother? My father? What do you mean?' Shock stole sense from her mind and tongue. 'I have no father. I was created by Elmira Connor. I'm her gene-daughter. She's my moth—'

'No.' Radan cut across her babbling. 'She's not, but I'm bound to silence on that matter. You must ask Elmira.'

'But—'

'Enough.' His grip on her wrist relaxed. 'Tomorrow the jundom will be in Ven's hands. You won't be safe. They won't believe you don't know. Take the gift and leave. Whatever you do, keep it safe and return it to your father. Tell him he *must* protect the iron. If he cannot, he must destroy it.' He fell into a paroxysm of coughing until blood trickled from his lips and each breath gurgled in his throat.

Alere snatched a glass of water from the bedside table. She worked an arm under Radan's shoulders, raised him and held the glass to his lips. He weighed nothing. He sipped at the water. Blood stained the remaining liquid pink.

He waved the glass away. 'You must go.'

'You aren't well, shenshi,' she said. 'I should call someone.'

'There's no point.' His eyes were weary and wise. 'Just take the gift. I'll try to buy you some time. Behind the first bookshelf is a hidden door. The catch is under the second shelf. A passage leads to the south wall, near the stables. No-one else knows of it.'

'Shenshi, I—'

'Do as I say.' The ghost of old arrogance flitted across his pale features. 'You are freed from your contract.' He touched her cheek. 'I'm sorry to drag you into this. I had no one else to trust. Mistress Li tells me you're the best she's ever trained.'

'What?' Alere flushed. Mistress Li thought her the best? The best what?

'Go, girl. Tell your mother and Nasra their secret is safe. But the time has come to set it free. And your father needs to know his creation is dangerous and must be destroyed.' Radan turned his hollow-cheeked face away and closed sunken eyes.

She clambered off the bed and opened a heavy drawer in the bedbase. Inside lay a small parcel in smooth silk wrapping. Her name was scrawled in shaky lettering on a card tied to the parcel with black ribbon – the Weishi House's colour. The wrapping was the purple-and-silver family colours of Jun Second Ma-Safra. Was there a message in the Jun's choice of wrapping?

'Wait.' Radan's faint voice made her glance up. 'There's something else in the drawer. Bring it to me.'

Alere tucked the package into her robe, felt inside the drawer and found a weighty object, the length of her forearm, shrouded in stiff silk that smelled of rank mel-oil. The cloth disintegrated as she unwound it and revealed a section of dull, silver metal. She bushed at the exposed surface, dusting away remnants of the wrapping. A knife, with a blade of what looked like steel.

With a corner of her under-robe, she cleaned off the oil residue and tested the dagger's balance. Perfect. When she gripped the hilt's leather covering, the brittle suede crumbled and revealed some sort of engraving on the metal tang. The light was too dim to make out any detail.

She climbed back onto the bed and presented the dagger to Radan. He touched the stone embedded in the pommel. The translucent, milky jewel resembled a yanstone but lacked that gem's inner fire.

'I destroyed the others,' he whispered. 'This one...well, I couldn't. Two hundred years ago, this dirk was left behind by the anti-slavery rebels who attacked the Alcazar and tried to overturn the Jun First.'

'It's beautiful, shenshi.'

'I want you to have it, since you're now a rebel, my dear.'

Alere eyed the dagger longingly. She'd feel better with a weapon in her hand, but the steel was far too valuable for someone like her. She stroked the blade.

'But,' Radan added, 'there's a condition attached.'

She froze. 'Shenshi?'

He opened her hand flat, his papery skin rasping on hers. He lay the dagger gently in her palm and curled her fingers around the hilt. His wasted fingers trembled as he wrapped them around her fist. With their hands entwined, he lifted the dagger and pressed the point to his chest, over his heart.

'You must kill me.'

CHAPTER FIVE

'Shenshi!' Alere snatched her hand away, releasing the dirk. 'I *can't.*'

'You must.' Radan's red-rimmed eyes flashed tepid fire. 'I'm weak. Celia will break through my Inner wards before I die. I can't let that happen. She would know everything.'

'But I—'

The door handle rattled.

'That's an order.' Radan groped through the bedclothes and grasped the dagger. 'I have no one else. I must protect my people, and you. Please. Help me die.'

'Shenshi?' The servant's voice called from outside.

Radan waved his hand towards the door. 'Tell him to leave us alone for the night. That'll give them something to gossip about.'

Alere tweaked the veil down, ran across the room and opened the heavy panel a handspan.

'Shenshi Radan wishes us to be left alone for the night. I'll assist him. And he requests the weishi be dismissed.' She intended to use the secret exit and didn't need the weishi reporting she'd never left the room.

The weishi and servant exchanged astonished looks. The servant hesitated, then shrugged and both men left.

Alere locked the door. Reluctance weighted her steps as she returned to the bed. She studied Radan's grey skin and sunken eyes. A surge of pity and anger swelled in her heart. No one deserved a slow death by poison.

'I know: I'm not the man I used to be, my dear,' he said, his mouth drooping. 'Once I held many hearts, loved many women, and had many children.' A tear tracked down his papery cheek. 'Now my heart lies in your hands. Will you help me?'

'Shenshi, I...' She paced a few steps away, smoothed a stray lock of hair behind her ear and tried to think clearly. How could she do this? How could she be responsible for the death of the Jun First? No-one would believe he'd asked for help. If she did this, she would be executed for murder. Yet, if she didn't...

'Please, my dear,' Radan said. 'I've done many things I regret. I don't wish to add betrayal of my people to that list. If you won't do this for me, do it as your duty to the Jundom.'

'My duty.' Her voice broke, along with her resistance. Alere blinked away tears. As Mistress Li always said: the important over the desired. Radan was right: the lives of everyone in the Jundom were more important than hers.

She sank on to the bed and held the dagger in one hand, Radan's blue-veined fingers in the other. With a heavy breath, she brought her hands together, encasing Radan's and the dirk within them.

She helped him position the blade between the ribs, over his heart, then hesitated.

'Are you sure, shenshi?'

Radan's eyes lit with hope and relief. 'Oh, yes.'

'Then forgive me.'

'I do. And I thank you, my dearest girl.'

Alere glanced at the closed door.

Radan's lips twitched into a wavering smile. 'I'll try to die quietly so the weishi don't break in too soon.'

She stifled a half-hysterical laugh and tightened her grip on the dagger, her palms damp with sweat. She lifted the blade an inch from his skin, angled the tip up a fraction, and gritted her teeth. His fingers twitched beneath hers and he nodded.

Together they plunged the steel into his thin chest.

Radan's back arched. He clenched his jaw shut on a gurgling cry. His body slumped and his head lolled to one side, eyes sightless.

Alere bit back a sob. Her hands were slick with the Jun First's blood, and tears poured down her cheeks. What had she done? She'd crossed the line. Kett was right: there was no going back.

The door handle rattled. Someone thumped on the panel.

'Jiaoji? Let me in!' Ven's voice sent a rush of fear through her body.

She tugged the knife free of Radan's body and wiped her hands and the blade on the sheet. She tore off a strip of cloth to sheath the steel then slipped the blade into the front of her robe. As an afterthought, she pulled the sheets to Radan's chin. Ven wouldn't be deceived for long, but leaving Radan uncovered and soaked in blood felt disrespectful. She closed his eyes.

The door flexed and jolted as something heavy thudded against it.

Alere ran to the first bookshelf and fumbled with the catch. The panel swung open, revealing a spiralling staircase. Two glass bulbs of antique design dangled from the low ceiling, bathing the steep steps in a sick yellow glow.

For a few seconds, she paused on the threshold. Any choice was fraught with danger. She touched the package and dagger, lying against her breast, and glanced at the Jun First. If Radan was right and there was an iron deposit, whoever held it could control the whole of Mamlakah – and even Melcor and Jadid. Who should she go to with this? Mistress Li? Elmira? But if Elmira wasn't her mother, then Alere's whole life was a lie; and Mistress Li most likely the architect of that deceit. Who could she trust? Who would believe her?

Her instinct was to seek out Kett but their parting was still a raw wound. She missed his steady presence and his abandonment hurt. What would he advise if he were here? As always, his first words would be: avoid the fight, if possible. For once Alere agreed.

Hurrying footsteps and Ven's raised voice outside the door sealed her decision. Ven would have her executed for his father's murder. The thought of facing him propelled her feet down the narrow stone staircase. She closed and latched the secret door. There was no time to collect her effects. The things she most valued, her throwing knives and bow, had been confiscated on her arrival, anyway.

Alere stopped in a cross-corridor at the bottom of the stairs, deep in the South Tower's base. A short corridor to the left ended in a door with peep-holes at eye height. To the right, a corner cut off any view of the hall's end. She hurried along the left corridor and pushed back the hole-cover but found only darkness and silence beyond. She flicked a switch by her left hand. A faint bulb glimmered, revealing five empty prison cells; bleak rooms with bare stone floors and stout timber bars. She turned the light off and closed the cover.

Distant shouts drove her to the opposite corridor. The Alcazar weishi would search the castle. She had to get out. Past the corner, the hall ended in a timber door studded with rusted iron. If the door didn't lead outside, she was in serious trouble. She found a switch, doused the lights and eased the door open a fraction.

Fresh, damp air brushed her skin. Cold rain spattered on the cobbles. Night had fallen and brought an evening storm. In the wet darkness, it took Alere a while to recognise the jumble of storage sheds and trade workshops abutting the outer wall behind the Alcazar. The stables were nearby; the air heavy with the scents of urine, wet horses and an acrid odour; sharp and chemical even through the rain. A door to the nearest workshop stood open. Several men moved about inside, focussed on shifting large barrels under cover, their lamps shielded. If she was quick, she should be able to pass unseen.

She hesitated. Her red robe was too distinctive, even without the veil. Jiaoji red was a specific blood-shade no other House or Jun family used. She pulled off the robe, flipped it inside out to show the dark burgundy inner lining, and tucked the veil, parcel and dagger away again. She slipped outside. Stone cladding camouflaged the hidden door against the surrounding wall. If she ever came back – which seemed unlikely – it would be difficult to find the door again.

Heedless of the icy rain, Alere strode away from the castle, holding her head high. Kett had once told her hiding sometimes entailed normality over stealth. As she rounded a corner, and joined the chaotic night market outside the Alcazar, she understood what he meant.

She rated barely a second glance amongst the bustle of housewives dickering with merchants, and unveiled jiaoji soliciting passing trade. Children laughed and picked pockets as they wove like mumit-wrigglers through the crowd. Alere clamped an arm across her stomach, protecting the parcel and dagger. A strolling musician plucked at an oud and sang a mournful song about a woman who'd lost her favourite jiaoji. The rich scent of stir-fried glass-rabbit meat wafted from a food-seller. Alere picked her way over slick cobbles and wove through the stalls, heading east to Xintou House.

Three Alcazar weishi jogged towards her, their weapons rattling and boots thumping in unison. Alere feigned interest in a cloth merchant's stall until they passed. She stole a black veil from the display when the merchant turned his back. Heart pounding, she ducked around a corner and awaited an outcry. None came.

She yanked out her hairpins and her hair tumbled free like a lower-class woman's. She could have paid for the veil with one of the pins, but the transaction would be remembered, for the copper pins carried the Jiaoji House lanhua flower symbol picked out in rubies. Alere snapped off the jewelled tips, pinned the veil in place, and tucked the gems into her breast binder. Her robe, darkened by the rain, could pass for black. Now she was weishi.

Behind her, the great bronze bell atop the Alcazar tolled. Its sonorous message rolled out across the rooftops, causing carts and people to stop. Heads turned towards the iron towers as all Madina counted the tones. Three meant a birth, eight a fortunate outcome, four a death. In the market a child wailed but was quickly hushed.

The tones stopped at four. Then, after a breathless pause, a single tone rang out a message of death. Now the whole city knew their Jun First was gone. Alere glanced around furtively at the shocked faces in the market. How long would it be before Hanna and Ven accused her of Radan's murder and circulated her description to every house and town? She had to get out of the city before they closed the gates.

Sick with fear, she shouldered through the crowd. Around her a babble of angry questions arose, like toxic fumes, from caustic tongues loosened by the silence. She hurried along the street to Xintou House and stopped in the shadows of the guard house. The weishi on duty was new.

She rapped on the window. 'I have an urgent, private message for weishi Kett Peter-kin. Please send him out.'

'Yes, Mistress.' The weishi fumbled with the door handle and sprinted into the House yard.

A few moments later Kett arrived, berating the boy for leaving the gate unattended. The young weishi scurried back to the gatehouse. Kett approached Alere, one hand resting on his sword hilt.

'You have a message for me?' His tone was cool.

'It's me, Alere.' She raised the veil a fraction.

He stilled. 'Very well,' he said, raising his voice. 'I shall pass that on. Now go, it's too wet to be out.' He added, sotto voce, 'Meet me in the alcove behind the stables. I'll be there as soon as I can. Don't come inside. Mistress Li is unwell. Alcazar weishi are here, searching for you.'

Alere bowed in formal weishi style, with both palms pressed to her chest. She marched into the darkness, resisting the urge to run. Kett was right. This was the first place Ven would send his people. She should have gone elsewhere. But where?

She had to speak with Elmira but couldn't risk compromising her mother's position as Xintou to the Jun Second family. Elmira knew something, some great secret – and she wasn't Alere's mother. That idea was yet to take root, so the fruit of understanding lay beyond Alere's reach.

The splashing march of many feet sent her darting into a vine-covered niche in the compound wall. Mel-oil lamps along the wall cast a glimmering golden half-light, just enough so Alere could see the niche was empty. To most passers-by the decorative plantings simply broke up the solemnity of the House's outer stone wall. But Alere and her house sisters had long since discovered their more useful function as hidey-holes and, for some, trysting places. To Alere, huddled now in the damp dimness behind the vines, such innocent enjoyment seemed surreal.

Endless minutes later, the vines shifted as Kett's big frame eased into the small space. He gripped Alere's shoulders and peered at her. His face was shadowed, but he seemed more puzzled than annoyed.

'Are you alright? The House received a message saying you'd killed the Jun. Mistress Li's confined to her bed. Mistress Renna's gone to the Alcazar to meet with the Jun-Heir and the other House leaders. What happened?'

She couldn't tell him; couldn't bear the look of horror if she told him everything.

'Now's not the time, Kett. Trust me, please. Radan was sick, dying. They...they poisoned him!' The dagger and package dug into her skin, beneath the robe. 'He entrusted me with a secret and a task. But I'm scared, Kett.'

'Poisoned him? Who?' His fingers tightened. 'What task?'

'Sh-Shunu Hanna and Celia and the Jun-Heir, Ven.' Shivers wracked her body. 'They p-poisoned him. I can't tell you more yet. I have to get out of the city. Speak to Elmira. Find someone called Nasra. The only Nasra I've ever heard of was Elmira's mother. B-but she's dead. I don't know who I'm sup-posed to find or where to go and—'

'Stop! Get control of yourself.'

His harsh command snapped Alere to her senses. She clenched her jaw against a resentful protest and hung her head.

'Bai, shifu. I'm sorry. I...I need to get to Elmira and work out what to do.'

A bell rang out overhead, with a higher, thinner tone. The Xintou House bell. Four tolls again, a pause, then two. Alere stifled a gasp. Not the House leader but the second in command. Mistress Renna was dead. But how was that possible?

An orange-uniformed Messenger House runner hurried past, his torch highlighting Kett's grim profile. Leaf-shadows, like grasping hands, clawed across the sandstone walls.

'I believe you, Alli. Only Celia has the power or the audacity to kill Mistress Renna. And if Hanna's pulling Celia's strings then the House isn't safe for either of us. Here.' He thrust a soft bundle into her arms. 'Put these on and tuck your hair away. Grime your chin to look like a beard. We're leaving. We'll pay a runner to take a message to Elmira. The Ma-Safra house is near the Eastern Gate so we'll leave the city that way.'

Only then did Alere see the haversack slung over Kett's arm, and the alzin metal and leather armour under his cloak. His bow and quiver hung across his back; sword at his hip. He'd meant to come with her all along. A warmth in her heart spread to her fingers and stopped their shaking long enough that she could undress.

The bundle contained trous, a dark high-collared shirt and a soft black hat. Male weishi apprentice clothing.

'There were no boots your size, sorry,' Kett said, watching the street as she changed.

'Doesn't matter.' She tucked away her long hair and stuffed the betraying red robe into the pack. Her dagger slid into the belt, and the parcel and gemstones went into a deep pocket. She grabbed a handful of damp dirt and rubbed it along her jaw.

As she followed Kett into the night, Alere glanced back at the golden house that had once been her home. A cacophony of wailing and sobbing drifted out as her house sisters mourned their mistress. Alere gulped back tears. A cold stone settled in her chest, alongside the one for Radan. But there was no time to grieve for either. The House would go on, but Mistress Li had long groomed Mistress Renna as her successor. Now Mistress Li was old and had little time to train another.

Alere turned away. What would happen if Mistress Li died now, without a replacement to stand against Hanna and Celia?

'It's not safe for you here.' Elmira hesitated then pulled Alere into a brief hug. Xintou normally discouraged physical contact, so she must be agitated. In response to Kett's message she had met Alere and Kett at the rear entrance to the Ma-Safra town house. 'The Alcazar weishi have already come once, looking for you. You must leave.'

Alere stiffened and pulled free of Elmira's arms, unable to put aside Radan's revelations. Now was the moment to discover the truth. There had always been something missing in her relationship with Elmira; something wrong with who Alere was and the life she led. Kett had dismissed her feelings as normal, said everyone felt that way, but now she was proved right.

'I need to talk to you,' Alere said.

Elmira frowned. Lightning danced, high in the clouds, casting shadows that highlighted Elmira's angular cheekbones and deepset eyes. 'Let me Read you. It will be faster.'

Alere shook her head. 'I need to hear this from you. Out loud.'

'But...very well. We'll have to be quick.' Elmira lifted her gold silk skirts clear of the muddy path. 'Come this way.'

She led them through the damp garden to a summerhouse of black bamboo and golden sandstone. The cold, earthy smell of winter rain and decaying leaves pervaded the empty building. Light drizzle pattered on the copper roof and dripped off the broad, navy leaves of an overhanging tacca tree.

Elmira raised her gold veil. 'Now, what is it? You know I'll do whatever I can to help.' She glanced back at the sprawling stone mansion. 'But you must leave the city immediately. Go to the Ma-Safra estates in Jiali. Petar and Leah are there. They'll hide you.'

Alere hesitated, deeply tempted. If she went to Jiali she could change her name, disappear and start a real life with no-one to dictate her path. But with no-one to turn to for help, either; no family, no friends – for she couldn't drag Kett into such a life.

The dagger shifted inside her robe, its point digging into her hip. She gritted her teeth. She'd made a promise to Radan, to her Jun First. That had to take precedence over everything. But to fulfil her promise, she needed to confront Elmira and expose a lie that underpinned the foundations of her life.

'Alere?' Elmira's expression held only concern. For twenty years Elmira had been her mother, though duties as Xintou had taken much of her time. Calm and distant though she was, her love had never been in doubt. That couldn't have all been a lie. Bitter accusations of deceit evaporated from Alere's tongue.

'The Jun First said you're not my mother. Is that true?' Tears pricked at her eyes.

'The Jun? How did he...?' Elmira paled and touched Alere's cheek. 'Oh, my dear girl. I'm so sorry you had to find out this way. Yes, it's true.'

Alere pushed Elmira's hand aside. 'Why? Why did you lie? Who *is* my mother?'

Elmira's breath hitched in her throat. She reached out again but Alere shrank away and let her false-mother gather only emptiness to her breast. Elmira's midnight-blue eyes fell, veiling pain.

'I can't...' Elmira's hands fluttered and stilled. 'It's not my secret. I'm sworn.'

'That's not good enough.' Alere clenched her fists. Stormclouds built in her chest and she fought to control the outpouring.

'I meant to tell you many years ago but there never seemed to be a good time.' Elmira's eyes shone with unshed tears. 'And I love you as though you are mine. I didn't want to lose you.'

The tempest raging in Alere's heart abruptly dissolved under that honest admission and she wrapped Elmira in a tentative, awkward hug.

'You won't,' she said, 'I promise.' She sniffed and gave a broken little laugh. 'At least now I know why I'm not a xintou. If I'm not your gene-daughter then it's a relief. I'm not a mistake and I can stop being angry at you.'

'No.' Elmira's arms tightened until Alere could barely breathe. 'Never a mistake. Never not good enough. Not xintou, and I know that's caused you pain. I'm sorry I had to hide the truth from you. It was a secret too dangerous to burden a child with.'

Alere broke free. 'Dangerous? How? This is about more than just me, now. The Jun just died for this secret.' She stared out the window behind Elmira. Night rain shrouded the Alcazar in a swirling robe of darkness. Lightning flashed. Tattered ribbons of silver mist fluttered around the steel towers where Radan lay, at peace in the centre of a storm. Alere breathed in the warm scent of ozone and tried to settle the roiling unease in her stomach.

'What do you know of Radan's death?' Elmira's sharp question cut through a rumble of thunder. 'I won't believe you killed him. Did Hanna have a hand in it? And Celia – has she Turned?'

When Alere nodded, Elmira paced away, one hand stroking back her tightly-pinned auburn hair. She threw Alere a doubtful look.

'Moth...Elmira.' Alere softened her tone. 'The Jun said I must find my real mother and see Nasra. Did he mean my grand...your mother, Nasra? Isn't she dead? What does she have to do with you adopting me?'

'Nasra is— Oh! Quickly, you must leave.' Elmira hastened to the window overlooking the front entrance of the house's walled enclave. Thudding on the gate echoed the thunder. Rough voices rose above the crackle of lightning. 'They're here again.'

Kett joined Elmira at the window and cocked his head, listening. 'Alcazar,' he confirmed. 'Demanding entry in Ven's name. Time to go.'

'Yes. That Khaler man is here this time.' Elmira shuddered. 'His mind is a sewer. If you fall into his hands he'll...You must leave. Now.'

'I can't!' Alere resisted as Elmira tried to hurry her out the door. 'Please, tell me who I am.'

A noise of frustration escaped the Xintou. 'There's no time,' she snapped. 'Go.'

'Go where?' Alere held her ground. 'I have to find out the truth.'

At the gate, weapons clanged and shouts reverberated. A scream of pain rent the darkness. The great timber portal swung wide and slammed against the stone wall. Angry voices rose and the crunch of boots on gravel echoed through the summerhouse.

Elmira whirled to Alere. 'Nasra isn't dead, though few know it. Go to Gaton. Speak to her. She'll tell you the rest. I can't, for I know very little.' The Xintou frowned. 'Go carefully and speak of Nasra to no-one. My mother's life depends on our silence.'

Metal clashed on metal. Lightning glinted off ceramic and bronze blades raised high, not fifty paces along the path towards the main house. Only a thin screen of decorative bamboo stood between the Alcazar weishi and the summerhouse.

Elmira addressed Kett. 'Take care of my daughter.'

'Always, shunu.' He bowed and took Alere's wrist.

'But what about you, Elmira?' Alere allowed Kett to pull her towards the exit. 'They'll ask if you've seen me. Celia will come.'

Elmira drew herself up in elegant hauteur. 'I can deal with the likes of *her*.' Her voice rang with scorn. 'Celia's been Bonded only eight months. She forgets I've been Xintou to the Jun Second for over twenty years. She can't strike at me without causing war between the Jun families. She knows that.' She gathered Alere into a final hug. 'The Ma-Safras are at their country estate in Jiali. I've just sent your sist...foster sister, Hallee, to start her training in Xintou House so she is out of Hanna's reach. I have twenty weishi with me. I'm safe enough for now. Go.'

Alere inhaled Elmira's favourite calla-flower perfume, felt the silken brush of her skin, and the warmth of her body, and knew Elmira's concern was real. A long-held twist of tension and doubt in her stomach unravelled. Some questions had been answered but the time had come to discover the rest; and learn who she was meant to be.

Drawing back, Elmira sighed. 'Go, please. I'll be alright, I promise. Be safe and give my love to Nasra. The back gate's unguarded and there are two horses waiting.' With a backward glance, Elmira vanished into a narrow side path in the direction of the house.

Heavy footsteps rattled on the walkway leading from the front gate to the summerhouse. Kett tugged at Alere's hand, pulling her away from the approaching Alcazar weishi.

'Will she be alright?' Alere whispered.

He didn't reply. Assailed by doubt, Alere stopped and yanked free. 'Kett, I can't leave her like this.' She turned back. 'That Khaler's a hmar. He won't listen to her. He'll hurt her.'

Kett uttered a bark of laughter. His breath condensed into a pale cloud, soon dispersed by the cold rain. 'I'd bet your moth...Elmira against a dozen of my best men any day. Yes, Khaler's a hmar, but don't forget who she is. She can drill right through his Outers and make him croak like a swamp-dafdae. She'll be fine. And I'm sure she'll have sent a flitter bird to warn Petar and Leah in Jiali. We have to go.'

'But—'

'Alli!' Kett gripped her wrist and hauled her towards the back gate. 'The one thing that could endanger her is Khaler finding you here. Celia is looking for an excuse to move against Elmira. If Elmira is found protecting Radan's murderer, not even Mistress Li could intervene.'

His words made sense but fear dragged at Alere's feet, anchoring her to Elmira's fate.

CHAPTER SIX

Elmira's clear, imperious voice rang out above the ruckus, demanding explanations. The noise of fighting died away. Alere chuckled in relief. She knew that tone. Right now the Alcazar weishi probably looked like apprentices about to be dragged before their master and whipped.

She followed Kett into the darkness.

Wet bushes slapped against her legs as she ran. Leaves clung to her ankles and slid into her slippers. Cold rain trickled down her bare neck and thunder rumbled in the roiling clouds. Rain and the brush of wet vegetation swept away the lingering perfume of Elmira's embrace. Far behind, the Ma-Safra front gate closed with a decisive thud.

Kett eased open the bronze-studded rear gate. The hinges shrieked, high and thin, like the whine of a hunting night-wing. Kett swore and beckoned Alere through, closing the timber panel behind. Outside, two horses waited in the rain. Heads lowered and hides glistening, they flicked moisture from their ears and stamped in the thick mud. Alere ran to the roan mare and stroked her nose.

'Rumi, how did you get here? I thought you were at the Alcazar.' The mare snuffled, pushed her nose into Alere's hand and nudged her with a shoulder. Alere threw an arm over the strong neck and petted Rumi's water-slicked hide, murmuring soft blandishments. Rumi nickered and shook her head in a spray of water. Alere checked the saddle's girth and stirrups. Her bow and quiver, complete with twenty or more arrows, were strapped behind the saddle.

'And my bow. How—?'

'The Alcazar sent Rumi and your bow back to the House.' Kett tested the girth strap on his horse. 'She wouldn't allow anyone to ride her so I thought she'd be better off with Elmira. I'm glad of it now.' He patted his gelding's strong nose. The animal nuzzled Kett. 'If I'm not mistaken this fellow is Bol, Shenshi Petar's mount.'

'My throwing knives?' Alere checked the saddlebags, but the knives weren't there.

'The ones I gave you for your nameday last year?' Kett grimaced. 'No. We'll get more. Somewhere.' He adjusted his stirrups then gathered the reins looped around a tethering post. 'Mount up. Someone might have heard that gate. The Alcazar weishi could be here any second.'

He swung into the saddle. Alere followed suit and kicked Rumi into a trot.

The East Gate lay not far from where the Ma-Safra's house abutted the city wall. A dozen or more hostels and taverns, catering to travellers from Jiali, lined the wide road leading to the gate. Lamplight and music poured from open doors, competing with the thunder and rain. The sound of pipes, ouds and drums intertwined with laughter and snippets of bawdy song. Drunks and unveiled jiaoji ran through the rain, holding cloaks over their heads, laughing and sloshing ale and jiu from wooden tankards.

A chair smashed through the front window of the Jiali Way tavern and splintered on the cobbles. Alere started, one hand on the dagger at her hip. The tavern door flew open and a black-clad weishi shoved a staggering drunk outside. Kett turned aside and twitched his cowl forward. A crier in the orange uniform of Messenger House sprinted past, shouting the news of the Jun's death. Thunder drowned his voice as he yelled Alere's description and a curfew warning. At the sound of her name, Alere's heart hammered against her ribs. The revellers ignored the runner and Alere breathed a silent sigh of relief.

She tugged her cap lower and kneed Rumi closer to Kett.

'Shouldn't we—'

'For once in your life, Alli, shut up and do as I say,' he muttered, his eyes on the runner. 'When we get to the gate, if I say ride, you do it. Don't stop and don't ask why. Got it?' The ice in his eyes brooked no argument.

'Ya-zheng, shifu.' The traditional student-weishi's response popped from her mouth. His uncharacteristic tension twisted through her stomach and the brief moment of relief vanished as reality sank in. How did he intend to get them through the gate? The curfew meant all the city gates were closed except to legitimate travellers. They had no hope of exiting. Cold sleeted across her skin and she looked to Kett, hoping for a solution.

Kett tugged a small copper hipflask from his pocket, took a swig and sprinkled the rest of the contents on his clothes. Alere wrinkled her nose as the raw smell of jiu overpowered the scents of wet horse, dung and mud. He never drank. What was he doing?

When the East Gate came into view, he launched into a hideously off-key song. Alere grimaced and plugged one ear. Now the jiu made sense. His forethought and quick planning was impressive. But would the guards fall for such an obvious ruse? She held her peace as Kett swayed in his saddle and belched. A young junren, in an ill-fitting uniform, challenged them. Kett listed to one side and Alere propped him up. A second junren, yawning and pot-bellied, lounged against the half-closed gate.

'I'mmm...mm gotta get home. Just two streets out the gate.' Kett held up three fingers then pointed unsteadily at the heavy portal. 'S'verrry late. Wife'll be soooo mad.' He chortled.

'Yes, I'm sure.' The young guard thumbed rain from his eyes and straightened his black-and-gold uniform. 'But the city's under lockdown. You're not allowed out until we confirm you're not the fugitive jiaoji, Alere Connor.'

Kett gripped the boy's shoulder and hauled him close. 'Do I look like a girl? Ha!'

The junren fanned a hand and raised a disdainful brow. Alere pitied the beardless youth. If he said the wrong thing now it could be the last words he ever spoke.

'No, but you are weishi and I thought they didn't drink.' His fingers whitened on the shaft of his spear.

Kett's shoulders slumped. 'Been posted.' He flung his arm out wide, barely missing the guard's nose. The boy jerked back. Kett scowled. 'To Hargo. Can you believe it? Me in that gouri pigsty of a farmer hole.' Kett thumped his chest. Bol tossed his head, shifting and stomping on the cobbles. 'Me, the best—'

'Yeah, yeah.' The youngster eyed Bol's hooves, 'I get it. I don't care. What about your apprentice? I'll need to check he's not the jiaoji.'

Alere ducked her head. This would never work. By now the rain must have washed off the dirt on her jaw. She didn't look like a boy. She resisted the urge to check her slight breasts were hidden under the damp shirt.

'Nope, he's not a girl, either, but there are times I sure wish he was.' Kett tapped the side of his nose and leered. 'Know what I mean?'

Weary distaste flashed across the boy's face. Alere hoped the blush rising in her cheeks wasn't visible in the guttering torchlight.

Kett renewed his grip on the junren's shoulder, swayed in his saddle and waved at the pot-bellied guard.

'Hey! You gonna come over and check my 'prentice out as well? Your friend here thinks he's a *girl.*' Kett sniggered and slapped his thigh.

The older junren waved a lazy dismissal, clearly more interested in staying dry and picking his teeth than a fight. Thunder crackled and rolled overhead. The clouds thickened. Rain pelted down, drenching and icy.

'Let 'em pass, Dar.' The older man scratched at his armpit.

'But Brendo,' Dar protested, 'Shangwei said we're supposed to—'

'Give it a rest,' Brendo snapped. 'Even I can tell the kid's not a red-robe. They're a lot prettier and they've got....' He cupped his hands in front of his chest, laughed and heaved open the gate.

After a long, suspicious look at Alere, Dar stepped back. Scowling, he waved them through. Alere let out a shuddering breath.

'Wait!' Dar thrust his spear shaft in front of Rumi's chest. The mare whickered and tossed her head.

'You're wearing house shoes?' Dar pointed accusingly at Alere's feet.

Alere's heart stuttered. She sought for some plausible explanation. Nothing. She had to say something. 'I—'

Raucous laughter cut across her half-formed words. Dar blinked in surprise as Kett giggled uncontrollably, almost falling off Bol.

'I told him.' Kett said. 'I told him not to bet on those dice. Loaded. Lose your gouri boots if you keep gambling with gouri cheaters, I said. And he did.' He clutched at his sides and pointed at Alere's feet. 'Lost his sword. Lost his boots.'

'Master, please?' Alere said, forcing her voice as deep as it would go. She sent Dar a sheepish look. 'I thought it was a sure thing.'

Dar sneered and shook his head. 'You two are a disgrace to Weishi House. I ought to report you to Master Anh. Get out of here. You deserve that posting.'

As they passed Brendo, he spat to one side and peered up at her through the downpour. 'Get your master home, son. He picked a bad night to be in town.'

'I will.' She kicked Rumi forward, dragging a drooping, chuckling Kett with her.

They carried on the ruse longer than Alere thought necessary. The guards couldn't possibly see them through the rain and night. Thunder rolled through the sky and lightning painted clouds and buildings in shades of white-purple and black. She led Kett past rows of mudbrick, slate-roofed houses, closed and shuttered against the storm. Bad weather might make their ride miserable, but rain also meant a delay in disseminating the news about Radan's death – and her description. Not even Messenger House riders travelled on nights like this, and flitter-birds remained nested in their cotes.

At last, Kett straightened and surveyed the road behind. 'We're good.'

'No, *you're* good. After that performance, I think you've missed your calling to the purple.' Her laugh held an edge of hysteria Alere couldn't hide.

'You're not the only one to take lessons.' Kett wiped rain from his face. 'But I think the Artist's House is safe without me. It's more a measure of the rot in the city than my acting ability. Our little charade shouldn't have worked. Jun Third Kennor Han-Asad commands the city guards and I wouldn't allow him to run a brothel of unveiled jiaoji.'

Surprised by his scathing indictment of a Jun as respected as Han-Asad, Alere held her tongue. The two rode in silence beneath the cloud-covered moons, past the last, straggling houses, until they reached a signposted crossroads. One cracked timber slab indicated the east road, to Jiali. The other pointed southeast, towards Faladon.

Kett rose in his saddle, peering through the rain. 'We'll ride east for a while, then go south, cross-country, until we meet the main south road to Jadid. From memory, the road forks about a day's ride south. Then we'll have to take the more easterly route to reach Gaton. Won't be long before Shangwei Penon, and Khaler realise you've escaped. They'll send xiongshou after you. With any luck, they'll think you're headed east to Petar's estate. Should buy us a day or so.'

'Xiongshou! You really think they'll send assassins?' Alere flipped up her collar as the wind slashed ice-daggers of rain through her clothing. She glanced over her shoulder at the city, just a glow in the mist behind.

Kett nodded grimly.

She gripped his arm. 'Thank you, Kett. You've left everything behind for me. I'm sorry.'

Lean, callused fingers entwined with hers, rough and warm against her skin. 'No need. My obligation to protect you is more important. Besides, I left everything else behind years ago.' He, too, looked back at the rain-smeared lights of Madina, his eyes haunted.

Before she could ask what he meant, Kett put his heels to Bol's sides. Rumi took off after him and Alere hung on, bending low over the mare's neck.

They rode without stopping, with only the cloud-veiled moons' dim light by which to navigate. Only when Luna-Er set, and the horses stumbled with exhaustion, did Kett call a halt. Alere slumped in the saddle, struggling to stay upright. At least the rain had eased to the barest drizzle.

Kett led them into a small village. How he knew which way to go was beyond her. She'd rarely travelled more than two or three gongli beyond the city walls and had no idea which way was south or how Kett kept them from travelling in circles. Maybe they had gone in circles. She didn't care, as long as the misery was over. Her clothes were soaked, her extremities numb with cold and her mind treacle.

In the stableyard of a tiny hostelry, Kett roused a stable boy from bed in the hayloft and handed Bol's reins over before helping Alere dismount. Her thighs ached and her feet sank into the cold quagmire of the yard. For a long time, she simply stood, unsure how to move her exhausted body. Kett urged her towards the squat, mould-blackened inn. He pounded on a warped back door until specks of green paint flaked off and a feeble light gleamed in a window. The door cracked open. A pale eye peered out.

'I know it's late.' Kett held up a tiebi. 'But we'd like two rooms, please.'

The door creaked, opened wider, and a scrawny hand snatched the steel coin. A woman eyed them suspiciously through the slit and nibbled at the coin with yellowed, broken teeth. The tiebi vanished into her pocket. The woman scratched at her wispy bun of greying hair. She opened the door and, with a grunt, ushered them inside. Her brown robe, embroidered with stylised images of big-eared xiao-cats, had seen better days. *She* had seen better days. She picked up a candle and shuffled along a low-ceilinged hall. The dull yellow light jumped, sending sharp shadows scurrying up the dark-timbered walls.

'Up there.' She stopped at the base of a staircase. 'Door on the right. Only one room, though. The other's taken.'

Alere protested. 'But we want—'

'Breakfast's two yinbi. If you've horses to feed, it's another two,' the woman droned on. Still muttering, she rounded the corner and left them in the dark.

'Well,' Alere whispered, 'I'll bet this place is famed for its service.'

'Far and wide. I knew it would live up to your high standards, shunu.' Kett chuckled when she growled at him. 'Let's get upstairs.'

Dim moonlight filtered through a window above the landing. As Kett opened the door, the hinges shrieked and the occupant of the next room moaned. Outside, the clouds broke and Luna-Yi's pale, reddish glow poured into the bedroom through a dirt-smeared window. The room was small, with one narrow bed and a spindly bamboo chair. A hint of mustiness caught in Alere's nose and she sneezed.

'There's dry clothes in the pack,' Kett said, crouching by the small stone fireplace. 'I'll get a fire started. You change.'

Alere rummaged through the haversack. She found a pair of black trous, a high-collared apprentice-weishi black shirt, and a rough sacking cloth to use as a towel.

In one corner of the room stood a plain bamboo privacy screen. Alere slipped behind it and changed. When she emerged, a fire crackled cheerily in the hearth and the smell of cooking meat made her mouth water. Her eyes stung as smoke puffed from the mudbrick chimney. Probably blocked, if the rest of the inn was anything to go by.

Kett rose, brushing his hands. Two quail were spitted on a bronze poker over the fire.

'Where on Kalima did you get those?' Alere asked.

Kett shrugged. 'I stole them from chef at Xintou. They were already cooked. Thought you'd appreciate something hot. Turn them while I change?'

Alere hurried to tend the birds, unable to even voice her gratitude or surprise. Kett, who never stole or deceived, had become a thief and a liar because of her. Guilt twisted her stomach. She didn't deserve such loyalty.

She sat on a low stool and rotated the spit, warming her hands and listening to the rustle of clothing as Kett changed. Without fuss, he wrung their wet things out the window and hung them near the fire, then crouched beside her. He pulled the sizzling birds off the poker and handed one to her. She ate, silenced by hunger.

After the meal, Alere barely had the energy to wipe the grease from her mouth. She stared into the fire's dancing orange light, her body heavy and mind floating. The world vanished behind the red-blackness of her heavy eyelids and she fell into delicious, if damp-smelling, softness.

Dawn's washed-orange light filtered into Alere's dreamless sleep. She swam to consciousness and opened her eyes to a low, timbered ceiling festooned with cobwebs. The straw-stuffed mattress beneath her rustled as she sat up. Kett must have carried her to the bed. He lay on the floor before the smoke-blackened fireplace. He was curled on his side, head pillowed on the haversack, fingers loosely wrapped around his sword's hilt.

The bed creaked. Kett's eyes snapped open, alert and unclouded by sleep. He rose and scrubbed a hand over his face.

'Get up. We need to get moving.' He thrust their laundry into the haversack.

Alere watched him move around the room and belt on his weapons. She was used to Kett as her shifu, brother-figure, and reliable, deferential retainer. Somehow, he'd assumed a leadership role, making decisions without consultation, and she didn't know how to respond.

'And I suppose you know where we are and how far there is to go?' Her sarcasm deserved the level look he returned. Mornings weren't her favourite time and guilt at dragging Kett into this mess sharpened her tongue. She also hadn't quite forgiven him for deserting her at the Alcazar.

He was right, though; they needed to go. She yawned hugely. Fine. If he wanted to run the show, then he could; especially if she didn't have to think before she'd had a cup of lancha tea. Still dressed from last night, she climbed stiffly out of bed and stuffed her feet into her damp house-shoes. She followed Kett from the room, tucking dagger into belt and hair under hat as she went.

Alere trailed him through a narrow, dim-lit hall to the front of the building. The scent of porridge, miso and dumplings set her mouth watering. Kett opened a door to what must be the parlour but stopped so suddenly she bumped into him.

'Hey!' She propelled him into the room and followed. 'Oh.'

A young woman, veiled and dressed in healer's grey and white, sat alone at a rough, slab-timber table by the hearth. She turned and her soft, pretty mouth dropped open.

'You!' The woman started to her feet, tipping the chair over. She pushed the veil up onto her forehead, revealing wide, black-as-night eyes.

'But you...you can't!' Alere gaped at Kett. 'She looks like me. Is this the same girl, Mina? You said—'

Kett shut the parlour door. 'I think we'd best sit down.'

CHAPTER SEVEN

Alere reached across the table towards Mina and hesitated. If she touched Mina's face, would it be real? Was this all some bizarre illusion; some trick of light; a reflection in a mirror? Alere's fingers met warm, smooth skin and she jerked her hand back, cradling it. Mina was real.

A soft-footed young girl in a stained, shapeless robe, entered the parlour, muttered an apology, and laid out breakfast. Kett slid out a wooden stool and gestured for Alere to sit. She sank into the seat and opened her mouth to speak, only to shut it again when the maid reappeared with a pot of lancha tea. Mina raised her eyes briefly, the wonder in their dark depths tainted with a hint of fear.

'Who—' Mina began.

Kett cleared his throat and glanced significantly at the servant. The girl hovered by the table, pouring steaming tea into cracked earthenware cups and dishing out dumplings onto scarred wooden plates.

Alere sipped at her lancha. The brew had been steeped to a deep blue and was almost too bitter. She drank it anyway, needing the jolt to start her brain. Mina drank a mouthful of her tea, screwed up her nose and set the cup aside.

Bacon and steamed dumplings appeared on Alere's plate and she ate, tasting nothing, anxious to be done. The meal passed in silence. Mina's eyes rose often and fixed on Alere, but fell each time Alere caught her looking. Alere was afraid to open her mouth lest she blurt out the questions hovering on her lips.

When the servant cleared the last plates, Kett rose and locked the door. He stood silently by the window, dividing his attention between the women and the road outside.

'I don't understand,' Alere finally said, unable to take her eyes off her reflection opposite.

A strange sort of recognition, a...rightness, settled in Alere's chest at being in close proximity to Mina. She sat back and Mina did the same, giving Alere an eerie illusion of being in two places at once.

Alere inspected Mina, searching for variances and finding few. Same dark hair. Same dark eyes and straight, almost-frowning brows. Same pointed chin and sharp cheekbones, though Mina's face was softer and fuller. The only visible difference lay in a small scar Alere sported on her upper lip.

'Who *are* you? Where are you from?' Alere fingered the scar, waiting for Mina's answer.

'I'm Mina Sura-kin.' Mina's cheeks flushed.

Alere hesitated, uncertain how to reply. The name meant simply 'kin of Sura'. Sura was a woman's name. Which meant Mina was the child of an unknown father to an unwed mother. Father-kin names weren't unusual; mother-kin were. Only the twenty-one Jun families still bore Funding-Family conjoined names. Minor nobility kept a single, First-Family name, like Elmira Connor, or Celia Edwards. The rest were mostly father-kin names, acceptable because their genealogy was traceable. But the colonial stigma of mother-kin names remained even though the population across the four jundoms now numbered hundreds of thousands.

Alere cleared her throat. 'This is Kett Peter-kin and I'm Alere...' Dismay knotted her stomach. She was no longer Alere Connor, daughter to a Bonded Xintou. She was name-bereft. Worse, she could not even claim mother-kinship. She was a wuming – nameless; the lowest of all castes. Less, even than she had been before.

'But why do we look alike?' Mina asked in her soft, country-accented voice. 'What's your family name?' Her gaze was abstract, curious almost. She touched Alere's cheek. Alere jerked back and frowned. Xintou were untouchable. Ordinary people maintained their distance. Mina withdrew her hand, blushing and muttering an apology.

'My family name?' Alere couldn't hide the bitterness in her tone. 'I don't—' She caught Kett's warning glance and steered the conversation in a safer direction. 'Are you from Madina?'

Kett was right. She shouldn't reveal too much. This girl was a stranger. No matter how alike in looks, she was not family and not to be trusted.

'I've been in Madina for four years.' Mina folded her hands on the table, straightening her back like an apprentice brought before the Masters tribunal for wrongdoing. 'I trained as a healer and have just been made journeyman. I'm going home to Gaton.'

'Gaton!' Alere looked to Kett. He shook his head, just a fraction, preventing her thoughts from dancing off her tongue. 'We're heading in that direction, too.'

Elmira had told them to go to Gaton, where both this girl and Alere's real mother lived. Impossibly coincidental. There must be a connection.

Alere rose and paced the cramped room. The timber floor creaked beneath her feet. She curbed her usual impulse to talk over her thoughts with Kett. That wouldn't do here and now.

'There's a mystery here I need to solve.' Alere stopped before the healer. 'Can we travel to Gaton with you?'

Mina's gaze lingered on Kett. She scrubbed her palms down her thighs. 'Very well. Ride with me in the huoche if you like.'

The prospect of sitting on a cushioned seat, rather than spending hours in the saddle, was tempting but Alere needed time to think and to speak with Kett privately. And the awkwardness of being cooped up with someone who was – but was not – herself…No. Better to take time to think about the situation.

'Thank you. Maybe later.' She smiled to take the sting out of the rejection.

A few minutes later Mina was safely tucked into her square-bodied huoche. Two large trunks, bulging with medical paraphernalia, were strapped to the back of the antiquated vehicle. The huoche, drawn by two thick-boned che-ma, was not designed for speed. The driver, a monosyllabic local contracted to take Mina as far as Pelon, sat hunched over the reins. Mina appeared content to travel at the slow pace he dictated.

Alere swung onto Rumi and groaned. Her backside and thighs *hurt*.

Kett chuckled and slewed in the saddle to look at her, his eyes alight with secret humour. 'It has cushions, you know.'

'Oh, shut up.' She flicked the reins lightly across Rumi's neck, wincing as the mare trotted ahead. She lifted her face to the pale, teal-green sky. The orange sun was only a hand's width above the horizon. The feeble light was yet to warm the earth and draw last night's rain from the ground so the air was still cool and dry.

They rode at an easy trot for several gongli then dropped to a walk as they neared a low range of hills and the road steepened. Alere eased Rumi alongside Kett and Bol.

'Who do you think she is?' She watched the huoche splash and jolt through deep potholes filled with muddy water.

Kett rested an elbow on the pommel and raised an ironic brow. 'It'd make more sense to ask *her*. I sure as diyu don't know.'

'I get the impression she doesn't know either.' Alere's head ached. She yanked the tight cap off and scratched at her scalp before tucking her hair up again. 'I wish I was enough of a xintou to Read her history. The best I can hope for is to find Nasra and some answers.'

Kett's eyes lingered on the lumbering huoche. 'It must have occurred to you that her mother might also be yours.'

Alere gripped the reins. Rumi, sensing Alere's tension, tossed her head and danced a few nervous side-steps. Settling the mare gave Alere time to regain self-control.

'Yes,' she said. 'And it scares me.'

Was Mina her sister? The idea had teased her but she'd pushed it aside. If true, it explained the niggling sense she'd carried her whole life: the feeling of being not quite whole; not quite right.

According to Mina, they were the same age, which would make them twins. Identical twins were rare on Kalima and treated with suspicion. If they were twins, her mother had deliberately chosen one daughter above another; rejected Alere. And that also meant Alere was a mother-kin child, and would have to live with the sense of shame that carried – unless she could discover her father's name.

'I thought you'd be glad to have close family.' Kett sent her a quizzical look. 'You left the Ma-Safra household before Elmira birthed Hallee. Mina could be a real sister to you. Wouldn't that be a good thing?'

'I...' Alere twisted the reins. 'I don't know. I have no idea how to be a sister. I spent so many years learning to keep my thoughts and feelings to myself in Xintou House; training to seem calm and cool. I wouldn't know where to start. I've always been alone, even growing up in the Ma-Safra's house.'

'Alli—'

She waved his sympathy aside, unable to bear it. 'I don't have time now, anyway. My life's been blown apart. Suddenly I'm not Elmira's daughter and I have no home. My House has been betrayed. Why the secrets? Why did Elmira and the Jun send me— Oh!' She clapped a hand to her pocket. 'I forgot: his gift. I haven't even looked at it.'

Looping the reins around the pommel, she pulled out the water-blistered silk package and tore off the black ribbon. Kett took the ribbon from her and read the blurred tag. Alere flung the purple and silver wrapper to him. He folded and carefully tucked the silk into his shirt. Orange sunlight turned to blood-red the zitan-wood box lying on her palm. A delicate marquetry of paler timbers picked out the letter 'S', in an exquisite floral design, set into the lid. The copper clasp, stiff and dulled with age, resisted as Alere flicked it open.

Inside, on a bed of dark green silk, lay a polished-steel bracelet set with eight silvery yanstones.

'Oh, my...' Alere showed it to Kett.

Each domed stone was the size of her thumbnail and glowed with shifting, silver-gilt cold-fire. The steel band was two fingers wide and crafted in square, articulated segments. The metal glittered with striations and geometric lines. Alere turned the box and watched the play of light across the design. No, not a deliberate pattern. The lines seemed to be integral to the steel, an internal crystalline structure, not etched onto the surface.

Kett held a hand out. Transfixed by the bracelet's beauty, she almost refused to pass the box over, but his ironic smile opened her grip. She thrust the jewels at him unsure why she was reluctant to let them go. She usually cared little for jewelry.

'Must be worth a fortune.' Kett angled the bracelet so the sun caught the stones. They absorbed the orange hue then exploded into a thousand glittering shards of blood-light. That was the appeal of yanstones: the gems gathered and intensified light, holding it for hours in their fiery hearts.

Alere tore her gaze from the mesmerising shimmer. 'But why did the Jun send me to Nasra and my mother? And why must I ask them who my father is? Radan must have known who my father was. Why not just tell me?'

Kett returned the bracelet to Alere and shook his head.

She snapped the lid shut and stuffed the box deep into a pocket. 'All I can do is hope they have the answers.'

'You do realise,' said Kett, measuring her from beneath dark lashes, 'you could sell the bracelet and disappear.' He gestured at the violet-forested ranges to the east. Misted in haze, beyond the foothills, white-tipped mountains clawed at the sky. 'You've always wanted to be free. You are now. There are settlers beyond the Ahmar Mountains. Or we could continue south, to Jadid. It's a big world and Mamlakah's a small jundom. Its troubles need not be yours.'

Alere pressed her lips tight, afraid she would blurt out how desperately she wanted to agree. The bracelet would fund years of comfortable living somewhere far from Madina. Somewhere no-one knew who she was – or wasn't.

'It's not mine to sell,' she murmured, then gave him a bright, false smile. 'I'm not a thief. You beat that into me, at least.' She slid a hand into her pocket and caressed the box's smooth timber. 'Besides, there's more to it.'

Kett waited. He was good at that. Should she tell him about the deposit? The less he knew, the safer he'd be. But this situation was too big to get her head around. The political implications alone were mind boggling. Kett excelled at thinking problems through and seeing angles she missed in her impatience to get things done.

The huoche rumbled on, out of earshot, but Alere kept her voice low, anyway. 'Celia, Hanna, and Ven were trying to force the Jun to reveal the location of a mineable iron ore deposit. The Jun said they intend to make weapons. They mean to topple Xintou House, then start a war with Melcor. Celia claims the Shah has been raiding the borders, taking slaves and training junren. Hanna mentioned something about *selb* fanatics.'

Kett stiffened, his eyes fixed on her, intent as he waited for her to continue.

She stroked the box's sharp edges. 'I'm sure Radan believed the deposit's located where my father lives. Maybe this bracelet is made from that very iron. He said the iron must be destroyed.'

'Ah.' Kett stared at the huoche. His jaw clenched. 'Interesting.'

'That's it?' she said. 'That's all you're going to say? It's ridiculous to think they could defy Mistress Li, of course. But is it true about the Shah?'

He lifted one shoulder in a shrug. 'The Slavemasters of Melcor have long raided our borders. Whether it's at the behest of the Shah or not, I don't know. But I've heard nothing from Weishi House about the Shah training an army.'

Alere shifted in the saddle, lifting one side of her rear end to ease the bruising. 'Not helpful. What the diyu is a selb, then?'

'I'm not certain, but Mina's attackers back in Madina called themselves selbs and I know I've read the word somewhere. It'll come back to me.'

'Kett, at times you can be really annoying.'

'That, I do know. You've often mentioned it.'

'So, do you think that much iron could actually exist?' she asked. 'If there's a big iron deposit on this planet, can you imagine what it could do for the Jundom that has it?' A world with an abundance of iron was hard to imagine, even though she'd read history books showing the luxurious lifestyles abandoned by the colonists who'd left Earth.

'Yes,' Kett replied after a long pause. He seemed unfazed by her irritation. 'I can see quite clearly what that much iron would do.'

'What does *that* mean?'

'It means,' Kett said, scanning the road behind, 'Hanna is afraid. As Jun Seconds, Petar Ma-Safra and Rafi Koh-Lin, are the only Juns with the resources to challenge her authority. If the iron's on their lands, then Hanna's desire for the deposit is as much about breaking them as about the power of Xintou House or any threat from Melcor.'

'But what am *I* supposed to do about it? Jun Radan said *I* had to stop Hanna.' Alere flung out her arms. 'Who am I? A nameless no-kin. What did he want me to do?'

'He wanted you to find your mother and give that bracelet to your father,' Kett replied evenly. 'Radan was weak and ineffective, but not stupid. If he thought that bracelet was important enough to defy Hanna and Celia for, then we need to move faster. It's possible Celia broke his wards before his death.'

'No,' Alere said, bile rising in her throat at the memory of blood on her hands. 'I'm sure she didn't.'

'How can you be so certain?' Kett asked.

Alere turned away, afraid he'd see the truth. Telling him the whole, wretched reality of Radan's death would destroy his faith in her.

'The bell tolled only moments after I left the Alcazar. There wasn't time.'

'Nevertheless,' he said, 'we can't delay. We need to find out what sort of man your father is.'

Kett nudged Bol into a canter and rode alongside the carriage. He spoke briefly to the huoche driver. It was a testament to Kett's persuasive skills that, within moments, the driver flicked the reins and pressed the che-ma into a trot.

For the rest of the day, Kett pushed hard, pausing only to feed and water the animals, and eat the cold meats and bread bought from the grudging innkeeper that morning. When Mina argued against the need for such a mad pace, Kett spoke with her at length, too softly for Alere to overhear. Alere's heart sank as Mina's stubbornness melted into butter-soft compliance beneath Kett's warm smile.

When Kett remounted and their journey resumed, Alere took several deep breaths to calm her unwonted displeasure. It hurt to see him smile so openly on another when his desertion at the Alcazar still stung.

'You're troubled.' His deep voice intruded on her thoughts.

Alere flipped her cowl up to shade her face from the sun – and from Kett's too-sharp scrutiny. 'It's been a difficult couple of days.' She nodded at the huoche. 'If we're in such a rush, why don't we leave her behind and go on?'

Kett looked at her steadily and a betraying flush warmed her cheeks.

'That was unworthy of you.' He touched his heels to Bol's flanks and trotted ahead, leaving Alere ashamed and angry. Was she really so petty? Kett was right: her childish jealousy was unworthy of her and unfair to him. She urged Rumi on.

'I'm sorry.' She came alongside Kett, matching Rumi's pace to Bol's. 'I'm...frightened and, I suppose, a little jealous. You...' She choked back remembered tears. 'You left me at the Alcazar and now...' Her throat tightened around the words so she indicated the huoche.

Kett was her best friend; her only friend. She depended on his steadying influence. Only now did she realise how much and that frightened her. A xintou should be aloof, bipartisan, focused on truth and what was best for the Jundom, not swayed by individual people.

Kett's stern expression softened. 'I know.' He squeezed her fingers. 'I've been too hard on you. These last couple of weeks have been difficult for both of us. It tore my heart out to leave you like that, but I had to.'

'Had to? Why—'

'Don't ask, Alli.' His eyes were haunted, his mouth hard. 'I can't...maybe one day, after this is done. Just know that we're bound, you and I. Be patient, little though you like it. I'll do my best to bring you through safe.'

She brought his palm to her cheek, as she had when she was younger and he'd rescued her from yet another reckless venture. Her heart brimmed with gratitude. 'Thank you. I missed you, in the Alcazar. I even missed you telling me to be patient.'

'And I, you.' He smiled. 'I had no one to point out my shortcomings, no one to school with the flat of my sword, and no one to tell to be patient.'

'Ya-zheng, shifu.' She bowed her head in mock humility.

Her heart sang at the easing of tensions between them, but she was also disappointed, although in what, she wasn't sure.

When at last they rode into the hamlet of Pelon, distant mountains nibbled at the garnet sun where it shimmered, low in the western sky, and Alere was a fair way to hating her saddle. She eased herself to the ground, balanced precariously between pride and pain, every muscle complaining.

Alere handed Rumi over to an ostler, relieved and guilty not to have to care for the mare. Even staying awake long enough to eat would be a challenge. She'd always considered herself to be fit, strengthened by daily combat training with Kett and weekly lessons at Jaioji House. Clearly, she'd been delusional.

The Crossroads Inn was small, but clean and hospitable. Built of neatly-squared sandstone, the internal walls whitewashed and bamboo floors scrubbed, the inn was a far cry from the previous evening's accommodation. The innkeeper and his wife bustled about making three rooms ready, and even provided copper hip baths with clean, hot water. Once alone, Alere sank into the steaming water and indulged in a few tears of self-pity before speaking firmly to herself. Things were never as bad as they appeared. The worst of her aches eased in the sulphur-smelling water, leaving her enough energy to wash her two sets of weishi clothing and hang them by the fire to dry.

She put on her red-robe and sat near the fire, staring into its crackling depths. Without boy's clothes, she couldn't go downstairs. Dinner in her room suited her mood anyway, and she could use the time to replace the perished leather on her dagger. The innkeeper had kindly provided her with several lengths of suede from his wife's stores. Alere picked out a green swatch.

Kett's light step fell on the landing and his knock sounded on the door. Squinting in the flickering lamplight, Alere called out for him to enter, busy with the leather.

'Nice dagger,' Kett said. 'Where'd you get it?'

'Radan gave it to me just before he…died.' Guilt fluttered, low in her stomach and she passed the knife to Kett. 'He said it was at least two hundred years old.'

'Radan…' Kett turned the dagger over in his hands, his gaze distant. He held the blade up to the mel-oil lamp's smudgy yellow light. 'Lovely balance and still clean and sharp. Amazing. I think this might be from the old world. They had a way of making steel so it didn't rust. I don't recognise that crest, or the stone. Must be one of the old family lines that died out.'

He gave the dagger to Alere who cradled it close against her stomach. Earth steel. She'd read about it in history books. Today, Earth steel was almost unheard of, the only pieces remaining were old machines brought to the planet by the colonists. A few still operated; most had long since been broken down and recycled because of the steel's high value. Even Kett's sword, a family heirloom forged of Kalima iron and many hundreds of years old, was of inferior quality.

Alere studied the play of firelight dancing across the metal. The weapon embodied the best and worst of the original colonists who'd brought it to Kalima: their strength, their ingenuity, their endurance; and the double edge of violent self-destruction that forced them to leave Earth.

'Do you think they knew?' she asked.

'Who?' Kett smiled at her.

'The colonists,' she said. 'When they terraformed this world, Kalima already had land and oceans, but no history of life and no iron.' She looked up at Kett. 'Did they know how hard having no – what were they called? – fossil fuels, and no iron, would make it for us? We have alzin and bronze and copper, but they aren't the same. D'you think they realised the lack of iron might start the very wars they ran from?'

Kett touched the blade, his expression grave. 'How could they? They would've expected the ships from Earth to keep supplying iron-goods. And Kalima had some volcanic iron-sand deposits to begin with. And a few asteroid-miners. Before the Sol-wars cut us off from Earth. Iron would've been valuable six hundred years ago, but not as rare as now.'

'So why does Mistress Li object to the Miner and Craftsman Houses trying to extract iron from the soil?' Alere stared into the fire. 'Wouldn't more iron make our lives better? At least we wouldn't fight over it.' She absently scraped her thumb across the blade's sharp edge.

'Does Mistress Li object? Interesting.' Kett scratched at the stubble on his chin. 'She's always espoused stability over change. After all, stability's part of the House motto: *"Clarity, stability, responsibility, and compassion".*' He grimaced. 'But even if we had all the iron we wanted, we're human. We'd find something to fight over. Humans are inventive when it comes to war. We've both read dozens of the Weishi House books on the subject. It's only surprising it's taken the colony so long to get to this point.'

Her heart sank at his words. 'If it's inevitable, how am I supposed to stop it?'

Kett crouched, searching her face. 'I don't yet know, but we'll work it out, Alli. Together.'

'But Hanna, Ven...Celia – they're not your problem, Kett. You shouldn't risk your life as well. Why did you give everything up to come with me? Why did you say the House wasn't safe for you?'

He bowed his head, his fingers white on her chair-arm. 'Hanna and Ven are everyone's problem,' he said at last, lifting his head. His eyes held the vestiges of dark pain that made Alere's heart contract. Then he smiled and the look vanished. 'Besides, Mistress Li charged me with your care when you were ten and hasn't revoked that. I'm coming with you, whether you like it or not.'

'Thank you.' She kissed his cheek. He hadn't answered her last question, but he'd retreated behind a calm façade that made asking twice seem rude. When he was ready, he would tell.

He hesitated then rose and stared enigmatically at her. 'Alli, I want—'

A knock sounded on the door. A maid announced that dinner was served in the communal dining room downstairs.

Alere leaned back in her chair and cut the length of green leather for the knife hilt. 'What did you want, Kett?'

He paused, wry amusement in his eyes. 'Dinner. Not coming down to eat?'

'Not in this.' She plucked at her robe. 'Would you mind asking them to leave a tray outside?'

'Of course.' He strode to the door. 'And sleep well. We'll start early. You must be exhausted. It's not quite like a few hours of training, is it?'

The door closed and Alere busied herself tying the scrap of leather around the exposed metal tang of her new dagger. The engraving did resemble a family crest, but not one with which she was familiar. The words were in an unfamiliar language. They read: *nunquam non paratus.* She wound the suede over the tang, and the spur and buckle motif was soon hidden beneath the soft leather.

When finished, she held the dagger up to the firelight. The weapon truly was beautiful. The milk-silver stone on the pommel's end caught the light and, deep in the stone's heart, a small glimmer of gold-fire answered. She rotated the dagger, hypnotised by the tiny flame. Maybe the gem was a yanstone after all.

The maid returned and left a tray of noodles and fried rong. Alere ate quickly, the rich golden straight-eel flesh hot and filling. After tucking dagger and jewelry box under her pillow, she climbed into bed. Luxurious spice-otter fur edged the quilt's top seam, lending the linen a cardamom-sweetness that soothed Alere's anxieties as she drifted into sleep.

CHAPTER EIGHT

Alere awoke to the creak of a floorboard and the faintest rustle of cloth. She inched a hand beneath the pillow, clutched her dagger and steadied her breathing, feigning sleep. Luna-Er's pale light glimmered through a chink in the curtain so several hours must have passed. A dark form loomed over her. Dagger-drawn, she slashed at the shadowy figure. Strong fingers bore her wrist down.

'Glad to see you're alert, but I'm reasonably sure you don't want to kill me.' Kett's hushed words barely reached her ears. 'The Alcazar guards are almost here. They've caught up faster than I expected.' He yanked open the curtain and pressed a fistful of damp clothing into her hand.

'How do you know?' Alere leapt from bed and dragged on the trous and shirt, shuddering as the cold cloth clung to her skin. Kett threw her remaining possessions into his pack. Alere stuffed the box and dagger into her pockets.

'I paid some children to camp up the road and signal if someone approached.' Kett peered out the window. 'You get Mina. I'll ready the horses.'

'She'll slow us down in that carriage. They're not looking for her.'

Kett frowned. 'We're not taking the carriage. The Alcazar weishi may not be looking for Mina, but they are looking for you. And she *is* you. We cannot, in good conscience, leave her to their mercy. Now go.'

Alere thrust aside the fleeting, appalling thought that if Mina's identity *was* mistaken, all their problems would be solved. How could she even think such a thing? Ashamed, she fled into the hall and slipped into Mina's room, relieved the girl was trusting enough to leave her door unlocked. Alere flung the bedcovers aside and shook the sleeping figure.

'Wha—?' Mina blinked, bleary-eyed in the silvery moonlight. 'Alere? I thought I dreamt of myself. Why are you here?'

'Get up.' Alere snatched a travel bag and pile of clothes from the floor and thrust them at Mina. 'Get dressed. We have to leave.' She peered out the window. Nothing but darkness and a single torchlight flickering in the stable.

'I don't understand,' Mina protested, rising from the bed. Her healer robe fell from one lax hand and puddled on the bamboo floor 'Why? It's the middle of the night.'

Alere spun, snarling her frustration. 'Jiche! Don't argue. *I'm* in danger so *you're* in danger because you look like me.' She yanked the robe over Mina's head. 'Believe me, if I thought we could safely leave you behind I would.'

Mina's mussed hair and wide eyes appeared in the robe's neck-hole.

'But I can't,' Alere added, 'so grab what you need and get moving – unless you want to stay and be executed for murder.'

'Murder! Who did you murder?'

'No one.' Alere looked away. 'But I will if you don't hurry up.' She glanced out the window to where Kett waited in the stable-yard below. Rumi and Bol were saddled, along with a rather rough-looking stockhorse, presumably from the inn stables.

A string of six red torches appeared in the distance, bobbing along the dark north road, moving closer by the second. Billowing fog smeared the lights into a bloody glow. The Alcazar guards added red-burning calcium salts to their torches to instil terror into the populace. Knowing that didn't make their appearance any less ominous. Alere watched, fixated, unable to shake the notion that three pairs of giant xiao-cat eyes stared back.

'Hurry! They're coming,' Alere urged.

'What about my trunks? I can't leave my medical equipment.' Mina stuffed her scant possessions into the bag.

'You can come back for them.'

'But—'

'Stop arguing and move. Kett's downstairs with the horses.' Alere grabbed Mina's hand. 'He sent me to get you.'

'Kett...oh, well...' Mina stopped resisting.

'Oh, zhenshide!' Alere rolled her eyes. She towed Mina downstairs and out into the chill evening air of the stableyard.

'Hurry.' Kett scanned the north road and beckoned to Alere and Mina. 'They're close.'

An irregular tattoo of hoof beats rattled off the timber buildings.

'Too late. Here, take the horses.' Kett thrust the bundle of reins at Alere. 'Get Mina to safety. I'll hold them here.'

'I'm not leaving you,' Alere said.

'Then move her out of harm's way.' He pointed towards the inn. 'And get your knife ready. You'll need it. Show no mercy, for they won't.'

Six hooded riders materialised, faceless wraiths of mist and red shadows. Their black and silver livery glinted in the carmine torchlight.

Kett swore.

'Hold these hard and be ready.' Alere shoved the reins into Mina's hands and dragged her away from the riders. 'Can you use a bow?'

Mina shook her head, trembling as she clutched the reins.

'Jiche! Then use the roan as a weapon. She's trained to kick on command. Things are about to go suilie.' Alere glanced over her shoulder to where the semicircle of cloaked horsemen blocked the exit. Fog swirled in spectral fingers that rose from the cold ground to stroke the horses' heaving chests and drooping heads. Foam flecked the animals' mouths and sweat darkened their hides. Alere grimaced. If only she'd been a little faster. Even Mina's stock horse could've outrun the exhausted animals.

After surveying Kett, Mina and Alere, the weishi leader nudged his mount closer to Kett. The man's countenance was obscured by his black and silver hood. He slid his sword free of its scabbard. The scrape of ceramic on leather drove fear into Alere's blood. With her head bowed subserviently, she stood before Mina, ready to protect the unarmed girl.

'So,' the guardsman drawled, circling the three, 'this is a strange time of night to be travelling.'

Alere stiffened. That voice; the sneering, arrogant politeness: Kahler, second in command of the Alcazar weishi.

'Indeed, it is, shenshi,' Kett replied, with a respectful inclination of his head. Alere had no way of warning him.

'Do you have an explanation?' Kahler leaned forward, his face still in shadow. The saddle creaked. His thick fingers stroked the ceramic blade across his lap.

'Of course,' Kett replied, still courteous. 'My mistress is a healer and we've received word that the next village is stricken by illness. She's summoned urgently. My apprentice and I are her escorts.'

'Really.' Kahler drawled the word. 'Now why don't I believe you?'

Alere groaned under her breath. In her rush to get Mina dressed, she'd forgotten the white veil. Had Mina worn it, Kett's story may have held. But Khaler knew Alere's face; and therefore Mina's.

Kett kept his hands open, raising his brows in innocence. 'I don't know, shenshi. Please, let us go. We cannot be delayed.'

Khaler gave a disdainful laugh. He drove brass spurs into the bloodied flanks of his mount. The mare lurched forward, foam dripping from her mouth. Khaler lifted a hand and his men shifted, almost encircling the travellers. Alere stepped back, pushing Mina behind her, trying to keep a gap in the wall of horsemen.

'You can, and will, be delayed.' Khaler flung back his hood, eyes glittering in the torchlight. His mouth stretched in predatory, savage triumph and he pointed at Mina. 'Because not long ago I had the pleasure of teaching this chouhuo a lesson. I daresay she remembers the sting of my fist on her cheek.'

Alere resisted the urge to touch the bruise. Kett's hand dropped to his sword hilt and his eyes hardened. Khaler kicked his horse closer to Alere and Mina, closing the circle and surrounding Kett with armed, mounted men.

'But perhaps she forgot I saw her.' Khaler's voice oozed false surprise. 'I know she's the jiaoji wanted for the murder of our Jun First and Mistress Renna of Xintou House.' He pointed the tip of his sword at Mina and spat at her feet.

She shrank away, watching Khaler with wide, frightened eyes as she pressed against Rumi.

Khaler swept his men with an irritated glare. 'What are you waiting for? Take her into custody.'

Alere faced Mina. Turning her back on Khaler was a risk, but was also the unexpected. Even a moment's hesitation on Khaler's part afforded a chance for Kett to act.

'Mistress?' Alere slid one hand to the hilt of her dagger. 'Is it true? Surely not?' Sotto voce she added, 'As soon as it starts, take the horses and get your back against the inn wall.'

Mina's fearful expression firmed into comprehension. She nodded.

'Boy, stop muttering and move aside.'

The flat of Khaler's sword stung Alere's arm. She yelped and barely stopped herself glancing up and exposing her face. Instead, she shuffled aside, bobbing and bowing in servile mock-fear.

Khaler laughed and fixed his disdainful gaze on Mina who, to her credit, raised her chin and moved backward. With Khaler's attention on Mina, Alere edged nearer to his horse. She hid her dagger flat along the inside of her forearm, then slipped the blade between the saddle girth and belly of Kahler's horse. Sharp steel slit the girth-strap leather like silk. Alere slapped the animal hard on the rump. The horse reared and tossed its head, dancing a few steps to the left. Khaler hauled at the reins, yelling as the saddle slid and he plunged to the ground.

Alere leapt forward and snatched the sword from Khaler's hand. He thrashed about on the packed earth, struggling to free his feet from the stirrups. He tore one foot loose and kicked at the saddle. Alere laid the swordpoint against his neck.

'Stay still, or I'll happily slit your throat.'

He smacked the blade aside and rolled away from her, untangling himself from the saddle. No! She couldn't give him a chance. He was weishi, and with years more experience. She closed the gap between them before he could get to his feet and dug the blade's tip deep into the hollow of his throat. Blood welled, dark in the silvery moonlight, pulsing with each beat of his heart. Khaler stiffened, nostrils flaring and teeth bared in animal fury. Alere pressed the blade deeper. Blood traced a glistening trail down his neck and dripped onto the packed earth. He growled.

'Don't try me, Khaler.' She touched her bruised cheek. 'I owe you.'

His eyes widened.

Behind her, steel clashed with ceramic. Alere risked a glance up. An Alcazar weishi lay on the ground, eyes emptied by death, Kett's throwing knife lodged in his chest. The dead man's horse whinnied and hauled frantically at the reins trapped beneath its rider. Two weishi swung off their mounts and advanced on Kett. Another stalked Mina, who cowered against the inn wall, watching his approach in wide-eyed horror. Wasn't there one more weishi? Alere frowned. A fading drum of hoof beats told their own story. She swore. Her bow was too far away.

At her feet, Khaler laughed. He shoved the sword blade away again, slicing open his palm. His large hands seized her ankle and yanked her off balance. Alere slammed into the hard earth, sword jolting from her hand. Winded and coughing, she lashed out with her free foot. Her heel connected with something solid that gave with a sharp crack. Khaler shrieked and spat a curse. He scrambled to his feet and pounced on the sword. He now had the advantage of height, reach and strength, while she lay on the ground. Alere swore.

She twisted and scythed her legs, catching him behind the knees. He staggered two steps away, but stayed upright. She rolled to the right, following him, and snapped a kick at the leg bearing most of his weight. The knee twisted and bulged. He screamed and clutched at her, dropping the sword. She kicked the weapon away. It skittered across the dirt towards Mina.

Khaler would have another weapon concealed in his clothing. She couldn't allow him time to regroup. She shoved upright and leapt at him, dagger in hand. He blocked the dagger with an alzin-clad forearm. His fingers latched onto her windpipe. She'd underestimated him. Kahler squeezed, grinning as Alere scrabbled at his arm. His bloated face filled her vision.

The grip on her throat tightened. The world grew silent, but for the blood pounding in her ears; muffling Khaler's triumphant laugh. Panic swelled. No. She knew what to do. Alere twisted to the right and brought her left arm over his. His grip broke. She sucked a quick breath into starved lungs. Red lights sparkled behind her eyes as blood pumped back to her brain.

Her legs trembled, but she had to move. With a quick left-step, she jammed her elbow into Khaler's nose, which crunched satisfyingly. He staggered back, blood cascading over his mouth and chin. She drove the steel dagger through his leather and alzin armour, hilt-deep into his chest. Khaler gasped and pawed feebly at the knife. He dropped to his knees and raised bemused eyes to hers. She yanked the blade free. He swayed and collapsed sideways, blood pumping from the hole in his chest to stain the earth.

Alere stood over his body and sucked great lungsful of air, trying to hold herself together. Her knees shook uncontrollably. She rode the ebb of adrenalin and the urge to throw up. Khaler's blood was on her hands. She had killed a man. Not a good man but, nevertheless... Her actions were not the same as freeing Radan from pain.

A torch guttered on the dirt nearby. The light flared, giving Khaler's face the illusion of movement. Alere turned away from his staring eyes. She pressed shaking fingers to her mouth and swallowed self-hatred with the bile that burnt her throat. Her tongue touched a metallic warmth on her lips. She jerked her hand away, staring in horror at Khaler's blood, dark on her fingers. Her stomach heaved.

'Alere!' Kett's sharp tone snapped her from the daze.

'Bai shifu.' She responded automatically, jumping to attention. His command voice yanked her back from the brink of hysteria. She clung to the steadying familiarity of his presence and blinked away sweat and tears.

Kett thumbed the blood from her lips and inspected her. 'Are you hurt?'

'No shifu, but I—'

'You did what was necessary. You did as you were trained and you did it well. Put it aside. We need to get moving. One escaped and he'll raise the alarm.'

Alere took stock. Five bodies littered the ground. Kett had accounted for three. One more bore Rumi's hoofprints in his collapsed chest. Mina crouched against a wall, sobbing. She clung to the horses' reins as though they were a lifeline and she was drowning. Kett took a half-step towards her. He glanced at Alere.

'I'm fine,' Alere lied. 'Go help her.' She jerked her chin at Mina, trying to overcome a deep desire to behave in the exactly the same fashion.

Alere wiped blood from her hands and cleaned her blade on a dead weishi's clothing. As an afterthought, she divested the smallest body of boots, socks and heavy woollen black and silver cloak; all too large but better than her house shoes and thin clothing as they headed south and the nights lengthened and cooled. She took his scabbard, belted on the ceramic sword, and added her dagger in place of his. The sword was large and unwieldy, but would do for the moment.

'A wise thought.' Kett threw an Alcazar weishi cloak around his own shoulders to replace his black and gold Xintou-badged one. 'Mina's calm enough now and the inn's awake with the noise. Let's go.' He handed a cloak to Mina and helped her mount.

Swinging into his saddle, he nodded to Alere. 'You take point. I'll bring up the rear. Get us off the road as soon as you can. Head for the mountains and we'll find a hiding place.'

Alere mounted and kicked Rumi into a trot, out of the stable-yard. Behind, a babble of voices arose as the innkeeper and his wife found the mess left for them. It seemed a poor way to repay their hospitality. Alere headed south along the broad, packed-earth road dividing the hamlet. She drew the cloak close as her damp clothing gathered the chill night and drained heat from her body.

'I know a place we can hide.' Mina's voice was faint, her teeth chattering. 'It's not far from here. Safe, hidden, and with water and grass for the horses.'

Kett twisted in his saddle and studied the road behind. 'Can you find it in the dark?'

Mina studied the clear, star-speckled sky. The gibbous crescent of Luna-Er rode low above the western horizon, spilling fae silver light between long shadows.

She nodded. 'Er will set in a little over two hours. That should give us time.'

'Ride then.' Kett glanced again at Pelon's wide main street. More lights shone in upper windows. Sleepy villagers poked their heads out of doors and asked questions of each other. 'Ride now before anyone gets a good look at the two of you,' he added.

Mina clucked at her mount and kicked it into a lumbering gallop. Rumi raced after, Bol pounding close behind.

The sun was well up when Alere woke. She stretched and sucked a sharp breath as the movement pulled at bruises and abused muscles. Her head was thick and eyes gritty with sleeplessness. Each time she'd closed her eyes, Khaler's sneering face appeared. Her stomach roiled with fear and guilt. Even now her heart thudded as she tentatively explored the bruises on her neck. She shied away from the memory.

Nearby, Mina lay huddled under her cloak, lips slack with sleep. Tear-tracks smeared the road dust on her skin. Alere sighed. Mina was annoying and oddly compelling; too sweet and gentle, too perfect. But she possessed an enviable, quiet strength, and had recovered quickly after the fight, especially considering she'd been unwillingly dragged into this escapade – although she wasn't alone in that.

Alere rose. The fire had died down and someone, probably Kett, had buried it. He wasn't in the cave so he must be either tending to the horses or hunting. They'd purchased only enough supplies for a day or two on the road, not a prolonged stay in the mountains.

Thirst and a need to relieve herself drove Alere into the morning sunlight. She pulled aside a curtain of blue-black leaves that concealed the cave's entrance and stopped, squinting against the glare. Bloody morning sunlight glinted and reflected in opalescent shimmers off the valley walls. Every facet of every rock glistened and sparkled. It was like being inside a vast diamond.

She touched the nearest rock. Ah. The glitter was simply a result of crystal alignment; beautiful, but not valuable or mystical. She smiled at the pragmatic streak her more romantically-inclined House sisters had always disliked.

Stretching in the warm sun, Alere inspected the valley. It was an excellent refuge: small and almost circular, extending for several hundred paces in each direction and bounded by glittering cliffs. Over the eastern cliff tumbled a misted waterfall, which pooled first amongst jumbled black rocks then fed a bubbling stream that meandered across the flat floor.

In the valley centre, a small, grassy hill broke the flat swathe of meadow. Around the hill were heaped piles of red dirt; some grassed over and some fresh. They were too big for either glass-rabbit or tunnel pig mounds. People had been excavating. Perhaps this valley wasn't as hidden as Mina thought. If the miners returned, Alere's party would be discovered.

The horses grazed close to the cave. Rumi raised her head. A massive, black and grey roc eagle launched from the eastern cliff-top; it's mournful hunting wail echoing off the cliffs. Rumi whinnied and galloped towards Alere, who watched as the reptile snapped its leathery wings open in the chill morning air and flexed its eight-taloned feet. The predator was big enough to take a human. With one more cry, the roc-eagle banked, showing its pale green belly, and vanished to the south. Alere relaxed.

She tasted the air – clean, free of humanity's stench and the filth tainting the city. She rested against Rumi's warm hide and gathered strength from the mare's affectionate nuzzling. The sun warmed Alere's back and she closed her eyes, safe and tranquil for the first time in many days.

'What's for breakfast?' She spoke without looking around.

Kett's deep chuckle sounded. 'You're getting better.'

She turned.

'What's wrong?' His smile vanished.

Alere stroked Rumi's soft nose. 'It's all happened so fast.'

'You're handling it well so far.' He lifted Alere's chin and inspected her neck. 'Those bruises look bad but they'll heal. You fought superbly last night. What's our next move, shunu?'

She shoved his hand aside. 'Jiche! Don't patronise me, Kett. All this has served to show me what an arrogant little shazi I've been. How much I took my place in the world for granted.'

Rumi whickered softly and pushed her head into Alere's hand. Alere stroked the long nose and leaned on the mare's neck.

'We all do,' Kett murmured, staring across the valley, 'until it's taken from us.'

'One minute everything was laid out for me, little though I liked it, and now...' Alere rubbed at a crusted smear of blood on her hand.

'Alli.' Kett stilled her hands with his own. 'It'll be alright. You don't have the luxury of falling apart right now. Forget the dead. They can only harm you if you let them into your mind. Stay focussed. You need answers and we need to clear your name if we can, or at least prevent a war. So, I repeat, what's our next step?'

He was right. Her duty to Radan and the Jundom had to take precedence. Alere swept fear aside. 'I guess we need to get to Gaton and find Nasra and my mother.'

'Yes,' he said, falling into step as she headed back to the cave. 'I was thinking about that. I'm not sure you going with Mina to Gaton is the best answer. She's not trained for this. She's afraid. She'll give you away by accident. I've got a better idea.'

'You want to what?' Mina reeled back against a glittering wall and sank to the ground, staring up at them in disbelief. 'You want her to pose as me, in my own village? While you keep me prisoner here?'

'No, no.' Alere sat beside Mina on the red dirt floor. 'You're not a prisoner. You'll be safe here.'

'While you pretend to be me? But why?' Mina gathered her cloak closer. 'Who are you? What are you running from? Why did those weishi want you? They were Alcazar men and Kett killed them. You killed one, too. Oh.' She hid behind her hands. 'I'm a healer and I murdered a human being!'

Alere hesitated. If she spoke, the horror of last night might resurface and destroy her own precarious equanimity. The last thing she wanted was to dissolve into tears in front of Kett.

Mina raised a tear-stained face. 'How can you be so calm? Who are you? You were dressed in the gold in Madina, but you're not xintou. Now you're acting like you're a real weishi, but you're not, are you?'

Kett ran a thumb across the throwing-star tattoo on his wrist. 'Alere doesn't have the black cap or the tattoo. But, to all intents, she is a member of the black. She's done her training proud.'

Alere turned aside, the sickening memory of blood warring with gratification. 'Who we are is a long story and I'm not sure you'd believe me. Basically, it boils down to one thing.' She looked Mina squarely in the eye. If only it didn't feel uncannily like looking in a flawed mirror. 'I need to speak with Nasra Connor.'

Mina gaped. 'How do you know Nasra?'

'I'm...Elmira Connor's daughter.' Alere grasped at the simplest explanation. 'I have a message for Nasra but I must deliver it secretly.'

'You're Elmira's daughter? How could you be? Her daughter is Hallee and she's ten.' Mina touched Alere's dark plait. 'Nasra, Elmira and Hallee all have red hair. Elmira would keep that gene. Nasra told me Elmira's a nai-xintou – a gene-sequencer – but you look nothing like...I mean...you look like...me. How could she achieve that?'

'I don't know,' Alere said, 'and that's part of the mystery I need to solve.'

'Why can't we both go into town and ask together?' Mina wrapped her arms around her knees, her mouth set mulishly.

'Because there's a good chance that escaped weishi will lead a regiment straight to Gaton. The innkeeper knew you were going there.' Alere touched Mina's arm. 'I'm sorry we were in the wrong place and got you involved. I'm trying to protect you and your family. If Mina shows up, then they can safely say they never met Alere, the wanted fugitive. See?'

Mina paled. She twisted a dead leaf in her fingers, crushing it. Shuddering, she brushing off the black dust.

'Did you kill the Jun?' She shot Alere a sharp look.

'No. I promise I didn't.' It took all Alere's jiaoji training to hold Mina's gaze without flinching.

Mina regarded her awhile longer then nodded slowly. 'I have no idea why but, for some reason, I believe you.' She squinted at the bright daylight outside the cave. 'But it's still a week's ride from here. More if we stay off the main road. There's another hidden valley, closer to the village, we can base ourselves in. Will you be long in Gaton?'

Relieved, Alere packed away her things. 'We'll have to ride hard and get there faster than a week. The Alcazar won't give up now. They'll be right on our heels. I should only need a day or two in Gaton. And,' she added reluctantly, 'perhaps it's best if Kett stays with you. They wouldn't expect you to come with a weishi anyway.'

Mina's brow cleared to thoughtful consideration. 'Well, I would feel safer. This is raider territory and they don't like trespassers. They're not as violent as they once were, but they'll have scouts watching.' She returned her attention to Alere. 'I'll lend you my robe and you'll need to know a few things about the villagers.'

She frowned. 'Apart from my mother, Sura, the person who knows me best is Rohne, my best friend.' Her eyes flickered to Alere and away again. 'But you won't be able to fool him for long. He's…different.'

'How so?'

'Best I let him tell you. Just…' Mina sighed. 'Try to withhold judgement. He's a good person.'

After threshing out the basics of a plan, Kett left to saddle the horses. As the vines closed behind him Mina cast Alere a quick look beneath long lashes.

'Are you and Kett lovers?'

Alere huffed a laugh. 'No. He's been my weishi, my shifu and almost a brother these last ten years. I don't think of him that way at all.' It was truth, but Mina's interest in Kett made Alere uncomfortable. 'Of course,' she said, shrugging, 'the girls at Jiaoji House were always glad to see him when he escorted me there for lessons. But if he's had a longer relationship, he's kept it discreet. None of my business, anyway.'

'And how does he feel about you?' Mina ask softly.

Alere folded Kett's cloak and placed it in the knapsack. The cloth smelled of wood smoke and dirt, and the rough material rasped across her skin.

'The same,' Alere said, matter-of-factly. 'We're friends but I know he'd do anything for me, and I for him.' She lifted her chin. 'I've tried to tell him I don't need him, but he's pledged to help me see this through. He's weishi; hired by Mistress Li to protect me. That takes precedence over everything.' She tried to shake off her discomfort. Kett was a friend and weishi, nothing more.

'I see.' Mina finished packing and silently left the cave.

CHAPTER NINE

ROHNE

A child's shrill scream sliced through the warm afternoon's peace. Rohne frowned and lowered his book. The distant cry was one of excitement, not fear, so he stayed in his comfortable spot beneath the midnight tree. From this hill he could see the length of Gaton's wide main street, to the central square. A dozen people clustered about a female figure in grey. More excited voices rose in a clamour of indecipherable words. Children tugged at the woman's skirts, demanding attention. A dog yipped, dashing back and forth.

Rohne squinted against the late afternoon flare of sunlight. Sura must be back from a midwifing in one of the nearby villages. He lifted his book then paused and studied the grey-robed figure again. No, only an hour before Sura had been here in Gaton, tending to Eshia, the cooper's wife. This newcomer couldn't be Sura.

Someone yelled a name and Rohne froze. His heart thudded. He scrambled to his feet, his shirt catching on the rough black bark of the midnight tree. The book fell from his lap. He snatched up his jacket, stuffed the thin volume into a pocket and slapped at the stains on his clothing. The red-earth marks refused to brush off. He'd been helping Henner prepare the fields that would supply Jiali with hemp next season. Now there was no time to change.

Mina had returned.

Rohne plucked free several night-dark leaves clinging to his hair. A layer of winter-death blanketed the ground around him, like a hole in the earth through which the skeletal midnight tree clawed towards the sky. The leaves crackled underfoot as he ran to join the villagers gathered in the dusty square.

Rohne peered over the villagers' heads, angling for a glimpse of Mina's dark eyes and gentle smile. He hadn't seen her for over four years. Had she missed him? He'd missed her. She was the only one in this forsaken hole of a town who'd always accepted him.

Her throaty laugh rose above the villagers' rough voices. Rohne glimpsed her face, half-hidden by the healer's veil, her long, dark hair braided severely back. He directed a thought towards her.

That was all it took. One touch of her mind and he knew.

The girl was an imposter.

Rage snaked through his stomach and curled his hands into fists. Who was she? What had she done with Mina? Fear displaced anger and he grabbed at the bakery porch-rail for support. Had this imposter murdered Mina and taken her place? No, surely not? He would have felt Mina's death. Resolutely, he pushed aside the knowledge that Madina was outside his range, even for someone he knew as well as Mina. She was alive. She had to be.

He tamed his spiralling fears. There was no point in calling this girl to account now. With most of Gaton's two hundred inhabitants gathering, the afternoon bid fair to become an impromptu coming-home party. No-one would believe him, for this interloper looked and acted like the Mina the villagers had known their whole lives. Rohne's abilities allowed him to distinguish between the women, but his skills had remained hidden for twenty-four years. Now was not the time to reveal himself. He would wait 'til the time was right to confront the fraud.

He avoided her eye and instead strolled around the edges of the crowd, watching. Did no-one else notice the difference? Turning up the fur collar of his jacket against the cool of dusk, Rohne ducked into the shadows and Read the Mina-look-alike. He probed her mind, more powerfully this time, and recoiled in surprise. She was xintou-trained; her Inners invisible. Her public Outers were so skilfully ordinary anyone else Reading would turn away in sheer boredom. Mina knew the basics, but her Outer wards thinned to transparency when she lost concentration. This girl's were stone, without a crack or flaw to be found.

Rohne withdrew and shifted so he could see her, irritated to be reduced to observing only the outside. Whoever she was, she'd been well-briefed about the people of Gaton. He watched her hug all the right people and speak all the right names in Mina's soft, sultry voice. But behind the white veil her eyes never rested, and her hand strayed often to the dagger on her hip. Rohne curled a lip. No-one questioned why a healer carried a weapon.

The girl's wards didn't falter, so Rohne turned his attention to Sura, Mina's mother. Surely she must have realised? He caught a glimpse of Sura's expression: disbelieving, bewildered joy. With great delicacy, Rohne Read her, but Sura had been trained by Nasra and warded closely. He learned nothing beyond a fleeting sense of wonder and a hint of worry for her daughter. Sura did know the newcomer wasn't Mina, but didn't consider her to be a threat.

Perhaps Mina wasn't in danger. Rohne grinned. In that case, exposing this intruder would be fun. It might even relieve the monotony of living in a small village that clung, like a beggar, to the skirts of far richer farmland to the northwest. The folk of Gaton were boring, their pleasures simple, their thoughts and conversation more tedious than Reading a hibernating xiao-bear.

As night fell, a dozen mag-nite celebration torches flared to brilliance, sparkling like yanstones, around the square. Children danced beneath them, holding up eager hands to catch the cascading snowfall of white sparks, laughing when the sparks bounced off skin and vanished. Neffa and Brid struck up a tune on the viol and pipes. Delar, the butcher, snatched at not-Mina's hands and dragged her, protesting, into a dance that kicked up dust and set the children giggling. Rohne lifted a brow. Whoever she was, this woman moved with extraordinary grace. Energetic confidence, bordering on arrogance, spiked through her constructed calm. Night-black hair, braided back, lent a severity that ill-suited her sharp features. Mina always wore her hair loose. Thoughtful and gentle, Mina could not have turned into this intense stranger.

Possibly the girl was just a scam artist. But was she alone, or with accomplices? Rohne studied the villagers and tasted the crowd's emotions, searching for strangers. There was nothing unusual. He extended his reach to sweep through the surrounding mountains. He wouldn't be able to Read the mind of someone he'd never seen, but he could sometimes feel a presence. It was worth a try.

In the nearest hills, among the winter-bare branches of the silk-mulberry plantations, he found only the skittish minds of a few hardy goats. Further east he tasted the blood-wild mind of a prowling xiao-cat, and a den of spice-otters.

He made note of their location. Otters rarely came this close and their presence attracted the xiao-cats, which were a threat to villagers and livestock. No point in going to the Jun Fourth for help, though. Hassan Wen-Gates paid Gaton no attention. Jada Marin-kin, kui of the local mountain raiders who traded with the villagers, was the logical person to deal with a hunting xiao-cat. He and his men would track the cat, take the skin and spice-otter furs as payment and give Rohne a cut of the profit. And, of course, trapping the cat would protect the village children.

As far as he could tell, there were no other minds close to Gaton so Rohne directed his thoughts to the chattering villagers. He slid his attention from one person to another, feeling an edge to someone, somewhere in the room.

Nasra glided across from the other side of the square, her dark blue eyes serious behind the gold veil. She reached his side and pressed one cool, smooth cheek to his.

'Mother.' Rohne nodded to her, keeping the not-Mina girl in sight. 'Sura's daughter has returned, you see.' He grinned at Nasra, inviting her to share in his secret knowledge.

Nasra smiled and Rohne heard the Outer revealed through her wards.

'Yes, I'd guessed as much.' He propped himself against a cool stone wall and watched the girl from beneath lowered lids. 'Who is she, then?' He shrugged at Nasra's next Outer, unsurprised at her noncommittal response.

He was used to these half-conversations with his mother. Nasra's muteness made her life difficult. She disliked physical and telepathic contact with untrained minds, but only Rohne and Sura were able to communicate with Nasra without touching her, so living in Gaton was a constant trial.

Rohne watched his mother as the villagers begged stories of Madina from the Mina-imposter. Did Nasra miss her life at court as Xintou to Jun Second Ma-Safra's family? The simplicity and isolation of Gaton was a far cry from the luxury of Jiali and Madina.

He studied Nasra critically. Sixty-four years touched her only lightly. Yes, her flame hair was now faded and salted, but her golden skin showed few of the life-lines of other village women her age. She walked firm and upright. Only her slender hands and neck showed the deepening lines caused by years away from her life in Madina.

If she did miss that world, Nasra warded her feelings with great skill, and etiquette prevented Rohne from taking them forcibly from her mind. She would reveal what he needed to know. Nasra was the one person he trusted.

Nasra flicked him a wry smile. He hadn't warded that thought. He flushed and Nasra laid a hand on his cheek, her expression gently amused.

A sharp thought speared through the babble of low key Outers in the room. Sura, in her excitement, had revealed the name of the girl at her side: Alere.

Rohne took a step towards the two women but Nasra laid a restraining hand on his arm. Yes, there was sense in her caution. This was still not the time or place for a confrontation, but there were secrets that must be uncovered. The set of his mother's shoulders betrayed tension beneath her serenity. She hid something, too. She caught his questing and shut him out with skill he couldn't penetrate. Rebuffed, he shook off her hand and strolled away. He was good at waiting; good at pretending, too, though he liked neither.

At the banquet table, he impaled a slice of roast lu deer with his dagger, and accepted a pot of ale from Halof, the brewer.

'Mina's come back quite the beauty, hasn't she?' Halof leered and winked. 'Better make nice with her again quick, boy, or someone else'll be in there first. I wouldn't mind a bit of that, myself.'

Rohne resisted punching him and inserted a false memory of payment for the ale, by way of revenge as he stalked away. A stool, shoved up against the warm wall of the bakery, gave Rohne a comfortable place to oversee the festivities. He sipped the thick ale and watched.

Nasra and Sura held a secret close between them; something to do with Mina-Alere. Although Nasra and Alere gave nothing away, Rohne caught snippets from Sura. Not enough to put a coherent story together; just her own face, younger; a memory of loss; a beloved man.

So Rohne curbed his impatience and waited. The evening wound down. Musicians played their last, the torches were doused, and noisy revellers staggered home. Full overhead, Luna-Er dimmed the stars and illuminated the square in cool brilliance.

Halof and his wife, Bella, lingered. Rohne entertained himself by inserting information about one of Halof's secret affairs into Bella's Outers. The ensuing screaming match caused the remaining folk to scatter. Nasra sent Rohne a chastising thought, which he ignored.

At last, when only Sura, Nasra and Alere remained, he strode over to where the three women stood, close by the fire. Alere's smile carried a hint of wariness as she held out her hands.

'Rohne.' She clasped his fingers and kissed his cheek, the fine silk of her white veil catching on his unshaven stubble. 'It's so good to see you. I wondered when you were going to come and speak to me. I've missed you, my friend.'

'How can you miss someone you've never met?' He released her hands. 'Where's Mina?'

A gasp from Sura and a silent warning from Nasra failed to deter him. Alere neither flinched nor panicked, but she tensed and one hand dropped to the dagger on her hip. Rohne curled a lip and waited.

CHAPTER TEN

ROHNE

'Is there somewhere we can talk, Sura?' Alere's focus stayed on Rohne and her hand on the dagger hilt. He let his smile broaden into triumph. Her eyes narrowed.

Sura led the way to her cottage on the village's eastern edge. She closed the door and secured the wooden shutters against eavesdroppers, then busied herself making tea. Nasra sat gracefully at the barra-wood dining table, a faint smile curving her lips. Rohne dropped into a chair, studying Alere.

Alere thrust the veil up onto her forehead, an unguarded look on her face as she watched Sura: a fleeting expression of longing, followed by a scowl. Sura placed cups of lancha tea, earthy and warm, on the scarred table. She sat, clutching her cup, never taking her eyes off Alere.

Rohne folded his arms. 'So, speak. What's going on?'

Alere inspected him coolly and for so long that Rohne caught himself shifting in his seat, like a naughty child.

'Who are you and why are you here?' he asked, refusing to let her take control.

Alere mirrored his pose by folding her arms. 'I've come to speak with Sura and Nasra. *Only* with Sura and Nasra.'

Rohne responded with an ironic smile. 'You'll need me if you want to speak with Nasra. If you were really Mina you'd know she can't speak aloud.' He raised one eyebrow. 'And you'd know that, as her son, I'm just about the only person who can communicate with her without physically touching her.'

'Her son?' Alere grabbed at the table edge, her fingertips whitening. 'But how? Mina never...I mean...Nasra, you're a *xintou*. The House nai-xintou always sequence foetal DNA to prevent xintou birthing boys. How did the House allow you to have a son?'

Nasra's smile held old bitterness and new scorn.

Rohne glared at Alere. It was true that Xintou House prohibited male xintou, but no-one knew why and the tradition went unquestioned. Nasra had rebelled, hiding in Gaton, rather than aborting. For that Rohne was grateful, even though he'd spent his life concealing his abilities. What right did this chouhuo have to question his mother, and speak as though he wasn't even in the room?

Through clenched teeth, Rohne told the story; so old now it had become tedious.

'These mountains are notorious for raiders. The village was sacked. I was the result. Not really your business.' He leaned forward, elbows on the table. 'I'm more interested in how you came to be here, where Mina is, and who you are.'

'But...' Alere smoothed a strand of hair into place behind her ear. 'Very well, but this has to stay between us. Mina's safe, I promise. But if anyone else finds out the whole village could be in danger, understood?'

'Prove Mina's safe, then we'll listen,' Rohne shot back.

'I don't have to prove anything to you,' she snapped. Quick anger flared and crackled in the silence between them.

'Please?' Sura's brown eyes were dark with worry.

Alere leaned back and gave a rueful laugh. 'She said you'd be tenacious, Rohne. She also said to tell you "the pies are finished baking" and you'd know she was unharmed.'

'Yes, that's Mina.' Rohne grinned and relaxed a fraction. 'Right, so tell us what's going on.'

Alere told her tale: the Jun First's death, her escape from Madina, and her meeting and exchange with Mina. Gradually, the feeling grew on Rohne that she might, possibly, be telling the truth, if not all of it.

Two days before, a Messenger House rider had arrived in Gaton bearing news of the deaths of the Jun First and Mistress Renna. That much of Alere's story was clearly true. But her meeting with Mina seemed too coincidental. What if she really was the escaped jiaoji who'd murdered the Jun? What if she'd stalked Mina, seen an opportunity to hide in Gaton, and was taking advantage of Mina and the villagers? And who was this weishi, Kett, travelling with Alere? Did he even exist?

Rohne sipped his tea and watched the play of emotion on Alere's face, irritated that her wards prevented the surest way of discovering the truth. He wanted to demand she lower her wards, but that would mean revealing what he was, and she hadn't earned that trust. She was strong-willed and too sure of herself and her ideas; and clearly too prepared to put others and herself at risk to achieve her goals.

When Alere finished, Rohne spoke into the silence she left.

'That's all well and good, but it doesn't explain why you look like Mina and why you're here.' He gestured at Sura's sparse cottage with its three small rooms and lack of security or wealth. 'Getting out of the Jundom would have been smarter.'

Alere laid a restless hand on the silver-metal dagger sheathed at her hip. Her other hand slid into the front of her robe. She studied Sura, then Nasra, and seemed to reach a decision.

'Because Elmira and the Jun First both said I should speak with you about your secret, whatever it is. The Jun First said the time had come to set it free.'

Nasra touched Sura's hand and they exchanged a long look. Rohne couldn't follow their silent dialogue without Nasra allowing access.

Alere gasped and pressed her palms to her temples. 'Nasra, I heard you. Just for a second. How's that possible?'

Nasra reared back, eyes wide. She recovered quickly, but her sharp frown revealed alarm and disquiet. After a moment's hesitation, Nasra pulled Alere's hand into contact with Rohne's, allowing all four to communicate. Rohne cringed at the feel of Alere's skin. He'd never been easy with close connections to anyone, except Mina.

I don't know why you heard me, but Sura can, so perhaps there's some genetic reason. Nasra's rich-timbred Outer dropped into his mind like soft rain.

'Are you saying...' Alere's fingers twitched beneath Rohne's. 'That Sura and I...that I *am* her...'

Yes, Nasra said, *but let me tell you the whole.* She patted Alere's hand and the tense atmosphere eased. *Twenty years ago, Sura was delivered of twin girls.* Nasra held up a finger as Rohne gasped. Sura flushed and looked longingly at Alere.

The midwife was late. I was on hand and Elmira was here, visiting. Sura took the decision to separate the girls, for their own safety, before the midwife came. Elmira adopted Alere. Sura kept Mina. Now, fate has returned Alere to her mother.

Alere ripped the veil off and tossed it aside. She stood and paced the room, her expression stormy.

'Separate us for our own safety? Why? And why send me away? Did you think I was xintou, or was it just inconvenient to have two children?' Alere's voice broke.

'You have to understand.' Tears spilled down Sura's cheeks. 'We thought it best. Twins are rare. People are superstitious of them. I'm a twin and what my sister and I suffered as children...' She paled, one hand stealing to her cheek. 'I'm sorry. I'm so sorry. I loved you both so much. It broke my heart to send you away.'

Rohne kept to himself the observation that Gaton now had four sets of twins.

Nasra grabbed Alere's hand as the girl passed and her thoughts speared into Rohne's mind again. *Sura and I agreed. In the past, ignorant villagers have been known to murder twins out of fear, though times are changing.* She squeezed Alere's hand. *Tell me. Where is Mina? You said she's safe, but where?*

'She's...' Alere restlessly smoothed a wayward lock of hair behind her ear and flicked a resentful look at her mother.

'Please tell me. When can I see her again?' Sura said tentatively.

Alere's shoulders drooped. 'She's with my weishi. Not far away. She'll come here when I leave – so no-one knows I've been. That way, if the Alcazar weishi do arrive, everyone can vouch for who she is.'

'So,' Rohne said, 'with Alcazar guards after you for murder, you come here to find your mother? You abandon Mina with some man she's never met and *now* you're worried for her safety?' He fisted his hands on the table. The fog of raw hurt, anger and worry emanating from Alere's Outers clouded his own thinking. 'No, there's more. Why are you really here?'

Alere's eyes flashed and her hand crept to the front of her white and grey robe. Did she conceal something beneath the cloth? Rohne straightened. Something related to why she'd come to Gaton, perhaps?

You may trust us, Alere. Nasra's reassuring thought drifted into the expectant silence.

Alere's gaze flicked to Rohne, who gritted his teeth. She didn't trust him. He growled low in his throat, rose and marched to the door.

'Rohne.' Alere's voice stopped him.

He looked back over his shoulder, still seething. She lifted her chin, every inch the haughty city noblewoman.

'I'm sorry.' The apology sounded stiff and forced. 'The Jun First and Elmira both bade me speak with Sura and Nasra, no-one else.'

Rohne yanked the door open and stalked into the frosted night. Outside Sura's house, he stopped and stared at the diamond-speckled sky, seeking calm. His angry puff of breath obscured the stars for a moment. Footsteps scuffed the ground behind him. He forced a smile when Sura approached. She was a healer by nature as well as by training. Of course she wouldn't let him go without checking on him.

Sura clutched a shawl around her plump shoulders and smiled tremulously at him. 'She's so different. So strong. I knew she wasn't Mina as soon as I saw her. She didn't mean to hurt your feelings. She doesn't know you.'

'I'll go with her when she leaves and bring Mina home to you, Sura.' He hid the anger simmering in his guts and kissed her cheek. 'Go back and hear what she has to say.'

She nodded, wrapped her shawl closer and returned inside. Rohne struggled to master his irritation. What was Alere saying? All three women were impenetrably warding. It was hard to believe Alere wasn't xintou, so solid were her wards. Even her Outers were invisible, now, yet he caught flickers of excitement from Nasra and fear from Sura. He yanked his jacket closed and strode to the cottage he shared with Nasra.

Ten minutes later Nasra arrived, her expression thoughtful as she hung her cloak near the door. Rohne stayed where he was, deep in a worn leather couch, staring at the fire.

'So?' He didn't expect a detailed answer. Nasra was good at keeping secrets.

She'll leave in the morning. You'll go along and bring Mina home. Alere's path is her own to follow after that.

'What's going on?' Rohne straightened. 'Who is she? Where's she going? Why did the Jun First send her here?'

Nasra sank onto the couch. *I don't know who she is. Sura would never tell me who the father was. Alere brought a gift from the Jun but it held no significance for me. A bracelet. Perhaps he thought Sura had told me. Maybe Sura will tell her.*

'She's come all this way for nothing?' He understood, a little, how she must feel. He'd spent the first seven years of his life not knowing who his father was; enduring the slights that went with being a mother-kin child.

I'm not sure if her journey was for nothing. Nasra rubbed a thumb across the back of her hand. *Once she learned I knew nothing about the bracelet, or her father, she refused to say any more to me. She said she didn't want to endanger me. Obviously Radan expected me to know her father. But I don't and I believe it's important somehow. Otherwise, why would he send her?*

Rohne draped an arm over her shoulder and squeezed. 'You can't blame yourself for not knowing. I'm sure she's exaggerating. She's young and frightened. Perhaps the Jun wanted to give you a gift?'

Nasra shook her head. *Everyone should have thought me dead these twenty-five years. The only one who knew I lived was Elmira. I can't imagine why she would have told him. Besides, I was Bonded Xintou to Jun Second Ma-Safra, not to the Jun First. I knew Radan, but only at Court. I wasn't raised a xintou.* Her mouth twisted into bitterness. *My parents were glad to sell me to Mistress Li when my xintou gifts appeared.* Hurt and anger knifed through her Outer wards and sliced into his mind.

'Mother!' Rohne flinched. Her rage vanished, leaving him stunned.

Forgive me. Nasra smiled wearily. *I'm tired and this has brought up memories I thought left well behind me. I'm sure you're right. Alere's exaggerating the drama.* She threw back her shoulders and stretched her neck. *Perhaps the Jun First is...was her father and that's why Sura refuses to reveal it. The laws Shunu Hanna brought in twenty years ago made kin-children illegal for the Jun families. And Hanna has been ruthless in hunting her husband's kin-children. Radan may have sent Alere away to keep her safe.*

Rohne frowned and tugged at the short mawei holding his unruly auburn hair back. 'But Sura's lived here her whole life, where would she have met the Jun First? Besides, if Alere were his daughter, she wouldn't inherit anyway. Ven is before her.'

The whole situation made no sense. Something was wrong, but what? Irritated and restless, Rohne rose and stalked around the room. He ran his fingertips across the spines of Nasra's vast library of books, taking comfort in their familiarity.

It's late and my mind is clouded. Morning will bring light into darkness, I'm sure. Goodnight. Nasra held Rohne's face in her hands and touched their foreheads together; a loving gesture she'd made every night of his life. It reassured him. Then she kissed his cheek and disappeared into her room.

Only a few minutes later, a sharp knock fell on the front door. Rohne sent a questing thought and came up against the wards of

Alere Sura-kin. He opened the door and Alere shouldered past him, carrying two bulging bags. Sura, weeping and protesting, followed close behind.

'Get Nasra. Pack. We need to leave, now.' Alere dropped the bags to the floor.

Nasra's bedroom door opened. Nasra emerged, fully dressed and holding two leather bags, one full and one slackly empty. She showed Rohne a swift, explanatory thought-image.

'Alcazar weishi?' He gasped. 'Already? But they'll tear the village apart if they think Alere's here and find us all gone.'

'They'll tear it apart anyway.' Alere grabbed the empty bag from Nasra and thrust it into his hands. 'Bring only what you need. They're only a couple of gongli away.'

'How do you know?' Rohne asked.

Her grin held a hint of mischief. 'I paid some children to camp out up the road and keep watch.' She gave him a nudge. 'Now pack. We have to get Sura and Nasra to safety.'

'Why? Surely the point of you coming alone was so Sura and the village would be safe. Why don't you just leave?'

'Sura and I have unfinished business, Nasra's meant to be dead and,' she said coolly, 'assuming I'm not mistaken, you'd be considered an abomination by Mistress Li. Unless you want to be dragged in chains to Madina for execution, I strongly suggest you pack.'

CHAPTER ELEVEN

ROHNE

'Wait.' Sura's breathless cry halted the little group. 'I can't see where I'm going and I've turned my ankle.'

Rohne planted his feet carefully on the slippery path and grasped a tree trunk for stability. He frowned at the three women straggling up the slope. Sura supported herself on a yar-pine and panted. Twenty years older than Sura, Nasra paused, barely out of breath. Alere, who brought up the rear, reached her mother and ducked beneath Sura's arm.

Rohne scanned the dark path behind them. Gaton lay far below, nothing more than occasional flickers of light. But burning a torch was still too risky until they'd reached the next valley. With both moons out he could see well enough to pick out the familiar path.

'Are we going much further, Rohne?' Alere pinned him with a glare.

He shrugged. 'You're the one who wanted to leave.' Although he and Nasra, together, could easily influence the weak minds of the Zah-Hill guards, he wasn't yet ready to reveal himself to the world. Alere's abomination label stung, but her suggestion to run was right – for now.

Leaving Gaton was no hardship; he'd outgrown the place and the parochial minds of the villagers. But he wasn't optimistic enough to believe the Alcazar guards would abandon the chase – especially once they discovered Mina had disappeared. The villagers would probably guess where Rohne and his party had fled, but no-one would tell. At least, not under normal circumstances. He grimaced. Hopefully the gruesome images cascading into his mind were not true Seeings of the future.

'Sura can't keep this up all night,' Alere said.

Rohne shook himself free of uneasiness and nodded towards the mountain. 'There's a raider encampment over this ridge. We'll be safe there for the night.'

'Raiders?' Alere clutched her dagger. 'How does that equate to safe?'

'Because,' Rohne said impatiently, 'they worked out that trapping, mining and trading is more profitable. Besides, my father is the raider kui, Jada Marin-kin. He acknowledged me when I was seven. He and Nasra are together. Him, you can trust.'

Alere narrowed her eyes, but said nothing.

'You alright, Sura?' Rohne called.

'Yes. I'm just not as young as I was.' Her plump bosom heaved and she mopped her forehead with her skirt. A night-wing fluttered past, chirruping, its six enormous wings buzzing in the darkness. Sura yelped and flailed her arms around her head. Alere snatched up a stick and struck at the insect, shuddering as it vanished into the gloom.

'They won't hurt you,' Rohne said scornfully. 'You're too big to eat and it's not egg-laying season yet, so your ears are safe.'

Alere sniffed, but touched her ear.

Nasra simply swapped her bag to the other shoulder and waved Rohne ahead. A few minutes later, at the ridge crest, he paused to get his bearings. Several days had passed since he'd travelled this way. Hopefully the raiders were still there. He didn't care to lead an unfit middle-aged woman, a grandmother, and an inexperienced city girl any further into the hills.

The Ahmar Mountains were riddled with old mine shafts and were hunting grounds for xiao-cats, xiao-bears and roc eagles. By the cool light of the moons, the hills were sharp-shadowed, black-holed and treacherous. Then there were Jada Marin-kin's raiders. Since Jada had become kui, the raiders travelled widely, seeking new yanstone mines, new spice-otter packs or simply new territory. Still, they did not welcome outsiders.

Alere caught up to Rohne. Nasra fell behind to help Sura.

'Do you know where you're going?' Alere said, peering into the darkness below.

Rohne scanned the valley for a campfire. 'I was here a couple of weeks ago.'

A sense of being watched grew steadily as he picked his way down the slope. The metallic clink and slither of broken rock underfoot echoed across the tiny valley. Khara! The raiders had to hear them coming even without lookouts stationed. Rohne gritted his teeth and carried on, checking occasionally on the women.

Near the valley bottom, the slope eased. Deeper soil meant larger trees. A stand of blood-pines, their trunks glistening with sticky red sap, hid the moon and gathered shadows into skirts of inky darkness. Behind Rohne, the distinctive slide of metal cut through the silence as Alere drew her dagger. He couldn't blame her. The hairs on the back of his neck rose and every nerve screamed panic. Unwarded minds were close by. Raiders. Men and women he knew but they'd likely shoot without warning before they recognised him.

The four travellers halted in a moon-washed clearing as Rohne studied the surrounds. Surely this was where the camp had been? He peered at the ground, nudging a mess of black charcoal, cold and half-buried under sand.

'Rohne.' Alere's soft warning reached him.

He stayed his impulse to reach for a weapon and raised empty hands. Fitful breezes sighed through the pines. Shadows moved as branches swayed; and moved again even when the branches stilled. Rohne caught the faintest scent of woodsmoke and sweat. Brittle needles crunched. A mis-step by one of the raiders?

Alere turned, moonlight glimmering off her dagger.

'Put it away,' Rohne snapped. 'Now.'

She slid her blade slowly back into its sheath and lifted her hands. The shadows slipped closer, resolving into human shape. Twenty of them. One, larger than the rest, shouldered through the group. He peered at Rohne, then threw back his head and laughed. Turned to the sky, his bearded face became visible, pale eyes and teeth gleaming in the moonlight.

'Why, Rohne.' Jada slapped his son on the shoulder, deep voice booming across the clearing. 'You've brought me presents. How nice.'

His massive arms engulfed Nasra, lifting her off the ground before placing her back down. He held up a palm and she pressed hers to it, their touch allowing a private greeting. Nasra's smile held secrets she shared only with Jada. Rohne long suspected his powerful xintou mother may not, actually, have been molested as she allowed the villagers to believe. Whatever the truth, he didn't particularly care. Nasra's love life was her business and Jada's.

The raider kui regarded Sura and Alere. He fiddled with a pendant that hung around his neck, as he did when he was perturbed. The miniature steel axe glinted in the half-light.

'Interesting.' he said. 'Let's get to camp and get you warm. We can swap stories later. We have other visitors, too.'

Rohne lifted a brow. The raiders weren't renowned for their hospitality.

Surrounded by silent-footed sentinels, Rohne and the women hiked over another ridge to the raider encampment. Ten khibas nestled amongst giant blood-pines and thorny ci bushes. The tents were well-camouflaged; only noticeable by blue smoke curling from holes in the top of the skin and bamboo constructions. Several dozen horses, lu-deer and small goats dozed in a makeshift zinzana made of ci shrubs.

Jada's men melted into the darkness. The kui lifted the flap on the largest khiba and invited the Gaton party into the warmth and light. Rohne, Nasra and Sura stepped in, but Alere hesitated. She gripped her dagger as she entered the tent. What was there to be afraid of? With a mocking smile, Rohne waved her in. She glowered and stepped past him, treading warily.

Rohne strolled towards the central fire, across handwoven, vibrant rugs that crowded the floor with clashing, perfect colours. To one side, on a raised dais, a pile of blood-red xiao-bear furs passed for a bed. Rohne sighed. Raider beds were warm and comfortable and he'd already missed half a night's sleep. He rotated his neck and breathed in the fire's jilla-fruitwood sweetness, allowing tension to dissolve. He was safe here.

In the centre of the khiba stood a circle of three-legged stools, two of them occupied. A dark-haired man, wearing weishi-black, raised his head, grey eyes sharp. His hand rested on a sword. A woman sat beside him, also in black clothing and wearing a black veil. Before the strangers stood a small yar-pine table, set with three wooden plates and the remains of a meal. The scent of roast goat made Rohne's mouth water. Dinner had been hours ago.

The two strangers rose; the man tall and lean with the strong forearms and watchful wariness of a swordsman. The woman lifted her veil.

'Mina!' Sura dashed forward and wrapped her daughter in a fierce, tearful hug.

Rohne observed Alere. What would her reaction to this reunion be? Unmistakable resentment, then regret, flickered over her face as she watched her mother and sister. Then the dark-haired man approached and Alere smiled at him with the familiarity of an old friend.

'Kett,' she said, indicating the Gaton party, 'this is Nasra, and her son Rohne, by Jada. And that is, of course, Sura: my mother and Mina's.'

Mina gasped. 'Sisters! Oh, Alere.' She threw her arms around Alere, who stood stiff then broke free with an uneasy half-smile. Mina's mouth drooped and she returned to her mother's side.

Kett raised an eyebrow and merely nodded a greeting, though there was speculation in his look. Rohne appreciated his lack of judgement. He sent a swift probe at the weishi's mind and met with wards as strong as Alere's. Perhaps Xintou House trained all their staff. Nasra had never mentioned it, though.

'How did you and Mina end up here?' Alere asked Kett. 'I left you in the valley.'

'Mina begged me to take her closer to Gaton so we could meet on your way back to the valley. She was worried,' the weishi said.

'We found them.' Jada's laugh rumbled through the khiba and his thick hand descended onto Kett's shoulder. 'This one certainly put up a good fight. If Mina hadn't intervened, three of my best men would be food for the roc-eagles. They'll need Sura's services for a few days to recover.'

Rohne was surprised to see Kett uninjured. The raiders gave no quarter.

From beneath her lashes, Nasra looked long at Kett, then her lips curved in a faint smile. Kett returned her inspection steadily.

'Sit,' Jada said. 'Sit and tell us why you've come.' He dropped into his seat, an ornately-carved zitan-wood chair, its rich, maroon timber glowing in the light of the fire. The group pulled up stools and Alere again told her story, this time mentioning the bracelet Nasra had seen. There was still something she left unsaid, but Rohne couldn't Read what.

Finally, after reassurances from Sura and a nod from Kett, Alere produced the boxed bracelet from inside her robe. As the jewels were passed around the small circle, Alere addressed Sura.

'Nasra doesn't know anything about this bracelet. We had to leave Gaton before you could tell me anything... Mother. So?'

The group fell silent, all eyes on the plump healer. Sura fidgeted and stroked the glowing yanstones. She shivered and thrust the gems into Mina's hands as though glad to be rid of the bracelet.

'Twenty years ago I came to Gaton from Shanzhai.' Her words were hurried and strained. 'I travelled in the train of Jun Forth Hassan Wen-Gates, my cousin. He visited Gaton after coming into his title.'

Rohne exchanged astonished looks with Mina. This was all news to him, although the expression on Nasra's face said she'd known.

'Why?' Alere asked.

'I was pregnant.' Sura held up a hand when Alere opened her mouth. 'My twin sister, Yasmin, is married to Jun Second Rafi Koh-Lin. After five years they were childless and asked me to help. Such arrangements used to be common.' Her mouth drooped. 'As the younger twin, I'd spent most of my life hidden away from the world. You know how superstitious people can be about twins. I wasn't able to contract a marriage, I cared for Rafi, so I agreed to help Yasmin.'

Sura fell silent and Kett shifted in his seat. As Rohne watched, a hint of relief flashed across the weishi's face.

'After I fell pregnant,' Sura continued, tears gathering, 'the First Shunu passed the law that kin-children could no longer inherit from a Jun. It became illegal for Jun to even have kin-children. Alcazar weishi slaughtered Jun kin-children on Hanna's orders. I had to leave, to hide. Hassan offered sanctuary.'

'Jiche.' Alere's oath fell softly into the silence. 'The kin-child massacres were so long ago. I didn't realise…'

'Hanna's law affected mostly people in the cities and towns near the twenty-one Jun-family estates,' Kett said quietly. 'It almost led to an uprising by the senior Jun. Almost.' Pain swept through his eyes. His hands were clenched between his knees.

'Yes,' Jada added, glancing at Nasra. 'Xintou House didn't support the Juns; Mistress Li advised them to lay down arms and obey the ruling.'

'Why?' Mina asked, pale and clearly shaken. 'Why would she do something like that? Those poor children.'

Alere straightened, lifting her chin. 'Mistress Li is responsible for the whole of Kalima. For the Juns to rise against the throne would have been all-out war. She must have done what she thought best.'

Mina's mouth set into mulishness. At a swift thought from Nasra, Rohne stepped in to prevent an argument between the sisters.

'Gaton wasn't affected,' he said. 'It's far enough from Jun Fourth Wen-Gates's estate and he's pretty much a recluse, anyway. Is that why you came here, Sura?'

'It was as far as I could get. The girls were birthed a few months after I arrived.'

Mina shook her head. 'I can't believe we're the children of Jun Second Koh-Lin.'

'Alere is the elder.' Sura nodded. 'We sent her to live with Elmira to learn city and court ways in the hopes that one day, should the law be overturned, Alere might take her place as Jun-Heir.'

'Oh, thank goodness it wasn't me,' Mina breathed.

Alere stood and paced two steps away before coming back to the circle. Her eyes gleamed and she pressed white fingers to her flushed cheeks. Then she stopped and stared blankly into the fire. The excitement drained away and she collapsed back onto the stool.

'But I'm not Jun-Heir, am I?' Alere cast a bitter glance at Sura. 'I mean: I'm kin-child, the laws are still in place, and Rafi and Yasmin Koh-Lin have a daughter. She's a year or two younger than me...us, I think. How did that come about?'

Sura shrugged. 'Yasmin got pregnant after all. But you're right: if your identity is revealed now, you and Mina will be executed.'

Alere put her head in her hands. 'So in the space of a week I've gone from being a Connor, to a Sura-kin, to a Koh-Lin and now what, do I...we...claim?'

'I'm sorry,' Sura said humbly.

'What I don't understand,' Mina put in, 'is what's so important about the bracelet? And why Radan told you to return it to our father? Rafi's the second most powerful Jun in the land, so he doesn't need the money.'

'Who knows.' Alere stared at the floor and clenched her hands in her lap until her knuckles whitened. 'Radan obviously thought it important enough to die for, though.'

Rohne felt a nudge at his elbow. Kett handed him the jewelry box. Prescience tickled the back of Rohne's skull as he opened the timber lid. Polished yanstones, set into gleaming steel, glowed with characteristic silvery inner fire. Rohne despised the Juns and their wealth, but couldn't deny the bracelet was a thing of beauty. He shifted so the firelight fell on the stones, and the silver glint in each stone flared into liquid red and gold. A desire to touch the stones spiked into an inexplicable compulsion, low in his chest.

'Rafi made the bracelet himself.' Sura's words distracted him and the urge faded. 'It was a gift meant for his heir. He gave it to me just before I left. I sent it with Alere to be held in trust for her. It belongs to Yasmin's daughter, now, I suppose. I have no idea how it came into the Jun First's hands. Perhaps Elmira gave it to him.'

Nasra frowned and made a chopping gesture with one hand. Rohne Read her Outer. Yes, that made more sense.

'Mother says Elmira could hardly return to the Ma-Safra family with an unexplained baby in her arms. She would have reported to her House.' He shrugged. 'Mistress Li must have given the bracelet and the story to the Jun First.'

Alere looked shocked. 'Mistress Li told...? But the danger to me...' She stared at the floor, her cheek pale.

Rohne shared her unease. Telling Radan had been a huge risk. One wrong thought around his Xintou and the secret would have been betrayed. Why would Mistress Li have put Mina – and Alere – in such jeopardy over something as trivial as a piece of jewelry? He snapped the box shut and handed it on to Alere, who tapped the timber restlessly. Mina reached over and stilled Alere's hands, her gentle smile reassuring.

Side by side the sisters were almost impossible to tell apart. Mina's eyes were a shade bluer and her hair a handspan shorter than Alere's. But in personality, they were poles apart. Alere exuded strength and impatient energy. Rohne preferred Mina's quieter femininity.

A strong sense of déjà vu derailed his thoughts. Somehow, some-when, he had Seen these two women seated together. He'd had precognitive Seeings before and recognised this for what it was: the memory of a vision. But why couldn't he recall the original Seeing?

How could he have forgotten something like that, about Mina? He would chase the memory later, when things were quieter.

Nasra sent him a frowning glance, her mind closed. She turned away.

'I need to give this to the Koh-Lins, do I? Jiche!' Alere opened the box and stared at the gems. 'Alright. Fine. Tomorrow I head west, to Shanzhai.'

'And after you give Rafi the bracelet?' Sura's question held a note of pleading. 'Then what?'

'No idea.' Alere's left hand rested on her dagger as she gazed moodily at the yanstone bracelet and stroked the blazing gems like a pet xiao-kitten.

A hint of uncertainty escaped her Outers. Rohne studied her profile. There was definitely more she'd left unsaid. Returning the bracelet, although noble, was hardly a good reason for traipsing across five hundred gongli with winter approaching and an army of Alcazar weishi on the hunt. Selling the bracelet and disappearing would be smarter. What was she hiding?

Rohne sent out a questing tendril of thought, delicately sliding across her wards, seeking a crack he could wedge his mind into. Nothing. For a non-xintou, this girl had extraordinary control. Intrigued, he tried again, this time sharpening his touch into a spear-point. She wouldn't be aware if her wards were breached. He stabbed through her Outer wards.

The room vanished into spiralling darkness. The roar of a thousand people, screaming abuse at him through a waterfall, drowned his thoughts. Rohne blinked up at the timber and leather ceiling and tried to pull his brain into place. The back of his skull ached.

Why was he lying on the floor? Sura's anxious face appeared above him. She peered into his eyes and her mouth moved but her words were ghosts, silenced by the hordes in his head.

Slowly, the overwhelming mind-din faded to white noise. Rohne groaned and struggled onto his elbows. Jada and Kett hauled him to his feet while Sura fussed around, examining his head and pupils. He batted her away and fumbled to a stool.

'What happened?' His brain pounded in time with his slowing heart.

'You tried to pierce my wards. It rebounded on you,' Alere said, folding her arms.

Rohne mumbled an apology he didn't feel. His attempt was an inexcusable rudeness in the world of a xintou, but a survival technique in his. But what he'd felt was no mere rebound, it had been a true *chuizi* – a hammer-strike; a psychic-weapon recorded only in one of Nasra's books on xintou skills. How had Alere done it?

Nasra touched Jada's hand.

Jada rose, towering over the group. 'I think It's time you all went to bed. You're tired and there's a lot to decide tomorrow. My men will show you where to sleep. Nasra?' He extended a hand and she took it, smiling.

Rohne strode from the khiba, into the starry darkness. Each step jarred a spike through his skull. When he dropped into his bed, even the lumps in the fur pillow hurt.

Shouts and the smell of burning leather wrenched Rohne from the silver-fire shadows of nightmare. He flipped aside the furs and snatched at his things, belting on sword and dagger even as he moved to the door flap. Kett appeared, grim-faced, by Rohne's side.

The bare sword in Kett's hand gleamed silvery by the light of the central hearth.

'We should cut a door in the back. Sounds like the Alcazar weishi have found us. Which,' Kett said drily, 'surprises me.'

Outside, Jada's thunderous voice shouted incomprehensible orders. Bronze clanged against ceramic, cutting through the scuff of feet on bare earth and cries of pained surprise. A horse whinnied and hooves thudded past the khiba. Fire crackled. The smell of smoke grew stronger.

'I'll get the women and meet you by the zinzana,' Rohne murmured. 'The girls will be frightened and we'll need mounts.'

Kett laughed. 'Clearly you haven't spent much time with Alere. She'll be in the thick of things, but yours is a sound plan. I'll find her.' He slashed at the back wall and the skins parted beneath his blade like water before a straight-eel fin.

Rohne leapt out after him and headed for Sura and the girls' khiba. In the clearing, Jada's men and women fought off thirty or more black-and-silver uniformed Alcazar guards. Swords glinted in the dim, pink moonlight. Cries of terror and pain rent the cold night. Black-clad bodies sprawled on the dust, attesting to the raiders' skill. This half-shadowed night-world of confusion and camouflage was the raiders' element; the advantage was theirs. Rohne hefted his weapon, tempted to add his arm to the fray. No, getting Mina to safety was more important. He skirted the worst of the fighting and reached the back of the khiba without being intercepted.

'Mina,' he called, and sent a thought towards Nasra. A dagger blade stabbed through the skin a hands-breadth from his nose. With an oath, he jumped back. Nasra appeared in the gap. Sura and Mina followed.

'Alere went to help,' Mina whispered. 'She'll meet us at the zinzana. Jada's men will cover our escape.'

'Keep to the shadows,' Rohne said.

He scurried across a patch of bare ground and ducked into the shade of a blood-pine. The others followed. He ran ahead, sword in hand, searching the shifting darkness for threats. A black shape leapt at him. Rohne barely lifted his sword in time to block the blade descending at his head. It was an instinctive, ill-judged motion. The swords met at the wrong angle and both ceramic blades shattered. Rohne and the weishi stared at the stumps in their hands.

Rohne snatched out his dagger and flung himself at the man. There was no time to try a psychic attack. That took concentration. The weishi caught Rohne's wrist with iron fingers, fending him off. A dagger slashed towards Rohne's neck. Rohne grabbed the black-clad arm and forced the blade back by sheer strength. He twisted, trying to hook a leg around the man's knee and bring him to ground. The Alcazar weishi was better-trained. He countered and Rohne landed flat on his back, winded and gasping. Rohne held the blade off his neck in desperation. The weishi's feral grin was inches away, his breath rank. His bitter sweat dripped into Rohne's mouth. The ceramic knife-edge scraped Rohne's skin.

The weishi collapsed, eyes closed, breathing heavily. A pair of hands rolled the weighty body off Rohne, who scrambled out from beneath.

Nasra helped Rohne up. *I shut down his cortical functions.*

'You mean you put him to sleep?' Rohne hid his shock. She could affect brain physiology? That spoke of power greater than she'd ever displayed.

In a manner of speaking. It's a little more complicated than that. Nasra picked up a dagger and plunged it into the man's heart. She watched with clinical disinterest as the weishi's breath rattled in his throat and he relaxed into death. Leaving the dagger in place, she spun on her heel and strode towards the zinzana. Sura and Mina followed, clinging to each other, pale and wide-eyed.

Rohne trailed behind. Nasra's ruthlessness had protected him for many years, so her action came as no surprise, but why had she hidden a skill that might help him survive? What else hadn't she taught him; and why?

At the zinzana Alere, Kett and two of Jada's men were saddling the frightened horses. Four Alcazar weishi lay, bloody and still, on the ground. Made skittish by the scent of smoke and blood, a roan mare almost yanked Alere off her feet. Mina gripped the mare's bridle under the bit, stroking the long nose and settling the animal with soothing words.

'Jada sent us,' Kett said. 'He seems to have everything under control. He asked his men to escort us. Nasra, Jada said he'll join you later at the winter-valley camp. You, Rhone and Sura will stay there. He'll keep you safe while the girls and I head west.'

Mina's head snapped around. 'What do you mean? I'm staying with my mother. I'm not going anywhere. Gaton is my home.'

Rohne drew her apart from the others, willing her to trust him. As a child she'd followed his lead but, when pushed too far, she had a knack for quiet resistence. Would the years in Madina have created too wide a gulf between them? Would he still be able to influence her?

'Mina, we have to go with them and you know it. Both of us.'

'But I just got here.' Tears shimmered in her eyes. 'I've been away four years, dreaming about coming home.' She waved towards the dawn-haloed mountains. 'I want this, Gaton and my family, not whatever Alere's involved in.'

'I know, but it's too late to hide.' Rohne caught her into his arms, wishing there was more time to savour the warmth of her body. 'Your life's in danger. Sura's and Nasra's as well. I know you see the best in everyone, but Jun Ven has a reputation for vindictiveness. He won't let this go. You can't stay here and I won't let you go without me. If they find us, they'll kill everyone. If you're gone Sura can claim you were killed in this skirmish.'

She broke free, her eyes still dark with doubt.

'Besides,' he added, 'Alere's your sister and there's clearly something between you. You used to say something was missing in your life. You can spend time with her. And you both need to know your father. He owes you that much.' Rohne stroked her cheek. 'Then we can come home again.'

Mina rubbed her hands down her thighs, a nervous gesture.

'Alright,' she murmured, sending Rohne a quick, worried look beneath her lashes. 'I'll come.'

He raised her chin and kissed her softly. She blushed and pulled away, glancing over her shoulder at Kett. With a murmured apology, she left Rohne's side and ran to her horse. Kett helped her mount, smiling at some comment she made. A hot fist of jealousy punched into Rohne's stomach. He swung into the saddle and jabbed his heels into his horse's sides, yanking at the reins when the animal tossed its head.

He watched Mina ride ahead. He'd wished for adventure and a reason to quit Gaton. He'd wished for Mina's return, so they could resume their relationship as friends and casual lovers. This was not the homecoming he'd imagined.

CHAPTER TWELVE

ALERE

The sun shimmered into view above dragon-backed eastern mountains and shafts of red light leavened the purplish gloom under the yar-pines. Alere twisted in her saddle and looked back through the forest. None of the Alcazar men seemed to be following. A curl of dark smoke spiralled up from the valley behind, into the brightening sky. Alere's party picked their way over a ridge, into a different valley where the sounds of battle faded to the occasional ring of metal on metal.

It went against her weishi training to leave Jada and his men but the raider kui had insisted. The fighting had been brutal, though Alere's contribution was minor. Jada's men were skilled and ferocious fighters who outnumbered the Alcazar junren three to one. The raiders showed no mercy and fought dirtier than the junren – gouging eyes and slicing throats without hesitation.

Alere pushed away memories drenched in blood and death. As Kett said: dwelling on them wouldn't change what happened, only cement the images into her mind so they would resurface to disturb her more often. She focussed instead on Mina, whose chestnut gelding struggled up the steep mountain path ahead. Mina's loose hair rippled like black silk as she leaned forward over the gelding's neck. Kett had been riding beside Mina, but now fell back, a slight smile curving his mouth.

'Careful there.' Alere dropped her voice and nudged Rumi closer to Bol. 'I think Mina likes you. And Rohne doesn't like it that she likes you.'

'I know.' The humour fell away from Kett and he glanced at Rohne's stiff back.

Kett's feelings for Mina were impossible to judge from his expression. Mina's fascination for him could cause trouble. Hopefully he'd handle her attentions circumspectly. He said nothing more and Alere grimaced. Perhaps it was best to remain silent, herself. Who Kett loved was none of her business. That notion caught the breath in her throat and she had to cough to set it free.

'Where to now, Shunu Alere?' Kett asked.

'Please don't call me that. You know it annoys me. I've no claims to it and the title just reminds me of what I'm not.'

'Why do you think I do it?' He smiled and Alere glared at him. 'Alright.' He held up a hand. 'I'll stop. But what's wrong with the title? What aren't you?'

'Not anything. Not a xintou; not a jiaoji – of which I'm glad – not a weishi. Apparently not a Jun-Heir either.' Alere tugged at a strand of hair behind her ear. Disappointment warred with relief. After years of slights from her Xintou House-sisters, part of her wanted to throw her rank in their faces. But a greater part shied away from the responsibility being Jun-Heir would entail. Luckily that wasn't an option, since her father had a legitimate daughter.

'Not a xintou?' Kett said. 'What'd you do to Rohne back in the khiba? That had all the hallmarks of a xintou-gift. Not an ability I've heard of, though.'

'I have,' she said, quietly. 'I think it's called *chuizi*. Mistress Li mentioned it, but the technique's considered unseemly because it's an attack, and xintou are all about peace.'

'That doesn't explain how you did it.'

Alere studied Rohne, who rode on a sturdy mountain pony two places ahead.

'I don't really know.' She shivered, not only from the cold. 'I felt Rohne trying to get through my wards. I just...hit back, I guess. Then I was able to talk telepathically with Mina. Just for a few seconds.' The connection had been fleeting. Mina was frightened at first, then had opened herself so unconditionally that Alere had retreated by reflex, overwhelmed and afraid of risking Fusion. Mina's hurt and disappointment was burned into Alere's memory.

Kett said nothing, leaving only the sound of hooves clattering on stone and birds twittering alarm calls in the brightening canopy to fill the silence.

When he spoke, his tone was thoughtful. 'That's never happened to you before, has it?'

'Not even close. No, wait. There was a moment in Gaton when I heard Nasra even though she wasn't touching me. I just put it down to her being a xintou. I haven't been able to do it again – I tried.'

'Maybe it's something to do with Mina?'

Alere's stomach sank. She'd always wanted to be xintou-gifted; always felt incomplete. Although the connection with Mina was strong, the thought of being tied to her sister for a gift filled Alere with bitter disappointment. How would she ever be free if she was close-linked to a twin sister? As much as the idea of a real family drew her, it also represented more people to whom she must answer. Her whole life had been bound by others' rules, tied to other people's agendas. She was tired of it. Tired of being told she wasn't good enough. Tired of trying to prove her worth and failing.

She sat up straighter in the saddle, inhaling pine-scented air and appreciating, for the first time, the taste of freedom. She *was* free. Radan had released her; Xintou House had no right to her life. It was a heady concept.

'Maybe you were right, Kett,' she said. Rumi crested a ridge and Alere flung her arms wide. Below, a vast spread of tree-filled valleys appeared, their rims afire with red sunlight and depths still purple-shadowed. A jin-bird alighted on a branch nearby, its golden-furred body glowing in the dawn light. The little reptile trilled a joyful descant to the jangling of bridles and bits, then fluttered into the forest.

'Maybe I should disappear,' Alere added, watching the last flicker of gold vanish. 'It's beautiful here.'

'It may be a little late for that,' Kett replied. 'We've left a trail of blood behind us. Hanna won't give up. It's about saving face now. She needs to make your execution public. Ven's first act as Jun First will be revenge for his father's death. I can't let that happen, Alli.'

Alere groaned and folded the reins over her hands, feeling freedom slip away like the leather through her fingers.

'If Hanna finds out who I am, will she go after the Koh-Lins?'

'They're the only family powerful enough to challenge her,' Kett said. 'If Hanna learns of the Koh-Lin's connection to you, or to the iron deposit, she'll find an excuse to wipe them out.'

Alere gazed west over the broad river plain, still mist-shrouded and grey in pre-dawn shadow. Somewhere out there, beyond the Aswad Mountains, Rafi Koh-Lin slept in the fortified hill-town of Shanzhai, his seat of power. She'd heard only good things of the Jun Second: his fair rule and care for his people. Now not only his future, but also that of his family and people, were intertwined with Mina's and her own.

The brief, exhilarating dream of liberty faded in the light of duty and Alere slumped. Returning the bracelet wasn't a choice, but an obligation. Important over what she wanted – again. She had to warn Rafi. Had to find out what the Jun First's cryptic words about the bracelet meant. And the iron deposit must be destroyed before the

First Shunu found it. With winter's cold hand stretching closer each day, time was short. In a few weeks, snows would close the pass to Shanzhai.

'I could do it for you,' Kett said. His matter-of-fact tone snapped her wandering thoughts back to the present.

'Do what?' She screwed up her nose in non-comprehension.

He cocked his head and smiled crookedly. 'It never occurs to you that someone else could take this burden, does it? Stay here with your family. Give the bracelet to me. I'll take it to Rafi, in Shanzhai.'

For a moment her heart leapt, then Alere sighed. He was, once again, testing her moral compass. When she had first come to Xintou House she had been certain of both her superiority; certain her xintou powers would flower at puberty. They did not, and her house sisters swiftly pointed out her unworthiness. She would never be xintou.

She sought Kett's company as an easier alternative to their company, but easy was not the path he had in store for her. He had a job to do and, if she wanted to spend time in his non-judgmental company, she had to train with him. As they trained, he forced her to question what she learned in classes. The House taught her duty and conformity. Kett had taught her honour and scepticism.

Alere rubbed at her forehead. 'I can't back out now. Partly Mistress Li's fault – I feel guilty if I do the wrong thing. And partly your fault.'

He raised his brows.

'You taught me to question everything. I have too many questions to let matters go.'

'I'm regretting that now,' Kett said. 'I'd be glad to know you were safely away from Jun-politics. Funny, but I often wondered if you were Petar Ma-Safra's child, hidden in the House for safety.'

'Why didn't you tell me?'

He shrugged, his smile a strange mixture of bitterness and resignation. 'There was never any point. The kin-child laws meant you'd never be Petar's heir. Besides,' he added, 'you were already full of outrageous plans for your life.'

Chuckling dutifully, Alere shook herself free of the past and faced forward. 'And now look what I've dragged us into.' She indicated Mina and the others of their party, riding ahead.

Kett straightened in his saddle, his gaze fixed on Rohne's back. 'Yes, we've certainly met some interesting people.'

Rohne, wrapped in a red xiao-bear-fur jacket, rode beside Nasra. Between mother and son lay a silence thick with significant eye contact. Unease trickled down Alere's spine.

'There's something odd about Nasra and Rohne. Apart from the whole xintou-thing, I mean. But I can't put my finger on what,' she said.

Rohne was handsome enough: muscular like his father, with dark auburn hair just long enough to tie back; and clear, amber-brown eyes. But he possessed a disconcerting trick of looking through a person; as though he'd already worked out what they were going to say, found it dull, and moved on to more interesting thoughts. He seemed extremely sure of himself and mentally always three jumps ahead. Alere found it unsettling and irritating to be so dismissed.

'Mind your thoughts, Alli,' Kett said, his eyes narrowing as he watched the xintou. 'Nasra was considered one of the most powerful Jun-Bonded Xintou ever known. A wild-gene triggered pre-puberty by her muteness. The first non-gene-daughter xintou in over a hundred years. Speculation was rife after her death-notice. I was very young at the time, but I remember her death being spoken of even much later.' He nodded at Rohne's back. 'Now we know why she chose to fake her death. We've been told male xintou are dangerous. The lost journal quoted in the Teachings of Lei states it clearly, but not why. Until we know the truth behind the tradition, we should be cautious, but don't be too quick to condemn him.'

Alere remained silent, aware of her tendency to make snap judgements about people – a fault Kett had been unable to train out of her. She'd give Rohne the benefit of the doubt and begin with basic respect. He could earn trust from there, if he would. But it was doubtful he'd care if she trusted him or not.

Jada's men chose a tortuous path through the foothills and the morning trudged apace with every slogging step through the dense forest. For the final half an hour of the journey the travellers dismounted and led the weary horses through a narrow gorge into an enclosed valley.

Thin plumes of smoke spiralled from the peaked leather tops of thirty khiba nestled among the skirts of the surrounding slopes. A long-range flitter bird spiralled down from the sky and landed on a large wooden cote set apart from the khibas. Dozens more flitters chattered and stirred within the structure. Children played at the edges of the campsite, giggling and mock-fighting with sticks. In a cleared central space, warriors of both sexes sparred with wooden axes and staves. The clash of timber and grunts of pain echoed off the steep valley walls.

Alere stretched aching muscles, welcoming the break. A sparkling creek gurgled along one side of the valley, promising a chance to bathe away the sweat and blood staining her clothing. Cooking pots bubbled over open firepits dotted around the campsite, and the rich smell of meaty stew made her stomach rumble.

A man and woman rode to greet the travellers. Both wore bronze lamellar armour and black and grey speckled xiao-catskin cloaks, and each led a pack-laden horse. The valley raiders greeted Jada's guides, Nasra, and Rohne with smiles and respectful bows, but watched Alere, Mina, Sura and Kett with suspicion. Alere and Mina, particularly, were the subject of wide-eyed, furtive inspections. After a hushed discussion, to which only Rohne, Nasra and Jada's guides were invited, Rohne rode back, leading the two pack animals.

'Jada sent word,' Rohne said. 'We're to be given supplies and sent on our way. Only Sura and Nasra will stay.' He held up the two sets of reins fisted in his hand. 'He doesn't want the Alcazar weishi to find this place. We leave now.'

Alere sniffed. 'Friendly.'

'You can't blame the man for trying to protect his people,' Kett said. 'If questioned he can deny ever hosting us here.'

Given no choice, the travellers lingered only long enough to say their goodbyes. Sura dissolved into tears and clutched at her daughters. Unused to overt displays of affection, Alere bore it, for her mother's sake. But her chest ached with the awareness of twenty years of missed family connection. She broke free.

Sura grabbed her wrist. 'Don't go, Alere.' Her cheeks were wet and reddened. She glanced at Mina. 'Either of you. Please? I'm scared I'll never see you again. Stay. Hide. They won't find you here.'

Alere twisted loose. 'I can't. I made a promise I have to keep.'

'But why?' Sura held Mina close against her side and frowned at Alere. 'It's just a bracelet. I won't let you put Mina in such danger over something so petty.'

Hurt roiled in Alere's stomach as Mina leaned into their mother.

Alere backed away a step. 'You gave up the right to tell me what to do twenty years ago, Sura. Mina can stay if she wants to. I'm not making her leave.'

'It's alright, Mother,' Mina said gently. 'Rohne's right: I do need to see this through.' She frowned at Alere. 'It's not that I want to leave...I don't know why, but I *need* to help Alere.'

Sura wept harder. 'No. Please don't go. I can't bear to lose you, Mina.'

Alere spun away, tears blurring the ground as she stalked to Rumi. She sucked a deep breath and centred herself, using weishi techniques to settle her hurt into acceptance. Her mother had done what she thought was the right thing, twenty years ago. It was just hard to remember that, sometimes.

Nasra stood near to Rumi and thoughtfully regarded Alere. When the older woman touched Alere's arm, Alere partially lowered her Outer wards.

You have a difficult path to tread. Nasra's Outers slid into Alere's mind. *I'm not sure you'll like what you find at the end. Be sure you're on the right side of what's coming.*

'What does that mean? I'm just giving back the bracelet.'

Nasra raised a sceptical brow and, with a swirl of skirts, turned away.

Alere remounted Rumi and absently patted the mare's neck. Could Nasra know more than she revealed? She seemed so smug. What did she mean by 'on the right side'? Helping the Koh-Lins and Shanzhai against Hanna and Ven was the right thing to do, but how could Nasra know Alere's task? Alere frowned. If the xintou had breached her wards... Cold foreboding sleeted across Alere's skin.

The xintou took Rohne's head in her hands and pressed their foreheads together for several seconds before releasing him. A silent interchange followed and, had mother and son been speaking aloud, would be a heated argument. Nasra glared at Rohne, shaking her head and gripping his shoulders. Rohne jerked free and, with a silent scowl at his mother, re-joined Mina by the horses.

Alere wasn't thrilled to have Rohne tagging along. She had no idea where his loyalties lay, what his skills were, or how he would act under pressure. Had Nasra instilled in him the primary, peace-keeping function of a xintou? Most female xintou could Read, Speak, and use Empathy to influence emotions. Could Rohne do the same? And could he See future events or Broadcast to many minds at once – which were rarer abilities?

Rohne was a wildcard and Mina was another unknown. Alere watched her sister's tearful farewell to Sura. The girl must be a hard worker and possess a strong stomach to have graduated to journeyman healer. She kept her head in frightening situations, but had no skill with a blade. However, having dragged Mina into this situation, Alere was honour-bound to get her sister out. Neither would have a settled life until Alere's name was cleared and the threat of war averted. To do that, were it even possible, Alere needed her father's support.

'So?' Kett's question broke her train of thought. 'West?'

Alere nodded and touched her heels to Rumi. 'West.'

It took the remainder of the day to make their way through the Ahmar Mountains' maze of foothills. One of Jada's men wordlessly led them out of the hills then, before he could be thanked, vanished into the darkening woods.

'Right,' Alere said, saluting the trees, 'and goodbye to you, too.'

Kett, practical as always, took a bearing on the blood-red setting sun and scouted the immediate surrounds. Alere studied the landscape. Not far away, a small stream gushed from between two hills and wound through a copse of twisted trees before running across rocky, uncultivated grasslands. The soil was too thin and the water supply too scarce to be good farmland. Only hunters and goat-herders were mad enough to traipse through this wilderness, so lighting a fire shouldn't attract unwanted attention. Alere was chilled enough to welcome the warmth.

Rohne chose a campsite near the stand of trees, in the lee of a granite outcropping. Kett put the horses on a long tether while Alere and Mina gathered firewood. An inspection of the packs provided by the raiders revealed enough dried meats, fruits and vegetables for four or five days. There were also waterskins, wineskins and waterproofed glass-rabbit furs sewn into sleeping bags.

Alere held the translucent grey furs in one hand and kicked at the ground. Even the hard pallet in her room at Xintou house was softer than the smooth swell of granite underfoot. Mina appeared, carrying a huge armful of bracken and heather. With a tentative smile, she dropped the branches at Alere's feet.

'It's better than the ground.'

'Thanks.' Alere spread the plants and shook out her sleeping bag onto the makeshift mattress. The earthy scent of crushed leaves unravelled a deep knot of exhaustion and tension in her shoulders. She plucked out a handful of bracken and studied it. Mina had added fennaro leaves to the mix. Alere sat and breathed deeply. Hopefully the sleeping-herb would help dispel the nagging sense of unease she'd carried all day.

A few paces away, Kett lit a small fire with twigs and leaf litter and arranged a tent of larger branches over the licking orange flames. Where on Kalima did he learn these skills? Hadn't he lived his entire life in Madina? Yet here he was acting as if wandering around the wilderness was normal.

Mina reappeared with another armful of bracken, dropped it to the ground and inspected her scratched arms. 'I wish I had my medical supplies.'

'Sorry about that,' Alere muttered.

'I think saving my life makes up for losing the medical gear.' Mina's smile was gentle.

Alere envied Mina's steady calm. 'I'm sorry I dragged you into this. And I'm sorry you had to kill that Alcazar weishi in Pelon.'

'I don't know how you and Kett do what you do. Killing those men like that...' Mina shuddered and wrapped her arms around her body. 'How do you get used to the nightmares?'

Alere gave a shrug of feigned casualness and studied the shimmering sweep of stars overhead, hoping her face didn't betray her torment. Every night Khaler's blank eyes and bloodied corpse haunted her dreams.

Rohne stood at the fringe of the firelight, staring east towards the mountains.

'Rohne?' Mina called, sounding worried.

He started, his gaze sharpening. 'Sorry, what? I've been Speaking with Nasra.'

'Oh?' Alere plucked at a loose shirt thread, concealing uneasy surprise. No female xintou was capable of either Speaking or Reading over such a distance. 'Is she well? She wasn't happy about you leaving.'

'She tends to be overprotective.' Rohne's sour expression held hints of puzzlement and anger. He filled a pot with stream water, sat by the fire and began to chop dried meats and vegetables, hacking at them as though they were the enemy. 'She says more Alcazar weishi and junren came to Gaton. They sacked the village.' He was outwardly calm, intent on his task, but his lips pressed into a thin line.

Mina gasped, one hand flying to her mouth.

Rohne's voice was tight. 'Luckily, Jada posted men on the north road. They warned the village in time. Almost everyone took refuge in the mountains. The Alcazar men burned Nasra's library. Books over five hundred years old.' His mouth curled in a snarl. He beheaded a tuber and threw it into a pot filled with stream water.

'Almost everyone?' Mina whispered. She sank onto Alere's bed.

Rohne named five people and silent tears tracked down Mina's cheeks. Alere hesitated with one hand poised above Mina's back, then patted her sister's shoulder, unsure of what to say. Mina leaned into her. Alere slipped an arm around Mina's waist and held her close. A small seed of warmth grew in Alere's chest, entwining her with tendrils of love...and fear. Mina was her sister; her family. Their intangible connection grew stronger each hour, filling a gap Alere had never understood, binding her a little tighter.

'What will they do now?' Kett's deep voice broke the silence. 'And your Jun, what will he do?'

Rohne stirred the pot and settled it in the coals. 'Our Jun Fourth will do nothing, as he always does. He controls our Fifth and Sixth, too. Jada will shelter the villagers, but it'll mean he can't claim to be uninvolved. He'll send the villagers, along with the oldest and youngest of his people, far into the ranges. Then Jada's fighters will buy us time. The Alcazar will lose more men than they find and it'll be messy.'

A breeze, sharp with the scent of snow, tumbled from the hilltops and danced with the flames, sending sparks spiralling into the sky.

Rohne flipped up his collar. 'With winter coming, the Alcazar men won't survive long in the hills. They'll give up as soon as the first snows fall.'

Alere wrapped her cloak closer. 'We need to be at Shanzhai before then. How long will it take to get there?'

Radan's words rang in her mind. The First Shunu and her son wanted control of the iron deposit before winter in order to produce weapons for a summer campaign. Winter was close upon them and only lasted two months.

'There's about two weeks of hard riding between us and Shanzhai, including crossing the Aswad Ranges.' Rohne pointed west into the darkness. 'But Jun Fourth Hassan Wen-Gates's home estate is a day's ride away, between us and Newmec – which is the start of the road to Shanzhai. To avoid the Jun Fourth's patrolled lands we'd either have to head back north towards Madina or southeast into the mountains again. North, we risk capture by Alcazar search parties. Southeast, we add two or three weeks. And we'll be caught in the mountains when it snows.'

'There is a third option.' Kett added wood to the fire. 'We can go straight through his lands.'

'No!' Mina said, blanching.

'Why? Is he dangerous?' Alere asked.

Rohne laughed. 'Mina's just overreacting. We were brought up on stories of our Jun Fourth. Nobody from Gaton has seen him for twenty years. Rumours abound.' His amber eyes sparkled as he ticked points off on his fingers. 'He never married because he murdered his betrothed. He sacrifices people on moonless nights. He has a harem of thirty jiaoji and seventy kin-children – he sells them to the slavers in Melcor when he needs money. Oh, I forgot, he's building a space ship to go back to Earth.'

'And,' Mina put in, giggling, 'my favourite is that he experiments on animals and tries to recreate the old terraforming techniques.'

'So.' Alere lay back on her bracken bed and admired the star-swept sky above. 'Not a homicidal maniac then? Apart from the betrothed, that is.'

'No,' Mina replied. 'I'm sure he's perfectly nice. But he hates uninvited visitors. Mother and Nasra go there to midwife the women of his estate. Mother says the only strange thing is the eight pairs of identical twins in his household. Hardly sinister.'

'How do we get across, then?' Alere shifted and breathed in the soothing scent of crushed leaves as the bracken rustled beneath her.

There was a long silence, broken only by the crackle of burning wood and the stew's gentle bubbling.

'What does he want most?' asked Kett.

'A new betrothed?' Alere suggested.

'Volunteering?' Kett raised an ironic brow.

'Ha ha. But that does give me an idea.' She sat up. 'Under Traveller's Law the Jun Fourth can't refuse entry to Jun or First Ship families travelling on business. He's a recluse so he won't know the minor nobles. Mina and Rohne can dress as well-born merchants. I saw some merchant-green clothing in the packs and we can blonde Mina's hair with white weed. Rohne can be from one of the First Ship families. If you take off the silver insignia on your Alcazar cloak, Kett, you can be a ronin weishi. I'll cut my hair, dress as a boy and be a servant. Mina and Rohne can be going home to…' She addressed Kett. 'What's the next major town past Shanzhai?'

Kett's amusement faded. 'Asalam. The country seat of the Jun First Zah-Hill family.'

'Perfect,' Alere crowed. 'No one would suspect us of wanting to go there. If the Alcazar weishi question the Jun Fourth, he'll be able to say he hosted a blonde woman and three men going to Asalam.'

She waited impatiently while the others voiced objections but, with no valid alternative, they were obliged to accept the idea.

'What name will you use?' Kett said. 'Choose carefully. Hassan may know which families are closely allied with the Zah-Hills and he's never liked Hanna.'

'How about Johnston?' Rohne suggested.

'Never heard it before,' Alere said. 'Where's it from?'

'Old First Ship settler name. One of the extinct lines, so he shouldn't know it.' Rohne said. 'I like the family motto: *nunquam non paratus.* Means "Never unprepared" which is a good idea to live by right now.'

Alere stilled, hiding her shock. That was the motto engraved on her dagger. But she'd never shown it to Rohne. She threw a twig into the fire and yawned, feigning disinterest. 'What made you pick that name?'

'Saw it in a history book, I think.' Rohne's mouth twisted into a knowing smile and he flickered a look at her from beneath his lashes.

She couldn't accuse him of breaching her wards without seeming rude so Alere said nothing. After all, his choice of name could just be a coincidence. Still, it made her uneasy.

With the immediate future decided, they demolished Rohne's stew in hungry silence, set watches and settled to sleep.

Alere took first watch hoping she'd tire enough to sleep well. But, when she lay down to rest, with dagger in one hand and bracelet in the other, she still couldn't relax. Every crack of a burning log, every whine of a night-wing, every sigh of a breeze in the trees overhead, startled her awake with the expectation of a sword at her throat. The rustle of leaves and bracken became the insidious murmur of voices, urging death to her enemies in order to save the jundom.

Kett roused Alere at dawn. Hoar-frost covered every surface and she shivered as her bare feet hit the ground. The sturdy socks and boots provided by Jada's men were a welcome relief. She shook Mina awake and went to locate white-weed. Its distinctive white-veined, lavender leaves were a popular source of dye and hair colour.

An hour later, their camp packed and the horses loaded, the four travellers mounted. They headed southwest with the rising sun's pale orange fingers stroking their backs. Mina's long locks shone white-blonde. With her night eyes – made vivid by the new hair colour – she'd be memorable. Alere touched her own dark hair. Short, fluffy curls met her seeking fingertips. Cutting her hair made sense, since she masqueraded as a boy not yet old enough to grow a man's mawei, but it would take some getting used to.

'Never mind...Alek.' Kett's amused voice broke into her thoughts. 'It'll grow back.' He guided Bol alongside Rumi.

Alere screwed up her nose at him and adjusted her scruffy green hat. 'I kind of like it. It'll be easier to look after.'

'It suits you,' he said.

She grinned. 'I'll tell you what suits me – not wearing the veil or makeup and jewelry every day.' She threw her arms wide and breathed in the winter-dry air, embracing the plains and distant mountains. 'This suits me. No classes, no rules, no Mistresses telling me to do better. Do you ever wonder what our lives would have been like without that jiche kin-child law? If I'd never gone to Xintou House?'

'Different.' Kett's fingers whitened on the reins.

'Well, we probably wouldn't have met,' Alere said. She sobered. That possibility didn't bear thinking about. She forced a smile. 'And you'd have had no-one to torture in training.'

Kett's smile didn't reach his eyes. 'Oh, I suspect we would have crossed paths. You're hard to miss.' He tilted his head, quizzical. 'But do you really feel like I was too hard on you?'

She flushed and shrugged. 'I guess not. I was pretty wild.'

'You were angry, hurt,' he corrected gently, 'and understandably so. Training taught you self-control.'

'Why? So I wouldn't hurt any of the precious xintou girls when they laughed and insulted me, you mean? Great.' She laughed bitterly. 'You should have let me go when I ran away.'

Kett's brow darkened. 'I couldn't have lived with myself if something had happened to you. Protecting you is my job, Alli.' He said no more, and dropped behind as the path narrowed.

His job. Her heart contracted. Was there anyone who cared about her for who she was, not for what she represented? To Mistress Li and Radan she was a tool. To Elmira, a dangerous secret; to Mina an intruder in her peaceful life who symbolised everything a healer disdained. Alere looked away across the plains.

The sun sparkled off frost and lit the blue grasslands in shades of silver and gold. When the stream narrowed and veered southeast, Rohne found a route across the shallow, rocky bed and so they could continue southwest across the grasslands. The horses splashed through the water and clambered up the steep bank opposite. As they topped the rise, Kett once more kneed his horse close to Rumi.

'Company.' He nodded forward. 'Loosen your sword and be ready. Our story is about to be tested.'

A heavily armed, nine-man patrol rode towards them in a precise v-formation, on matching grey horses. The riders wore Wen-Gates purple-and-copper colours. Their commander rode at the head of the formation, his copper and leather armour glinting in the clean morning light. A dusty breeze fluttered his mulberry cloak and rippled the blue-grass meadows like waves on a lake.

Alere slid her sword a handswidth clear of the scabbard. Kett shook his head and pointed at Rohne. Kett was right. She had to give Rohne a chance. Fighting Wen-Gates's men would be counter-productive, and outrunning the patrol would be impossible with the short-legged mountain pack ponies in tow. Unfortunately, Alere had little faith in Rohne's ability to talk his way across the xenophobic Jun's border.

CHAPTER THIRTEEN

Several hours later Alere silently kicked herself for stupidity. Things were not going as expected. Although Rohne had overawed the guardsmen with suspicious ease the weishi had, instead of allowing safe passage, escorted the party into the Wen-Gates fortified estate. Rohne's doing, or theirs? Alere had no way of knowing.

As the four companions and their escort approached the estate, Alere's uneasiness grew. Everywhere in the compound were signs of preparation for siege and war: stockpiles of grain, meat smoke-houses, thick stone walls around the central villa, a well close to the main living area, ranks of junren training in the courtyard.

Alere's party was ushered into the foyer of the great hall and stripped of their swords. She managed to secrete her dagger in one boot, and the bracelet in the other. Then she and her companions were ushered into the Jun Fourth's presence. As her bootheels tap-tapped on the slate floors and echoed back off the stone walls, the full madness of their plan hit home. Dozens of armed weishi and junren lined each wall. There was no way out but through them.

Hassan Wen-Gates sat on a plain zitan-wood chair at the western end of the vast, arched hall, his back to a jewel-coloured window, his face in shadow. At his side, dressed in shimmering gold silk, a Bonded Xintou also watched Rohne and Mina's approach.

Alere shored up her wards and groaned, low in her throat. She hadn't anticipated being brought before the Jun and his Xintou. Mina had no distraction-ward training – thinking innocuous Outers to appear normal. Her thoughts would give them away. Why hadn't the

Xintou already raised the alarm? Mina had the distracted air of someone concentrating hard. Maybe Nasra's training would get her through, after all?

Rohne told their story and Hassan sat motionless on his throne. When Rohne finished speaking, the expectant silence stretched into anticipation of axe-fall. Mina twisted the edge of her green robe. Rohne touched her hand. She stiffened. Alere and Kett stood the regulation three paces behind, caps in hand, heads bowed, helpless.

On the dais, the Xintou leaned forward and sunlight painted her cheek the gold of her robe. She appeared to be around fifty, with mahogany hair touched by grey. She exuded the regal, self-contained assuredness common to Xintou, but Alere didn't recognise her. The Xintou's pale eyes narrowed. When the woman didn't speak, Alere released a silent breath. Rohne's guise held, somehow.

'You're merchants?' The Jun's reedy voice emerged from the shadows. He tapped an impatient tattoo on the chair's arm.

'Yes, Shenshi Hassan.' Rohne inclined his head.

'And your goods for sale?'

Rohne didn't hesitate. 'Raiders from the Ahmar Mountains ambushed us. Stole the huoche carrying our trade goods. We humbly request to pass through your lands on our way to Asalam. We have family there that can assist.'

There was a long pause before the Jun turned to his Xintou. Light caught his face and Alere started. Hassan Wen-Gates was the image of the old Jun First. No, not quite – around forty years old, whereas Radan Zah-Hill had been fifty, so perhaps a younger brother, or a cousin. The resemblance was uncanny.

The Xintou touched the tip of her nose with two fingers in an obvious signal. Did that mean the woman couldn't transmit thoughts? Bonded Xintou were always the most powerful telepaths so it was more likely Hassan was too paranoid to lower his wards.

Was there an advantage in that for Rohne's talks with the Jun? It was hard to think how, unless the Jun and his Xintou could be separated.

The silence became oppressive. Mina's shallow breaths rasped, over-loud in the vast space of the hall. Alere resisted grabbing the dagger hidden in her boot. She focussed on thinking harmless Outers appropriate to a servant boy. Beside her, Kett kept his head bowed, but his weight balanced on the balls of his feet, hands held away from his body, ready to uncoil into battle.

The Jun leaned back in his throne-like chair. He raised a finger and a servant scurried to his side. Hassan murmured something inaudible and the servant left. His Xintou relaxed. Alere allowed herself a small sigh of relief.

'So, what news from the capital?' Hassan chose a glossy pink hada from a blackstone bowl beside his chair. He bit into the eight-pointed fruit, scarlet juices dribbling down his chin. Alere's stomach growled.

Rohne placed a hand over his heart. 'Only the tragic news you've probably already heard. About the Jun First, Radan Zah-Hill?'

The Fourth stiffened, clutching at the arm of his chair. He surged forward. A dusty beam of sunlight, made bloody by the stained glass, touched the copper circlet on his dark hair. There was a wildness in his gold-brown eyes; a hint of passions uncontrolled. A suggestion of madness, even.

'What news is that? We've heard none.' He glared at his servant. 'Why have we had no rider-news?'

The servant cringed. 'Shenshi, you gave orders to forbid entrance—'

'Silence! I didn't mean riders in the orange uniform, you kalet! The Alcazar doesn't send official news by flitter.' The Jun hurled the fruit at his man and refocussed on Rohne. 'What news?'

Rohne swept a deep bow. 'I regret to be the bearer of sad tidings. The Jun First is dead of illness; about a week ago now. His son, Ven, sits on the Steel Throne in his stead.'

The Xintou gasped, a hand to her throat, her washed-grey eyes fixed on the Jun. Hassan froze; only his fingers moved, opening and closing around the chair arms. He sank back, consumed once more by shadow.

'Radan, dead.' The Jun Fourth's voice was a faded whisper. 'Ven on the throne. Ven and Hanna...' He rubbed at his forehead and removed the copper circlet, passing it to a waiting servant. With jerky movements, he stood and paced before the dais, his guests apparently forgotten. The juice on his chin glistened red. He wiped his mouth, gazing at the blood-coloured liquid before curling his fingers into a fist.

'Jilla, it's come sooner than I'd hoped. The time of the *er*—.' He seemed to stare through his Xintou, even while speaking directly to her. 'No. I mustn't tell you...you aren't...and the House can't be trusted.' He wiped his hand on his robe, leaving a smear of red on the purple fabric. 'But my work isn't finished. They aren't ready.'

'They? Who aren't ready, shenshi?' The Xintou, Jilla, touched his arm but he jerked away. 'Shenshi Hassan, we've planned for this. We'll be safe here. Remember the flitter-bird from Mistress Li?'

Alere started. What had Mistress Li to do with Hassan's plans? Isolated as Alere had been in the House, it had never sunk in that frail Mistress Li was the true power in the jundom; that she controlled, though her Xintou, all twenty-one Jun families, from the First to the Sixths.

'Get me the shangwei and a flitter-bird,' Hassan snarled at a hovering servant. 'We need to make ready.'

Rohne cleared his throat. Hassan paused in his pacing and stared at the four travellers, his frown deepening. He flicked a hand at them.

'Go. You have rooms in the guest quarters for tonight. You leave in the morning. Meals will be sent to you. Speak with the housekeeper about replenishing supplies, if you must.' Hassan sent Rohne a keen look. 'And don't spin me any more tales. I'm not interested in what you're running from. If what you say about the Jun is true, then there are more important things to worry about. Be on your way with first light. *Molian*.' He turned his back, ignoring Rohne's polite bow and murmur of thanks.

A servant led the way to austere, sombre guest quarters in a distant wing of the building. He led Alere's party into the main sitting room, indicated two bedrooms and left without speaking. The thick timber door clicked shut with the finality of expensive metal locks and imprisonment. Alere and her companions stood, frozen in the middle of the room, listening to the servant's retreating footsteps.

'For a moment I thought the Jun was going to order our execution.' Mina sank into an over-stuffed chair. Dust clouded the air and she sneezed. 'What was that he said? Molian? What's it mean? And the time of the *er*—? The *er* what?'

Kett moved around the room, methodically opening doors and inspecting every corner.

'Molian is an old word,' he said. 'It means something like: *to temper oneself*, or *to endure*.'

'But Hassan used it like a farewell,' Alere said.

Kett said nothing. He paused by the window of their second-storey room, twitched aside thick, purple curtains and flung open the clouded glass panes. Daylight and cool air flooded into the quarters. Kett tapped his fingers on the windowsill, uncharacteristically restless and ill-at-ease.

'Why does he look like Jun First Radan?' Alere asked.

Mina and Rohne looked at her in surprise. 'Does he?' Mina asked.

'Very much.' Kett stared outside. The clash of weapons and stomp of feet carried into the room; junren trained in the yard below.

Alere curbed her impatience. He would answer in his own time

'He's kin-brother to the old Jun,' Kett continued. 'Hassan's mother was Lalla Wen-Gates. Mistress to Peter Zah-Hill, Radan's father. When Hassan inherited this estate, he changed his name to Wen-Gates. He was safe here, even when Hanna started her kin-child campaign. At that time Radan was strong enough to resist Hanna, and wouldn't allow her to march against his kin-brother. But Hassan has never returned to the capital.'

Alere put her hands on her hips. 'How on Kalima do you know all of this? Before yesterday all I knew was his name and title.'

Kett's lips twitched and he sent her a half-exasperated look. 'A weishi is silent more often than not. It means we listen more than we speak. Try it sometime.'

She glared but it was an old argument, not worth pursing now.

'And you think we're in danger here.' Rohne joined Kett at the window and leaned out, inspecting the outside wall.

Kett nodded. 'Hassan won't let us go. We've seen his siege preparations. He can't risk us going to Asalam and warning Ven and Hanna. In retrospect naming the Zah-Hill's seat of power as our destination was a poor choice, but we couldn't have known.'

'Hassan's paranoid and thinks we're spies from the Alcazar.' Rohne picked up a small, wooden ornament; an image of a pair of girl-children entwined around a double-headed axe. He tossed the carving and spun it between his fingers with distracting dexterity. 'He didn't believe our story. Reading his Outers was easy'

'Wasn't he warding?' Alere said. 'I thought he must have kept his wards up to stop Jilla Reading.'

'Oh yes, he was,' Rohne said, dismissively, 'but not very well. *I* had no trouble getting through his Outers. His Inners were too strong, though. His mind was so disorganised that I'd probably risk Fusion if I broke through to his Inners, anyway.'

'Disorganised sounds like a polite way of saying insane,' Alere said, forcing herself to sound calm. Rohne's ability to get through a Xintou-trained ward so easily was frightening. She strengthened her Outer wards. 'Do you think Jilla suspects you?'

He flipped a careless hand. 'She hasn't the skill to penetrate my wards and I helped Mina shore up hers. The gold-veil saw what we wanted her to see.' He flicked the ornament deftly back onto its stand. 'Hassan's delusional, but he's probably right to believe Hanna's his enemy. We need to get out of here.'

'Agreed,' Kett said. 'This evening after Luna-Er sets. When the weishi and junren are on night-watch.'

'I can't believe Hassan would...' Mina gulped as Kett directed a bleak look at her. 'But what about our equipment?' she whispered.

Yes, escaping from the room would be simple enough, but Alere had no intention of leaving Rumi behind, nor walking all the way to Shanzhai. She had her dagger, cloak and the bracelet on her, but travelling comfortably was easier with horses, tents, sleeping bags and cooking gear.

'If we can get to our gear and load up without being found,' Kett said. 'If we can't, we'll just take the fast horses and get out.'

Mina rose, straightened her robe and twitched down the green veil. 'Then I'm going to chat with the housekeeper. The Jun said we could. If Hassan's going to pretend we're guests then I'm going to act like one. I'll get medical supplies and food in case we have to leave everything Jada gave us.'

'Good thinking.' Rohne quirked a grin at her. 'We might freeze to death trudging horseless and weaponless across the Plains, but we'll have willowbark if we get a headache.'

Mina sent him a withering glare. 'We can take blankets from the beds.'

'And swords from the armoury if we can't find ours,' Kett said, cutting across a potential spat. 'But I would be loath to lose mine.' Kett's steel sword was priceless; a family heirloom rarely out of his sight.

Mina rang for a servant and went off to consult with the housekeeper.

Two hours later, indifferent meals of overcooked lu-deer and tasteless steamed vegetables were brought and consumed. When the sun set in a blaze of blood light and Mina still hadn't returned, Alere began to worry. Rohne seemed unperturbed, a slight smile on his lips, his gaze abstracted as he stood at the window staring out into darkness.

'Can you tell where Mina is?' Alere asked. Surely he'd be more concerned if Mina was in danger?

Rohne let the curtain fall, before nodding. 'Yes, she's in the kitchen. She's fine. She's spying for us and feeding me information.' He chuckled. 'It's a game we played as children. She'd find out when the baker was making pies, distract him and let me read her Outers. I'd steal the pies from the window.'

'What's your range?' Kett, who had been reclining with eyes closed on the couch, sat up, refilled Alere's wineglass and held it out. She shook her head and he set the glass aside.

'If I haven't met the person,' Rohne said, 'or seen them, zero. They're invisible. If I have seen them, it depends on how well I know them. Someone I've touched, maybe thirty gongli. Someone I know fairly well, about sixty. I've never had the chance to test it, but I'm fairly sure I could Speak with Nasra up to about a hundred.'

Unease slithered down Alere's spine, and she guarded her face and wards. He might still be communicating with Nasra, which was disturbing for some reason. Connecting over that distance was unheard of and Alere had the uncomfortable notion Rohne held something back.

She fingered the bracelet-box, now tucked back inside her shirt. So did she, if it came to that.

'What's Mina found out?' Kett asked.

'Not a lot we didn't already know.' Rohne sank into a chair, yawning, and flung a leg over the arm. He tipped the chair back and stared up at the vaulted timber ceiling. 'Hassan's understandably paranoid. But his staff are loyal out of fear so bribing the weishi isn't likely to work. Ah!' He sat up and faced the door. 'Mina's got good news. She's warding it until she gets here.'

A few minutes later the door opened to admit Mina. She thanked her weishi escort, who handed over a large haversack before closing the heavy timber panel. The lock clicked from the outside. She glanced at Rohne, who nodded.

'All clear,' he assured her. 'The Xintou is in conference with Hassan and isn't Reading us at the moment.'

Mina dropped the haversack and collapsed onto the couch next to Kett. He gave her Alere's glass of wine and she smiled gratefully.

'Thank you. You have no idea how exhausting that was.' She sipped the wine. 'The cook talks non-stop and likes to brag, and the housekeeper has an obsessive need for control. They hate each other. I played the helpless female to the hilt, but I got what we need.'

'What's that?' Alere eyed Mina. This was a new side to her sister.

'Supplies and a way out,' Mina replied, looking slightly smug.

Alere blinked at her. Kett gave a slow grin of approval that brought a flush to Mina's cheeks.

Rohne frowned and sat up in his chair. 'How'd you get that information out of them?'

She scrubbed her free hand down her thigh. 'I asked lots of questions about the estate and the staff and grounds. Mostly encouraging them to dispel rumours we'd heard in our "travels". Eventually the cook mentioned a service entrance. From the stables to the end of the hall on this level. This place is a warren of hidden tunnels.' She grimaced. 'The servants call them "the sorrows".'

'Unsettling. Why?' Alere asked.

Mina shrugged. 'No idea. But the cook seemed uneasy after she'd talked about the tunnels and wouldn't say anything else.'

'Nicely done.' Kett leaned forward, ran a hand over his mawei and stared absently at the threadbare purple and gilt rug on the cold timber floor. 'So how do we get past the weishi outside our door? And the ones guarding the stables and gates?

Mina sent him a mischievous grin. 'I took care of that, too. When I was in the kitchen I salted the stew the cook made for their dinner – with runweed.'

Alere muffled the giggle welling up from her belly.

'You did learn something useful in Madina.' Rohne's amber eyes danced with delight and he let out a guffaw.

Kett chuckled, his admiring gaze resting on Mina. Alere sobered and turned away, appalled at the strength of her reaction to that look. Was she so petty as to deny her best friend some happiness? She walked to the window and stared at the torch-lit courtyard below, trying not to think of Kett and Mina together. It was like trying not to think about green plants: impossible and unimaginable at the same time.

'That means the weishi should be otherwise occupied 'til around lunch, tomorrow,' Rohne said. 'The sooner we get away tonight the better. Well done, Mina.'

'Indeed.' Kett unfolded himself from the couch and extended a hand to Mina, helping her rise. 'We should all get some sleep, if we can. I'll wake you when it's time to go.'

Mina blushed and smiled. Alere headed for the bedroom she was to share with Mina, not wanting to see any more. Mina's light footsteps followed.

'Keep your wards up,' Rohne called. 'We don't want our plans leaking to the Xintou.' He blew out the mel-oil lamp, plunging the sitting room into darkness.

Somewhere in the distance, a weird, ululating cry echoed through the building, followed by hysterical laughter. The sound wasn't quite human, yet unlike any animal Alere had ever heard. She shivered in the chill of the darkened room. Her hand dropped to her hip, but her scabbard was empty.

Mina gave a nervous laugh. 'Maybe he really does do genetic experiments on animals?'

Alere relaxed, curled under a feather quilt, warm and comfortable for the first time in days. She blew out the mel-oil lamp by the bed and bid Mina goodnight.

'Do you think our father will welcome us?' Mina's voice drifted out of the gloom.

Alere dragged herself away from the borders of sleep, reluctant to think that far ahead.

'I don't know,' she admitted. 'All we can do is show up with the bracelet and hope he can help.'

'But what are you expecting from him?' Mina asked. 'He can't acknowledge you without bringing the Alcazar down on all of us.

What's he supposed to do? How can he clear your name? Or protect you…us…from Hanna and Ven?'

Alere had anticipated and dreaded this moment but she'd expected the questions to come from Rohne. Mina's gentle quietude made her intelligence easy to overlook. What should she say? Surely she could trust her own sister. But Mina might be blood, but she was still almost a stranger. She also had a history with Rohne and something about him troubled Alere.

'I don't really know,' Alere said. 'Radan told me to take the bracelet to Rafi. He must have had a good reason. After all, he knew who I was all along and didn't betray me to Hanna.'

There was a long silence. Had Mina fallen asleep?

'There's more, isn't there?' Mina's voice was barely audible. 'There's something you're not telling me. Something important. I don't know how I know, but I do. What's going on? Why are you willing to risk your life, mine, Kett's and Rohne's for a bracelet? It's madness.'

Alere gritted her teeth. Telling Mina was too dangerous. The iron was a secret that could start a war.

'I can't tell you, Mina. I'm sworn to silence. This is my responsibility and I have to see it through.'

'So doing what Radan asked is more important than the lives of people you care about?'

'Yes,' Alere said shortly. 'You'll just have to trust me.'

'Like you're trusting me?'

'Mina—'

'Oh, don't.' There was a rustle of bedclothes and a heavy sigh. 'You don't trust me. You don't trust anyone except Kett. And you don't tell him everything, either, do you? I think that's sad. You've cut yourself off from people who could love you. What are you afraid of? You cling to duty like it's some sort of shield against bad things happening to you. Well, it's not. And if you keep pushing people away, you'll find yourself alone when you most need help. Complete freedom is a two-edged sword, Alere.'

'Mina…' Alere's throat closed. The words cut deep and she chewed on her bottom lip to hold back a defensive reply.

'Just go to sleep,' Mina said. Cloth rustled again, then silence fell.

Alere closed her eyes. In Xintou house, keeping her thoughts private had been vital. If her wards failed, the outcome was the humiliating revelation of her fears. She'd spent her spare time in the library or with the weishi, comfortable in their bluff, undemanding company. Female friendships were untrodden ground and Alere had no idea how to open up without Mina discovering everything Alere was – and wasn't.

Alere woke to a night-black room and the sense someone moved in the darkness.

'I'm awake.' She flipped the blankets aside and fumbled on the floor for her boots.

Kett squeezed her shoulder before returning silently to the main room. Alere bundled up a blanket and tucked it under one arm.

She shook Mina awake, one hand over her mouth to prevent a cry. 'It's time. Get up.'

Mina nodded and Alere released her.

In the main room, by the light of Luna-Er's last, feeble rays, Alere and a yawning Mina joined the others at the door. Rohne shouldered the haversack, which bulged with supplies. Alere yanked her knife from her boot. At a nod from Kett, she tried the door handle. It gave easily. She hesitated. It had been locked when they went to bed.

Kett grimaced and nodded again. She eased the door open. The hinges protested with a teeth-aching shriek that cut like an axe through the silence. Alere paused, unsure whether to pull the door closed or throw it open. The bronze door handle dug into her skin. Mina gave a little whimper.

No other sound broke the building's oppressive hush; not even a whispered breath from the guard outside their door. Rohne touched Alere's shoulder. He tapped his temple and raised his little finger in the signal used between xintou wishing to communicate.

After a moment's uncertainty, Alere relaxed her Outer wards.

The runweed must have worked. His thought slid into her mind. *As far as I can tell, the corridor is clear. Go.*

But if there's a guard out there you haven't met you wouldn't be able to tell, would you?

Well, no, but—

Alere cut him off with a sharp gesture. He scowled. There was no point arguing. They had only one option, anyway. Alere flung the door open. The hinges' squeal quietened to the high-pitched squeak of a terrified glass-rabbit. The hall lay empty, the chair by their door unoccupied. Alere slipped into the corridor, treading carefully so her heels made no noise on the timber floor. The others followed. Rohne eyed the chair and raised a mocking brow. Alere ignored him. Hopefully there would be no need for further telepathy with him. Hearing a male voice in her head made her uncomfortable for some reason.

He collected a mel-oil lamp from the guard's table and held the tiny flame aloft. Smoky-orange lamplight danced on the timber-panelled walls. Mina pointed into the darkness, down the corridor. Alere, with dagger ready, led the way. Rohne's lamp illuminated a path and Alere's murderous shadow stalked ahead.

Timber creaked somewhere behind in the black of the sleeping house. A floorboard?

Alere held up an open hand – the weishi signal to halt. Kett froze and the others followed suit. She closed her eyes and listened to the silence. Was that the rustle of cloth? The thick hush remained unbroken. Rohne's eyes blanked; he shook his head and shrugged. Alere tiptoed on.

At the end of the corridor, Mina lifted a hidden latch, tucked into a join between timber slats. The click of the mechanism cracked the stillness. Alere tensed and glanced behind, but no weishi appeared to challenge them. Rohne thrust the lamp into the gaping doorway, revealing a narrow staircase that clung to the stone wall and curled downward into the sorrows' cold gloom.

An icy gust of wind snuffed out the lamp, smothering vision with an impenetrable blanket of night. Rohne swore.

Something brushed Alere's arm. She jerked away. Warm fingers encircled her right wrist.

'It's me,' Kett whispered. 'We've no way to re-light the lamp. We'll have to go on. You lead, Alli. I've got Mina. Rohne, take Mina's other hand. Stick close to the wall.'

Alere transferred the knife to her left hand and put her back to the cold stone. She slid a foot forward, feeling for the edge of the stairs, and took the first step. The blackness pressed on her eyes and she blinked to make sure her eyes were open. Colours danced at the edges of her vision. She edged downwards. One misstep on the narrow stairs would end in disaster. The soft scrape of shoe leather on stone and the harsh rasps of her breathing were amplified in the stairwell. A chill crept up from the lower floor, bringing with it the scent of mould and damp.

Alere stumbled off the last riser onto a level floor. She hesitated.

'We're at the bottom. Where to, Mina?'

'The cook said to go left,' Mina whispered. 'She said the door to the stableyard is a few steps that way.'

Alere inched along the wall until the rough stone surface ended in a sharp corner. The cold numbed her fingers and goosepimpled her arm. She clenched her teeth to stop them chattering. The smell of mould grew stronger and she resisted the urge to sneeze. She twisted free of Kett's grip and swept her hands back and forth across the stone, searching for a latch.

'Hurry up!' Rohne's harsh whisper cut through the silence. 'We forgot to close the top door. I think I heard something.'

'Not helping,' Alere snapped. She found a metal slide bolt. 'Ah. Got it.'

The door swung inward and night air rushed in. An icy breeze wormed beneath Alere's cloak and brought the clean smell of wet earth with a flurry of snow.

She held her knife ready and stepped into freedom.

A torch flared to life, blinding her. Three swords flashed in the light.

CHAPTER FOURTEEN

Alere flung her blanket. The thick woollen cloth enveloped the middle guard's head. He yelled, flailed at the blanket and staggered back. She darted to one side and struck the closest man with the heel of her hand. His nose crunched.

She grabbed his sword hand and used her momentum to deflect the point away from Rohne and Mina. The weishi pulled back. Alere followed his motion, folding and twisting his wrist. Hauling him off balance, she yanked the sword free. He stumbled and fell awkwardly, his hand still imprisoned. She changed her grip into an armlock and trod on his neck. He gargled a half-choked scream and she pressed harder. If he woke anyone the escape was doomed.

The middle guard threw off the blanket and raised his weapon. Alere thrust the captured sword at him. The tip pricked his throat. Blood beaded into rubies that shimmered in the torchlight and slid in scarlet trails down the white ceramic blade. The guard gulped and retreated a step.

The man underfoot struggled against Alere's armlock. She kicked and her heel struck just above his ear. He sagged, his head lolling to one side, eyes closed. She dropped his wrist and shortened her sword-arm for the final thrust through the standing guard's body.

'Stop!' Jilla rushed into the torchlight and grabbed Kett's arm, thwarting his lethal open-hand strike at the third guard's throat. Kett elbowed the Xintou aside, his grey eyes steely, focussed on his opponent. The guard's sword arced towards Kett's head. Jilla shoved between the two men. The guard pulled his strike, his blade skimming the Xintou's gold robes. He gasped and paled.

'Alere. Kett! Mistress Li sent me to help.' Jilla's agonised cry stayed Alere's arm.

Alere froze. The guard standing before her shifted his feet and raised his sword. Alere lifted her weapon. Jilla repeated her order to stop. The guard hesitated then withdrew another step and lowered his blade, showing the throwing-star tattoo on his wrist in the traditional weishi signal for peace.

'These are my men so hold, please.' Jilla cast a horrified look at the unconscious man on the ground.

Alere held her stance, still poised to thrust. Kett hands remained up in a defensive position, his gaze fixed on his opponent. He didn't strike, so Alere waited.

'Why would a Bonded Xintou go against her Jun and help his prisoners?' Kett asked. 'How did Mistress Li even know where Alere was?'

'Mistress Li sent a flitter. She said you might be through this way and asked me to help.' Jilla signalled to the man in front of Kett. The guard bowed and retreated. Alere's opponent did the same.

The easy escape from Hassan's fortress was now explained, even if Mistress Li's knowledge of Alere's whereabouts wasn't.

Alere looked to Kett, who eyed the Xintou narrowly then nodded. Rohne's expression blanked and he studied Jilla. He gave a non-committal half-shrug, and turned away to comfort Mina, who clung trembling to the door frame.

'Very well.' Alere lowered the sword. A Xintou betraying her Bonded Jun was deeply suspicious, but one obeying Mistress Li's orders was a different thing altogether.

The weishi at her feet staggered upright, and Alere reversed the sword, offering it to him hilt-first. He shook his wrist and wiped the blood trickling from his nose. He took the weapon and sheathed it, bowing respectfully as he edged away.

'Come,' Jilla said, glancing over their shoulders at the estate building. 'We must get your horses. Runweed notwithstanding, there's a chance someone will discover your escape.' With a swirl of gold silk, she led the way to the stables.

Behind the stables, Rumi, Bol and the other horses waited, saddled and loaded. The mountain pack-ponies had been replaced with leaner, swifter steeds suited to the plains ahead.

As the others mounted, Alere caught Jilla casting several furtive, worried glances back at the castle.

'You're afraid of him.' Alere paused in the act of lifting a foot into the stirrup. She eyed Jilla curiously. 'Why?'

Jilla studied the castle's unremitting grey stone wall. High in the western tower, a single window glowed and a shadow crossed back and forth before the light.

'Hassan's hiding something from me, even though we're Bonded. He's planning something, and I risk Fusion if I try too hard to discover his intentions. I suspect he intends to make a bid for the Steel Throne. Short of killing him, I don't know how to stop him. The Jundom shouldn't be run by Ven, Hanna *or* Hassan. Somehow, you're part of Mistress Li's plan to prevent disaster. I trust her.' Jilla's troubled gaze rested on Alere. 'Go. Stick to the river while it's dark. The watercourse will take you south for about ten gongli. Change direction to southwest when the sun rises. I'll keep your escape secret as long as I can.'

'What'll happen if Hassan discovers you helped us?' Alere swung into the saddle.

'He won't, dear.' Jilla looked down her nose at Rohne. 'I do have enough skill to prevent *that*.' She backed away, hand raised in farewell, and was swallowed by darkness.

The travellers nudged their mounts through the open side gate, into cold freedom. With the faintest creak, the heavy timber swung shut behind them.

Alere tugged her cloak close. What, exactly, had happened there? Rohne had underestimated Jilla and, once more, Alere was a pawn in some enormous game of qi played by Mistress Li and the House. Was there anywhere in the Jundom it was possible to slide under the House's gaze and be free?

She touched her heels to Rumi's flanks and fell into line behind the others as Kett led them south along the river. Darkness forced a slow pace and Alere struggled to stay awake, lulled by the steady rhythm of Rumi's steps.

The first faint glow of dawn found them still following the watercourse. Kett called a halt.

'We should rest and water the horses.' He indicated the shallow waters. 'As soon as the sun clears the mountains, we'll ride hard and get off Wen-Gates lands. How much further, Rohne?'

Rohne studied the deep emerald western horizon. Slewing in his saddle, he frowned behind at the Ahmar Mountains, haloed in dusty orange dawn light.

'Hard to say. I've never been on this side of the estate. From memory, the maps show the boundary as that next low ridge of hills to the southwest. Maybe half a day's ride. Once we're past that ridge we should be close to Newmec, on Jun Fifth Smith-Lun's lands.'

'He's a loyal vassal of Jun Second Ma-Safra,' Kett said. 'We'll be well out of Hassan's reach there.'

They rested long enough to eat and drink, and allow the horses to do the same. The companions were back in the saddle as the sun cleared the horizon. Blood-orange light speared between the mountains and drew long, purple shadows across the grasslands.

Then the sun rose above the peaks and lit the world afire as frost on the grass sparkled and melted into glittering diamond drops.

An hour later Rohne hauled his mount to a stop.

'What?' Alere caught up.

He rose in the saddle and pointed back the way they'd come. A faint column of dust smudged the brightening sky.

'They're following.' He cocked his head, listening to minds only he could hear. 'I can only sense two. They were in the patrol that escorted us to Hassan's estate. But there must be more to make that much dust.'

Silently, Kett strung his horsebow and handed the reins of a packhorse to Rohne. Alere unsheathed her bow, bent it around her thigh, and slipped the string into notches carved in the midnight-wood limbs. She caressed the smooth, purple-black timber and tested the bow's draw. Mina, her eyes huge, gravely took the other set packhorse reins from Alere.

'You two ride on.' Kett's gaze was fixed on the rising dust column. 'Get to the tree line. Follow it to the border. We'll lead them away and try to slow them down.'

'But—' Mina began.

'Go,' Alere snapped. 'We'll be fine and we'll catch up.'

Mina looked back twice as they rode away; Rohne not at all.

Kett kicked Bol into a canter and headed northwest. Alere rode beside him, seeking out the dustiest patches of bare ground in the hopes of drawing the Wen-Gates junren away from Mina and Rohne. Their pursuers were now tiny but distinct figures, riding hard; at least twenty-abreast in a wide line.

'Ready?' Kett asked, calm. He tested the draw on his bow and brushed a thumb along his arrow fletching.

Alere's heart pounded as she studied the oncoming regiment. Just her and Kett against twenty trained junren and weishi? Rumi sashayed sideways and tossed her head, picking up Alere's nervousness. Alere wiped slick palms on her thighs. She was not going to let Kett see her reaction. Besides, the sickness churning in her stomach was excitement, not fear. Definitely. She slipped on her thumb-ring, drew forth an arrow and laid it across the bow on her lap, hooking a finger over the nocked shaft to hold it in place.

'Let's make it a competition, shall we?' she suggested. 'Highest score gets to relax at camp tonight. No cooking or cleaning up.' Anything to make the approaching skirmish less real, more like a training exercise. The riders neared, almost within range of her furthest shot and certainly within Kett's.

'Oh?' Kett drew four more arrows from his quiver and held them ready in his bow-hand. 'You know how to cook?'

Alere managed a laugh. 'No, but I won't need to, will I?'

'We'll see.' He pressed a knee into Bol's side and headed south. Alere swung Rumi in the opposite direction, riding at right angles to the line of approaching men. Both horses jumped into a gallop at the touch of a heel. Alere eased into rhythm with Rumi's smooth gait. At Kett's whistle she dropped the reins and used her knee to guide Rumi in an arc towards the Wen-Gates men. Kett rode from the south, since he was equally skilled left or right handed. In a moment, they'd turn to ride across the line and strafe the riders – a manoeuvre she and Kett had rehearsed many times.

But shooting straw dummies was different to shooting live men on horseback.

Kett whistled again. Alere rose in the stirrups, steadying herself against Rumi's motion. She hooked the bowstring, pulled it back, took aim at the only archer in the line-up and released just as he did. Their arrows arced past each other. Hers lodged in the enemy archer's breast and he fell with a cry. His arrow skimmed past Alere's back, tearing her shirt as she ducked forward. She straightened, sweat prickling her skin. Her fingers trembled as she nocked another arrow, drew and fired; and again. Arrow after arrow found its mark. Six shots, two fatal, only one miss. Her sixth target ducked and slid over the side of his horse, using the animal as a shield.

With a twinge of regret, Alere shot the horse. Not a killing shot; horses were valuable. The arrow lodged in its shoulder. The animal squealed and reared, throwing its rider. A quick check forward and Alere nudged Rumi a fraction to the right to avoid colliding with Bol in the crossover.

The attacking line was in disarray. More than half the guardsmen were unhorsed – on the ground motionless, or writhing and screaming. Others yanked at reins and kicked sweat-darkened flanks, trying to manage their frightened animals. One man's horse bolted, neck outstretched, the bit firmly in its teeth. Frustrated oaths rang across the plain as the rider fought for control. The shangwei screamed orders. The remaining men struggled to obey and re-formed into a ragged line.

The rhythmic thud of Bol's hooves drummed louder. Alere and Kett passed each other to the jingle of bridles, the *twang* of Kett's bowstring and the horses' heavy breaths. The warm scent of animal sweat and churned earth caught in Alere's nose. Her eyes stung and teared in the swirling dust. She wiped them clear, relieved to see Kett upright and uninjured in the saddle.

Rumi galloped past Bol and Alere's targets came back into view. Seven men remained, including the one Alere had unhorsed. They were close to re-organising and charging. Their line needed to be broken again. The shangwei lifted his arm and screamed the order. Alere released another arrow. It drove through the shangwei's throat. The bloodied tip protruded from the back of his neck. The pain and shock on the shangwei's face twisted a rush of nausea through

Alere's stomach. Gritting her teeth, she drew again and aimed at the second in command. Her arrow missed.

She focussed on her technique to calm the swell of guilt. Archery required a clear mind and identical movements for each shot. A stray thought led to a stray arrow. Deep breath. Calm draw. Smooth release. The next point found its mark and the rider pitched backwards off his mount.

Rumi galloped past the line's chaotic remains. A nudge brought the mare around sharply for another run. Alere swapped the bow to her right hand and thumb ring to her left. She nocked and drew as Rumi picked up speed. Left-handed wasn't Alere's strong side, but it didn't matter. Only three junren still moved: two ahorseback, another on the ground, his face bloodied from a head-wound. All were closer to Kett than Alere. One of the horsemen screamed a challenge. He raised a scimitar and bore down on Kett, who threw aside bow and drew blade. The weapons clashed, the ring of ceramic on steel a clarion call in the cold morning air.

Alere lined up the last mounted junren, a stocky brute with two fingers missing on his left hand. He bent low over his horse's neck and Alere's arrow glanced off his alzin armour. Beneath his bronze helmet, the junren's lips twisted into a triumphant snarl. He kicked his animal into a gallop and charged, ceramic blade gleaming, straight towards Kett. On the ground, the injured junren snatched the bow from the fallen archer and nocked an arrow. He shot at Alere, but missed. He wiped blood from his face and pointed his next arrow at Kett, who was closer and focussed on the scimitar-wielder.

Alere leaned back and Rumi skidded to a straight-legged halt. Kett kicked Bol. The gelding reared, striking with its front hooves at the opposing stallion. Kett's back was to the charging horseman with the missing fingers. The junren on the ground drew back his bowstring. Alere couldn't protect Kett against both attackers. She aimed her arrow at the bowman.

His arm wavered.

Alere switched targets and lined up the fingerless junren, now only seconds away from Kett. She slowed her breathing. The rider raised his sword. She released. Her arrow speared through the junren's alzin armour. He dropped his weapon and slumped in the saddle. His horse skittered away, tossing its head. Alere covered her mouth to hold back a cry of relief.

The bowman on the ground released his arrow, aimed at Kett. Alere followed its path. The shaft whistled through the air, on target to hit Kett.

'No!' She loosed one of her own arrows hoping, by some miracle, it would strike the other mid-flight.

Hers missed.

'Kett, watch out!'

The arrow pierced Kett's alzin armour and lodged high in his back. His sword arm faltered. His opponent struck and knocked Kett's sword loose. The junren raised his scimitar. Alere swapped hands and drew the string again. This time her aim was true. The junren clutched at the arrow protruding from his neck. His scimitar fell to the dust. He slid from his horse and lay motionless on the winter-dry grass.

Kett slumped forward over Bol's neck.

CHAPTER FIFTEEN

Alere aimed the next arrow at the bowman, but he took shelter behind a riderless horse. Alere's throat tightened with unshed tears. She snatched up the reins and urged Rumi on. Kett swayed in his saddle. The enemy bowman laid a new shaft and drew it back. Hooves thudded behind Alere. She slewed in the saddle, unsure of which enemy to face and how best to protect Kett.

She cried out in relief. Rohne rode low along his horse's neck, galloping towards her.

'The bowman.' She pointed. Rohne dragged at the reins, changing direction. Silent and fierce, he bore down on the archer, drew his sword, and ended the threat with a single stroke. Alere turned back to Kett and brought Rumi alongside Bol.

'Kett.' She grabbed his arm and steadied him in the saddle. 'Stay with me.' He'd be alright. He had to be.

Kett groaned and slumped further forward, his breathing shallow. The reins fell from his hands and Bol stumbled to a halt, chest heaving. Kett listed to one side. Blood darkened his shirt and glistened on the matt black alzin. At least he was alive. Alere fisted his sleeve and dragged him upright. He gasped and coughed, blood spraying from his lips to speckle scarlet on Bol's mane. Rohne cantered up and grasped Kett's other arm.

'Thank you,' Alere said, unable find better words to voice her gratitude.

'Sorry I wasn't here sooner. Let's get him to Mina.' Rohne slid off his horse and collected Kett's dropped sword.

'Kett?' Alere squeezed Kett's arm and he raised his head. His grey eyes held such stoic acceptance and such pain that she gasped. 'Oh, I'm so sorry.'

He managed a shuddering breath. 'Not...your fault.'

'But it was,' she said, tears stinging her eyes. 'I shot the wrong man.'

'Not now, Alere,' Rohne snapped. 'Help me get him to Mina. I'll ride behind and hold him.'

'Bol won't let you,' Kett said. He coughed and winced. 'Alli can, though. He knows her.'

Irritation flashed across Rohne's face but he jerked his head at Alere. She swung down and tied Rumi's reins to Kett's saddle. Kett managed to stay upright as she clambered up behind him, though he grunted, his skin ashen.

Alere leaned to one side to avoid bumping the arrow. She was tempted to drag the shaft free, but perhaps it was safer to leave it in until Mina had a chance to inspect the injury. Alere reached around Kett's waist and gathered the reins. He sagged and she tensed, taking his weight. Her arms trembled with the effort of holding him upright.

'Sword,' Kett muttered. 'Get my sword.'

'Rohne has it,' Alere said. 'I know it's important to you. I promise we have it.'

Rohne remounted and caught one of the riderless horses skittering nearby. Helpless and worried, Alere clicked her tongue at Bol. Guilt tightened her throat. She'd made the wrong choice, but wallowing wouldn't fix Kett. He would be alright. He would. Grimly holding back tears of doubt, she followed Rohne to the tree line.

'Will he live?' Alere hovered, watching Mina's deft fingers and intent expression. Kett lay, face down and unconscious, on a hastily-made bed of leaves and blankets. The patch of trees sheltering him was still within Hassan's realm. Once the Wen-Gates troops failed to report back, Hassan was sure to despatch more. He'd be furious at the decimation of his men. She thrust aside the memory of bodies, blood and death at her hands. There was no time for indulging in regret. She needed to get Kett across the border to safety and medical attention.

'For the fifth time, Alere.' Mina focussed on packing the wound with adang moss and securing the poultice with a bandage. 'Be quiet and let me work.'

Alere spun away and strode to the small clearing where the horses were tethered and grazing. Inaction and patience had never been her strengths. She patted Rumi and leaned her head against the animal's neck. Tears, held back through sheer force of will until now, spilled, but failed to ease the burden on Alere's heart. Even a river of saltwater wouldn't wash clean the stain of guilt. Rumi snorted and jerked her head.

'You alright?'

Alere jumped at the sound of Rohne's light voice. His cool hand dropped onto her shoulder. She forced herself to stay still and scrubbed away the tears. How had he snuck up on her, unnoticed?

'I'll be fine. I'm just worried about Kett. I hate doing nothing.'

Rohne passed her a bundle of arrows – her grey goose-feather fletched shafts and Kett's white-fletched ones. He must have gone back to the battlefield to retrieve them. They were damp and cleaned. Alere accepted them gratefully, since making new ones was time consuming and difficult. He brushed aside her thanks.

'I needed to do something. I know how you feel.' Rohne reached out to pat Rumi, who jerked her head away. 'Besides, there were a few of the junren still alive. Badly injured. We don't have the time or resources to care for them.'

Alere shuddered. She hadn't considered the need for mercy. Thankfully, he hadn't asked her to help. She'd been so focussed on Kett she hadn't spared a thought for the men left on the battlefield. Rohne had dealt with the problem, but how did he stay so sanguine; find it so easy?

'And,' Rohne added, 'we can't afford them talking if Wen-Gates sends more men.'

Alere averted her face and bit back a gasp of horror. Had he killed men who could have been saved, just to shut them up? It was the logical thing to do, but her stomach heaved at the idea. Her hand shook as she mechanically patted Rumi's neck.

'We need to get Kett to Newmec,' Rohne said. 'It should be just over the border. Maybe two hours at a walk, but I'm not sure.' He squinted at the sky. To the south, storm clouds, heavy with snow or rain, piled up against the ragged southern peaks.

'We've got about two, maybe three, hours before the sky opens up,' Rohne added. 'Early winter storms can get pretty bad around here. If it's not snow, it'll be sleet and freezing rain. We should make a sling. If we hang it between our horses, we can carry Kett and rig a canopy over him.'

Alere set to work with a will, breaking branches and lashing them together to form the framework for a litter, over which they stretched blankets. Before long, they had a serviceable sling.

'We can't move him,' Mina protested as Alere and Rohne lay the sling on the ground beside Kett. 'The wound will start bleeding again.'

Alere grabbed Kett's ankles. 'Rohne says a storm's coming. If we don't get Kett to Newmec, he'll die of exposure. Is that what you want?'

Mina scrubbed her palms down her thighs. She felt Kett's forehead and stroked back a stray lock of his dark hair.

Rohne turned aside and finished tying a knot, his movements jerky and sharp.

'Very well,' Mina said. 'But don't lift him onto it like that. Slide it under. And make sure he's on his side, wedged so he won't roll.'

Alere and Rohne strapped Kett into the sling. Mina fussed over her patient, tucking the blankets around his body and tightening the bandage.

'Back off, Mina,' Rohne said. 'You've done your bit. Let us finish.'

Mina flinched and mounted her horse in stiff silence. Alere focussed on the task and ignored her companions, too frightened to look at Kett's waxen face.

Bol jibbed and refused to be tied to the sling, so Alere roped him in train with the other horses behind Rumi. With Kett in place between Rumi and Mina's mare, Alere mounted. Rohne galloped ahead to check the distance to Newmec, and find shelter and healers. Alere loosened her sword in its sheath and surveyed the broad, bluegrass plain. Rain swept hazy brushstrokes across the eastern horizon, softening the open country and sharp mountains into mist.

Alere stared resolutely forward, towards the low western hills. Rohne's dark figure was a dot in the distance. Mina and Alere were alone, with no way of running or hiding if the Wen-Gates junren caught up.

The ride to Newmec stretched out endlessly, time dragging beneath the weight of guilt, fear and unshed tears. The trip seemed to take longer than the rain-soaked night Alere left Madina. Then she'd followed in Kett's wake; trusting, naïve. Now she was responsible for his welfare and it felt wrong.

A cold drop of rain feathered Alere's cheek. She wiped the liquid away and studied Kett, his skin pale, dark-lashed eyes closed.

He had to live. Had to. If only he didn't look half-dead already. Without his steady support she wasn't sure she could handle what lay ahead.

Her heart stuttered and she stared at Kett, aghast. Was she so self-centred that his life must revolve around her comfort? What about his needs? What about his family? Did he even have one? Years before, she'd asked about them, but Kett had never given a clear answer and she, self-focussed, never asked again.

In that moment, as the sky wept for him, Alere understood the one-sided nature of their friendship and knew shame. She bit back a sob. For ten years Kett had stood by her; pushed and helped her to womanhood. He'd been her safety net; the one person who listened to her crazy dreams, her self-doubt, and her railing against duty to the House, without judgement. What had she done but complain about not being free – of the House, of him? Overhead, thunder rumbled a lament to the memory of clear days.

Alere leaned over and touched Kett's cold skin.

'Please stay, Kett. I'm sorry.' She stroked a wayward strand of hair from his eyes, hoping for a flicker of an eyelid to show he'd heard.

Nothing. He remained unconscious, his breathing slow, his body jolting as the horses fell in and out of step.

'I've given him istilqa,' Mina said. 'He can't hear you.'

Alere hid shame and worry. 'I know.' She straightened and scrubbed a sleeve over her cheeks, clearing away rain and tears. 'Here comes Rohne. Let's hope he has good news.'

Rohne trotted towards them, his horse dark with sweat and rain, its head bobbing.

'Newmec's over that next rise.' He indicated a low hill. 'There's an inn that looks snug enough. I've bespoken rooms.'

'What about a Healer House?' Mina inspected her patient.

Rohne nodded. Raindrops sparkled in his dark hair as orange rays of light shot through the clouds. 'It's small, but well-respected. Not far past the inn. I've already spoken to the healers. They're ready, so you can go straight there. I'll take the rest of the horses to the inn.'

'Thank goodness.' Mina's soft exclamation heightened Alere's unease.

It was agony to keep to a slow walk when help was so close. The sky darkened and rain blotted out the distant buildings. Water dripped through the cloak tented over Kett's still form. His lips took on a bluish tinge. Mina glanced back and forth between the injured man and the outlying buildings.

Lightning flared and the sky unleashed a flurry of stinging, icy rain and hail as Alere and Mina reached Healer House. Three grave-faced healers waited at the door. Sidelined by their efficiency, Alere watched them carry Kett into the building. She tried to follow, but was stopped at the door by the house weishi.

'Sorry, kid. Healers only past this point until he's in recovery.' The man was firm but not unsympathetic. 'Where are you staying? I'll make sure they send a message if there's any change in his condition.'

'But...' Alere's view was blocked as Mina and the three healers bent over Kett's inert body. The wooden door swung shut, closing her out of the building, out of Kett's life, perhaps forever. Freezing rain soaked Alere's green cap and saturated her cloak until the cloth hung as heavily on her shoulders as the weight of worry and blame she carried.

The weishi eyed her sympathetically from his covered guard station. 'Go back to the inn. I promise they'll send word. You'll catch your death standing there.'

Alere left, her boots squelching in the mud. Clasping two sets of reins in frozen fingers, she trudged to the inn, oblivious to the mud and worsening weather. The main street of Newmec was empty save for a stray pig, squealing and trotting through the sleet and driving wind.

At the inn Alere left the horses with a stableboy and plodded across the boot-sucking stableyard. A housemaid opened the back door, exclaimed over Alere's bedraggled state, and showed her upstairs. Numb inside and out, Alere locked the room's door, stripped and climbed into the standing tub that steamed before the fire. The warmth did nothing to ease the chill in her heart.

Half an hour later, she climbed from the cold water, dressed and sat in front of the fire, blind to the dancing orange flames. A knock at the door made her jump.

'Al..ek?' Rohne's hesitant question drifted through the thick wood.

It took Alere a moment to remember her boy's name.

'Yes?'

'The rain's easing. I've sent a runner to the Healer house. Landlady's sending up some food for you.'

'Thanks.'

The floorboards outside her door creaked. She went to the window seat and leaned her head on the glass, ignoring the icy cold that seeped through and chilled her skin.

'Please be alright, Kett,' she murmured. Her tears dripped onto the glass, freezing into glittering icicles before melting under her breath.

An hour later, brisk footfalls outside her room preluded an equally brisk knock.

'It's me.' Mina's soft voice was unusually strident.

Alere hurried to the door. With a sob, Mina threw herself into Alere's arms. Rohne entered behind, scowling as he shut the door. Alere's heart dropped. She held Mina away and scanned her sister's tearful face.

'Kett?'

Mina sniffed and scrubbed a palm over her cheeks. 'They operated and removed the arrow tip. It nicked an artery and he lost a lot of blood.' She laughed, tears sparkling on her dark lashes. 'But he's going to be alright.'

CHAPTER SIXTEEN

ROHNE

Rohne endured Mina's raptures over Kett's survival and suppressed a surge of resentment. He propped himself against a wall near the fireplace, staring into the flames. Behind him, the two girls sat on the bed holding hands and discussing Kett's condition. Rohne turned around and folded his arms, eyeing the women sardonically.

'I was there when Kett woke,' Mina said, a hint of colour staining her cheek. Her lips curved into a small smile. 'He recognised me and there's no sign of fever.'

'Oh. Good. That's good.' Alere's smile seemed forced.

Rohne sneered at his own stupidity. How the jahim had he got himself into this, what was it, a love triangle? No, even worse, a quadrangle; like some clichéd romantic comedy the travelling purple-hats staged for swooning village girls in Gaton. Those performances, full of mistaken identities, girls dressed as boys and mock sword fights, always ended with the hero and heroine kissing and the villain vanquished. Only shazis and gullible girls believed such rubbish.

'How long 'til he recovers enough to travel?' Rohne interrupted Mina's blow-by-blow description of the surgery. Hurt flashed through her dark eyes.

'Don't get me wrong,' he said. 'I'm glad he'll be alright, but we can't stay. Winter's not far away. The Alcazar guards will catch up with us, even if they have to go around Wen-Gates lands. How long before we can leave?'

Mina thought a while before replying. 'I'd say a week, perhaps two if the cold settled in his lungs. He needs to stay warm and rested. He can't travel.'

Alere made a hasty gesture as though to push aside Mina's words. She bit her lip, scraped damp hair behind her ear, and stared at the fire. She paced the room twice, running a hand through her short, dark curls until they stood out wildly from her head.

'But we have to…I can't wait…How can I leave him?' She half-whispered the words, speaking to herself more than Rohne and Mina.

Rohne shrugged, impatient. She needed to face reality. 'Up to you. This is your show. You've got three options.' He held up a finger. 'You stay here and get captured by the Alcazar weishi.'

'No!' She shot a frightened look out the window.

He raised a second finger. 'You and Mina go on to Shanzhai. I'll stay here to keep track of Kett's progress. We can catch up when he's better. Doubt you'll agree to that one, Mina. Which gives us: Alere and I go on and Mina stays here with Kett. He can bring her to Shanzhai once he's recovered.'

Alere tapped her lips and studied Mina for a moment. 'That would leave Mina here alone if the Alcazar weishi came. Blonde hair or not, someone might recognise her from my description.' She raised her chin, but fear sparked behind the defiance in her eyes. 'There's a fourth option: I go alone. That way you'll be here to protect Mina or get her away if they come.'

Rohne caught the hint of guilt and a plea in her eyes. So she wanted him to play chaperone? Nice. As much as he disliked the thought, he had to accede to her logic. Mina wasn't fit to be alone and unprotected in a thief-haunted, mudhole town like Newmec. The town had nothing to recommend it but access to other places in the Jundom.

'You can't travel alone,' Mina cried, leaping up and clutching at Alere's hands. 'You…you just can't! It's too dangerous and you can't *want* to leave Kett here. He's your best friend. He'll need you. He's more important than any bracelet. Tell her, Rohne.'

Rohne shrugged, unwilling to get in the middle of the sisters' disagreement. Kett's survival was irrelevant, anyway, but neither woman would want to hear that.

'Of course I don't want to leave him.' Alere snatched her hands free. 'Do you think this is easy for me? But as Mistress Li said many times,' she continued, cynicism sharpening her tone, 'what I *want* and what's *important* isn't always the same thing. I have to see this through. I'm quite capable of looking after myself, Mina. I can hire myself out as a male yongbing. The caravans have a high turnover of hired swords, especially those going through Eagle Pass to Shanzhai.'

'But we can hide if the Alcazar men show up,' Mina said. 'It makes no sense to put risk your life just to return a stupid piece of jewelry. And Kett isn't out of danger. You—'

'Enough.' Alere laid a hand on her dagger.

Mina shrank away, her eyes wide.

'I have to go and that's all I can say,' Alere said quietly. 'I'm entrusting Kett's care to you, and yours to Rohne.'

In the thick silence, the sisters stared at each other. Rohne smiled. Mina's stubbornness might have met its match in Alere's arrogant confidence. Alere clearly had another agenda. Mina was right: if avoiding the Alcazar weishi was her main goal, then simply hiding in the hills made sense. What was so vital about getting the bracelet to Shanzhai? So imperative that she would risk Kett's capture?

Alere's jaw hardened and she drew herself up. 'Go through the baggage. Separate out what you'll need. The spare horse we can sell. But first strip off the Wen-Gates livery. I'll need a plain cloak or snow jacket, too. Here.' She thrust a bejewelled, broken hairpin into Rohne's hand and strode to the door. 'I'm going to say goodbye to Kett.'

The door closed behind her and Rohne rubbed at the back of his head, trying to shake another low-key headache and strong sense of déjà vu. He'd experienced both several times in the last two days. Each instance coincided with a moment when the sisters were together. But how could he have forgotten that many Seeings? Maybe this enforced stay in Newmec would provide the chance to search his memories for answers.

He turned to find Mina huge-eyed, her lower lip trembling. He sank onto the bed beside her and held her close.

'It'll be alright. She'll be fine,' he said, hiding his skepticism. The road between Newmec and Shanzhai were notorious for bandits and thieves who made Jada's men seem like friendly puppies. And her boy's guise was thin at best, too graceful and feminine to withstand close scrutiny.

'I don't understand her,' Mina said. 'How can she abandon him? How can anything be more important than someone you love?'

'Who knows,' Rohne said. 'But her mind's made up, so we need to stack the odds in her favour. C'mon. We've got work to do.'

ALERE

Alere crept into the darkened chamber and waited, just inside the door, as her eyes adjusted to the dim light of a mel-oil lamp in the corner. She strained to hear Kett's breathing. Was he awake? Alive? Her heart skipped and she took a step closer to the bed.

The small room was shuttered against the grey afternoon light, but redolent of sweet-reed and an acrid hint of antiseptic ginnong root. Bare, except for a bed and two small tables, the room's starkness felt hygienic rather than poor. Cloth rustled in the heavy silence and Alere muffled a sob of relief.

'Alli?' Kett's sleep-roughened voice drifted through the darkness.

She carried the lamp to the bedside table so she could see him. She gulped back a gasp of shock. Pain had carved deep lines in his drawn face. Sitting on the bed, she took his hand. His grip felt frighteningly weak.

'I'm sorry, Kett,' she whispered. 'It's my fault. I should've shot the bowman.'

He shook his head. 'You take ownership of something not yours to own. You made the right choice. I didn't know the horseman was there. His sword would have done the work the arrow didn't.'

'Mina says you'll be alright?' Alere gritted her teeth and forced tears back. He needed her strength, not her doubt and weakness.

'So I hear. Hard to imagine right now. But the healers here seem to know their craft.' He coughed and winced.

She always felt helpless around sick people and seeing Kett like this was even worse. He was the foundation on which her confidence was built and now the ground underfoot was uncertain. The self-centred trend of her thoughts dawned on her and Alere almost groaned aloud. What kind of friend was she?

'Can I get you anything?' She forced a smile.

'No, nothing,' he said. 'Oh. My sword?'

'It's back in our lodgings. Safe, I promise. Anything else?

'No. Unless you're going to cook?'

'What? Oh, yes.' She chuckled. 'You did win the shoot-off, didn't you? Well, if you want to get better then eat someone else's cooking.'

'You're not getting out of it that easily,' he said. 'When I get to Shanzhai I expect to find a home-cooked meal waiting.' He ran his thumb over the back of her hand. 'Thank you for coming to say goodbye.'

'How—?'

Amusement chased pain from Kett's grey eyes. 'It's what you ought to do. Leave me and get to Shanzhai before winter sets in. I'll follow with the others as soon as I can.' His mouth twisted into irony. 'Besides, you get an air of guilty anticipation when you're planning something you're not sure I'll like.'

'But…I don't want to abandon you. And I'm not sure I'm capable…' She rose and paced the small room, conflicted and unsure how to voice her fears without sounding cowardly. 'I never thought I'd have to go without you, Kett. I ran away from the House a dozen times but I always knew you were there. Now…' She waved a helpless hand at him. 'I thought I could do this. I thought I wanted freedom, but this isn't…and I'm still Mistress Li's puppet. And I'm scared, Kett. What if I fail?'

Kett smiled. 'Well, that made hardly any sense.' He held out a hand. She took it and sat.

'Alli, you need to let go the belief you're unworthy. You're more than capable and freedom isn't in your location, or who you answer to, it's in your mind and your choices.'

She brushed that aside with a headshake and stared at his calloused palm in her hand.

His fingers closed around hers. 'You're not a mistake and you're not flawed,' he said. 'Mistress Li must have seen something special in you as well – after all, she's the one who authorised your training with so many Houses. You're one of the best martial artists I've ever seen. You're meant for more than just someone's jiaoji. Go. You don't need me. You haven't for a few years, now. It's time to start choosing your own path.' Regret coloured his faint smile. 'But I'll find you in Shanzhai, I promise.'

Could it be true Alere's extra training was more than compensation for a lack of gold-veil skills? Had Mistress Li been planning something that long ago? But what? She must have known Alere wasn't Elmira's daughter, but did she know Rafi was Alere's father? How could she?

Alere stared at the dancing mel-oil flame. The situation was complicated with too many 'what ifs'. The only way to find out was to push on; to stay ahead of the Alcazar weishi and get to Shanzhai as soon as possible. She needed to see her father, find out if he knew what was expected of her, and stop a war.

But that meant leaving Kett and even the thought made her chest ache.

Kett raised her hand to his lips, the rough stubble on his chin scraping her skin. 'Go, Alli. It's your duty and you know it.'

'Duty first, huh?' She gave a bitter laugh.

'In this case,' Kett said, his mouth twisted, 'yes.'

'Is there ever a case where it comes second?'

'That's a decision only you can make.' He smiled bleakly. 'I'm probably the wrong person to ask, anyway. Go. Just be careful. I expect to find you in one piece when I get there.'

'You too,' she whispered, the words catching in her throat.

She embraced him carefully, kissed his forehead and ran from the room without looking back lest she change her mind, fling herself at his feet and beg his protection. The time for that was past. She needed to do her duty by the Jundom and that meant becoming her own weishi.

Even if she wasn't sure she wanted the lonely freedom that entailed any more.

Her feet found their own way back to the inn while her mind dwelt on Kett's pale, pain-ridden face. In her room, she discovered Rohne and Mina, full of plans and ideas. Rohne laid out on the bed a set of throwing knives and a ceramic sword, smaller than the one Alere had taken from the Alcazar weishi. He'd also found a chance for employment with a trade caravan leaving the following afternoon for Shanzhai. There was much to do.

Silenced by uncertainty, Alere submitted to their ministrations, allowing Mina to tidy her hair with borrowed shears, and half-listening as Rohne instructed her on the fine art of being male. By the time he'd pointed out her various, innately-feminine gestures and the pitch of her voice, self-doubt threatened to overwhelm her decision. She frowned at him and clenched her teeth to hold back a sarcastic comment. Surely it couldn't be that difficult? After several minutes, Rohne made a noise of frustration. He plucked a small, bespeckled mirror from the wall and held the glass before her.

'What do you see?'

Alere inspected her reflection. 'Me dressed as a boy, so what?'

Rohne crouched in front of her, his amber eyes intense. 'You can't be "you dressed as a boy", Alere. You have to *be* a boy; no, a young man. You have to *be* Alek Marin-kin, warrior from birth, son of Jada Marin-kin the feared raider.'

'I *know,* Rohne. I can take care of myself. Stop lecturing me.' She thrust the mirror aside.

'Take care of yourself?' He laughed. 'You've been wrapped in silk and privilege your whole life. You've no gouri idea how brutal these people can be. Well, you're about to find out the hard way.' He jerked his head at Mina. 'Mina has something else for you. I'll go and finish repacking. When I come back, I expect to see Alek, not Alere.' He stalked from the room and slammed the door.

'What's wrong with him?' Alere glowered after him. 'I don't need anyone else telling me I'm hopeless.'

'He didn't mean that.' Mina screwed up her nose and tugged open the string on a herbalists bag. 'He's torn and angry. Stuck here protecting me when he wants to go with you.' She glanced at the door. 'Rohne's always wanted to leave Gaton. Nasra wouldn't let him, because of what he is. She can be quite strong-minded. They clash but Rohne knows she only wants him to be safe. I think, this time, she ran out of excuses for keeping him home.'

'I can't believe he stayed there this long,' Alere said. 'It'd drive me mad to live somewhere that small. Where everyone expects something from you and knows exactly how to pull your strings.'

Mina pursed her lips. 'Funny, I'd give almost anything to be back there, with people I've known and loved my whole life; looking after them.'

Alere flushed but said nothing. Mina's upbringing had been different from her own. There was no way of reconciling their viewpoints on people. And Alere was no longer certain Xintou House's policy of keeping emotional and physical distance was right, anyway.

'As for Rohne…' Mina produced two small bags from within the larger one. 'When I left for Madina he was angry. He wanted to come. I know it hurt when Nasra said I'd be safer without him. He'd never admit it, but he hates the fact his very existence endangers Nasra, me and Mother – and now you, too.'

'Because he's a xintou?' Alere asked. 'I think that's the last thing anyone's chasing me for at the moment. Besides, he doesn't seem to care what people think of him.'

'I'd have thought you, if anyone, would understand how it feels to be alone in a crowd of people you know well,' Mina replied with a short laugh. 'Rohne's…complex. He's one of the most intelligent people I know. He's read every one of Nasra's books, but no-one's ever challenged him to *think*. No-one's taught him to question what he reads or how he views the world and other people. I can't match him. He's been isolated his whole life, hiding who he is. He's driven but there's no outlet for his ambition. And in need of an equal – in a world that kills anyone who might be like him.' She flicked a quick look under her lashes at Alere. 'And now he has to stay here and watch me care for Kett. You get to leave.'

Alere froze, a tumult of emotions roiling in her chest, trying to make sense of Mina's words. There was no point avoiding the issue of Kett any longer. Truth was the smartest path, even if it hurt.

'You're in love with Kett, aren't you?' she said in a rush. 'And Rohne's in love with you.'

'Yes and no.' Mina studied at her fingers, playing with the strings of the herbalist bag. 'Rohne's clinging to the one friend who's always accepted him for who he is: me. He's not in love with me. He's afraid to let me go. Not unlike you and Kett, really.' She raised her eyes, calm and frank with a hint of trepidation in their black depths.

Alere gripped the back of the chair, holding in by sheer force the angry denial on her lips. How dare Mina make such assumptions? How dare Mina imply her feelings for Kett were somehow more profound than Alere's? Mina had known Kett only a matter of days. What was the rush of hormones compared to half a lifetime of trust and respect?

Heartsick, Alere paced the room. She stopped by the window. Rain pounded the thin glass and wind whistled through a gap around the ill-fitting window, sending cold swirling into the room. She dared not look at Mina's tranquil expression lest she lose control and slap the girl. But Kett – what about his happiness? Alere needed to put his wellbeing before her own, for once. If he wanted Mina, then he deserved a chance to make the relationship work.

She bowed her head, breathless with the ache in her chest.

'Fine.' Tears pricked as she cut the last tie to her childhood. 'You and Kett have my blessing, if you need it. Should I convince Rohne to come with me?'

Mina rose, eyes sparkling. 'Thank you, and I promise I'll look after Kett. He's strong. The Healers sent word: there's no sign of fever, so he should recover quickly. He is...' She flushed and cleared her throat, her smile embarrassed. 'But you were right about Rohne needing to stay here. I know my limitations. I'm not a fighter like you. I'll send Rohne after you as soon as Kett's fit to ride. We'll follow more slowly.'

'Fine,' Alere repeated, rubbing her forehead. She needed to put aside the image of Kett caring for someone else. She had a job to do. That was more important, anyway. 'What was the other thing you had to give me?'

'Oh, yes.' Once more the brisk, skilled healer, Mina pressed a small cloth bag and tiny jar into Alere's hands. 'Two things. The jar has ghost-wood sap. Keep your hair trimmings and use the sap to stick them on your upper lip.' She dimpled. 'Nothing says "young man" like an attempt at a moustache. If you're careful, it should last three or four days.'

Alere dipped a finger into the tacky stuff, sniffed and screwed up her nose at the smoky smell. She dabbed the sap above her upper lip, pressed on some small hair clippings, then tucked the jar into her belt-pouch.

'And nothing says "woman" like your xue cycles,' Mina said, pointing to the small bag. 'Where are you?'

Alere had to think. Her five-weekly cycle usually coincided with the dark of Luna-Yi. She counted and groaned.

'Any time in the next day or so.'

'Then take one of these every day for the next week. After that, once a week until you come out of disguise. In tea if you can, but chew it if you're camping cold. They taste disgusting. Herbal tea's good to hide the flavour.'

'What is it?' Alere tugged open the bag and inspected the shrivelled, brown lumps inside. Thirty, by her best estimate.

'Dried xuezhi mushroom. Six months worth, just in case.' Mina curled Alere's hand around the bag. 'They'll stop your cycles completely. But don't take it for more than two months in a row if you ever want children. This is an emergency or I'd never recommend it.'

'Where on Kalima did you get this?' Alere asked. 'Jiaoji use a powdered form to prevent pregnancy, but it's so expensive. This must have cost more than that spare horse.'

Mina fussed at putting away the shears and brushing loose hairs off her robe. 'I stole it from the Healer house.'

Alere gaped at her sister. Her heart dropped. 'But… you…that means you took it when you were with Kett. Before I even said I was going. How…?'

'Kett guessed. He knew what you'd do.' Mina lifted her chin. 'To be honest, he seemed relieved. Now sit. I'll tidy that moustache so you can present a true Alek to Rohne.'

Alere sat and tried to shelve the resentment and hurt burning in her gut. Was everyone in the world one step ahead of her, controlling her like a puppet? Kett was relieved to be left behind? That didn't sound like him. Why would he be?

Then again, why wouldn't he? After all these years of responsibility for her, he must be tired of dealing with the consequences of her rash decisions. She swallowed the lump in her throat and ground her teeth. She was better off on her own, anyway. Mistress Li had always warned that friendships were an anchor and made one vulnerable.

Grimly, she focussed on becoming Alek Marin-kin. Mina went to work. The result, a short while later, was enough to surprise even Rohne.

Part II

CHAPTER SEVENTEEN

CORIN

No amount of conducting would improve Hellor's ear-twisting rendition of *The Gentleman from Jiba*. Corin Mal-kin waved his drinking-hand in time to the song, anyway, and grimaced. Watching the rigid Hellor descend into gibbering intoxication was always an amusing way to spend the afternoon. Arm in arm, Corin and Hellor rounded the grey-stone corner of Newmec's only grain warehouse and emerged into the main street. Corin stomped through the red mud, chuckling as the thick muck spattered on Hellor's pale trous. Hellor aimed his unsteady steps at the next tavern, the Wander Inn, focussed on his unattainable goal to drink Newmec dry of its piss-weak ale.

Halfway there, Corin stopped in consternation. Ahead, che-ma bawled, shaking their stiff manes and tugging against their huoche harnesses. Fifteen three-humped tuo, loaded with saddlebags, unfolded their legs and rose, spitting and grunting at their handlers. People milled about in semi-controlled confusion, waving arms, shouting orders, loading wares into the huoches and fending off beggars. A small man, dressed in gleaming bronze lamellar armour and a Merchant House green tunic, scurried amongst the chaos. He directed the goods-loading with words as sharp as the steel stiletto in his hand.

Corin grabbed Hellor's arm, steadying neither man. Hellor dribbled to a halt, peering at Corin in drunken perplexity.

'Wha?' Hellor tipped his cup upside down. Two sparkling jewels of ale splatted onto the soggy ground. 'You're right, we're outta beer. Tha's bad. You're a kid, Cor, but you're not a shazi. Tha's why I like you.' Hellor's huge hand landed on Corin's shoulder and he grinned sloppily.

Corin staggered under the weight and laughed. 'Twenty-six is not a kid. Just 'cause you're almost old enough to cut your hair short again…No, woman, you may not have my purse.' He shook off the jiu-raddled unveiled jiaoji who'd attached herself to him at the last inn, glowering until she pouted and flounced away.

The sound of stomping hooves recalled his train of thought and he stared at the caravan ahead. There was something important he had to remember.

'What day is it?' He shook Hellor's arm to get the man's wandering attention.

Hellor squinted up at the sun's orange glow, which was diffused by a thin layer of clouds. At least the rain had stopped, though the churned road was ankle-deep in red mud and animal dung.

'Sitta.' Hellor's thick brow knitted. He held up six fingers, folding each one and counting aloud the days of the week. Scowling, he held up the thumb. 'No. Sitta was yesterday, when I beat that cocky little guisunzi at arm wrestling in the tavern. It mus' be Ahad the nineteenth of Shisanyue. Why?'

'Gaisi!' Corin downed a final mouthful of beer, snatched Hellor's cup and tossed both vessels away.

A nearby watering trough promised a quick and easy path to sobriety. Corin dragged his companion to the trough, dunked Hellor's head then yanked him out by a clump of matted hair.

Cursing and swatting at Corin, Hellor shook himself free and swiped dripping hair from his eyes. 'Corin Mal-kin, you gouri dog. What was that for?'

'We're in Newmec, festering boil on the arse-end of Ma-Safra lands, remember?' Corin indicated the motley collection of weather-worried buildings squatting amongst the low foothills of the majestic southern mountains. 'Gateway to the frozen wastes of Jadid, and packed with thrilling adventures for those who place little value on their lives.' He pointed at the small man managing the caravan. 'And trade for the likes of our employer, Jacksa.'

Hellor sobered. 'You're a wisix hundan and Jacksa John-kin's a gouri little haraami. I hate both of you and this huozui of a job.'

'Tell him that to his face, my friend,' Corin said, slapping Hellor wetly on the back, 'and see how long you keep your huozui of a job. C'mon. Looks like the caravan's ready. Cheer up. You have some new yongbing recruits to whip into shape.'

Hellor smirked and sized up the caravan. 'You're right. Fun times.' He rubbed his hands together.

'Yes.' Corin re-tied the thong holding back his wayward blond hair and eyed the recruits sympathetically. 'Three weeks of terror for them, three weeks of entertainment for you. Let's see who Jacksa's hired for the suicide run. Who knows, maybe this time you can beat your record. Make it back to Shanzhai without killing more than four.'

'One of these days I'll run out of yongbing and it'll be you on the watch, musician.' Hellor spat the word. 'How will you play instruments or women if your fingers are chopped off?'

Wiggling said digits, Corin grinned. 'I'm a man of many talents, Hellor. It's not just my fingers women love, you know.'

Hellor snorted, straightened his sodden shirt and threw back his shoulders. Marching in an almost-straight line, he bellowed orders at the small knot of bewildered, newly-hired swords. Prepared to be amused, Corin sauntered across to the inn, collected his gear and paid his tab. He sat on the front deck, idly strumming the small oud he carried on all his travels. The railing offered a good footrest, so he put his feet up, tilted back the chair, and chuckled at the confusion generated by Hellor's often conflicting orders.

Amongst the caravan's yongbing were a dozen seasoned veterans. For several years, they'd travelled the Shanzhai-Newmec run with Jacksa's caravan. The veterans understood Hellor and how to handle him. They knew he was a ruthless instructor and leader for a good reason. If they listened and followed orders, he'd get them through alive. They respected him, even if they didn't much like him.

The new recruits were where the fun began. A couple of older men, scarred and silent, sized Hellor up, much as he did them. In front of them stood four younger men, each a painful mix of uncertainty and enough experience to make them brash. Corin changed to a minor chord sequence. Well, this trip would sort the wise from the zifts who felt the need to show off.

And last of the new yongbing were raw recruits: ten this time. More each trip, it seemed. Jacksa always picked youngsters with some skill at arms so Hellor wasn't obliged to crash-train them in how to hold a sword without cutting off their own legs. Corin memorised each face. Who would make it through and who would die on the road through Eagle Pass with a raider's sword in their guts? They were just children; desperate young men, escaping poverty or boredom. They reeked of bravado and fear as they shifted under Hellor's scathing tongue and bloodshot glare.

All but one.

Corin's fingers stilled on the strings. He lowered his feet and leaned forward, the bamboo chair creaking. The young man in question held still, watchful, impassive, weight balanced. He sported a barely-there moustache, but the shortness of his hair, delicacy of his slender form gave away his extreme youth. He seemed familiar, too. Perhaps a youngster who'd been sent home last year and now considered himself old enough to fight? Surely Jacksa wouldn't allow this child to come along. He was barely into puberty; not even old enough to tie his hair in a mawei.

Corin slung the oud across his back and gathered his bag and sleeping gear. He squelched through the mud, heaved his bags into the luggage huoche, then hunted for Jacksa amongst the crowd. He found the man upbraiding the animal handler responsible for a den of breeding spice-otters being transported live to Shanzhai.

'The cage is too gouri small to hold five, you hundan!' Jacksa tapped his blade on the bamboo bars, already scarred by the otters' knife-sharp claws. His straight, black brows twitched together.

In the cage, a large female snarled and bared four-inch, yellow fangs. She rounded on a smaller male and raked him with curved claws, setting him squealing. At this rate the thick fur, so valued by Shanzhai nobles for its silvery colour and sweet scent, would be shredded before the caravan arrived.

The animal handler, a good head taller than Jacksa, shrank away. 'But—'

Jacksa cut him off with a chopping gesture. 'Feddan, find another cage in ten minutes or I'll find another handler.' He stabbed the point of his stiletto into the wood next to the handler's arm.

Feddan flinched and hurried off. For a small man, Jacksa housed a forceful personality few of his staff could withstand.

Corin grabbed the caravan leader's shoulder to get his attention.

Jacksa shrugged him off. 'Not now, Cor. We're leaving in a few minutes. I'm yet to get word the pass is still safe.'

His scowl lightened as a black dot appeared in the northwesterly sky. A long-haul flitter bird. Corin waited impatiently until the white-furred reptile landed on the bird-handler's huoche and hopped onto Jacksa's wrist. The animal was larger than a man's head and made growling, throaty noises as it writhed in Jacksa's grip. He swore and pinned the flitter, holding its wings to stop them flapping. The curved, toothy beak dug into Jacksa's knuckle, drawing blood. He flicked the creature's skull with a fingertip. The flitter's beady red eye fixed on him but it stuck out a clawed foot and allowed the message tube to be removed. Afterward, squeaking and growling, the reptile fluttered away to the flitter handler, who cooed at it like a clucky mother.

Jacksa sucked on his finger, read the message and stuffed the paper into his belt-pouch. 'Still no sign of snow, or bandits.' He frowned and stared westward.

Corin followed his gaze, but the mountain ranges were too far away to see, even on a clear day. 'That's good news.'

The caravan master eyed him cynically.

'Alright, alright.' Corin held up a hand. 'I'll check it out when we get there. I agree, it's not normal.'

Jacksa's expression lightened. He slapped Corin between the shoulderblades. 'Good. Now, what troubles you my friend? Can't find a woman you haven't bedded in this forsaken hole of a town?' He walked the caravan's length, his black eyes flicking from animal to wagon, inspecting each. His attention to detail and skill at managing people made him the most successful trader on this route.

The stiletto on his hip helped, too. Few people crossed Jacksa John-kin twice.

Corin ignored the jibe. The women he visited in each town were well paid and served their purpose. He jerked a thumb at Hellor and the yongbing.

'Why're you hiring children now? There's a boy in the new recruits who's barely left off sucking.'

'Oh, you mean young Alek?' Jacksa raised narrow black brows, reviewed the group and laughed. 'He's seventeen, he tells me.'

'Fifteen if he's a day,' Corin retorted. 'Send him home. He can't be experienced enough for this trip.'

Jacksa grinned. 'Let me be the judge of that. Don't you spoil my surprise for Hellor. Pity you two weren't at the testing when I took the boy on. Most interesting. Let's just say I'm quite looking forward to tonight's initiation.' With another slap across Corin's shoulder, he strode off, shouting commands to the drivers to make ready.

With one more pitying look at the youngster, Corin found his mount and swung into the saddle, resigning himself to another three weeks of boredom, leavened only by the possibility of raider attacks. Maybe this would be the last trip. He could use a break. Corin chuckled wryly and nudged his gelding into a walk as the huoches squeaked and squelched their way out of Newmec.

Once the chaos of departure settled into order, he tugged on the reins and pulled away from the caravan, circling until he located Hellor. The man was a source of entertainment, as long as one didn't expect profundity or mind the occasional bout of flatulence. Corin passed the knot of new yongbing who followed Hellor like fresh-hatched flitter-chicks. The youth, Alek, returned Corin's curious gaze with a raking assessment which lingered on Corin's sword-hilt and the dagger protruding from his boot. Then the boy turned away, dismissive.

Corin grinned. Jacksa was right. Tonight would be interesting.

CHAPTER EIGHTEEN

The caravan's late start meant it was dark when Jacksa called a halt at their first stop, by the Metsa River's clear, broad waters. Corin led his horse to one of the trade-goods huoche and unstrapped his gear, listening with half an ear to Hellor's familiar bellowing at the hapless yongbing. In the morning, Hellor would use fording the shallow river to run some training exercises. Tonight they had only to take turns on watch – after the ceremony, of course. Corin grimaced.

Once the huoches were arranged to Jacksa's satisfaction, and the animals corralled, the cooks kindled a fire in the camp's centre. Before long, the smell of cooking meat and baking bread wafted across the clearing, setting Corin's mouth watering.

Corin spread out his bedroll in his usual sleeping spot beneath the trade-goods huoche. He tuned the oud, then dug out two bronze whistles and few rudimentary percussion instruments. There were usually one or two musically-minded men in the group to accompany his songs. He pocketed the bronze finger zills he kept for Yilan, the cook's daughter. Her rhythm with the zills was spasmodic and her dancing enthusiastic, at best, but it kept everyone happy if she performed – especially tonight.

The first night was always Hellor's favourite, if not Corin's. Before dinner, Hellor pitted the new recruits against the veterans to weed out the useless. The wood and bamboo weapons left a few cracked skulls and broken bones, but the process was less harsh than what the recruits would encounter in two weeks. On every trip a quarter of the newcomers crept away in the first night; cowards, but alive.

The camp buzzed with expectation. The raw yongbing gathered next to a rope-circle on the ground, the youngest huddling together. Flickering light from the fire caused the new recruits' shadows to jitter and jump; their fear revealed and dancing at their feet. Young Alek stood apart and hefted a wooden sword, swinging it in a professional manner. He glanced around. Judging who might have observed? Ego or caution? Corin watched, interest piqued.

Hellor bellowed the names of the first combatants. The audience jostled into place, forming a large circle around the fighting space. Hellor always started with two experienced fighters. The ferocity of their bout would send one or two scurrying into the darkness. Shirtless and barefoot, the scarred veteran grinned at one of the older recruits.

Alek's face caught Corin's eye; the boy's calm, analytical expression out of place amongst the crowd's sickening bloodlust. The onlookers cheered when the veteran took his opponent down with a solid strike to the head and a sword point to throat. Alek simply nodded.

The next round paired a cocky youngster with another veteran. Corin edged around the crowd to where Hellor stood with his arms folded. After a few seconds in the ring, the youngster collapsed to the ground, gasping through a frozen diaphragm and bleeding from a cut over his eye. The mob groaned. The injured youngster was dragged from the ring and Hellor called out the next two names.

'Who're the bets on?' Corin nudged Hellor, who spared him a disinterested look and a shrug.

Everyone but Hellor laid bets on the fights. It was standard first-night fare. Corin usually abstained, but this time he was curious.

Hellor jerked his chin at a tall, broad-shouldered lad with hands the size of frying pans and a nose that had already taken a few hits.

'Most are taking young Ferat to stick it out and take a beating even if he loses; and the pipsqueak Alek Marin-kin to faint before he even takes the first blow.'

'Marin-kin, huh?' Corin said, stroking his chin. 'Well, with that name he'll have something to prove, won't he? Think I'll go see Turin and lay some coin on the boy.'

'Not like you to take an interest. Know something I don't?'

'Nope, just trying new things. My father always said travel would broaden my mind.'

'Yours must be the size of a brothel-madam's ass, then.' Hellor sneered.

The audience gasped as a veteran sidestepped a wild blow and laid his sword across an exposed neck.

Hellor curled a lip. 'Well, I hope you're right about the boy. The rest of these hmari are a sad group. They'll all be dead in two weeks.' He growled the next names and Corin sauntered off to lay a bet.

Having surprised the enterprising Turin, Corin shouldered his way through the crowd to the rope circle in time to hear Alek's name called along with that of Gavon Abdul-kin. An astonished murmur swept through the onlookers. Corin kissed his coin goodbye. He shouldn't have told Hellor his plans. This pairing must be payback for the water-trough dunking. No-one, not even Hellor himself, could best Gavon. Thirty summers old – the last ten spent as a professional yongbing – Gavon tended to break bits of people.

Head down, Alek shuffled into the ring. Gavon strode in, twirling his wooden sword in whistling arcs. Alek edged away and moved to a position outside ma'ai – optimal fighting distance – with his back to the firelight that glimmered through gaps in the crowd.

Smart or accidental? He wielded two wooden swords, rather than the traditional sword and shield. Most interesting.

Standing flatfooted, the boy held both swords away from his body in a loose grip. Corin chuckled. This kid had style.

Gavon sneered and ran at him, screaming, attempting to intimidate. Alek held his ground then spun aside at the last second. Gavon's vicious overhead stroke sliced air. Gavon skidded to a halt, barely avoiding ploughing into the crowd.

He spun and came in slowly, smacking the sword on his wooden shield. The audience took up the rhythm, stomping and clapping, chanting Gavon's name. Dust swirled up from underfoot and Corin coughed. Alek circled with the yongbing and kept a long ma'ai between them. Someone yelled. Alek's attention shifted for a second. Gavon closed the gap, sword whistling. Alek brought up one sword and deflected the blow aimed at his head. The wooden weapon slapped into his shoulder instead.

Alek struck with his second blade and caught Gavon's exposed ribs. Gavon gasped and clutched at his side, snarling at the boy. Alek rotated his shoulder, wincing. Corin grimaced in sympathy. If the blow had struck the boy's head, his skull would have cracked. He would have a deep bruise, at the very least. Gavon now had the advantage, if his size and experience hadn't given him one before.

The crowd noise died away to silent, breathless tension. People pressed close, those at the back craning to see. Corin muttered encouragement under his breath.

Gavon waded in and drove the boy back with a series of heavy blows that whip-cracked into the silence. Alek's guard held against the onslaught, but he retreated, step by step, to the rope. If he stepped outside the circle he would lose.

Corin resisted the urge to shout a warning. The boy feinted another step and leapt aside. Gavon stopped, one foot on the rope, arms wheeling. The crowd parted, eager to see him fall. He regained balance and stayed within the safety of the ring. Corin noted Alek didn't take the opportunity to shove the older man out of the ring, but waited for him to return. Unwise, but interesting.

Alek watched Gavon narrowly, perhaps searching for a weakness. Gavon strode forward and slashed at the boy's legs. Corin groaned. It was a bluff. Alek fell for it and dropped his high guard to protect his thigh. Gavon jabbed his shield into the boy's cheek. The smooth wooden edge connected. Alek's head snapped back. He collapsed, rolled over one shoulder and shot straight to his feet. Blood streamed from a cut on his cheekbone. He wiped at his face, saw the blood and glared at Gavon in the first show of emotion Corin had witnessed.

Instead of signalling for first-blood end to the bout, Hellor said nothing. Corin raised a brow. Surely the boy had proved himself? What more did Hellor want? Hellor simply grinned.

Alek stalked towards his opponent. He raised one sword overhead and dropped the second into guard position. If the shoulder injury pained him, it didn't show through his set expression. He swung and the wooden sword connected hollowly with Gavon's shield. He followed with a slice at Gavon's unprotected ribs, catching the same spot as before. Gavon winced but brushed the blade aside. Alek retaliated with flashing strikes almost too fast to see, anger in each sharp move.

Gavon fell back, defending. Astonishment creased his forehead; laughable under different circumstances. He bore the attack for a few seconds then rallied and closed on the boy. They locked sword to sword. Gavon pinned the second weapon with his shield. His superior strength and height overpowered Alek's resistance. Alek tried to twist free. Gavon sneered, released one arm and drove the sword's pommel into Alek's head, felling the boy like a young tree.

Alek folded to the ground, eyelids fluttering. Gavon stood over him, the point of his sword to the youngster's throat. The onlookers groaned.

'Yield.' Gavon's gravelly voice broke the tension.

'No.' Alek knocked the sword aside with his blade and swept Gavon's knee with one foot. Gavon staggered but recovered his balance. Alek regained his feet, swayed and shook his head. Gavon's face darkened. He hurled the shield aside, gripped the sword in two hands and stalked forward.

'Enough!' Hellor's command cut across the whispers that rose like steam from the audience. 'The boy yields. The match is yours, Gavon. Time to eat, everyone.' He clapped and applause rippled through the spectators, who drifted away, talking animatedly. Money changed hands; laughter bubbled. Tensions dissolved. It had been a good fight.

Corin shoved his hands deep into his pockets and swung across the bare ground to where Gavon still faced the boy. The veteran sneered and threw his sword to someone in the crowd. He pointed a callused finger at the youngster, but said nothing. Alek lifted his chin and held his proud stance until the older man turned away.

As soon as Gavon showed his back, Alek dropped his arms, hung his head and sank to his knees in the dust. Corin knelt beside him and laid a hand on Alek's shoulder. The boy flinched and Corin belatedly remembered the first hit.

'Let's get you to the healer, lad,' he said, lifting Alek by the uninjured arm. 'You need to get that handsome face fixed. You'll have an interesting scar to show the girls.'

The boy blinked vaguely at Corin. Well, he had taken two head strikes. Corin raised Alek's chin and angled the boy to the light. The pupils of his dark eyes contracted evenly. No concussion then, only dazed.

Alek pulled away. 'Who are you?'

'Corin Mal-kin, musician and entertainer to this fine caravan. Come, let's get you stitched up.'

'Why do you care?' Alek's tone hardened into suspicion. 'I saw you watching with the rest of them.'

'Two reasons: one, you won me a tidy sum of money by not fainting.' Corin raised a finger. He lifted a second. 'Two, you've made a rather powerful enemy. I thought it behoved me to be a friend – to balance things out. I'm a big believer in balance.'

'Liar,' Alek replied. 'You don't strike me as the sort who believes in balance. You strike me as the sort who looks out for himself first, and opportunity second. I saw you speaking with Hellor just before he called me up. And with the bet-taker.'

Corin laid a hand on his breast, surprised and pleased at the boy's insight. 'You wound me, but of course you're right. I do see an opportunity – to befriend a young man with potential. And you're right: it was my fault you were paired with Gavon. Not intentional, though, I promise. Hellor trying to get even with me. This is me trying to make up for my mistake.' He spread his arms wide. 'The main point is: I'm probably the only one of your new companions who *won't* strike you – if you'll forgive the pun.'

Alek laughed, winced and touched the cut on his cheek.

'Alright, I'll accept your friendship, Corin Mal-kin. But forgive me if I don't trust you yet.' He bowed. 'Alek Marin-kin.'

'That's fine, Alek.' Corin returned the bow with a deep flourish. He grinned, liking the boy more every moment. 'I don't trust anyone.'

They found the caravan's healer. Attar, with a delicate touch at odds with his thick fingers and cynical attitude, cleaned and sewed the gash with fine silk and tiny stitches.

'We'll take those out in a few days,' Attar said, stowing the surgical kit away. 'Now let's have your shirt off, lad. That hit to the shoulder could've fractured the collarbone.'

Alek jerked back and clutched the lacing at his shirtfront. 'No, it's fine, see?' He lifted his arm but there was a catch in his breath.

Attar's eyes narrowed. 'Young zift. Use this. Comfrey and bone-root.' He thrust a small ceramic pot at Alek. 'If it's not feeling better in a day, or if you have any numbness or tingling in your arm, come back. No argument, mind, or I'll tell Jacksa to send you home.'

Alek nodded, his cheeks paling.

'Tell me,' Corin said, drawing Alek's hand through his arm as they strolled to the campfires. Corin inspected Alek's narrow, callused fingers. 'Do you happen to play an instrument?'

'What?' Alek's eyes widened and he snatched his hand away. In all fairness, it was probably the last question he'd expected to be asked. 'Yes, why?"

Corin dug amongst his clothing. 'Which would you prefer: sticks, darbuka, pipes or finger zills? Be warned: if you take the zills you may have to dance in Yilan's place, which we'd all appreciate.'

Alek chuckled and his eyes sparkled with some secret amusement. 'Yilan can have the dancing.' He pointed to the oud across Corin's back. 'I'll take that.'

'No, my boy, not unless you know all the words to every dirty song ever written.' Corin backed away in mock horror. 'In Shanzhai I used to play songs of courtly love and loss for Shunu Yasmin Koh-Lin. Now I play bawdy tunes for a bunch of – your good self excepted – lowlife scum who wouldn't know a book from the paper they use to wipe their arses.'

'I see we're going to get along fine, Corin,' Alek said, laughing again. 'I'll take the pipes. But my fingers are a little stiff and out of practice, I warn you.'

'Never mind.' Corin waved Alek into the food queue. 'Most of these men are tone deaf anyway. I think the few ladies along on this trip won't be interested in how stiff your *fingers* are, either.'

He noted with interest the boy's scornful eye-roll, and that Alek hadn't denied being able to read. This youngster was no blushing virgin and no mere uneducated raider's son.

'How many women travel with the caravan?' Alek asked.

'This trip, five.' Corin held out his bowl and allowed Yilan to slosh stew into it. She winked at him. He ignored her and guided Alek to a seat near the fire. 'There's Shina, Attar's wife. You won't see much of her. She's got a new baby. Yilan and her mother, Peta, are the cooks. Then there's Kalla and Leena, the large-animal handlers.' He nodded across the circle at two dark-haired women engrossed in conversation. 'But if you're after female companionship tonight, they won't help.' He flashed a grin at Alek. 'They're a couple – known to pointedly discourage men who think three might be company. Yilan's your best bet, but she's...rather popular.'

Alek coughed around a mouthful of wine. 'No, I meant...'

Corin gazed guilelessly at him, inviting elaboration.

'Never mind,' the boy said, sending Corin a speculative look before focussing on his food.

Corin laughed. He caught Jacksa's eye across the fire and shared a grin with the caravan master.

CHAPTER NINETEEN

ALERE

Alere sat on an upturned wooden bucket and ate in silence, letting the conversations around the campfire wash over her. The stew was surprisingly good, its gamey lu-deer flavour balanced out by the spiciness of greenberry and salt of black-root. Alere took another bite and winced. Chewing stretched the cut on her cheek, highlighting her stupidity. The first night and she'd succumbed to ego, then lost her temper. She deserved the beating. Kett would've been disappointed.

The hot food stuck on a sudden lump in her throat. Kett was only a day's travel behind but the void he'd left, loomed larger than the physical distance. Had she made the right decision, to leave him behind? The bracelet box dug into her ribs and she grimaced. Duty first. There was no choice.

Alere ground her teeth and thrust the image of Kett's pain-weary face aside. What would he advise in this situation? To study her companions; learn their strengths and weaknesses. She focussed on the caravan folk's chatter and her sense of isolation eased.

Forty or so people encircled the roaring central fire, some huddled in blankets against the chill evening air, many swigging from leather wineskins. Most of the yongbing were thugs or inexperienced boys. The rest of the caravaners were huoche drivers, animal handlers, the weapons master, healer and a couple of what might be passengers travelling under the caravan's protection to

Shanzhai. Across the fire from Alere, Gavon sat with his cronies, his dark eyes fixed on her. He squirted wine into his mouth and, when she accidentally caught his gaze, grinned and spat a mouthful at her. The purple liquid sizzled in the fire.

Alere put the half-empty bowl of stew aside, her appetite gone.

The back of her neck prickled. A few seats to Gavon's right, Jacksa John-kin watched her, his small, dark eyes thoughtful and amused. Had he seen through her disguise? There was no way to be certain, but she thought not. Anyway, nothing prohibited women from being yongbing, but it was unusual.

Corin nudged her with an elbow and handed over a pair of bronze whistles, one tuned to the scale of C and one in D. Yilan chimed the brass zills. The clear, high tones cut through laughter and conversation. The first notes from Corin's oud fell into almost-silence. His fingers flew over the strings and plucked out a melody Alere didn't recognise.

'Think you can keep up?' His green eyes twinkled. 'Use the C for this one.'

'I'll try,' she said, running an experimental scale on the whistle. It had a fine, mellow sound, neither shrill nor too soft.

'Are we all ready?' Corin's call was met with clapping and hoots of encouragement.

Ohhhhh, the gentleman from Jiba
He barely left his khiba
Said his boyfriend's fong
Was two foot long
But I think he was a dreamer.

Hoots of laughter followed the first verse. Corin had a warm baritone voice, well-trained and smooth. He nodded encouragingly as Alere put the whistle to her lips. She was glad of a reason not to sing the words. Jiaoji House trained in the elegant, sensual arts;

seduction of both mind and body. Subtlety, not the coarse lewdness this bawdy group enjoyed.

'Looking a little flushed there, lad,' Corin muttered.

'Fire's warm,' she replied.

Corin chuckled and launched into the second verse. He was a skilled musician, adding unusual chord variations and chromatic note runs anywhere the tune became repetitive. Alere kept her accompaniment simple, admiring his technique. But the next song was so predictable she picked up the harmony halfway through the second line and was able to improvise around the tune. Corin flashed an approving smile. A small seed of warmth grew in her chest. She might not be prepared to trust him, yet, but he was definitely likeable.

He next chose a slower, sensuous dance number Alere knew from Jiaoji House. A melancholy story of a male jiaoji who couldn't bear to break contract with a woman who didn't love him, and eventually suicided when she set him free. Alere lost herself in weaving a complex counter-melody around Corin's singing. Yilan rose and rucked up her long, midnight-blue skirt, revealing slender legs. Her hips swivelled and her arms flexed gracefully as she sent sultry looks at the men. She wasn't a bad dancer, just untrained, and by the looks on the new recruits' faces, would have her pick of bed-partners tonight.

An hour or so after dinner, Alere caught a significant look between Jacksa and Corin. The musician switched to more mellow, minor-key pieces that slowed the heart and set the mind adrift. When Hellor announced who would stand night-watches, the crowd dispersed willingly enough.

As Alere and Corin strolled towards their bedrolls, Corin tucked his arm through hers.

'You've quite some skill with the whistle, lad,' he said, his words crisply articulated for someone who'd drunk an entire skin of wine. 'Apprentice in an Artist House?'

'No.' She tugged free. 'I'd best get my things for first watch. Don't want to be late.' She headed for the cook's huoche, where her gear was laid out.

'Alek.' Corin nodded at the huoche. Yilan and a male companion were thoroughly occupied on the steps, their activities loud. The huoche rocked and creaked with their motions.

'Perhaps you should relocate to somewhere quieter? Yilan's been known to entertain all night. There's space under the trade-goods huoche, with me. You shouldn't sleep alone tonight.'

'Jiche!' She eyed Corin with suspicion. Had he seen through her disguise? Or was he interested in men? Was he trying to get into her bedroll? He was undeniably attractive, but she wasn't willing to compromise her disguise. After a long day, and three hours of watch still ahead, sleep was more appealing, anyway.

She watched the cook's huoche uncertainly.

Corin's eyes lost their sparkle and softened to understanding.

'It's okay, lad. That didn't come out the way I intended. You've no cause to trust me yet.' He squeezed her shoulder. 'But do believe me, you've less to fear from me than from Gavon and his ilk. I like you and I only meant I'd hate to see you fall prey to his bullying on your first night.'

'Second night's fine, I suppose?' she said.

'By then you'll have found your feet,' he said. 'And Gavon's weakness. In the meantime, I'll sleep easier if you watch over me. And I over you.'

A night-wing whined past, the breeze from its huge wings tossing Alere's hair. She flinched.

'If it helps,' Corin said, 'I installed netting around the bottom of the huoche.'

'You think of everything, don't you?'

He grinned and flung his arms wide. 'Never unprepared, that's me.'

Alere gaped at him and gripped her dagger. 'That's...an odd way of phrasing it.'

The lightheartedness fell away from him for a moment and his smile became strained. 'My father used to say that.' He shook his head and the sparkle resurfaced. 'So, what do you say? Cook's huoche and a sleepless night, or no?'

'Well,' she said, trying to keep a straight face, 'I suppose my job is to protect members of the caravan. I can always say you were afraid of the night-wings.'

He laid a hand over his heart. 'Alas, you've found my greatest fear. You're right, lad. Terrified. Do, please, protect me?'

She gathered her gear and spread it near his, bid him goodnight and went to stand first watch.

Three hours later she returned, tired and relieved to have finished the watch without incident. She crawled into her sleeping bag, unable to suppress a groan as she jarred her bruised shoulder. Shivering, she hauled the glass-rabbit fur up to her neck. Her toes and fingers were numb with cold, and the healer's anaesthetic had worn off, leaving her cheek tender and swollen.

'All right, lad?' Corin's soft drawl reached her ears.

'Yes. Go to sleep.'

'I was. You woke me with your great tromping feet.'

Alere inspected Corin's profile, silhouetted against the distant glow of the fire. She'd moved with deliberate, silent care. He was far more alert than his sleepy, sparkling eyes lead one to think. Who was he? He was no more than five or six years older than herself. He'd mentioned playing for Yasmin Koh-Lin in Shanzhai. What had he done to be sent away? Rumours of his womanising had already reached her. Had he cuckolded some nobleman and been banished? Surely he was smarter than that. She wasn't immune to his charm, so she'd need to exercise great care around him. If anyone pierced her disguise, it would be Corin Mal-kin.

The morning broke sooner than Alere liked, the first hint of dawn rousing the camp to action. Yilan and her mother clattered pots at the fire and the spice-otters set up a ruckus, squealing to be fed. Hellor bellowed orders and Alere scrambled from her bedding, hurrying to pack her gear away. Corin smiled drowsily and rubbed a hand over his face.

'Why the rush, lad?' He yawned. 'Hellor's a xiao-bear in the morning. You're best off staying abed until he's had half a pot of lancha and can be relied on not to rip your head off.'

'Easy for you to say. You're not reporting to him about your watch last night.' She widened her eyes in mock-innocence. 'Oh, wait, you didn't have to take watch.'

'You have me,' he said, laughing. 'Can I give you some advice, though, on how to handle him? And Gavon, if you like.'

'I suppose so,' she said.

'Don't show off.' He scraped his hair back. 'And do go straight to Gavon this morning. Last night his status took a knock, but it's hard to hold a grudge when someone admires you. Be humble. Agree you're an arrogant little zift. Ask him to train you. Flatter him, but not too obviously. I think you can be relied on to tread that line.' He burrowed under the furs and rolled away.

Alere stood by the huoche for a moment. Was he sending her into a set-up or genuinely trying to help? What would he gain by either? It was impossible to know. Whatever his motivation, the advice was worth considering. Using flattery and sycophancy as a defence against bullies had never occurred to her. In the House she'd used her fists and the girls learned to leave her alone. Here, she had no hope of beating the worst of her tormentors. Yet if she did nothing, she would spend the trip isolated in fear.

She reported to Hellor then went in search of Gavon and found him sitting with his cronies around the central fire, eating thick red grenporridge.

Alere dropped her proud stance. She held her battered fur cap like a shield before her body, stepped into the circle of men and cleared her throat.

Gavon looked her over. An old scar puckered the left side of his mouth into a permanent sneer, making it difficult to guess at his feelings. His creased, sun-darkened skin made him appear older than his true age. She bowed her head, ignoring his friends' derogatory mutterings. This would only work if she controlled the conversation, so she spoke before Gavon did.

'Shifu.' The word silenced the group. It was used only by weishi students to their masters and implied utmost respect and humility. Dropping to one knee, she repeated it. 'Shifu, I've come to apologise and to respectfully ask for your help.'

Gavon's jaw dropped. He scratched at his dark hair which was cropped short in the manner of Jadidan men. He swiped a hand over his short beard.

'My help?' He waved the whisperers around him to silence. 'What do ye need from me, whelp? I got the idea ye think ye're better than me.' His accent was a mixture of Jadidan and Melcori, with lilting vowels and back-of-the-throat rolls on the hard consonants.

'No, shifu, last night taught me how much of a shazi I have been; how arrogant. I was lucky and you held back. I humbly ask your forgiveness.' She looked up and met his dark suspicion with open admiration. 'And I ask to be your student. I have much to learn.' Bowing her head again, she tried to gauge his reaction from the corners of her eyes.

His feet shuffled in the dirt. He rotated the leather armguards on his wrists, but didn't reach for dagger or sword. The silence lengthened and sweat pricked Alere's skin. Had she overdone it? Did he think she was mocking him? As Corin said: it was a fine line.

Gavon rose. Alere's heart pounded but she remained still.

'Get up, boyo.' His voice was gruff. When she hesitated, he hauled her upright by the arm. His scarred mouth twisted into a lopsided grin. 'Ye've guts, I'll say that for ye. More 'n most.'

He stroked his beard and walked around, inspecting her like a runiu at market.

'Skinny, but strong. Fast, I know that. Smart, too. Maybe too smart?' His dark eyes glittered beneath bushy brows and she revised his intelligence up several notches. 'But ye've been trained t' fight weishi style, with honour. Ye've learned in a dojo. All that teaches ye is how *not* to hurt people ye like.' He spat in the dirt. 'There's no honour or friends where we're heading, just death – either yers or theirs.'

Alere quashed a surge of resentment. Defending her training wasn't going to achieve anything. He smirked and slapped her shoulder; the bruised one – deliberately, by the nasty little twinkle in his eye. She gritted her teeth and rode the pain.

'All right, boyo, we'll see what ye're made of. Consider yerself my student. I'll tell Hellor ye're to be in my team.' He gestured to the pot of porridge bubbling over the fire. 'Eat, then get ready for travel. Part of yer duties'll be caring for my gear, horse and weapons, too. Hop to it, boyo. We break camp in less than half an hour.'

Bowing herself out, Alere grabbed a bowlful of porridge and scooped it into her mouth, ignoring the sticky burn in favour of a full stomach. Done, she ran, trembling in relief, to where Rumi was corralled and threw the saddle onto the mare's back.

A slow handclap made Alere spin, dagger-drawn. Corin leaned against the animal handler's huoche, beaming. He sauntered over, patting Rumi admiringly. The mare, usually picky about who touched her, leaned into him.

'Oh, that was masterly.' Corin's eyes gleamed. 'I don't think I've ever seen Gavon quite so off balance. I may need to take you on as *my* student.'

Alere finished tightening the girth. 'One master is quite enough, thank you. Taking orders is not my strong point. I'll be swallowing enough ego having to take Gavon's, let alone yours.'

So much for freedom and independence. Every time she tried, people anchored her with responsibility and duty; told her what to do. She gritted her teeth.

Corin laughed, scratching Rumi between the ears in the spot she most liked. 'Don't let that same ego cause you to miss the opportunity, lad.'

Alere said nothing, not wanting to sound churlish. He leaned against Rumi, stroking the mare's nose.

'Gavon is one of the best and the dirtiest fighters I've ever seen,' he said. 'He spent over a decade as a warrior-slave in Melcor. One of the few to ever escape. He knows how to fight to stay alive. You may not believe it, but your words were truth. He was going easy on you. You were lucky. Swallow that ego. Do listen to him. It may save your life up on the mountains.' He gave Rumi one last pat. 'Of course, my lessons would be equally useful. And much less painful.' He wandered off, whistling a cheerful tune, hands in the pockets of his much-worn trous.

Alere stared after him. What could he teach her? Music? Hardly helpful. Shelving the question for later, she finished preparing Rumi and went to find Gavon's horse.

Her new shifu's animal was a massive black stallion with a vicious bite and an evil temper. When she led the beast to Gavon, Alere sported a bruise on one arm where the wretched animal had laid its teeth into her. At this rate she'd be purple all over within the week.

Gavon spotted the tear in her sleeve and laughed. 'I see ye've made friends with Iblis, then. Never mind, boyo. He only bites people he likes. Wait till ye see what he does to people he doesn't like. Nice mare, by the way. What's her name?'

'Rumi.'

'Trained for that bow on the saddle?'

'Er...yes?'

'Well then, mount up.' He waited until Alere was in the saddle. 'Ye'll ride point with me across the ford. Once the caravan's over we'll scout ahead. Ye can show me what ye can do with that fancy bow. Then we'll start yer training until the caravan catches up. It'll be a long day, boyo. No rest and ye'll eat in the saddle. At camp we'll spar for an hour before ye eat dinner.'

Alere pressed her lips together to stop a protest.

'Think I'm being tough on ye?' Gavon's eyes narrowed.

'N...no.'

He laughed, showing yellowed teeth. 'Ye will, boyo.'

Gavon started with lessons on riding point and scouting: what to look for; what signs in nature could indicate an enemy lying in wait. Alere found the information useful and the day seemed promising. As the last huoche straggled across the river ford, Gavon swung his beast of a horse to the west.

'Ready?' He pointed at the horse-bow on Rumi's saddle. 'Get that sticker out and we'll see what ye can do.'

He ran Alere through several shooting drills, not unlike those Weishi House taught, but gave no sign of approval in the results. As she gathered the arrows and remounted for a third time, Gavon slapped the flat of his sword across her bruised shoulder. Alere yelled, arm half-raised in automatic defence, glaring and rubbing the injury.

'Just wanted to see what ye'd do. When ye don't have a sword or shield to block with, that reaction'll lose ye an arm, boyo.' He kicked Iblis and cantered off.

Remembering Corin's words, she swallowed her pride and caught up.

'What should I do instead?'

Gavon cocked his head. 'Yer reactions are all about weapons. Have ye done no unarmed combat training?'

'Yes,' she admitted, 'but I'm better with a weapon.'

'Aye. And with ye it's all about being better, isn't it? What're ye trying to prove, boyo? Life's not about being the best, it's about surviving and protecting people ye care about.' Once more, Gavon cantered away, leaving Alere clenching her teeth.

When the horses rested, Gavon demonstrated a pared-down, lethal form of unarmed combat used by the slaves of Melcor. He slammed Alere again and again to the ground until her head hit the packed earth once too often and the world blurred before her eyes and roared in her ears. Her wrists, elbows and shoulders ached from being twisted. When she could barely stand, and barely breathe through burning lungs, Gavon ordered her back into the saddle and rode on.

Training continued the whole day. He alternated between sword-work and archery when a-horseback, and unarmed combat when the horses grazed. When they reached the evening campsite, he pounded her through one last sparring session until she lay in the dirt, sobbing with exhaustion, surrounded by Gavon's sniggering comrades as the caravan rode in.

Gavon nudged her with a toe. 'Get up, boyo. Keep getting up again, even when ye feel like ye can't. Get up.'

Legs and arms shaking, eyes gritty with dust and stinging with tears of anger and shame, Alere took a fighting stance again.

Gavon laughed. 'Like I said, ye've got guts, boyo. But fighting's not just about guts and it's not about being patted on the back for yer skills.'

'What's it about, then?' She swiped away tears and dust with the back of a grimy hand and swallowed a lump in her throat.

'What's up here.' Gavon tapped his temple. 'It's a survival mindset ye don't have, boyo. Yer all…' He frowned and twirled a fingertip around in circles. 'Knotted up inside hiding how ye feel and trying to prove yer the best. Let that go. All ye need to know is what's worth fighting for, and what yer really prepared to do to survive. When ye know that, ye can switch it on when ye need to.' His lips thinned. 'And ye can sleep at night knowing ye did what ye had to and no more.'

Alere said nothing. He was right, but thinking that way changed a person. Like the elite xiongshou assassins of Xintou House. They were the xiao-cats of humanity: cold, ruthless and focussed only on the kill. Did she want that? Yet, with such a mindset, perhaps the faces of the dead would cease to haunt her sleep. And perhaps leaving people behind wouldn't hurt so much.

'Ye've got potential, boyo,' Gavon said gruffly. 'But I can't teach ye any more until ye decide what's important. What's worth killing for. Maybe *who's* worth killing for? Think on it.' He jerked his head at the huoches rumbling into the campsite. 'Caravan's here. Go clean up. In the morning, if ye've decided, come back.'

By the evening's end, after first watch, Alere was so stiff with pain, even crawling into her sleeping furs hurt. Tears scalded her cheeks. Was Gavon trying to humiliate her? He'd undermined the one thing she thought she was good at; the one bit of self-belief she treasured. No. She sighed and scrubbed fiercely at the tears. He'd revealed the truth, nothing more. Kett's teachings had brought her this far; taught her to be a good martial artist; a good weishi. But Gavon's path carried on, past duty and honour, into brutal reality. Dojo combat wasn't the same as fighting for survival.

Doubt seized her. What if she couldn't keep up? What if she couldn't handle what Gavon doled out? And what did he mean *who's* worth killing for? She was trying to protect the whole Jundom. Wasn't that enough? Who was more important than the people of Mamlakah?

She rolled over, trying to find a place that wasn't bruised.

'All right, lad?' Corin's voice from the darkness startled her. 'You weren't at the fire tonight. We missed your harmonies.'

Alere's throat closed on an answer. Fresh tears burned her cheeks but she held back a betraying sob.

'Are you all right?' Corin repeated. There was a rustle of cloth and a soft scraping as he shifted closer.

'I'm fine,' she snapped. 'I was looking after Rumi, then I was on watch. Jiche! Go to sleep.' Her voice broke.

His deep chuckle sounded. 'Swearing at me helps does it? Go ahead, I can take it. Rough day?'

Alere rubbed a sleeve across her nose, laughing and crying at once, grateful for the attempt to lighten her mood.

'You could say that. I don't think there's an handspan on me that isn't bruised.' She rolled over, just able to make out his face in the golden glow of the dimming fire. 'Whose stupid idea was it to beg to be Gavon's student?'

'Mine, and you can thank me later.' His teeth gleamed in the half-light.

'I haven't decided yet whether to thank you or hit you,' she retorted. 'No, yes I have. I'll hit you – when I have the strength.' In truth, the thought of resting her aching head on Corin's shoulder appealed. But he would discover her gender and she wasn't ready for that.

Corin rose onto one elbow and spread his other arm wide, presenting his cheek. 'Go ahead. Hit away. I can take that as well. I'm used to it.'

Alere laughed feebly. 'You're impossible. I should, you know. You sent me into a beating and you expect me to thank you for it?'

He dropped his arm and amusement fell away. 'Alek, in all seriousness, I've seen many bright young men come through this trek. Few make it unscathed, or even alive. It's distressing to see them die, so I try not to form attachments.' He cocked his head. 'But I like you and I do think you'll benefit from Gavon's teaching.'

Alere tried to hold in doubt but it burst forth. 'I just don't know if I can do it. I'm not good enough.'

Corin grinned. 'No-one's as good as Gavon, lad. That's the point.'

'Why are you helping me?' She got control of her unruly tongue.

'No idea, lad. Possibly you remind me of myself a few years ago: callow, naïve and seeing the goodwill in all mankind, and...' His eyes held a gleam of mischief.

'And?'

'And,' he said, patting her cheek, 'I feel it behoves me to throw you to the tame xiao-bears now to save your life from real ones, later. That way you'll live long enough to become as cynical as I. Then we can wench our way around this great planet as careless entertainers plying our talented…appendages, in trade for dinner everywhere we go.' He kissed his fingertips to the dark sky.

Alere shoved away, face aflame, trying hard not to think less of him for his attitude to women. 'I'm not interested in wenching my way around the world. Thanks anyway.'

'Oh? What is your mission in life, then, my lad?' Corin lay back and tucked his hands beneath his head. 'Do tell. What's in Shanzhai for a young man like you, if not wine, women and song? It's a dangerous trip to make for no reason.'

Deliberate casualness coloured his words. A loaded question then; one for which the answer held some importance. Why? And why use the word "mission"? How should she reply? She couldn't tell the truth. Then again…There was a useful jiaoji trick Mistress Houlia taught: when in doubt of how much someone knew, tell the truth as if it's a lie.

'Can I entrust you with a secret, Corin?' Alere whispered.

'Of course.' He sounded surprised.

'I'm not…' she said, pausing for effect, 'a raider's son. I mean, I'm also…umm…the kin-child of a First-Family's daughter. I'm going to find my family.' She gulped audibly. 'Or, I'm hoping to, anyway.'

'Ah.' Corin chuckled. 'You're good, I'll give you that. You almost had me fooled. No wonder I like you so much. Well, when you're ready to tell me the truth, please feel free. Good night.'

Alere smiled into the darkness.

CHAPTER TWENTY

Alere presented herself to Gavon straight after breakfast and passed over Iblis' reins without comment. The yongbing eyed her with a hint of respect.

'So?' he said. 'What'd ye decide?'

She hesitated. Would he mock her reasons as trite?

'Freedom,' she said. 'My freedom and that of the people of Mamlakah. *That's* worth fighting for.'

Gavon stilled, his dark eyes flat and hard. His hand fisted around Iblis' reins, knuckles white. He gave a slow nod.

'Aye, boyo. Yer right. But these "people" ye speak of – it's not yer job to free them. They make their own choices. But *yer* freedom is worth fighting for. And the freedom of people ye love.' He twisted the leather guard around his left wrist. 'Remember that. If it's important to yer, then ye'll do whatever it takes to win, won't ye?'

'Ya zheng, shifu.'

'None of that rubbish, boyo. Mount up. We've work to do.'

The first day became a template for the next twelve as the caravan trundled like a giant miayapede across the open farmland and bluegrass plains that lay between Newmec and the towering peaks of the Aswad Ranges in the west. Beyond the Aswads lay a fertile valley sheltering Shanzhai and the lands of Jun Second Rafi Koh-Lin.

Alere yawned as she rode ahead of the caravan on the twelfth day. Gavon guided Iblis alongside Rumi and pointed at the mountains.

'Third saddle to the right of the highest peak is Eagle Pass,' he said. 'That's where we're headed.'

With a sinking heart, she squinted at the mountains. The Aswads' tallest peaks adorned their white heads in gossamer grey scarves that trailed north with the wind. Below the snow-line, sharp-pleated black rock segued to rich deep-blue foliage and draped to where the bluegrass plains worshipped at the mountains' feet.

'That's the lowest and easiest pass?' she asked. It still appeared immeasurably high and distant.

Gavon grinned. 'Good thing ye've been training so hard, boyo. Steals the breath from yer lungs, that one.'

Alere groaned. The pass presented a daunting climb. The last two weeks had improved her abilities and strength. At the end of each day she was less exhausted; less despairing, less terrified of inadvertently revealing herself. She'd even been able to play the pipes in the evenings again. But she was still far from being able to defeat Gavon, although she'd earned a grunt or two of praise in their unarmed combat bouts. After the third day, he'd taken to staging surprise attacks – much as Kett used to, but harder and more painful if she froze instead of reacting.

At least, for the last few nights, her dreams had been free of nightmarish visions of death.

'Hold up, boyo.' Gavon halted Iblis and scowled behind at the column of dust raised by caravan and visible for miles, then at the mountains ahead.

Expecting another bout of training, Alere swung off Rumi's back.

'No, boyo. Mount up. Ye get a reprieve today,' Gavon said. 'From me, anyway. See that?' He pointed out a curve in the road. On either side, steep hills rose. The road cut between them like a tight belt on plump hips. 'There's our first danger point. Very popular spot for an ambush, is that little gorge. We need to regroup with Hellor and plan a defence. That bow of yers will come in handy.'

They cantered back to the caravan, where Gavon dismissed Alere to get lunch while he conferred with Hellor and Jacksa. She smiled at Yilan in the cook's huoche and was rewarded with cold roast, cheese and bread. Alere spotted Corin, his blond head thrown back in laughter as he rode with Brant, a quiet veteran yongbing with a dry sense of humour and lethal knife-throwing accuracy. Hellor called Brant, who bowed to Corin and joined the caravan leaders.

She watched Corin for a few moments. Why did he frown as he eyed Jacksa and the others? He turned his head and smiled, waving her over. Corin never failed to lighten her heart and she'd been grateful for his humour these last two weeks. His ironic observations and sly wisdom had guided her through the sometimes-incomprehensible world of yongbing. Unfortunately, she was also finding it difficult to hide her attraction to him. He must have seen through her disguise by now. She wasn't that good an actor, so his seeming ignorance of her gender left her uncertain. Was he attracted to her, or not? Did she even want his attention in that way, when their relationship now was so comfortable and uncomplicated?

As Alere approached, Corin nodded at the four men deep in conversation. 'Not yet invited to advise on matters of strategy?'

Alere laughed and handed him a sandwich. She gave an exaggerated sigh. 'Not yet. They don't know how much they need my sage wisdom. How is it they don't include you?'

'For some strange reason, Jacksa doesn't entirely trust me.' Corin flung an arm wide. 'The whole world wrongs me. I am unappreciated.'

She applauded. 'Ah, Corin, why aren't you on stage? The world's missed a great purple-hat in you. Just think: all the women you want. Fame. Fortune – if you attract a great patron.'

Corin blew kisses to an imaginary audience before bowing to Alere. 'You're right, of course, lad. I was meant for better things, as were you. I hear the men whispering good things about you. What's your first move after arriving at Shanzhai? Jacksa would welcome you back.'

She flushed, annoyed the praise pleased her; irritated he'd turned the conversation back to her. Though he'd never again asked directly, Corin hadn't given up trying to discover why she travelled to Shanzhai, and every chat became a subtle dance around the subject. But, often, ignoring him was the best option.

'Gavon says we can expect an ambush.' She pointed to the gorge ahead.

'Yes, raiders never tire of that location, although they do vary their tactics occasionally and try to surprise us.' Corin grinned. 'You'd think they'd learn. Not very bright these lowlanders. The ones higher up are more desperate and therefore more creative. Although even they have been slack lately. I should probably be prepared though, don't you think?'

He reached under the pack strapped to his mount and drew out a genuine steel sword. He sliced the air with a deft twist of the wrist before sliding the blade into a sheath and belting that to his hip.

'Ah, Hellor's calling the merry band together for a briefing. Shall we, my lad? Then you can show me all the fun things you've been learning.' He cantered forward to join the others.

Unable to think of a witty reply, Alere could only follow.

All the able-bodied attended Hellor's briefing and were allotted to defensive positions. The weapons master handed out extra blades and, to Alere, fifty new arrows measured and fletched, over the last two weeks, to her specifications. She tied Rumi to the weapons huoche and climbed onto the roof, reaching down for the spare arrows in their specially-designed quiver.

Each huoche was constructed like a small castle, the roof built with knee-high crenellations to shelter an archer. Fixing the quiver in place on the roof, Alere strung her bow, tested the draw and sat down to wait. On four other huoches, four other archers, including Yilan and her mother, did the same.

Below, Corin trotted past and hailed her. 'Good shooting, lad. Have fun up there. And if you see an unpleasant hundan with one eye and an axe, put out the other eye for me?'

'Surely, why?'

'He had the gall to kill my last horse,' Corin said. 'My favourite by far. Put an arrow through my leg, too. Most irritating.'

'For the crime of killing your horse, I shall do my best to exact revenge.'

'That's the way.' His expression softened. 'Do stay out of trouble, won't you? At the risk of sounding dramatic, try not to let yourself be captured.'

Sobering, Alere cocked her head in query.

'These raiders have a deal with Melcori slavers,' he said. 'You get captured and you'll end up in the loving embrace of a Slave Master in Chengdu. For a handsome young lad like you, not a good place. Ask Gavon sometime, if you're feeling brave. So do be careful. I've grown used to having you around.'

'And you,' she responded. Corin saluted and rode off, whistling. She resolved to keep an eye on him.

Silence reigned as the other fighters geared up for battle. All eyes studied the hills ahead; hands tight on weapons. The only sounds were the huoches' creaking rattle, the steady thud of hooves and the squealing of spice-otters in their cages.

Alere balanced her weight on the swaying huoche roof and took several deep breaths to settle her fluttering stomach. She flexed tense fingers around the bow and wiped a sweaty palm on her trous. A cold breeze from the south sprang up and wafted the sulphurous stench of stagnant swamp water and dead animal. She gagged, coughing.

As the caravan approached the gorge, and the rocky walls steepened, tensions ramped up until the air was thick with expectation. Soon the hills blotted out most of the sky and still no attack came. Alere scanned the ridges for movement, for misplaced lumps, for unexplained shadows. Nothing. A small rock bounced down the steep slope. Something moved, higher on the hill. Alere half-drew her bowstring, only to relax when a glass-rabbit bounded out from behind a rock. The animal sniffed the air. The rabbit's translucent fur rendered it almost invisible against the lichen-covered boulders. Tiny, pointed ears twitched and the rabbit bolted into a burrow.

What had frightened it? Alere relaxed her shoulders and peripheral vision. She released tension, expanding her awareness as Kett taught.

There! She drew and released in one smooth move. The arrow flew true and impaled a lookout concealed amongst boulders halfway up the slope. His agonised cry became the signal for raiders to emerge from hiding. A screaming, filthy mob flooded down the hillsides. Alere shuddered as the raiders came into view; their clothing in tatters, hair matted and lank, weapons dented and chipped. What armour they wore was a patchwork of leather, bamboo, and badly-hammered bronze plates. And there was no mercy in the raiders' eyes, only desperation and murderous intent, as the wave descended on the caravan.

'Fire!' Hellor's order cut through the noise. Alere steeled herself and loosed an arrow. It drove through a raider's eye and the man collapsed, face-first, in the dust. In swift succession, she put arrows into four attackers hurtling towards the line. The caravan defenders closed ranks and the tsunami broke upon a wall of weapons.

From her vantage on the roof, Alere saw danger spots and called out to the men below, even as she shot.

'Ferat, on your left. Brant, behind. Jacksa, look left!' Pausing only long enough to be certain they heard, she drew and loosed again and again. Adrenalin kicked in and her hand shook in time with her racing heart. She slowed her breathing, concentrating on making each draw smooth and steady.

Corin had three raiders in close quarters. He fell back. His sword glinted silver in the sun, licked out and rang against bronze. He stabbed one raider and snatched the bronze blade from the man's hand. Corin danced aside as a spear jabbed at his stomach. He blocked two blades slicing at his head, but staggered under the force of the blows.

Alere's arrows skewered one of Corin's opponents in the back, another through the leg. Corin dispatched the wounded men with two casual strokes and blew Alere a kiss. She took a second to admire his sword-work, and his steel blade, as another attacker swung wildly at him. Did he laugh as he killed the man? Hopefully not.

The raiders poured between the huoches. Cries and the clash of swords filled the air. Alere focussed, closing her mind and nose to the stench of blood, excrement, and vomit. She clenched her jaw, hardening herself against the knowledge she'd already killed half a dozen. She was doing what was needed to survive; to stay free; to protect those in the caravan.

Below, Rumi whinnied, tossing her head and prancing. Her eyes were wild and she yanked at the rope that tied her to the huoche. A raider crept up behind the mare.

'Rumi, left!' Alere called down. Rumi's hoof lashed out and struck the man in the chest with a wet, cracking sound. He staggered and collapsed, blood spilling from his open mouth. Rumi neighed in distress.

'Stand, Rumi.' The mare obeyed but her eyes rolled and her hide darkened with sweat.

Not far away, Hellor bellowed and lay about him with sword and dagger like a wild man. He was in no danger but Alere put an arrow into one of his opponents, just for the sake of seeing his disappointment. Hellor scowled. She saluted.

An arrow thwacked into the woodwork beside her foot. She jumped, heart thudding. High on the hill, raider-archers shot at Alere and the others on the roofs. The raiders had the advantage of height and were out of her range. Oh, for Kett and his hundred-pound bow.

She ducked behind a crenellation, peering around to sight her next shot. The far end of the roof offered a better vantage. She crawled until a stand of trees blocked her from view of the southern hill. Now she only had to watch north. Kneeling, she found a new target and loosed.

'Alek!' Corin pointed at the centre of the line. Half a dozen raiders surrounded Gavon, who held his own, but only just. Alere loosed four times and dropped four men at his feet. Timber creaked behind her and she spun, the fifth arrow drawn and ready.

She released. One of the men clambering onto the roof fell backwards with a cry. Another replaced him. Her back quiver was empty. The larger quiver stood where she'd left it: at the other end of the roof. She dropped the bow and drew sword and dagger. Three men swarmed up the ladder onto the roof. The huoche trembled and creaked as the raiders inched towards her.

Alere backed away. The men leered in chilling, rapacious excitement. She needed to get onto the ground, off the exposed roof. But there was no easy escape. If she jumped, she'd break a leg at best, and there was no-one who could help. The raiders had broken through the caravan's line of defence and stormed the huoches. Hellor bellowed an order to regroup. Dozens of small skirmishes erupted. It was impossible to tell friend from foe and the other archers were similarly beset.

Alere gripped her weapons. She switched off thoughts of rescue and watched her attackers instead, looking for weaknesses. None moved like seasoned fighters. One raider held a chipped ceramic sword; another swung a ji pole-axe like a farm-worker scything hay. He was in more danger of slicing open one of his comrades than Alere. A third hefted a bronze axe. A strip of dirty cloth covered his left eye. Corin's horse-killer.

The swordsman and Corin's nemesis rushed forward. The roof under the pole-axeman exploded into a shower of splinters. An oversized crossbow bolt, covered in gore, protruded from his chest. The weapons master had shot blind through the roof and, by an astonishing piece of luck, hit his target. The raider collapsed and blood sprayed across the timber underfoot.

The remaining two raiders paled and looked down. Alere gulped. Hopefully the weapons master wouldn't shoot again while she was still on the roof.

Both raiders edged forward, the swordsman jabbing tentatively at Alere. She flicked the blade aside with her dagger and thrust with her sword. The ceramic slid through a gap in the patchy armour and between his ribs with a sickening squelch. He coughed and crumpled. She tugged at the sword but it was wedged in his body. The one-eyed man leapt over his dead companion. With a cry of triumph, he swung the axe at Alere's head. She released the sword-hilt and twisted aside.

The raider's axe passed so close its breeze stirred her hair. Continuing the turn, she slammed an elbow into the man's floating rib. He grunted. She swapped the dagger to her right hand and stabbed. The raider snarled and skipped back, out of reach. He hefted the axe and jumped forward on light feet. A cut at her right side drove her closer to the roof's edge. He struck again, forcing her back.

With her calves pressed against a crenellation, Alere had nowhere left to go when he swung again. Jiche! She'd run out of options. She moved inside his reach. If he carried a hidden dagger, things could get messy. She blocked his axe-bearing arm and forced it down. His wrist twisted and the axe-blade scored her ribs. Fire and ice burned a trail into her skin.

A stifled cry of pain escaped her lips and he grinned. She slashed at his throat. Steel gleamed, but he grabbed her dagger-hand. If it became a contest of strength she was hopelessly outmatched. She folded her elbow, drove it into his throat and hooked her ankle behind his knee. Now his back was to the edge of the roof and he balanced precariously over the drop.

His eye widened. His grip tightened on her wrist. The raider let out a terrified cry; foul breath gusted in her face. The axe dropped from his hands and shattered on rock below. He snatched at her shirt. With a strangled yell, he fell backward and dragged Alere over the edge.

As Alere twisted in the air she glimpsed Gavon's horrified expression. He would be so annoyed if she died in such a stupid way, and Corin would be annoyed if she lived to be taken prisoner.

Hands lifted her. Unbearable pain split the world into flashes of light and agony. Someone ripped the shirt from her back. She tried to fight, but her arms hung heavy, immovable.

'No,' she whispered, only conscious of the secret she must protect at all costs. 'No.'

'Do shut up,' a familiar voice murmured. 'It's me and the healer. You're safe. It's over. Relax, lad.'

The dark sea of unconsciousness surged in and she drowned gratefully in its depths.

When Alere awoke, it was so black she blinked twice to make sure her eyes were open. Silence met her ears; cloth her seeking fingers. With every small movement, excruciating pain lanced through her body.

Something rustled in the darkness, close by. The brush of cloth. The slow, cautious sounds of someone trying to be silent.

Alere's heart jumped. She gritted her teeth and fumbled at the bedclothes, searching for a weapon. A small, smoky light flared and illuminated Corin, drawn with weariness and, unusually, frowning. His expression lightened to relief. He set the lamp on a shelf lined with dozens of earthenware jars. The smell of herbs and liniments filtered into her senses. The healer's huoche.

'What happened?' Her mouth was dry, her voice a mere croak.

Corin rested his elbows on his knees. The makeshift cot beneath him creaked. 'You fell, rather spectacularly, off the roof.'

'I remember the fight,' she said. 'But not the fall.'

'Be glad of that,' he said, gripping her wrist. 'The rest of us will never forget it.'

'What about the raiders?' Her fingers found his. 'They were winning. Is everyone all right? How am I even alive?'

He laughed and tied his loose hair back. 'Don't tell Hellor you thought that unruly bunch was winning. We lost only three of the newer yongbing, Berrat, Fodd, and Cho.' He grimaced.

Alere swallowed a sudden ache in her throat. Cho had been from Madina. He was her own age, the others not much older. All three good men.

Corin shook his head. 'The raiders lost about three quarters of their people and quit the field shortly after your fall.' He plucked a horn cup off a nearby table. 'As to how you survived, consensus is you're half xiao-cat.' He raised the cup in salute. 'Which would explain a lot, actually. Somehow you managed to turn in the air. Landed on top of your opponent. He broke your fall and the ground broke him.'

She shifted and pain speared through her ribs and left wrist. 'What did I break?'

Corin raised her gently, holding the cup so she could drink. The liquid was cool but bitter with willow-bark. She drank, but the motion of sitting up made her stomach churn and she vomited the mixture back up. Corin snatched a wooden bucket off the floor and held the container under her mouth.

Agony engulfed her mind in fire and burned her thoughts to ash. Tears of shame slid down her cheeks. Corin raised her again and put the cup back to her lips.

'No,' she protested, trying to push it away. 'It tastes disgusting. I'll throw it up again.'

'Stop being a child and do as you're told.' The harshness of his tone was so uncharacteristic it shocked her into obedience.

This time she managed to keep down both nausea and medicine. She lay back and he placed a cool, damp cloth on her forehead.

'You broke that stubborn head of yours,' he said. He stroked her cheek and smiled. 'Cracked a rib and sprained a wrist. Oh, and Attar has stitched up a shallow cut across your ribs. He thinks you'll be fine in a couple of days. Recommends you stay off roofs for a while.'

'Where are we?' Alere closed her eyes against the too-bright lamp and listened for camp noises, but there were none. 'Have they left us behind?' Alarmed, she grabbed at the bedclothes and tried to sit up. Corin gripped her shoulder, his smile quizzical.

'I do believe you'd actually try to catch up if they had. No, we're in the last village before the ascent to Eagle Pass. It's rather misleadingly called Paradise. However, it's a safe enough place to tend the wounded and prepare for the ascent. We'll be here another two days. You won't miss out, I promise.'

Relieved, she pressed a thumb into her temple, trying to ease the throbbing in her skull. She prodded at the lump over one ear. Memory surfaced.

'My dagger. My bow. Rumi! She was frightened. Is she all right?'

'Your things are safe, as is Rumi. I think she likes me,' he said, grinning. 'Gavon stood, rather fiercely, over your small, broken body. He took charge of your weapons before anyone could steal them.' Corin produced a cloth-wrapped bundle. 'You may, however, need a new box for this. The original smashed when it broke your ribs.'

With shaking fingers, she opened the cloth. Rafi's bracelet slithered out intact and she breathed a sigh of relief. The yanstones gathered the lamplight and turned to liquid gold, the lights flaring and dancing as she stroked the stones. She rewrapped the bracelet and stowed it under her pillow, muttering a thank you.

Corin propped his chin in one hand, staring in apparent fascination.

'You know,' he said, 'I think I've vastly underestimated you.'

She dared not look at him lest uneasiness betray her. Instead, she fussed with the bedclothes and straightened her soft bamboo-cloth shirt; a shirt several sizes too large.

'Jiche,' she said.

Wry amusement creased Corin's eyes. 'Not precisely the word Attar used when we brought you in. He cursed both Gavon and I for being useless hundan and allowing a slip of a girl to do our fighting for us.'

Alere inspected the whitewashed timber ceiling overhead, afraid to find condemnation in Corin. 'Attar knew?'

'Why do you think he used his finest silk and most delicate stitches for that cut on your first night?'

She groaned and covered her eyes. 'Who else?'

With a soft chuckle, Corin pulled her hand away, his expression one of unholy amusement. 'Jacksa spotted you the minute you applied for the job. Hellor and I noticed the first night. Gavon says he realised when you came and asked to be his student. He said, and I won't repeat his exact words, no boy would ever have the courage to do that.'

'I feel like such a shazi.' She faced the huoche wall. 'Go away, will you?'

'You're not a shazi at all.' His fingers turned her chin. His expression was warm, gentle and more serious than she'd imagined he could look. 'Every trip we get one or two women trying to join as yongbing. Most have had little or no training. Never, in the last two and a half years I've been working this run, have I seen Jacksa take one on. Not because they're female. Because they weren't good enough to survive. But you...Hellor's never commented so favourably on a yongbing. Nor have I seen Gavon drive one as hard.' Corin sat back. 'You singlehandedly killed fifteen raiders – not including the horse-murdering hundan you fell on. Or the one Rumi kicked.'

'Killing seventeen people is hardly something to be proud of,' she snapped, quashing guilt.

'Here, it is,' he said. 'The others are most impressed.'

'So? That won't mean anything when they find out I'm a—' She shut her teeth on the word. Now she'd experienced a taste of what life could be outside the House, she didn't want to give up the freedom of trous and a sword for all the feminine luxuries in the world.

'You've earned your place, Alek. No, that's not right, is it?' Corin tilted his head and waited.

'Alere,' she supplied, sighing in resignation.

'Oh?' He straightened, his brows lifting.

She pressed her lips together, angry with herself. The Alcazar weishi had undoubtedly spread her name far and wide by now. Had the knock on the head scrambled her brains?

'Perhaps you're right,' Corin said. 'We should continue with the masquerade until Shanzhai. Finding a sword-brother is a sister would disturb the men's neat vision of the world. Most won't see past the haircut and the moustache.' He stroked his own upper lip, with its habitual two-day growth. 'Nice touch by the way.'

'And Gavon and the others? What's to stop them telling?'

'So untrusting. And here I thought you were the one who saw the good in all mankind. Have I corrupted you so soon?'

'Just answer,' she said, weary of his games. 'I do *not* want to spend the rest of the trip in a robe and veil.'

'A veil?' Corin leaned forward, his green eyes were intent. 'What colour, may I ask?'

Alere cursed herself again. These days the veil was unfashionable and worn only by high-ranking Jun women, and

Houses clinging to the old traditions. To mention it had been a mistake.

'Please go away. I'm tired.' She closed her eyes.

He said nothing, but his lips brushed her cheek. After a few moments, the lamp snuffed out and the door creaked open then shut. Would he keep his word? Would Jacksa and Hellor betray her to the other yongbing?

For the first time in her life she felt accepted and valued; free to find out who she was; free of Mistress Li's, Elmira's and even Kett's expectations; free to make her own choices. Was she about to lose it all, and the men's easy camaraderie, because of one moment of stupidity? Tears stung her eyes. No. No matter what happened, she would never go back to the veil; to Xintou House. Kett was right: there was more to her; more to life than waiting for someone else to choose her path. There had to be a way. A place where she could be accepted, appreciated, and still be herself – whoever that was. She'd had enough of walking the wrong path.

Time to choose her own way.

She struggled to stay awake, to plan, but sleep was impatient and gathered her into its comfortable arms before she formulated a strategy to deal with what lay ahead.

CHAPTER TWENTY-ONE

'Stop being a stubborn fool, girl. You've nothing to prove by being in pain. Drink.' Attar passed her a willow-bark drink. He dropped a small sack of dried leaves into her lap. 'And chew one of those every day as we begin the ascent. Are you using the comfrey and bone-root ointment on those ribs?'

'Yes.' Alere drank the bitter liquid and inspected a nondescript little leaf. 'What is it?'

'Jabal fern,' he said. 'For altitude sickness. We'll be heading up the mountain faster than your body can adjust. Jabal helps your blood take in more oxygen.' He shook a stained finger. 'If you get any headaches – *any,* mind you – let me know. With that head knock you shouldn't be climbing mountains at all, but I know your type. Useless to tell you not to. Promise you'll tell me if anything ails you.'

Alere agreed meekly, put a leaf into her mouth and tucked the bag in with the one Mina had given her.

'When can I get out of bed?'

Attar raised his brows. 'Tired of my hospitality already?'

'I mean,' she said, flustered, 'I appreciate you letting me stay here, but I've already put your family out for two days. Hellor wants me back riding point.' Truth was, she'd had enough of the cramped quarters and medicinal smells of the healer's huoche. Even though Attar and his wife had moved into a tent with their baby to allow Alere to sleep undisturbed, she felt like an intruder and a prisoner at the same time.

'Tomorrow then,' Attar said. 'But no training or fighting for three days.' As he gathered bandages and his surgical kit, she felt compelled to ask after the one person who hadn't come to see her in the last two days.

'Where's Corin?'

Attar appeared to put considerable thought into his next words. Why did he hesitate? Was Corin injured or unwell?

'On a task for Jacksa. He'll be back before we leave tomorrow. Or he'll catch us up on the first day.'

The door creaked shut behind Attar, sending a chill breeze across her neck. What sort of task could a musician, even one who fought as well as Corin, be sent on? She groaned. She was an idiot. There was no task. Everyone in the caravan made jokes about Corin's reputation with women. That's why Attar hesitated. Paradise wasn't big but, according to Gavon when he'd visited, it did have a brothel. Alere closed her eyes against a sharp pang of regret and grimaced at the uncaring wall.

The next morning dawned fair and Alere left the healer van to again drink the wine air of freedom. It smelled of human waste and mud. She stood on shaky legs outside the huoche and squinted in the sunlight, inspecting the village. If this was Paradise, it was mislabelled. Barely thirty dwellings – patchwork huts constructed of bamboo and daub – a brothel, a general store, a workshop of some sort and an inn.

A mud-spattered child, with a thumb lodged in his mouth and a scrawny black dog sniffing at his backside, emerged from a nearby house and stared solemnly at Alere. A hollow-eyed woman appeared, snatched the child up and kicked the dog before vanishing inside and slamming the warped bamboo door.

Alere skipped a village tour and instead sought out Rumi. The mare nuzzled Alere's neck, whuffling and lipping at her hair. Alere spent a few minutes checking Rumi's feet and legs, feeling for heat or strain, relieved to find her in good health. The mare generally let very few people near her, but must have taken a liking to Corin. Rumi had good instincts about people, so maybe Alere was judging him too harshly for his interest in unveiled jiaoji. These caravan trips were long and difficult, after all.

Seeing a tendency for her thoughts to drift back to the feckless musician, Alere spoke sternly to herself. She gave Rumi a final talking-to about falling for the swift patter of charming men, then strode away in search of food.

She stowed her gear back in the luggage van and headed over to the fire for breakfast. Half a dozen men slapped her on the back, or commented on her bravery. She winced and mumbled thanks.

Brant invited her to sit near the fire. Alere scooped up a bowl of porridge and joined him and his companions. Her feat had broken some sort of barrier between her and the veteran yongbing, for they inquired after her with genuine concern. Their warmth spread through her body and she relaxed.

'And your duties?' Brant asked.

She screwed up her nose and shrugged. 'Attar gave me leave to get out of bed, but not to fight. I should be able to draw a bow, though.'

Brant levelled an ironic look at her.

'Well,' she muttered, 'he didn't say I couldn't.'

Hellor joined them and sat on a bench nearby. The timber creaked beneath his bulk and he half-rose, alarm on his face. He kicked at the bench. Apparently satisfied it wouldn't break, he sat and sipped a mug of almost-black lancha tea.

'You'll be point today?' His eyes narrowed.

'Yes, if that's alright?' she said, relieved he wasn't treating her differently.

'Your father's a raider back in the Ahmar Mountains, Corin tells me. Got any ideas how to deal with the scum here?' Hellor gestured with his cup at the Aswad Mountains looming behind the village.

Alere shuddered. She fingered her tender ribs and thrust aside the memory of the axe-wielding raider. 'Sorry. You've far more experience than I. My father's become a trader now.'

Approval glimmered in Hellor's dark eyes and he nodded, sipping his tea in silence.

Brant rose and tossed the dregs of his tea onto the grass. 'Gavon tells me that rib of yours will preclude your unarmed combat lessons. He's asked me to instruct you in knife-throwing instead. Are you agreeable?'

'Thank you, yes,' Alere said. 'I have some training but I'm not used to my new blades. I'd value your advice.'

'Come see me when we halt for lunch.'

Delighted, she finished breakfast, skipped to the animal zinzana and dragged a recalcitrant, head-tossing Iblis to find Gavon.

The morning passed easily enough. Gavon, when not teaching, was a minimal conversationalist, so Alere enjoyed the spectacular scenery as they rode in advance of the column. The Aswad Ranges gnawed at the sky like dragon's teeth and curved away south into mist and north into farmland. The range bisected the jundom, finishing near Madina and separating the two Jun Seconds' domains. With any luck, another four days would see the caravan over the pass, and onto the plains, heading to Shanzhai.

And another six or seven days would bring Alere to that city and to a new dilemma: how did she get into the palace and see Rafi? She pushed the thought aside. Something would present itself. Best to keep her mind on the current job and make it through.

Her thoughts drifted to Kett, Mina and Rohne. Kett had been much in her thoughts these last weeks. Had he recovered? Abandoning him still felt wrong, even though he'd insisted. Somehow she knew Mina was all right. But what about Kett? Declaring independence was one thing; actually being without her best friend was another entirely. She missed him. Had they followed her? Would the raiders attack them as well? She shivered and glanced back down the road towards Newmec. Gavon seemed to think the raiders would take some time to recover, so perhaps her actions had helped clear the way for Kett and the others.

Cheered by the thought, she nudged Rumi into a trot to catch up with Gavon.

By lunch the caravan had made good progress up the steep, crushed-rock track. Gavon eyed the surrounding mountains with deep suspicion and twice sent her back to warn Jacksa of partial landslide blockages. Deliberate landslides were the most common way of halting a caravan, so Hellor had all the yongbing on high alert and sent armed men forward to help clear the slides. No attack materialised and the caravan laboured up the road unmolested. She thought the tight switchbacks would cause difficulties, but Jacksa's bespoke, articulated huoches negotiated the corners with ease.

After lunch, Alere stood at the edge of the path and looked back, through a break in the violet bamboo stands, at the patchwork of farmland and bluegrass plains below. The dirt road from Newmec to Paradise sliced a blood-red path through the broad body of the Newhome Plains. Was it her imagination or was there a faint smudge of dust on the horizon?

Jacksa strode past, his expression distracted as he read through a message delivered by flitter-bird. The man kept an entire huoche for the pesky, twittering reptiles, sending and receiving messages almost hourly.

'Jacksa?' She pointed at the plains. 'Can you see that?'

He frowned impatiently then sighted along her finger. 'Never fear. You're not being followed if that's what you're worried about.'

She started. Had Corin betrayed her? Had Jacksa discovered she was a fugitive or was he just teasing?

'It's Ahkma's caravan.' Jacksa wrinkled his nose at the distant dust column. 'He always leaves a week after me, hoping to catch my leavings.' Jacksa re-read the message in his hand, dark eyes twinkling with unshared knowledge. 'With any luck we'll get through the pass and the first winter storms will snow him into Paradise for the next month.'

Alere squinted at the horizon. 'I was hoping some friends might be in that caravan,' she said. 'Can I get a message to Ahkma to find out?'

'No.' Jacksa sniffed scornfully and turned away.

'Please? I'm worried about them.'

He paused, eyed her narrowly, and softened. 'Sorry, lad. I don't carry birds that home to him and he doesn't carry mine. We're competition, not friends. You'll have to wait and see if they make it through to Shanzhai before the pass closes.' With a wave, he strode away. 'Brant's waiting for you, by the way.'

Much to Gavon's puzzlement and despite his dire expectations, the rest of the day was also uneventful. Brant showed her a new throwing style that made it easier to find her range with an unfamiliar knife, then she rejoined Gavon riding point. Corin was still missing and Gavon still grumbling about unpredictable raiders as the sun slipped behind the mountain and threw long purple shadows across the plains. Just after dark, the caravan straggled intact into the next camp.

A giant overhang had been hewn out of the mountain's solid rock; the site designed to shelter and protect caravans. Sheer cliffs, above and below, made access impossible from any direction other than the road. Spring water seeped through the basalt to form a clear, deep well in one side of the cave. A latrine built out over the cliff's edge was practical but terrifying.

Attar took a sample from the well before anyone drank. He scowled at a brash young yongbing named Belic, who complained and tried to edge past the healer to get to the water.

'Six months ago,' Attar said, sweeping a cool look across the eager men lined up to fill their waterskins, 'the raiders poisoned this well and an entire caravan died. Easy pickings.' He offered Belic the sample cup. 'Care to go first?'

When the yongbing mumbled a refusal, Attar stalked to his huoche to test the water. He returned shortly with the all-clear.

Hellor gave Belic the midnight watch.

In the cramped conditions, and with Corin nowhere to be seen, the usual nightly carousal was subdued and broke up early. Alere, her ribs and head aching, crawled gratefully into her furs and fell asleep.

Something warm covered her mouth. She stabbed upward. Iron fingers seized her wrist and bore it down.

'Do be a little discerning about who you kill or you'll run out of friends. It's me.' Corin's breath tickled her ear and his grip relaxed. 'Ah. Apologies.' He brushed at his hand. 'I seem to have removed your adorable moustache.'

Heart racing, awake and breathless, Alere rose onto her elbows, barely able to make his face out in the faint glow of the watch fires.

'Where've you been?' she demanded.

'Busy,' he replied, shedding stained and torn clothing and replacing them with clean, dark trous and shirt. The stench of animal faeces wafted from his discarded clothes.

'Ugh, you reek!'

'Thank you, I hadn't noticed.' He tipped his waterskin and wet a cloth, then scrubbed at his face. 'Animal crap on your clothes is a helpful trick for getting a tracker-doquan off your trail. But can we critique my personal hygiene later? Get your boots on. Bring your bow and knives. Leave your sword. You'll need a dark shirt, too.'

'What the—?'

He held up a finger. 'Just, for once, please stop arguing. There's something going on up the mountain in the raider stronghold. I need your help to find out what. Are you with me?'

She hesitated then slid out of the furs and shoved one foot into a boot.

'Have you got something with thinner soles?' Corin pointed at her heavy boots. 'We need to move quietly.'

Alere rummaged in her pack and produced a pair of lu-deer-leather moccasins she hadn't worn since leaving Newmec. He nodded. She laced them on and dragged a dark shirt over the top of the grey one she slept in. Then she shrugged into a dark suede jacket and belted on her knives. Her stomach fluttered.

'Where are we going?' she whispered.

'Not far. Your ribs all right? You up for this?' His teeth gleamed in the dim firelight.

'Of course.' She lifted her chin at the challenge in his tone. Why her? Why not someone hale, like Gavon. She debated for a moment, but curiosity won. Stringing her bow, she then grabbed half a dozen arrows and carried them so they wouldn't rattle.

The sharp air bit into every inch of exposed skin and condensed her breath into thick, white clouds. Thousands of jewel-stars sparkled overhead. Luna-Yi balanced, half-full and luminescent, on the peak of the Aswad ranges. In camp, only snores, the crackling of burning wood and the occasional stomp of hooves on stone disturbed the silence. Somewhere up the hill a xiao-cat yowled territorial rights and a night-bird shrilled an alarm. At the watch line, Hellor lifted a lazy hand in acknowledgement as Alere and Corin strode past. His greeting gave Alere some relief. This little trip must be with Jacksa's knowledge.

Once Corin led the way beyond Hellor's earshot, and Alere's eyes adjusted to the moon's pale red glow, she grabbed Corin's arm. He halted, irritation in his quick movements.

'What's going on?' She stopped and folded her arms. 'You can't vanish for three days then show up in the middle of the night and demand help. An explanation would be nice. Why me? I'm injured. I'll hold you back.'

He stared at her, eyes hooded, then his body relaxed.

'Ah, yes, I forgot.' He flashed an ironic smile. 'You don't like taking orders.' After a glance up the road, he pulled her into the shadows, close to the sheer black-stone wall. 'Why you? I trust you more than the others and I know you can keep a secret. I've been scouting for Jacksa. He believes the raiders haven't hit us because they don't need to.'

'What exactly does that mean?'

'Can we discuss this and walk at the same time?' Corin didn't wait for her answer, he strode away. After a moment, Alere growled and hurried to catch up. Disproportionate relief surged through her. Attar hadn't lied; Corin had been on a task for Jacksa.

'The raiders' stronghold is just up the hill, on a side track.' Corin pointed up the road, a pale scar in the dark mountainside. 'Caravans coming through either pay a toll or get hit as the raiders prepare for winter.' He moved faster, forcing her to jog to keep up. 'But, in the last month or so, caravans have passed through unmolested.'

'And?' Her ribs twinged.

'And we want to know why. Something's going on and we need to find out what.'

She opened her mouth to speak but Corin stopped and grabbed her shoulders. His expression was serious for once, clear-lit by the pale moon.

'Listen. Just for the next hour or so, I need you to pretend you *like* taking orders and do what I ask. Can you do that? Please?'

'Shi.' Alere spoke the term of agreement reserved for formal occasions, for Corin seemed unusually intense. Handing over control sat uncomfortably, but there was no alternative unless she abandoned him and returned to camp. She was free to do so, but with freedom came choices. Not all were simple or enjoyable. Corin trusted her enough to ask for help and she'd agreed, though he was still hiding something.

He spun away, breaking into a long-legged run, his feet silent on the crushed-rock road. Swearing, she dashed after him, conscious of her crunching steps.

CHAPTER TWENTY-TWO

Just as the pain in Alere's ribs became unendurable, Corin stopped in a switchback that looped around the inside of a steep, heavily-wooded ravine. He vanished behind a large rock marking the apex of the bend. Alere followed, dagger drawn.

From the deep shadow behind the rock, Corin whispered, 'Now it gets fun. Put the blade away. It catches the light. Stay close. It's about a ten-minute climb to where we can overlook the compound. I'd like to avoid killing the scouts. Better if they don't know we're here. Got it?'

She nodded, but of course he couldn't see her. 'So why am I here if you don't need anyone killed?'

'You know how I like an audience.' He breathed a laugh, peered around the rock then withdrew. 'Move. Now.' He leapt from their hiding place and ghosted up the hill, following a faint animal track into the forest.

Alere struggled to stay close to him without crashing through the trees like an angry xiao-bear. Silence was harder to achieve than it looked. Watching him in the half-light she caught the trick of picking out bare ground and distributing her weight carefully from toe to heel. Twigs and leaves broke less often and Corin grinned back at her.

When he finally slowed, Alere was almost out of breath and her ribs sent sharp warnings of which Attar would be displeased to hear. Corin slipped into the shadow of a large tree. Alere squeezed in beside him, trying to gasp quietly.

'Wait,' he whispered. 'There's a patrol ahead. They'll be back in about half an hour so that's our window.'

Alere peeked around the tree. Just beyond the tree line, two men picked their way down a bare-rock slope. Dressed in furs and sturdy leathers, they looked well-fed and fit, a far cry from the desperate mountain raiders Corin had once described. Each man carried a scimitar on his left hip and a dagger on the right. One wore a quiver on his back and carried a horse-bow. Corin clamped a hand on Alere's shoulder and hauled her back as the bowman glanced around.

'Didja hear somethin', Frad?'

'Nah,' his companion replied. 'Probably another gouri xiao-cat. They're gettin' too close to base. Smellin' the new horses. Is the pelt from the one you shot last week ready?'

'Ya. See if I can sell it to one of the weishi come in with the goods train. Only hole it's got is the one in the neck so it's worth a bit, I reckon.'

'Yer a fine shot, Beldor, that's the truth.' There was a grunt and a scuff of boots on rock. 'C'mon, we need to get to base and report before second walk-round.'

Corin waited until the sound of their movements died away.

'Right,' he said. 'From here things get a little uncomfortable. Best view into the compound is further up. But keep low or we'll be silhouetted against the sky.'

He crouched, so low his head was almost level with his knees, and crab-walked across the steep stretch of near-bare rock, dodging from shadow to shadow. Alere fingered her ribs, sighed, and followed as best she could, casting anxious looks downhill in the direction taken by the two raiders.

By the time Corin chose his final hiding spot, Alere's ribs ground together almost audibly. Pain spiked into her back as she eased onto the cold rock. Corin lay motionless in the shadow of a boulder, gazing downhill through a small brass telescope.

Cold oozed through Alere's thin jacket, freezing the sweat on her skin. She leaned closer to Corin.

'What are—'

He held up a second scope. She accepted and extended it. An arrow-shot down the slope, a fortress of black basalt was a child's toy castle glued to the mountainside. Luna-Yi's reddish light bathed a compound large enough to house maybe a hundred people. As Alere watched, guards appeared, patrolling the top of a narrow wall surrounding the complex. In the protected area, stone shelters jostled with skin tents much like the khibas used by Jada's people. Off to one side of the compound, a dammed mountain stream created a pool. Horses, che-ma and goats dozed in a nearby zinzana.

Alere focussed on the centre of activity: a large building of stone and timber from which drifted shouts of laughter and occasional snatches of music. Firelight shone between chinks in the mortar. Smoke seeped through the thatched roof and blurred the stars.

Corin touched her wrist and she started.

'There,' he said. 'Look at the men coming out of the central building.'

A twist of the scope brought the two men into focus as they emerged into a golden oblong of light before the door. One was short and solid, even beneath his furs; his face a mass of scars and half-hidden by a black beard. A vicious-looking double-bladed axe hung from his belt. His hand strayed to it often.

'The bearded one with the axe is Yaku,' Corin supplied, 'the raider kui here. The taller one's his guest. I saw him arrive yesterday with a dozen laden che-ma and horses. Food and weapons, but money as well I'd warrant. He's been getting the royal treatment.

I'm hoping you might recognise him. I suspect he's from Madina. A merchant, maybe, though he's not wearing the green.'

Alere studied the tall man. His back was to her. He was well-wrapped in furs and, by the urgency of his hand movements, in deep discussion with Yaku.

'Whoever he is,' she said, 'Yaku isn't comfortable with him. See how he keeps putting space between them?' Turn, she silently instructed the taller man. Turn into the light.

He shifted at last, into full view. Alere suppressed a gasp and her heart jumped. Sweat prickled her skin, but she held still lest shock betray her into unwary movement. The telescope trembled so much the world blurred. She collapsed the scope and wriggled back. She gathered bow and arrows and eased away from Corin, hoping the pounding of her heart wasn't as loud as it sounded in her ears. Without speaking or looking back, she half-ran, half-crawled across the hillside and headed for the shelter of the forest. A rock, dislodged by her foot, bounded down the hill, loud in the clear night air.

Safe in the tree line, she paused, holding her chest as pain stabbed through her ribs. She had to put distance between her and the raider compound; had to get to the safety of the caravan where Hellor and his men could be relied on for protection.

'I tell you, Frad, I heard somethin'.' The raider's voice was too close. Footsteps scraped on the rock nearby.

'Ah, c'mon Bel. Ain't nothin' there but animals. I just wanna do this last round and get to bed. Cora's waitin'.'

Alere froze. She couldn't afford to be found. But killing the men was out of the question. Their disappearance would alert the fortress.

The footsteps neared, slowing. A bowstring creaked.

'Should we get the doquan?' Frad whispered.

Alere cupped her hands around her mouth and yowled, imitating a xiao-cat.

'See, Bel? Just another gouri cat. Leave it. Huntin' them at night's a zift's game.'

An arrow whistled past Alere, inches from her stomach.

'Now look what you made me do, Frad. Lost a gouri arrow. Gaisi cats.' Beldor continued to mutter and argue with his companion, but their voices faded.

Alere covered her mouth to muffle a sob and ran down the mountainside, struggling to keep calm. A mistake would precipitate capture or injury. Every step jarred her aching head. The forest distorted into dark, unrecognisable shapes as tears of pain and fear drowned her vision.

She reached the wagon-road and ran until the ache in her ribs forced her to stop. Gulping at the thin, chill air, she rested in the shadow of a rocky overhang and clung to the stone's cold, solid support. Still too close to the raider compound. She straightened.

'Hey!' At the sound of Corin's whispered shout she shoved off the rock and strode away. He caught up and grabbed her elbow.

'Let go.' She twisted free. 'I have to get back to the caravan.' She took off again, relieved when the warm glow of the caravan campfire appeared, promising safety.

'Why did you run?' Corin peered at her. 'Khara! You're crying. Did you hurt yourself? Did that guard's arrow hit you?'

'Get out of my way, Corin.' She shoved him out of her path. 'I shouldn't have come. Shouldn't have trusted you. Leave me alone, or I swear I'll hit you, like I promised three weeks ago.'

He stopped and opened his arms wide, cocking his head. 'Go ahead then.'

She drove a fist into his diaphragm. He collapsed to the ground, gasping. She stood over him, glowering, until he regained breath control and stood.

'I suppose I deserved that,' he said, coughing. 'Though most women would have slapped me.'

'I'm sure you're speaking from vast experience, too,' she snapped, pacing back and forth before him. 'You...you used me. You think you know who I am. You already suspected who the *guest* at the raider fortress was.'

'I'm sorry!' He grabbed her arm, digging into an elbow pressure-point and stopping her short. 'I'm sorry,' he repeated more quietly, sincerity in his eyes. 'It was important to me. It still is.'

'Oh!' She broke free and flung up her hands. 'It's always about *you* and what you think is important.' She prodded him in the chest. 'You could have asked for my help *and* told me why. You have no idea what would happen if that man caught me. What's worse, you don't care either.' With a shudder, she checked the road behind. Empty. The caravan wasn't far away and she edged in the direction of security.

'Again, I'm sorry, and I do care.' Corin smiled ruefully. 'And I did tell you I have trouble trusting anyone.' His hands slid up her arms onto her shoulders. 'We can have this out later, in the ring if you like. I deserve it. You're scared, but I promise I'll protect you. These men are not here for you. That, you can trust me on.'

Alere backed away. 'I hear a "but" in there.' Her heart slowed as panic and anger ebbed.

'But right now I must know for certain: who was that with Yaku?' Corin's hands opened, palms towards her; guileless. 'Think what you like of me. It's vital we know who's arming Yaku and why. They aren't interested in you. They don't know you're here, so please, help us find out why they *are* here.'

'We? Us?' She studied him. The tide of fear and frustration receded further. Who was he working for? Just Jacksa? She knew he had another agenda. She should have trusted her instincts and stayed in camp.

'This is about more than me and what I want,' he said. 'It's bigger than the safety of the caravans, too. There's more going on than you know. Please, I need your help.'

Alere breathed deep the crisp mountain air and tried to regain a weishi's calm perspective. If Corin was right, and the raider's guest wasn't after her, then the situation wasn't immediately dire. With the raiders so close the danger still existed, but if she wasn't their guest's target, why was he here? Could it be somehow connected to her mission? Radan's wasted face flashed into her mind, his blood bright on her hands. She rubbed at her palm.

Of course. She froze, staring blankly uphill.

Pay off this hairy mountain man. Hanna Zah-Hill's words. But why? How did arming Yaku and his men help Hanna?

Corin obviously knew more than he was saying. Perhaps if Corin got the information he wanted, he'd return the favour. She needed to tread carefully, though; keep more distance. He was too likeable. Too untrustworthy.

'His name's Penon.' Alere flicked up her fur hood and brushed away cold tears. She stalked towards the camp. 'He's the Shangwei at the Alcazar. That's who's funding the raiders: Jun First Ven Zah-Hill.'

Corin trod silently beside her. 'How do you know Penon?'

'Don't pretend you haven't heard the rider-news. You're not that good at hiding your reactions.'

'Yes, I thought I'd underestimated you,' he said. 'But what did you mean by "I *thought* I knew who you were"? If you're not the Alcazar jiaoji who murdered Jun Radan, who are you?'

She folded her arms, trembling at the memory of the dagger blade sliding into Radan's thin chest. 'It doesn't matter. You're not just a musician, are you? We both have secrets. If you want to stop Ven arming the raiders, you'll have to trust me. I'm going to Shanzhai to stop a war. That's all I can tell you. You decide.'

'A war!' Corin's body tensed with unreadable emotion. Then a lightning smile swept away his seriousness and he extended an elbow. 'Very well, Alere, but I reserve the right to change my mind.'

Although said in the lightest tone, steel underlay his words. Corin believed his trust was hard to earn and easy to lose, did he? His reaction hurt, but spoke more about Corin than her.

'That's "Alek" to you,' she said. 'Don't think of me as a woman or you'll forget in front of the others.' She ignored his proffered arm and started walking again. 'Besides, I've heard how many women find you entertaining, and I'd rather not be one more. I'll stay as Alek, thanks.'

'Ah.'

Was that regret? She couldn't be certain and didn't want to think about it. Corin might be charming and intelligent, but he was also a philandering hmar, with unknown allegiances and an unknown agenda. She'd do well to remember that each time he made her laugh at some joke; each time the warmth in his eyes made her stomach flutter. Her Jiaoji House teachers had warned against people who used charm to get what they wanted. But it was hard to keep that in mind when Corin smiled.

He stopped walking and tilted his head, eyes holding a hint of something that, annoyingly, made her heart race.

'So that's it?' he said. 'No room for anything else between us?'

Alere said nothing and Corin stepped forward. She backed away. He advanced again until her shoulders pressed against the cold basalt. Her quickened breath frosted the air between them, a barrier as insubstantial as her resolve to keep him at a distance. Her heart pounded for another reason now. She wasn't afraid. He wasn't the sort to overstep the mark, physically. Mentally, however, he affected her and knew it. He wasn't above using that attraction to his own advantage.

But what, exactly, did he want? Why did he chose now to ask if she was interested in more than friendship? He'd never shown anything beyond comradely affection before. Was it just another method of getting information from her?

Corin slid cool fingers into the hair at the nape of her neck, thumb brushing her cheek. He drew Alere closer until their lips were mere moments apart, breaths mingling, eyes locked. His held a heart-stopping mix of desire and, surprisingly, wariness. He pulled her close, his lean body warm and tempting. Her skin heated under his touch. Her back arched of its own accord. A faint smile curved his lips and one knee slid between hers. His hand stroked her back, slipping under her shirt. Electricity slickered across her skin and she sucked in a quick breath. Oh, yes.

Corin's lips brushed her cheek. Alere released the breath in a groan. Her hands shook and almost dropped her bow. Corin plucked it from her grasp and propped it and the arrows against the rock-face. His fingertips traced fire up the soft inner skin of her arm, all the way to her neck. He feathered a kiss under her jaw. Alere dug her nails into her palms, holding onto sanity.

'So?' he whispered, smiling with raffish confidence.

That assurance was like a dousing with cold water. Alere studied his handsome face. He believed her to be a jiaoji without the protection of her veil, so he could only be interested in short-term, physical pleasure; and possibly information. A veiled jiaoji held herself in deep respect and shared the intimacy of sex only to her contracted partner or where her heart was engaged. Casual liaisons undermined the esteem in which Jiaoji House was held. And one of the first jiaoji lessons was how to keep secrets, even in the afterglow.

Although Alere wasn't a true jiaoji, the House's philosophy was sound. Her training had given her pleasurable experiences with male and female jiaoji, and skill. But she wasn't prepared to unveil herself for a single night of enjoyment with a man who respected neither her nor himself. And Corin's certainty was his weakness. He didn't understand how well-trained jiaojis were; how controlled their reactions.

So, she stayed still beneath his hand; firmly suppressed the thrill of his touch; did *not* kiss him, however much she wanted to. With ruthless self-discipline, she ignored her body's clamouring and remained motionless, watching as he unbuttoned the top toggle of her jacket.

Corin caught her gaze and paused. A moment, thick with anticipation, passed. Then he released her. His brows contracted, more in puzzlement than anger.

She rebuttoned her jacket with trembling fingers.

'Yes,' she replied to his question, 'that's it. There's no room for anything between us.'

He said nothing. His face blanked and he stepped back, inclining his head like she'd politely refused tea.

'Don't forget your bow and arrows,' he said and headed towards camp.

Alere spoke sternly to the part of herself that registered disappointment.

They passed Hellor and parted ways; Corin, she presumed, to report to Jacksa while she climbed into a cold bed. Corin didn't return to his bedroll and her restless dreams were of him, Penon and Ven all tangled into one person, pursuing her relentlessly.

CHAPTER TWENTY-THREE

The next day brought a sharp wind off the snow-dusted slopes and the thin air froze into icy flurries. The orange sun rose late and weak in a pale, teal-green sky. Winter nipped with icy teeth at the caravan's heels. Jacksa urged the caravan onwards and glanced anxiously at the southern mountains where heavy grey clouds lurked low on the horizon.

Surprisingly, Corin joined Gavon and Alere in riding point to the top of the pass. Corin seemed unaffected by last night's events. He greeted Alere, smile undimmed, his eyes sparkling with amusement. Alere fell behind, leaving the men to converse. Snippets of conversation drifted to her – the possibility of snow, raiders, landslides and anticipation of the warm pleasures of Shanzhai. Not yet cleared for unarmed combat training, Alere was disgruntled to be denied even Gavon's scant words of advice. By the time they arrived at the top of Eagle Pass, she was panting, headachey and annoyed.

Gavon called a dismount to inspect the trail ahead. Alere slid from the saddle, suppressing a groan. She chewed on a jabal fern leaf and the headache and breathlessness eased. Rumi, her sides heaving, drank deeply of the water Alere poured into a stone depression by the roadside.

The men stood at the apex of the pass, using Corin's telescopes to study the route to Shanzhai. When Alere approached, Corin offered his scope and she accepted with an awkward murmur of thanks. How could he act as though nothing had happened? Clearly her assessment was right: she meant nothing to him.

She pushed aside hurt and focussed on the horizon, hunting for Shanzhai, still a week's slow travel away. Gavon pointed out the city, nothing more than a dirty smudge in the air above the horizon; the smoke from thousands of hearth fires.

She lowered the lens and looked north, to Madina, but it was out of sight behind the mountains. Northeast of Shanzhai, a dust-cloud dirtied the sky to ochre. She raised the scope expecting to see, perhaps, a caravan with huoche strung out along the northeasterly route to Madina. Instead, there appeared a dark, indistinguishable mass from which flashed the occasional gleam of metal.

Pointing, she passed the telescope back to Corin. 'What's that? I think it's on the Madina road. It's too spread out for a caravan. Looks to be about a four-day northeast of Shanzhai.'

Corin followed her finger and nudged Gavon. Both men directed their scopes and stilled as they found the target. Corin lowered the glass and snapped it shut.

'That wisix, saafil, gouri dog!' He gripped Gavon's shoulder. 'Gav, we need to warn Jacksa. He has to turn the caravan around. Head back to Newmec.'

'Aye,' Gavon growled. 'I think yer right, Cor. This looks nasty.'

He jogged over to Iblis, mounted and cantered downhill.

'No! I have to get to Shanzhai,' Alere said. 'What's going on, Corin? Who's a gouri dog?'

'Last night,' Corin said, his gaze intense. 'You said you were going to Shanzhai to prevent a war. What did you mean?' He grabbed her arms. 'What did you mean, Alere?'

The stone of realisation sank in her stomach. She stared over his shoulder at the smudged sky. 'No. She couldn't. She wouldn't!'

Corin's nails dug into her skin. 'What do you know? Who couldn't? If you're hoping to prevent a war, it may be too late.' He pointed. 'That's an army out there. Marching on Shanzhai. Why?'

Alere's knees weakened. She swayed, dizzy with altitude and shock, her eyes drawn again to the dust cloud and the ominous blackness below it. She clutched at Corin, shaking her head, not in answer to his question, but in denial of a reality too awful to contemplate. It couldn't be true. Had she failed? Was the Alcazar marching on Shanzhai? Was she too late?

No. She had to try. She owed it to Radan and to her yet-unknown father. Steadying herself, she straightened.

'I have to get to Shanzhai, Corin. I need to speak to Rafi Koh-Lin.'

Corin gave a sarcastic shout of laughter. 'The Jun? Why would he see you? What could you possibly have to tell him?' His green eyes narrowed. 'And why should Rafi trust you not to kill *him*?'

Alere flinched then frowned at him. Something in the way he said the Jun's name solidified suspicion into certainty. Corin could help. She had a hunch that telling the truth was worth the risk.

'I'm his daughter.' She lifted her chin.

'Lianna? But Lianna is...' Corin froze, his eyes widening. He released Alere's arms and rubbed at the back of his neck. 'No, not Lianna. Though I must be blind not to see the resemblance.' He slapped a hand to his forehead. 'Oh, how could I be so stupid? You even told me on the second night. Kin-child. Not to a noblewoman but to Rafi.'

His eyes glittered with excitement and some secret knowledge she had no hope of understanding. He cupped her jaw and inspected her features.

'Jahim! You're right. We need to get you to Shanzhai. Rafi must see you. You might do more than just prevent a war.' He shouted a laugh. 'I could kiss you right now, just for existing.'

Joy slipped from him and he released her. 'Is that why you turned me down last night? Because you're Rafi's kin-child and that makes you better?'

'No,' she retorted, shocked by the bitter tone and accusation.

Corin cocked his head, studying her. 'Why, then?'

'I...because...' She hesitated, unwilling to accuse him outright of being an untrustworthy womanizer when a large part of her didn't believe it to be true. Or didn't want it to be true.

He glanced towards Shanzhai and gave a self-deprecating chuckle. 'Y'know what? It doesn't matter. I'm a zift. Let's go. I'll take you to Rafi. That's more important, anyway.'

Bewildered by his mercurial mood changes, Alere gaped as Corin strode to his horse.

'Wait,' she called as he mounted. 'What do you mean by "more than just prevent a war"?'

'Ah.' His grin flashed, not reaching his eyes. 'You'll have to trust me – until we get to Shanzhai, at least.' He nudged the gelding and cantered down the road, leaving Alere confused and blinking in his dust.

She caught up just as Corin reached the caravan. The huoches had stopped, but were not yet moving downhill. Che-ma whickered, and camels grunted and stomped their feet. The spice otters set up a howling racket, clawing at their cages. When the handler tossed them handfuls of dried glass-rabbit meat and fish, it did nothing to abate the noise.

Alere and Corin arrived to find Jacksa in a one-sided argument with Gavon. Jacksa yelled and gestured emphatically, while Gavon waited in silence, arms folded. As Corin approached Gavon threw up his hands.

'Maybe ye'll listen to Cor, then, ye hundan,' he grumbled, stalking away.

'Get your gear,' Corin murmured to Alere, 'and mine too, please. Give me a few minutes to convince Jacksa that losing the profit on one run is better than dying in a war.'

Alere hurried away, dug out her gear and strapped it behind her saddle. She piled Corin's gear on the ground next to his horse and hurried to bid farewell to the men. She sought out Gavon last, reluctant to say goodbye, and found him roping sleeping gear onto Iblis's saddle.

'Where are you going? Jacksa'll need you more than ever, you know.' Surely he wasn't running away?

'Ye didn't think I'd let ye and that haraami, Corin, ride into a war without me, did ye? Yer not ready, boyo.' He cast an eye over Jacksa who fussed around the huoche carrying the most expensive trade goods. 'And I'm due for a change of scenery. I'm coming with ye.'

Alere hugged him, her heart full.

'Away with ye, boyo,' he said, and broke free with a scornful laugh, 'or I'll lose me reputation as a hard-hearted hundan.'

Alere dashed away to speak to Jacksa. The little merchant marched to the head of the caravan, cursing Corin's name and muttering about the difficulty in turning the huoches.

'There's a new landslip,' she said, pointing up the road, 'A big gouge from the inside slope ahead. Plenty of room if you go past the slip and turn the final huoche first.' Maybe having a solution to one problem would make him amenable to her next request.

'All right, all right.' he grumbled. 'But you make sure Corin knows that if this supposed war amounts to nothing, he can make up my profits by working free for the next four years. Kalima's never had a war yet. Why the jahim would anyone start one now?'

'I guess they never had a good enough reason or enough spare lives to expend.'

Jacksa sent her a sharp look and she regretted speaking. The merchant was smart and had a habit of noticing things most of his caravan staff preferred he didn't.

'Jacksa,' she said, smiling. Hopefully he wouldn't see through her now. She needed his help. 'I'll be going on ahead to Shanzhai with Corin and I need to get a message to my friends in the other caravan. How can I do it?' Alere leaned her head to the side, showing vulnerability and leaving an expectant silence for Jacksa to fill.

He growled in frustration, his dark eyes darting about the chaotic string of huoche. Two che-ma were tangled in their traces, and three tuo folded themselves to the ground, ignoring their handlers' orders to stand. A huoche hit a pothole and listed to one side, threatening to spill the valuable cargo of zitan wood.

Jacksa flicked a dismissive hand at her. 'Alright, alright. Ahkma and I do have one bird each that will home to the other. But a reply won't reach you before we part company.' He pointed at the bird huoche. 'Go see Haffa. He'll send the message. Tell your friend to pass on the news to Ahkma as well. You owe me, lad.'

She kissed him on the cheek, smiling at his shocked reaction. 'Take it from my pay. Thanks.'

At the bird-huoche, she scribbled a message to Kett in the childish code they'd developed years ago for fun. He'd remember the key. She sealed the message and attached it to the bird's leg. The bird soared into the sky. A light step sounded behind her.

'Who's that going to?' Corin's tone was sharp.

'Just my friends.' She laid a soothing hand on his arm. 'Kett was injured in Newmec and couldn't travel. They should be with

Ahkma's caravan. The message lets them know I'm carrying on to Shanzhai and why the caravan turned back. Nothing more.'

Corin pursed his lips and followed the vanishing dot in the sky. 'Will they join you, do you think? Is this task of yours as important to them?'

'I hope so,' she said. 'I don't want to put them in danger but I do miss...them.'

With a shake of his head, and a baffling hint of resignation in his expression, Corin added, 'Let's go. Gavon's waiting. I'd rather not get stuck helping Jacksa turn these monstrosities around.' He swung into the saddle and rode away without looking back.

Jacksa allowed Corin to take three extra horses and supplies, but his indignant demands for full payment followed Alere's party up the mountain.

At the top of Eagle Pass, Corin chose the more northerly of two well-trodden paths down the mountainside. By noon, he'd led Alere and Gavon to the bottom of the mountain. An hour later they passed through a neat village of stone and stout timber; a far cry from the slovenly destitution of Paradise.

Several people watched them go by, some greeting Corin and Gavon by name. A middle-aged woman, slender and with sparkling dark eyes, appeared at the window of what was obviously a brothel. She called to Corin, twitched open the front of her pink robe to expose more cleavage and blew him a kiss. Corin responded with a wave and, with amazing accuracy, threw a small, paper-wrapped parcel straight into her hands. She blew him another kiss and disappeared inside.

Alere gritted her teeth. Corin's love-life was none of her business. She'd made a choice last night and had no right to be jealous. She pretended not to see the speculative look Corin sent her way.

Having six horses allowed the travellers to ride further than with only three, so Corin called a halt only when exhaustion set in and the horses needed rest. He drove them on until darkness crept across the land and brought biting cold. Even then he paused only long enough to light a torch that illuminated the white-painted road markers. Alere sagged in the saddle; numb with cold, the world sliding into dreams that dragged her eyes closed. She woke with Corin holding her upright as she swayed in the saddle. Rumi plodded along the road, head down, breath heavy and short.

'Stay with me,' Corin said. 'Not much further tonight.'

'It's here.' Gavon's rough voice called from the gloom ahead. 'Looks empty.'

Alere raised heavy eyelids. Just off the road, a travellers' shelter caught the torchlight. The hut was a simple cube of black stone, roofed with timber shingles and secured by a weather-beaten door. The finest inn had never appeared so welcoming. Gavon disappeared inside. Moments later, flickering orange firelight glowed through the gap under the door.

'Here.' Corin appeared beside Alere, hands upraised to help her dismount.

She was so tired she didn't cavil, but when Corin's fingers pressed into her ribs, she gasped.

'Gaisi! I'm sorry.' He snatched his hands away. 'Go inside. Rest. I'll take care of Rumi.' He unstrapped Alere's bag, passed it to her and vanished behind the hut, leading all six horses.

Alere stood on the dark road, shivering, her mind hazy with fatigue. She lifted her face and her breath obscured the starry brushstrokes that lit the dark canvas overhead. What was she doing? This trip was madness. What if she went through all this and Rafi wouldn't see her, or wouldn't listen? What if he despised kin-children as much as the rest of the Jundom now did? Or if he thought her a threat to his rule or that of his legitimate Jun-Heir, Lianna? But she'd promised Radan, and Kett. She had little choice but to continue.

Inside the hut, Gavon already had a pot, filled with the makings of lu-deer stew, over the fire. Alere vacillated, drawn by the thought of lying flat. Gavon levelled an expectant look at her. She went to help Corin with the horses. Only sheer, stubborn determination got her through the job of unloading, feeding and currying the animals. She stumbled as she left the stable and Corin caught her up, an arm firm around her waist.

'Thanks,' she mumbled, resting her head on his shoulder.

He kissed the top of her head. 'Zift.'

CHAPTER TWENTY-FOUR

When Corin shook her awake the next morning, Alere was too sleepy to snatch at the dagger under her pillow. The three travellers took to the road with the first red light of dawn teasing the sky. By late evening, when the horses trudged into the next stop, even Gavon showed signs of exhaustion, his brows almost meeting over his nose and bloodshot eyes. Corin had been silent for most of the day, his mouth set in a grim line each time he looked towards Shanzhai or beyond to the faint dust haze northeast of the city.

Alere was past noticing much of anything. Her ribs ached and her head pounded with each heavy step as Rumi stumbled into the stable yard of a small, wayside inn. With a grateful pat, she left Rumi in the hands of the stableboy and followed Corin into the building.

Corin escorted Alere to a room and handed over the key. She pressed a thumb to her forehead.

'Headache? Attar said you have willow-bark and to stop being a little zift and take it.' Corin laughed when she rolled her eyes. '*I* don't think you need mothering, don't get annoyed at me.'

She hadn't the strength for a witty comeback.

'I'll have them send food up.' Corin squeezed her shoulder. 'Get some sleep. Only a short ride tomorrow morning. We'll be at the city around mid-morning, even with a sleep-in.'

'Will you take your own advice?'

He shrugged, saluted and strolled off in the direction of the taproom. Alere envied his boundless energy.

The bed beckoned and she sank willingly into its cool, damp sheets without removing her clothing or waiting for dinner.

Not long after mid-morning, Rumi splashed through the Kuaisu River ford, a few gongli south of Shanzhai. The freezing water spattered Alere's face, soaked her legs and roused her from a half-doze. She shaded her eyes and peered at the track ahead. The road emerged from the ford and speared across a wide floodplain, up a shallow escarpment, onto a grassy plateau. As the horses topped the final rise, Shanzhai appeared in the distance and Alere groaned in relief.

The city began as a scattered collection of sulcrete-brick or sandstone houses strung out along the road. Children played in the shade of huge yilder trees. Behind each house small vegetable patches backed onto larger cultivated fields of rich, dark-red soil, now fallow as winter approached.

Closer to the town's protective wall, the dirt road became cobbles and bigger buildings appeared. Metal rang on metal as a smith hammered at bronze in his open workshop. The scent of bread, from the bakery next door, made Alere's mouth water. A stout woman flung open the red shutters on a white-washed inn and shook out a rug. Dust motes sparkled in the sun.

Corin led the way through the south gate of the city's massive stone wall. Inside, buildings grew atop one another and shops outnumbered dwellings. Tables and display shelves bore delicate glassware in translucent reds and blues, or ranks of brilliantly dyed leather shoes that made Alere conscious of her worn boots. The unpleasant odour of raw meat and blood wafted from a butcher's shop, where a pig carcass hung in the window. A fine soprano voice, lifted in song, floated from the window of a shop selling musical instruments.

Rumi shied as an orange-clad runner leapt a pile of horse-dung, dodged a laden huoche and dashed across the street. A crier shouted news of Jun-Heir Lianna Koh-Lin's eighteenth name-day celebration in three days. Alere grimaced. What would her half-sister say to the appearance of an older kin-sibling? Would Rafi introduce Lianna to Alere or even let Alere into the castle? She thrust aside the thought.

As the crowds swelled, so did the smells and noise. Overwhelmed, Alere glanced back at the clean, snowy mountain peaks. How had she borne the squalor and press of Madina for so long? But, in all fairness, the two cities were poles apart. Shanzhai had fewer beggars and the people walked with a purpose. Bamboo scaffolding spoke of new construction and growth. The paved streets were clean, the timber and stone houses tidy and well kept. When Alere commented on the lack of filth, Gavon pointed out great wooden plates set into the street.

'Sewers and storm drains,' he said. 'The Jun who founded Shanzhai six hundred years ago spent a lot of time and effort building them under the city.'

'Madina's got sewers,' Alere said.

'Oh, I know.' Corin said. 'I've spent quite a lot of time in them. Believe me, the ones in Madina are crap, if you'll forgive the pun.'

Gavon groaned. 'He means Madina wasn't planned. It grew in a hurry at the Landing Site, so its infrastructure isn't as good. And not well-maintained. The Jun First's spent no money on the city in decades. The folk here are grateful to the Koh-Lin family.' He jerked his chin at a towering black-stone castle that came into view as they rounded a corner.

The castle seemed to grow out of the hill, but its angular rooflines cut, sharp and clean, across the bright sky.

'It certainly dominates the city,' Alere said.

'Shanzhai folks call it "the watcher",' Corin said. 'You get used to it.'

Shaking off the fanciful notion that the castle did, indeed, watch her, Alere followed Corin to The Ploughman, a double-storey stone inn with leaded-glass windows and ornate timber-work. Although not yet lunchtime, the inn was alive with laughter and the clink of cups. Corin dismounted and tied the horses to a hitching post.

'Is this really the time for a drink? Shouldn't we...?' Alere pointed at the castle.

'We need information before barging in and demanding to see the Jun.'

'Like?' Alere swung down from the saddle and looped Rumi's reins over a post.

'Like: what the townsfolk are thinking; the mood of the city. If there's a war coming, the people of Shanzhai will probably know it before word gets to the castle.' Corin grinned. 'Besides, I'm thirsty and what's life without a mug of ale and a little adventure.'

'Free of headaches and injuries?' Alere muttered, pressing her aching ribs.

'And how dull that would be.' Corin pushed her gently towards the door.

Gavon grunted and pointed across the road. 'I see the new House is finished.'

Opposite the inn, Messenger House buzzed with activity as dozens of orange-clad runners and riders scurried in and out of the two-storey stone and timber edifice, bearing communications across the city and the Jundom. A nearby flitter-bird cote added to the noise as a constant stream of birds circled and croaked to each other.

'And,' Corin said, leading the way inside the crowded tavern, 'Rafi's approved laying those experimental copper wires. If they work as the Messenger House Master claims, within a few weeks we could have almost instant communication between the House and the Castle.'

'Copper wires?' Alere shed her cloak in the too-warm room and sat with her back to the wall, both exits in sight. She coughed. A smoky haze hung against the ceiling.

Corin remained standing, his gaze travelling around the room. 'Old technology rediscovered, apparently. Something to do with using electricity and copper wires to transmit messages. I heard Petar Ma-Safra's already using it in Jiali. Word is he went against his Xintou's advice and is laying a line right through to Messenger House in Madina.'

'Petar defied Elmira?' Alere frowned. 'But that's...' She faked a cough and hid behind her hand.

'You know them?' Corin's curious gaze flicked to her face.

'I was jiaoji at court, remember.'

Gavon raised bushy brows. Alere flushed, glad of the distraction when a barmaid plonked three mugs of dark ale onto the table.

'There's a lot of common folk who think the xintou have too much control,' Corin said mildly. 'That the world needs to change and Xintou House is holding us back from progress.'

'But Mistress Li is—' Alere snapped her jaw shut and looked away. She no longer had a clue what Mistress Li's agenda might entail, but the idea that everyday people were beginning to distrust the House was disquieting.

'Wait.' Corin's eyes narrowed. 'Elmira…*Connor*. Is she your—'

'No!' She glared at him.

His frown deepened. He leaned over the table and lowered his voice. 'Are you a xi—'

'No,' she said more quietly, staring at her own hands, clenched on the table. 'No. Just leave it, Cor.' It still hurt. For so long wanting, *aching* to be xintou, only to have even the hope of it finally stripped away with Elmira's admission. Now she was so close to finding her real family. What if they rejected her, too? Or wanted to use her, as Mistress Li did?

Corin hesitated, then squeezed her shoulder. He addressed Gavon. 'Gav. Watch for my signal. Excuse me. There's someone I need to speak to.' He threaded his way between tables to the other side of the room and struck up a light-hearted conversation with a weishi clad in dark green and silver – Koh-Lin family colours. Gavon, too, wandered away from the table.

Alere sighed, put aside useless resentment against Elmira, and studied the room. The taproom was large, with whitewashed walls and high ceilings. The scent of roast pork and baking sweet pies almost masked smells of old alcohol and vomit. Square timber tables were crammed with people eating and Alere's stomach rumbled. Several diners wore the orange messenger uniform with the embroidered horse or shoe symbol indicating their rider or runner status.

Content to be still, Alere watched the comings and goings of the messengers across the road. She sipped the ale, half-hypnotised by the systematic streams of orange, trying to imagine a world with runners replaced by wires.

Corin slid onto the hard bench opposite Alere and almost inhaled the tankard waiting for him. After the last mouthful, he winked and gestured Alere closer.

'See the two men, three tables behind me?' He laughed as though she'd said something amusing. Alere chuckled, going along with the deception. Her gaze slid around the room until it brushed over the men in question.

She'd already seen them and noted the watchfulness of professional weishi, at odds with the tavern's jovial atmosphere; marked them as potential threats. Although a low fire in the eastern wall-hearth warmed the room, both men wore cloaks and nursed their tankards but didn't drink. They wore black, with no identifying House, family, or trade affiliation colours. Ronin weishi, perhaps, looking for work?

One turned and said something to his companion. Alere stiffened and averted her face, kicking herself for showing even that much of a reaction.

'What?' Corin murmured, raising his tankard.

Alere did the same, hiding her mouth. 'I recognise one of them. His name's Prato. He was weishi at the Alcazar. I don't think he'll recognise me. I bumped into him once, but always wore the veil.'

Prato rose from his seat. Alere rubbed at her forehead, pretending to study the people in the street. He neared her table and she slid a hand to the dagger at her hip. Corin shook his head a fraction. Prato paused, his black-trousered leg a mere hands-breadth from Alere's shoulder. His hand rested on the hilt of his sword.

'The privy?' Prato addressed a barmaid weaving through the tables.

The barmaid pointed to the back of the room and Prato strode off.

Alere relaxed and Corin grinned, watching the weishi's back.

'Excellent. Ven's sent a few spies ahead. I was hoping we'd find some here. Let's give them a rousing welcome.' Corin pointed at his jaw. 'When he comes back, hit me.'

'What?' Exhaustion must have affected her hearing. 'Don't get me wrong, I'm happy to, but it'd be nice to know why.'

'I'm sure you can think of a few reasons,' Corin said. 'But right now, you're going to start a brawl.'

'Oh, good. I was worried it'd be something stupid.'

'Just hit me, will you?'

'Well, remember you asked for this,' Alere said.

'Once the fight's going,' Corin added, 'Gavon – who is lurking inconspicuously in the corner – will help me get those two men out without anyone noticing. I'll whistle when we're ready. Got it?'

Prato returned to his table.

Corin put down his cup. 'And do try not to kill anyone. Rafi doesn't like that kind of thing. Come on.'

Alere leapt up. She raised her voice over the hubbub and pointed accusingly at Corin. 'Say that again, you gouri kalet!'

Corin shot to his feet and faced her in the clear path between tables. 'You're a cheat and a liar Alek Marin-kin. You owe me fifty yinbi and I want payment *now.*' He thumped the table. The cups jumped. Patron's heads whipped around.

Recognising her cue, Alere swung a big roundhouse punch with her right hand. Her knuckles skimmed his cheek. She slapped her own thigh to mimic the sound of a punch. Corin turned his face and staggered back with a hand to his jaw.

'You gouri hundan!' Corin launched himself at her.

She sidestepped and let him fly past. He crashed onto an adjoining table. Drinks, chairs and food flew into the air, drenching everything and everyone close by.

'Hey!' A thickset man in Trades House brown shook ale from his hands.

People scattered like panicked herd-beasts. The barkeeper waved his arms in a futile attempt to stop the fight. Corin clawed his way upright and leapt at Alere again, hands outstretched. She grabbed his arm and head and threw him at the two Alcazar weishi. He did a neat forward roll then tripped over Prato's outstretched foot. Prato rose, yelling abuse. Corin came up swinging and drove a fist into the weishi's stomach. Prato folded, his mouth opening and closing like a landed straight-eel. His partner shouted and grabbed at Corin. Gavon jumped into the fray. Alere left them to it. Now was the time for that diversion.

Behind her, the tradesman, whose table was now kindling, tossed his empty tankard aside.

'You guisunzi!' he yelled. 'You can pay for that.'

He set up to throw a punch at Alere's head. His movements were so slow and obvious she didn't react. It must be a feint. No, apparently not. He swung. She stepped inside his reach, cupped her hand under his jaw and shoved his head back and down. He flailed backwards, tripped on an upturned chair and crashed onto the broken table.

Corin and Gavon were still working on the Alcazar weishi. Chaos rippled through the room. Punches, glasses and chairs flew. The noise faded to a background roar as Alere's heart hammered in her ears.

A tradesman with a crooked nose glared at Alere. 'That's my friend, you little hundan.' He moved forward on light feet, raising fists to guard his face.

Jiche! Someone who knew how to box. The shakes hit as adrenalin pumped into her system. She rotated her shoulders and neck and drew a long, slow breath. Time to finish this fast and get the diyu out.

With her footing secure on the slippery floor, she relaxed her vision to catch peripheral movement. What were her options? He was almost twice her weight and a good head taller, ugly as diyu and stinking of jiu. He jabbed and she swayed aside, judging his speed and strength. Closed-fisted punching was stupid. He probably wouldn't even feel her best punch and she'd break a few hand-bones. And there was no space to sweep his leg.

A tankard flew past her head. She ducked and used the motion to snatch up a full jug. She dashed the contents into the face of her would-be attacker.

He blinked and shook his head, his fingers opening and relaxing. Alere grabbed his jaw with one hand, his hair with the other and yanked his head back. A leg sweep unbalanced him. She let go. The big man windmilled backwards, squawking like an angry flitter. His head hit the table and he shuddered into unconsciousness.

A shrill whistle pierced the melee, barely registering through the wall of noise. Someone grabbed Alere's shoulder. She drove an elbow up and back. It connected with something fleshy-hard and breakable. A man in miner grey staggered away, blood dribbling from his wrecked nose.

A nearby window exploded in a shower of glass and broken timber. Between Alere and the door was a field of thrashing, flailing, screaming bodies. Corin and Gavon had vanished, along with the two Alcazar weishi. Exit time. She snatched up her cloak, leapt onto a bench and scrambled through the broken window, kicking out shards of glass still wedged in the frame.

Outside, she leant against the inn's stone wall, took three long breaths and rode the blood-rush, trying to settle her heart.

'You going to stand there all day?' Corin smiled and leaned forward in his saddle. 'We have things to do and people to see, you know.' Draped across two of the spare horses were the bound, unconscious weishi.

Corin's smile changed to concern. 'There's blood on your arm.'
Alere checked. 'Not mine.'

She grabbed a fistful of a prisoner's hair and inspected him. Prato. A sharp, chemical scent clung to his clothes and caught in her throat. She let his head fall and brushed dark dust off her fingers. Her knees trembled but she managed to climb into the saddle without falling and nudged Rumi forward. The noise of the brawl faded. Her heart slowed. Did it ever get easier?

Corin led the way through crowded streets and halted at the castle gates. Alere studied them with interest. Heavily guarded and thick, the curtain wall and gate looked impenetrable. If Corin worked for Rafi, as she assumed, getting inside should be straightforward.

Corin's grin became quizzical. 'Out of curiosity, how would you get through, Alek?'

Gavon laughed.

'What's funny?' Alere eyed him quizzically.

'Asked me the same question the first time I came here, boyo,' Gavon said. One of the prisoners groaned and Gavon tapped him over the head with a dagger-pommel.

'What'd you say?'

'I said I wouldn't.' Gavon shaded his eyes and squinted up at the castle. 'Who wants to be inside that monstrosity? Give me the road any day.'

Alere laughed but didn't agree. The castle was beautiful in its own way: solid and imposing. White sulcrete mortar between the black basalt blocks gave the building a sharp, angular strength that contrasted with the soft gold sandstones and rich violet bamboos of other Shanzhai buildings. She looked forward to seeing the interior; and to having a decent bath.

'If it was just me trying to get in, then runner,' she said. 'Even your weishi are conditioned to give right-of-way to the orange. Daily passwords are good, but I guarantee I could get the password and a uniform.'

'I'll bet you could.' Corin chuckled. 'Thank you. I'll keep that in mind when we next discuss castle security – which I think will be quite soon. Let's go. Oh, you'll need to hand over your sword at the door, too.'

Alere waited until Corin's back was turned, then tucked her dagger into her boot. Gavon sent her a half-smile and a nod.

He kicked his horse into motion, following Corin. As Corin approached the gate, the weishi on guard snapped to attention, saluted and, without question, opened the huge timber panels. Not just an itinerant musician, then.

Inside the courtyard, Corin gave directions to a servant.

'Take these two to the cells.' He dismounted and pointed at the prisoners. 'Gavon, go with them and supervise. They're weishi so make sure you find every gaisi hidden weapon. We need them alive to interrogate.' He grabbed Alere's hand. 'You're coming with me.'

'Where?'

The massive front doors swung open and Corin towed her towards the gaping castle entrance.

'To see your father.'

CHAPTER TWENTY-FIVE

Alere hesitated on the threshold and, seized with sudden dread, wrenched free of Corin's grip. This was the ancestral home of the Koh-Lin family. Jun Seconds, not just any householder. Could Corin really get her an audience or was he all bluff? And if he arranged a meeting, would Rafi reject her – would he even hear her out? She was kin-child; most-despised rank; illegal amongst Jun. Her very existence endangered his family.

She ran a hand over the zitan-wood front doors. Their ornate, geometric carvings and rich red timber made an imposing entrance. Once inside, with the doors closed behind, she'd be committed. She glanced at Corin, who waited a few steps away with brows raised in question.

What if this was a trap? Corin knew her identity. What if he handed her over to Rafi for murdering the Jun First? Handing over Radan's killer to Ven Zah-Hill would put Rafi in favour with the new Jun First. Alere's heart stuttered. Had she trusted Corin too far?

'Coming?' he asked, his expression one of mild concern. No guile in his green eyes, but he was an exceptional liar.

'I...' She glanced over her shoulder at the bright freedom outside. A servant swung shut one of the great doors. The thud rang with chilling finality through the vast hall.

'It's all right,' Corin said. 'I promise.'

Alere threw back her shoulders, quashed the sick trepidation in her stomach, and stepped inside.

The second door closed and she hesitated again, oppressed by the heavy strength of the room. The black basalt walls were a spear's thickness, with narrow, high windows. A bronze chandelier hung from the arched timber ceiling and illuminated the room with shimmering gold light from fine glass bulbs. On one wall hung a tapestry depicting a scene from the landing of the colonists on Kalima; thousands of brilliantly-coloured figures pouring from spaceships against a backdrop of dark blue foliage and pale green sky. Alere touched the images, awed.

The temptation to wander around the castle distracted her. She spun in a circle, trying to absorb everything. A fire crackled in a hearth in the western wall giving off the sweet smell of burning yar-pine logs. The hall held none of the soft opulence of the Ma-Safra family estate with its airy gardens, white walls and purple bamboo floors. Nor was it austerely functional, like the golden sandstone of Xintou House. The Koh-Lin house managed to be both homelike and intimidating.

Corin grinned and indicated a wide timber staircase that swept up to a mezzanine floor overlooking the hall.

'You'll have time to explore, later,' he said, heading up the risers. 'C'mon. This way.'

She ran her fingertips along the smooth stair-rail – perfect for childhood sliding – and took the stairs two at a time, catching up with Corin. On the mezzanine, thick timber railings with measured gaps provided a clear line of sight to the front door and protection for hidden archers. Ironic that, on a supposedly peaceful colony, this building was designed by a warrior.

Corin knocked at a plain timber door five paces from the top of the stairs.

'Wait here,' he said, and disappeared inside.

Alere brushed at her dusty clothing, assailed again by a rush of uncertainty. Picking at the sticky gum on her top lip, she teased off the moustache.

What if Rafi wouldn't listen? What if he was ambitious, like Hanna, and wanted the iron deposit himself? Maybe it would be wise to discover more about the Jun Second before handing him the key to power in this region. Maybe she should do as Kett always advised: stop and think before rushing in. Bit late now.

A hand gripped her left shoulder. 'Who are y—'

She drove an elbow back in a defensive reflex. Black-and-green colours of the Koh-Lin house weishi flashed into view. House weishi. She changed what began as an elbow strike into an arm-bar, but couldn't stop the leg sweep that dropped the man to the floor. His head cracked against the floorboards and he lapsed into unconsciousness. Alere released his arm and bit her lip. Knocking out the house weishi was not a good start. What now?

'You!' Two unarmed weishi appeared on the balcony.

'Wait.' Alere held up open palms.

They ignored her gesture and leapt over their fallen companion. Alere spun aside and drove an elbow into the ribs of one, shoving him into the other. They fell in a jumbled heap against the wall.

She tried again. 'Just give me a chance—'

An arm snaked over her shoulder, trying to get a sleeper hold on her neck. She dropped her hips and grabbed the arm and a little finger. A hip throw sent him crashing to the floor. His finger bone snapped. He screamed and clutched at his hand. Alere dodged a fifth man's swinging truncheon. It caught her shoulder. Pain lanced through her arm and numbed it.

She backed away and raised empty hands. 'Look, I don't want to fight—'

The truncheon-wielder growled and struck at her head. She swore, ducked inside his strike and drove the heel of her palm into his cheek, snapping his head back. She caught his arm and hurled him into the pile of moaning bodies.

The sound of running feet and shouts echoed in the hall. Five armed weishi sprinted up the stairs, swords drawn. Her dagger was hidden inside her boot. Alere wanted to avoid killing, but it was harder to not fatally injure. Leaving enemies at her back went against her training, but killing the Jun's weishi would hardly endear her to Rafi.

Four more men appeared at the opposite end of the mezzanine floor behind her, blades out.

Alere edged away from the fallen weishi, who were struggling to their feet.

'I've got a message for the Jun Second,' she called out. 'I'm not a threat. Your man just surprised me.'

The leader hesitated, scowled at his fallen comrades and signalled to his companions to fan out.

Alere swore under her breath and glanced over the railing at the stone floor below. Too far to jump. Two pairs of hands seized her arms. She didn't resist. There was no point. She was outnumbered and someone would die if she fought back – possibly her. A knife blade appeared at her throat, the bronze tip pressing into her skin. She froze.

She'd trusted Corin. Had he betrayed her?

The lead weishi glanced over her shoulder, His eyes widened and he lowered his weapon. The others followed suit.

'Thank you, gentlemen, but your diligence is unnecessary. The lad's with me. Let him go, please.'

Corin's request triggered an instant release of her arms. Yes, he was far more than a musician, and probably more than a spy.

Relieved, Alere massaged blood back into her fingers and tried not to glare at the weishi as they skulked off.

Corin leaned against a timber-panelled wall, hands deep in his pockets. Behind him, the door to the Jun's conference room stood open.

'You are *very* good, you know.'

'You could've warned them to leave me alone before all this,' she said.

He chuckled. 'I did mean to, but it slipped my mind in the hurry to see Rafi. Besides, it was amusing to watch. Thank you for being so restrained, by the way. Do come inside where we won't be overheard. Hopefully, you won't be tempted to kill anyone – apart from me, of course.' He waved her into the room. 'Rafi'll be back in a second.'

The subdued, masculine luxury of the room was daunting. Dark-timbered walls, crowded with portraits, rose to a high, white-painted ceiling. A gleaming zitan-wood table dominated the room, its deep red hue adding warmth to the dark space. Alere's dusty boots sank into a rug swirled with abstract greens and silvers. There were no windows or other exits, which made Alere uneasy.

Corin tugged off Alere's worn leather cap and studied her. He glanced behind her, laughed ruefully and shook his head.

'Khara! There's hope yet. Stay right there.' He pressed a section of timber panelling at the back of the room. A door slid open. 'Come in, shenshi.'

The man who strode in was familiar and yet a stranger. Alere had seen him, once, at court during her short stay at the Alcazar. Glimpsed through a screen as she spied on the formal proceedings, she'd known him then simply as Jun Second Rafi Koh-Lin. Now she knew him as her father.

Unlike many older rich men, he had kept his youthful fitness, moving with the grace of a trained fighter. His clothes were dark green and silver; Chala San colours, but severely cut and functional. One wrist was cocked in the manner of someone used to wearing a sword, although he was now unarmed.

Rafi stopped short, his sapphire eyes widening. He glanced at something behind her and his expression shifted from surprise to disbelief. He paled. The hand he swept over his short, dark hair trembled. His eyes fixed on Alere but he said nothing.

'Shenshi.' Corin bowed. 'This is Alere.'

Regret flickered in Rafi's eyes and pain momentarily shadowed his face before he straightened and hid behind a mask of urbanity.

Hurt snaked through Alere's chest. He didn't want to acknowledge her. She was a disappointment. This meeting was a mistake.

'*This* is the girl you met in the caravan?' Rafi's voice was deep and quiet, but not weak; a man deliberately controlling his ability to intimidate. A hint of humour lit his eyes. 'And you travelled in close quarters for three weeks and didn't recognise her?'

Corin laughed. 'I'm sorry shenshi, I'm a fool and a zift. The first day we met I thought she was familiar. Then she practically told me who she was, and I still didn't make the connection. I think I'm getting old.'

Alere repressed the urge to remind them she was still in the room and kept her expression blank. Her throat ached with held-back questions.

Rafi raised his eyes to the wall behind her. Again, a fleeting look of deep pain followed. Unable to resist any longer, Alere turned…and her jaw dropped. A portrait of a young, dark-haired woman hung on the wall. Alere stepped back to take in the whole picture, unable to process its meaning. The woman in the painting wore an indigo ball dress with a silvery gauze wrap around her plump shoulders. An emerald and sapphire pin glittered in her elaborately curled hair. Her dark eyes sparkled with mischief.

'But...' Alere whispered, 'that's...'

'Yes.' Rafi's voice was strained. 'The resemblance is remarkable, but it's not you, my dear. That's your half-sister, Lianna.'

Weak-kneed, Alere clutched at the table. 'You know who I am?'

'Your face told me.' Rafi pulled out a chair. 'Sit, we have much to discuss. Corin? Kindly ask the servants to serve lunch in here. You may join us, for I believe this concerns you as well.'

Corin bowed himself out, winking at Alere as he closed the door.

Alone with her father, Alere sank into a chair, finding her tongue intractable. Rafi's expression softened.

'I know how you feel.' He reached towards her, then stopped. Another glance at the portrait and his eyes returned to Alere.

'You look as she should.' His words were cryptic, bitter. He ran a hand over his face and seemed to regain his poise, though his smile was slightly forced. 'Although that's not a surprise, given who your mother is. Before we bring you to meet your aunt, Yasmin, tell me how Sura fares? Is she alive and happy?'

'I...she...I hardly know her, shenshi,' she admitted, confused by his rapid changes of emotion. 'But last I saw her, less than a month ago, she was safe enough.'

The door opened and Corin entered the room. Lacking his usual flamboyance, he dropped into a chair. His encouraging half-smile helped ease her tension.

Rafi cleared his throat and she flushed.

'How is it you hardly know your own mother?' Rafi leaned forward, intent. 'Why? And are you, as Corin says, the Alere Connor for whom the Alcazar is searching?'

Alere nodded and lifted her chin.

'How did Radan die?' Rafi's tone was calm, but he studied her narrowly.

'I...' How did she begin?

'Shenshi,' Corin said, leaning forward, 'if I—'

'I'm not going to attack her, Cor, so keep silent for once.' Rafi waved him off. 'I'm sorry, child. I know you're exhausted. Let's begin with something easier. Corin tells me you know something of this army of five thousand junren at my doorstep. Ven's message says they're an honour escort for his visit for Lianna's eighteenth name day.' Rafi's expression hardened. 'Should I doubt that?'

'Yes, shenshi,' she said. 'You should.' With one last look at Corin, Alere launched into a shortened version of her life, and her two weeks in the Alcazar – leaving out her part in Radan's suicide, Nasra and Rohne's existence, and the iron deposit. The iron's existence was so disturbing she wasn't sure how to share the information, or how deeply Rafi trusted Corin.

A servant delivered laden trays of pork dumplings and steamed, spiced kasa-root, but Alere couldn't bear the thought of eating. She was too unsettled; waiting for a judgment to be called on her life; on herself.

'Separated from your twin. I'm sorry, my dear child,' Rafi said, laying his hand over hers. 'If I'd been able to give you a different life, one less...isolating, I would have. Sending Sura into hiding was the right choice at the time.'

Uncomfortable that he'd seen so clearly what she'd tried to conceal, Alere withdrew her hand, stood, and paced the room.

'I didn't tell you all that to gain your pity,' she said. 'Only because you asked. I am who I am because of that choice and I'm glad of it.' She swallowed bitterness, dragged the cloth-wrapped bracelet from a pocket and tossed it on the table. 'Here – the bracelet.'

She turned away, angry at herself for wanting more and but not quite knowing what. Given her birth-status, any formal acknowledgment was impossible and they both knew it. Disappointment fisted in her stomach. She would get no approval from Rafi and had been stupid to hope for it.

Radan touched the bracelet and sighed heavily. He shook himself, his jaw firming. 'Tell me again what Radan said when he gave this to you?'

'He said: the gift is the key. I don't think he knew what he'd created. Surely he couldn't have? It could change...' she shrugged. 'He didn't finish that sentence. Then he said: Whatever you do, keep it safe and get it back to your father. He must destroy it.'

Rafi ran his thumbs across the gleaming yanstones.

'There's more, isn't there,' he said. 'None of this explains Ven's unexpected visit. He's not here for Lianna's name-day, is he?' He briefly covered his eyes. 'Come, tell me what else Radan said. It's important I know. He wouldn't have sent you on such a dangerous journey for the sake of a piece of jewelry.'

Rafi followed Alere's doubtful glance at Corin and chuckled low in his throat. He laid a hand on Corin's shoulder. 'You mustn't mind Corin. He may seem an unreliable kaddaab, but I'd trust him with my life. He's been my eyes and ears in the land for many years. No-one knows the tenor of the Jundom better.' With a condescending nod to Alere he added. 'You may speak your mind and it won't go beyond this room.'

With a short laugh, she folded her arms. 'I think the question is more whether he trusts me, shenshi. After all, why should either of you? I might be your kin-child, but aren't I also the jiaoji who murdered the Jun First and Mistress Renna?'

'Ah, I see,' Rafi said, wryly. 'Allow me to put your mind at ease. Before you interrupted our conference by proving my house guard to be ineffective bunglers, Corin had just finished briefing me on his latest trip with Jacksa's caravan.'

Corin picked up a roast fowl leg, tearing into it with apparent unconcern.

'In fact,' Rafi continued, 'he told me he'd met the girl rumoured to have killed Radan, and didn't believe it to be true. He trusts you and if he trusts you then I do.'

Alere grasped at a chair back, disturbed by the depth of both her guilt and relief. Had Corin got so far into her heart as all that? Since the incident at the raider compound she'd suspected much of his behaviour to be a front, but what about his reputation with women? Was that a lie, too? The image of Radan's brittle fingers, wrapped around the dagger hilt, intruded and she shuddered. It didn't matter. She had no time for romance and Corin's faith was unfounded. She was unworthy of it – she *had* killed the Jun. Corin and Rafi must never know.

'Very well.' She resumed pacing the room. It settled her nerves. 'Hanna, Ven and Celia poisoned Radan.'

'Khara!' Corin's chair legs hit the ground with a thump.

'Poisoned!' Rafi's fingers clenched into a fist. 'I knew he was ill, but poison? But I thought you said he'd killed himself?' Suspicion crept into his tone.

Alere scrubbed her hands together, but nothing would remove the memory of Radan's blood, slippery on the knife handle; or his rheumy eyes watching her as his life faded away. Would she ever be able to tell someone the truth of that moment? Corin frowned across the table at her and she shook free of the useless guilt.

'Yes,' she said, 'but only because he knew he was so weak that Celia would break through his Inners and find out…'

'Find out what?' Rafi prompted.

'Hanna said they were in debt to Shah Jahil.' Alere ignored the question. Part of her was afraid to reveal the iron existed. What if Radan had misjudged Rafi? 'Hanna wants to stop the Shah raiding Mamlakah's borders. Then she talked about controlling the *selb* fanatics, whoever they are.'

Corin rubbed the back of his neck and glanced at his Jun.

'I see.' Rafi's brow furrowed. 'But how does that relate to your visit here? Tell me: what did Celia need to find out from Radan?'

'Ven's here for the same reason Radan was poisoned – there's an iron deposit on your lands,' she stated. 'They must've guessed it's here, somewhere. Ven's at your gates to force you to give it up. They intend to overthrow Xintou House and use the iron deposit to make war on Melcor.'

Rafi displayed no shock or horror, but only exchanged a heavy look with Corin. The Jun Second slipped the yanstone bracelet restlessly through his fingers then lay it on the table, smoothing and lining each link up in perfect order.

'You knew,' she said, leaning over and placing her hands on the table. 'You already knew about the deposit?'

'I feared that might be the reason for Ven's sudden arrival. Thank you for the warning, my dear. You may leave this unsettling news with me.' Rafi touched the bracelet. 'As for this bracelet, it was meant as a gift for Sura. She must have misunderstood. Yasmin has its match. If Sura gave it away, that explains why—' He snapped his lips shut, rose and bowed to Alere across the table. 'You've discharged your duty with honour, Alere.'

'Shenshi,' Corin said. 'Perhaps she can—'

'This is my decision now, Cor. I won't endanger her further.'

'What do you mean?' Alere asked. 'I can what?'

'Nothing.' Rafi scrubbed at his dark hair.

'But, shenshi,' Corin said, gesturing vaguely northeast. 'If you refuse Ven entry, you'll be branded a traitor. But you can't allow five thousand enemy junren into the heart of heart city. He must be here because he knows—'

Rafi held up a hand and scowled. 'Yes. That's my challenge, however, not Alere's.' He turned a tired smile on her. 'Yours, my dear girl, is completed and we are grateful. You will, of course, stay with us tonight. Then it's best you leave before Ven arrives. Things are about to get...untidy. I'd rather you were out of danger. Corin will show you to your room. Please stay there until I send for you.'

Corin strolled around the table and bowed Alere to the door.

Alere eyed both men in angry confusion and hurt. One night? She'd come all this way to meet him, been burdened with this secret for a month and this was the extent of his reaction: leave it with me and go? She pushed aside the sting of rejection and snatched at anger, instead, holding tight to the burn in her stomach. He had no right to throw her away; ignore her existence; treat her as without value. She could cope without him as a father, but he owed her freedom from fear. And he owed Mina, and Sura more than a hand-to-mouth life in a backward village.

Rafi stood straight, looking down his aquiline nose at her, cool and assured. But his eyes drifted back to the painting of Lianna and that deep-seeded pain flared again. What was that about? There had to be something else to this. She raked Rafi's face for more clues. He hid something. Politics was all about secrets and lies.

'No, I'm sorry, shenshi.' She lifted her chin and gritted her teeth, throat tight. 'That's not good enough. I didn't come all this way to be sent to my room like a child then thrown aside as an inconvenience. I came to prevent a war. Clearly, telling you something you already knew isn't enough. I want answers.'

'Alere.' Corin laid a calming hand on her arm.

She shook him off, concentrating on Rafi. 'Why did Radan send me? He could have sent a rider with this news in code. Instead, months before he even got sick, he arranged to have me brought to the Alcazar on my twentieth name-day so he could tell me in person. He knew who I was. And I'm certain Mistress Li knew as well.' She pointed at the floor. 'If you don't want me, why am *I* here?'

Rafi stiffened and drew himself up to his full height, his eyes icy. Alere held her ground, meeting his glare with her own, ready to defend if he so much as raised a hand, Jun or not.

Corin's guffaw of laughter shattered the silence. Rafi rounded on the musician. Corin grinned wider and held up both hands in surrender, but the tension eased and Rafi's mouth twisted into a reluctant smile.

'I know she resembles Lianna,' Corin said, 'but she's your image when you face off like two spitting xiao-cats. If you want my opinion, I think you should tell her now.'

'Actually, I could do without your opinion in this instance, Cor,' Rafi said wearily.

He walked around the room, head bowed, hands clasped behind his back. He reached Lianna's portrait and touched its gilded frame. When he came back to the table, the change shocked Alere into dropping her defensive pose. His face was drawn and grey; a window to such misery it was painful to see.

'Shenshi!' she said, wanting to help; afraid to offer and be rejected again. She touched his arm.

He sank into a chair, covering his eyes with one hand. Corin poured a glass of dark purple wine, holding the goblet to Rafi's lips when the Jun made no move to do so. Rafi sipped and the haunted expression faded, though it still lingered in his eyes.

'Come with me, both of you.' Rafi set the wine aside, rose again and strode from the room.

Rafi led Alere and Corin through several corridors and up a level, stopping in front of double timber doors. Rafi paused. His jaw muscles jumped.

'This is Lianna's room. She's...not here. Come.' He led the way inside and closed the doors.

Alere hesitated inside the threshold, uncomfortable in her unknown half-sister's bedroom. Wouldn't Lianna be annoyed? It was a young girl's room: a haphazard jumble of clothes, memories and mismatched furniture. Clothing lay draped across a carved timber chest. Books were scattered across the polished-wood floor, near the window seat. A small midnight-wood chest sat on a stand beside the bed.

Alere smiled. Her own childhood bedroom in the Ma-Safra house in Jiali had looked the same – a mess.

The bed was stripped bare and the curtains were open, but the room smelled musty. It felt forlorn, expectant, and fluffy with its girlish decorations; like an abandoned pet awaiting the return of its owner. Why?

In one corner, a steel cage held a golden jin-bird. The reptile's fur shimmered in the sunlight as the animal clambered around the cage, twittering.

Rafi moved over and stroked the little reptile's round head until it trilled a scale.

'Poor little Reya,' he muttered. 'We need to...' He glanced up, his eyes glistening with tears. 'You tell her, Corin. Now I'm here I find I can't.' Rafi left the jin-bird and wandered about the room, touching things at random.

Pulling Alere aside, Corin glanced at his shenshi. There existed deep respect and love between the two men and Alere liked both of them the better for it. It was a dimension to Corin she hadn't seen before.

'About two years ago,' he said, softly, 'just after that portrait was done, Lianna fell ill with a wasting disease. She was only sixteen. Nothing the healers did worked and her health deteriorated. From about a year ago, she couldn't even make public appearances. Rafi and Yasmin gave out that Lianna had gone on a retreat to a meditation and healing centre in the Aswad Ranges.' Rafi's pain reflected in Corin. 'Six months ago, she passed away.'

Alere gasped, covering her mouth. That was the last thing she'd expected. Her sister gone before they had a chance to know each other. No wonder Rafi was so shuttered.

'Why didn't we hear of it in Madina?' she whispered, studying Rafi. He sat by the window, eyes closed, mouth slack, nursing a book and a tattered ragdoll in his lap. 'I'm sure I'd have heard such news. Rafi came to the Alcazar when I was there and said nothing at court. Oh!' Realisation dropped a stone into her stomach. 'Six months ago was when Radan asked for me as jiaoji. He knew. He...No!' She put her hands to her head, reeling with the ramifications. 'Mistress Li. *She's* behind this. She and Radan kept Lianna's death quiet.'

Corin grabbed her wrists. 'The Jun succession for the Koh-Lin lands must not be in doubt right now. Rafi did send a rider to advise Radan at the time Lianna died. Rafi received a direct order not to reveal it. Nothing else. Just a suppression order. Radan obviously knew his days were numbered, even then. He knew that, if Rafi had no heir, the lands – and the iron deposit – would fall into Hanna and Ven's hands.'

She stared helplessly at Rafi. 'Radan said my father needed my help. But he couldn't have meant...'

Corin's eyes were grave with shared understanding. 'I didn't understand Radan's order at the time, and I know Rafi and Yasmin were bewildered by it. They couldn't see how Lianna's death could be kept secret for more than a few months. None of us saw any benefit. Rafi went to court, but Hanna wouldn't let him see Radan.' Corin pointed out the window. 'Now, with Ven on our doorstep, there's no way Lianna's death can be kept hidden.'

He gripped Alere's shoulders. 'You asked why you were here. I think you know.'

In the corner, the jin-bird carolled shrilly, rattling at its cage.

CHAPTER TWENTY-SIX

'Radan sent you to take Lianna's place,' Corin said.

Hearing it aloud made it too solid, too real and Alere recoiled. 'No, that's *not* why I came. No!'

She smoothed a loose curl behind one ear and paced the room. Mistress Li, Elmira, Radan, even Sura – they had all conspired in this. The weight of responsibility dragged freedom from her hands; but perhaps the last few weeks had been a delusion. No. This was *her* life. Mistress Li had no right!

Alere rounded on Corin, glaring. 'I won't be someone's tool in this filthy game of politics. I wanted to know Rafi. I came to warn him. To return the bracelet and get on with my life. See the world. I thought maybe Rafi might recognise me, not as Jun-Heir, but unofficially, as family. But I never expected…I can't be…It's not *right*.'

'Hush. Do you see him?' Corin pointed at Rafi, who rested peacefully with eyes closed and worry lines smoothed away. 'This is the first time in six months he's slept without healer medication.'

She flung out a hand. 'He doesn't even want me here, Corin. You heard him tell me to leave tomorrow. He wanted his daughter back, not me,' she said bitterly.

Corin grimaced. 'No, you've misunderstood. Don't you see? The minute Rafi saw you, he understood the implications of your existence. He's no fool. He knew how it would feel to you – to be trapped in someone else's lie again.' He gripped her shoulders again and stared intently into her eyes. 'So he gave you the chance to leave. He tried to set you free of all this. *You* insisted. You've given him hope, Alere. You will *not* reject him for some selfish, childish whim. Neither he nor the Jundom deserves such treatment.'

'How is it selfish to be wanted for myself, not for who I happen look like?' she shot back.

'It's not all about you, Alere,' Corin said, sternly. Then his tone softened. 'He's got a whole jundom of people to consider as well. Don't let Ven strip the iron and crush these people. You can prevent that. If not for the kin-laws, the inheritance would be yours. What else will you do? Be a jiaoji? Or a yongbing?' Corin cupped her jaw with gentle hands, his expression wry. 'I once said you were meant for better things. This is your chance. Don't throw it away out of fear.'

Corin's closeness tempted Alere to bury herself in his embrace and lean on his strength. Wracked with doubt, she instead moved away and stared at her reflection in the dressing table mirror. It was true that Rafi has tried to give her an out. And his people needed an heir; stability; protection. But who would she be, if she stayed? She glanced out the window, towards the distant purple mountains. Duty and the temptation of a family warred with longing for the weightlessness of no responsibilities, no pressures, no expectations.

'What about Mina?' she asked. 'Couldn't she—?'

'From how you described her, Mina sounds too gentle. The people need a warrior. Lianna was like you: strong, smart, opinionated.'

'I'm not sure that was a compliment,' Alere said. 'If you knew Lianna, why didn't you recognise me?'

'She'd been unwell for two years.' Corin stood behind Alere and studied her reflection. 'There's also a big difference between sixteen and twenty. Nor was I expecting to see her in Newmec – she'd been gone for six months. And, of course, I didn't know you existed.' He indicated Rafi, slumbering in the chair. 'When I first began travelling for Rafi, he asked me to track Sura. I traced her to the Wen-Gates estate, but the Xintou there said Sura and her child had died years before. Rafi and Yasmin were devastated.'

Alere shivered. 'Even that long ago Mistress Li's hand was at work. Why? She couldn't know Lianna would fall ill. Jiche!' She clenched her hands. 'I'm playing into Mistress Li's plans if I agree to do this. I'm nothing to her; to anyone. Nothing but a tool. She's manoeuvring me like a qi piece, just as she does to everyone of the House. I thought I'd be free of her control by now.'

Alere's likeness to Lianna was certainly the reason Mistress Li insisted Alere wear the veil at the Alcazar. Towards what end was the old woman manipulating the Jundom?

'We're all part of something larger. All answerable to someone and bound by duty.' Corin glanced around the room. 'Your responsibility has simply become bigger than most.'

Alere groaned. She'd come to relish the taste of the sky and the sound of the wind. 'But I don't want the Jundom, or any of this political feihua. Why does everyone want to use me? To drag me into their stupid wars?'

Corin made a sound somewhere between frustration and annoyance and moved closer, stroking her cheek, a look a regret in his eyes. 'Do you think *I* want this for you? Being Jun-Heir puts you so far out of reach – ah, gaisi!' He thrust her away as Rafi shifted and opened his eyes.

While Rafi and Corin discussed the situation, Alere paced Lianna's room. She stopped by the window, craning to see the northeasterly plains where Ven's army of junren crawled like a black swarm of flesh-ants, a day's march away. Corin was right: Ven would strip Rafi's people to the bone and leave them to rot.

What was the right course? Where was Kett? He would know what to do. Rafi was a good man and if she could prevent a war by simply existing, shouldn't she? It was clearly the right thing to do, so why did the thought leave her so empty? If she were a true xintou – dedicated to selflessly helping the people – she wouldn't hesitate.

She glanced at the golden jin-bird preening in its steel cage.

Alere stood before Rafi and tilted her head to soften her words. 'I don't know if I can be Lianna, shenshi. Right now, it's hard enough to be sure who *I* am.'

'I don't want you to give up being who you are. I'm looking forward to learning who you are. You'd be Lianna in name only.' Rafi stroked a thumb across Alere's cheek. 'In doing so, you'd give me a reason to stand up to Ven and protect my people; protect you, Yasmin, and Mina. A reason I thought lost forever; a family I never dreamed to have again.'

Tears blurred her vision. Yes, this was about more than her personal freedom, wasn't it? And more than just helping the unknown people of the Jundom. Ven's invasion would affect people she knew and cared about. She looked at Corin, who smiled understandingly.

Reluctantly, she nodded, resignation a cold stone in her stomach. 'Very well. I'll...I'll try.'

Rafi smiled and kissed her forehead. He swept the room with a critical gaze.

'You'd be uncomfortable here. Adult quarters will be better. However, you should familiarise yourself with Lianna and this room is the best place to start.' He picked up a worn, leather-bound book and caressed its cover. 'I gave this to Lia for her tenth birthday. She insisted I read it to her over and over. I got sick of it, but she never did.'

'*Tales from Faraway Earth,*' she read aloud. 'One of my favourites, too. Elmira used to read it to me.'

'I've met Elmira numerous times, at court and at Petar's home.' His frown held a wistful regret that warmed Alere's heart. 'Why did I never meet you?'

She forced a smile. 'Because I was the grubbiest, least presentable child you've ever seen. Elmira said I was never fit to be in polite company.' She tapped her lips. 'But I saw you, once. In Jiali, a few weeks before I left to join Xintou House. I was hiding at the top of the stairs and remember thinking you looked nice. And you had a lovely voice.'

'Petar's a good man.' Rafi smiled. 'I'm glad you were part of his household, even if only for a while.'

'I didn't see much of Petar and Leah. I think my presence was painful because they have no children. They were kind, but I always felt...' Alere cleared her throat. He didn't need to know about her lonely, privileged childhood.

She touched the small black chest by the bed. 'What's this?'

'Lia keeps...' Rafi grimaced. 'Kept a few trinkets and letters from her friends. Go ahead, open it.'

Alere lifted the lid. A spicy, sugary scent, redolent of cinnamon, wafted through the room.

'I recognise that smell.' Corin peered into the box.

A small black and gold silk bag lay atop a bundle of pink papers bound with golden ribbon. Alere plucked out the bag. Corin reached past her and picked up the letters. He undid the ribbon and unfolded one.

'Sorry to hear you're still not feeling well,' he read. 'I hope these sugarfires reach you before Landing Day, so you can celebrate in style with your favourite sweets. Miss you. F.' He inhaled. 'That's what the smell is. Fires are delicious. Not surprised they were

Lianna's favourite. There's a specialty shop in Asadia. I used to buy them there for—' Catching Alere's ironic look, he grinned. 'Someone whose name I've completely forgotten.' He flipped through the letters. 'The crest and colours are those of the Jun Third Han-Asad family.'

Tucked beneath the letters was a delicately-painted miniature of a sweet-looking girl of about sixteen with charcoal eyes and hair, and nut-brown skin. She had the plump face and bosom of an overindulged, beloved daughter.

'Who is she?' Alere held the image up for Rafi.

'Farima Han-Asad. Jun-Heir to Jun Third Kennor Han-Asad,' Rafi said. 'Farima was a good friend to Lia. They met when Lia visited the Han-Asad estates in Asadia one summer. Farima was forever sending those horrendous sugar treats. Lia hid them and ate them in secret.'

Alere picked a sugarfire from the sticky mess inside the bag. 'They don't look all that appetising. Are they always that odd shade of yellow?' She sniffed the sweet. 'That's…not right?' She put it under Corin's nose. 'Close your eyes and try to ignore the strongest notes. What do you smell?'

He sniffed. 'Cinnamon. Stronger than I remember. Clove, definitely. A good helping of sweet xun. But you're right: there's something else. Almost sour. I'm sure I've smelled it before. Why do you ask?'

She turned the sugarfire about in her fingers. Something wasn't right. Where did she know that smell from? 'Maybe they're just off.'

Corin scanned another letter. 'No, I don't think so. Each letter mentions sending sugarfires, but there's only one bag in the chest, so they can't be too old. The last letter's dated a week before Landing Day, seven months ago. Sugarfires last forever. I found a packet I'd forgotten in my bag, still fresh, a year later. Not yellow and sticky, either.'

Rafi came over, carrying the tattered ragdoll. 'The girls hadn't corresponded for quite a while, but a letter arrived just before Lia's sixteenth nameday. Lia was thrilled and after that they wrote regularly again. A few weeks later, Lia stayed with the Han-Asads in Madina when both girls were presented at court.'

Alere stared at the silk bag. She sank onto the mattress and held the sweet to her nose. The sour smell was almost overpowered by cinnamon. Was she imagining things? No, Corin had noticed. She'd smelled it before, recently. But where?

She studied the stripped bed and untidy room for clues. The pillows, piled high against the dragon-carved bedhead, caught her eye. The bed. Why did that trigger an association with the smell, too?

Alere gazed in horror at the sweet. She lifted the sticky thing towards Rafi.

'What if Farima sent more than a letter two years ago? What if she also sent the first packet of sugarfires then?'

Corin groaned, deep in his chest.

'Han-Asad.' Rafi clutched the bedpost, his body shaking. 'How could I have been so stupid? Farima is Hanna's niece. Hanna poisoned my daughter and I was too blind to see it.'

Alere dropped the sweet into the bag and handed it to Corin. 'Ask the Healer House to test it, but I think I recognise the smell – manxing root.'

'How do you know?' Corin asked, frowning.

'Jiaoji training teaches poisons and drugs.' Alere said. She smoothed the loose lock of hair behind her ear. 'I always thought using poison was dishonourable. That no-one would stoop to such measures. Guess I'm naïve.'

Corin said nothing, but his lips thinned.

'Shenshi.' She addressed Rafi. He ignored her, his eyes closed and fingers white on the bedpost. Grief carved deep lines around his mouth. She raised her voice to pierce the anguish that had him in thrall. 'My guess is that Celia or Hanna coerced one of the Alcazar jiaoji to get the manxing – probably one of the junior women.'

Rafi remained silent, his whole body shaking.

'Shenshi, this isn't just about Lianna.' Alere squared her shoulders.

Corin's head lifted. 'What?'

'In the Alcazar. Radan's death,' she continued. 'Only female jiaoji have easy access to both manxing and Radan's food.' She pointed at the bag. 'I smelled manxing on Radan's breath. At the time I was too scared to pay much attention. The scent of the sugarfire reminded me.'

Rafi slumped into a chair, the ragdoll clutched in his hand. 'I should have seen it.'

Alere dropped to her knees and gripped Rafi's arm. He raised a grief-ravaged countenance, revealing the misery and guilt he'd hidden for six months. She had no comfort to give but Rafi couldn't afford to wallow in despair right now.

'Please listen to logic, Rafi,' she said, matter-of-factly. 'You may not hear it now, but I ask that you think on it later.'

Rafi's brows snapped together and he focussed on Alere.

'I've no doubt,' she continued, 'the healers asked Lianna if she'd eaten anything unusual. You said she hid the sweets knowing you disapproved.'

'But,' he said, swiping a hand over his hair, 'surely she must have wondered if the sugarfires had some connection with her illness? Why keep eating them?'

'You know nothing of women if you ask that question, shenshi,' Alere said, with a wry smile. 'It's a rare woman who'll give up her favourite indulgence when she's depressed or unwell. In fact, she'll usually eat more for the brief joy it gives. But it wouldn't have mattered, anyway.'

'What do you mean?'

'Manxing is named slow-poison because it can be given in the tiniest of measures over a long time. But it's also so named because one large dose will have the same effect – a slow, natural-seeming deterioration of health. The sour taste is difficult to disguise, but these sweets are perfect.' She indicated the empty bed. 'If I were planning an assassination I'd put the largest amount I could into the first package, just in case. Most girls won't eat just one sweet a day. Lia would have eaten them all within a day or so at the most. And there is no cure.'

Tears rolled down Rafi's face. Alere cleared a lump in her throat. Lianna was dead from the first parcel. It had just taken a year and a half for the toxin to destroy her young, strong body. Rage swelled in Alere's heart. Radan's death was one thing; an innocent child was something else.

She rose. 'If you'll forgive me for being blunt, yes, mourn for Lianna, but don't waste time blaming yourself for something you couldn't have stopped.'

Whatever Radan and Mistress Li had in mind was irrelevant – Alere's task here was more than pretending to be Lianna, and more than preventing Ven from taking over the city and the iron deposit. Whatever else was at stake, Hanna and Ven must pay for this. She helped Rafi to his feet and met his doubtful gaze.

'I'll do whatever you need, shenshi,' Alere said. 'Use me to exact revenge on Ven and Hanna and Celia. They'll expect to find a broken man mourning his heir. Let my life be worth something. Let me help you destroy them. For Radan, for you, for Yasmin and for your daughter. Lianna was my family, too.'

There followed a long silence and Rafi searched her face. Then he straightened.

'Are you sure?'

Alere swallowed trepidation and clung to black anger. She nodded.

'Thank you.' He glanced at his daughter's empty bed, caught Alere in a tight hug, released her and strode from the room.

The door slammed shut and Alere sank, trembling, onto the bed. What had she just agreed to? Then she took in Lianna's empty room, full of lost promise and potential, and her resolve strengthened. Yes, Lianna deserved retribution and Mina, Yasmin, Rafi, Corin and the people of Shanzhai deserved protection from Hanna, Celia and Ven.

'How could they do it, Corin?' she whispered. 'How could they kill an innocent girl?'

Corin stared broodingly out the window. 'I wish I didn't understand the depravity of people like Hanna, Celia and Ven, but in the past ten years I've seen the worst side of humanity. Returning to Shanzhai after each trip, spending time with Rafi, Yasmin and their people always renewed my faith and gave me the strength to go back out again.' He rubbed the back of his neck, drawing his mawei through restless fingers. 'Madina's rot has infected Shanzhai. I need to stop it taking more people I care about.'

Who had he lost? Alere joined Corin at the window.

He drew her close against his side and kissed the top of her head. 'You've done a good thing, Alere. Rafi's a great leader and his people respect him. Thank you.'

She leaned into him, seeking strength. Shanzhai lay visible below, the imperfect window glass warping and corrupting the city in a portent of Ven's invasion. Thousands of people living their days, thousands of businesses trading, thousands of lives over which either Alere or Ven would have ultimate control. The next few days would determine the city's future.

But, if she won against him, could she live a lifetime as Lianna? Only valued as someone else, not herself.

Across the river, beyond the ragged edge of the city, lay a patchwork of farmland, gold and rich brown as the last few crops were harvested and the stubble ploughed back into the soil for winter. Beyond that towered the sun-tipped peaks of the Gharb Mountains, and the Hepan: a great swathe of uncolonised, forested land that stretched hundreds of gongli into the continent.

Alere lifted her gaze to the horizon. What waited past the Hepan? Had anyone managed to build that far away from the original settlements? Should she have taken up Kett's suggestion; sold the bracelet and run like diyu to start a new life somewhere else? No. This was the right path. And something in her warmed at the look of gratitude in Rafi's eyes, and the admiration in Corin's.

She turned from the window. The jin-bird fluttered and squeaked in its cage. She ignored it.

'C'mon.' Corin jerked his head towards the door.

'Where?' She hesitated. 'I'm supposed to leave word at the Healer House so Mina can find me. But, if Ven takes the city, I should warn them to stay away. How can I reach them?'

Corin opened the door with a flourishing bow. 'Leave it to me, shunu. I'll undertake to find out if they are with the infamous Ahkma and his caravan. We'll leave a message with Healer House as well. Arrange to meet them at the Ploughman, if you like.' He waved a hand at the room. 'So you can break all this to them gently. Assuming, as you say, Ven hasn't taken the city. Personally, I think he'll make a diplomatic show first. He'll want to discover where the iron is before he kills everyone who might know.'

'Oh, thanks,' she said, 'I'm so glad I chose to stay. Didn't we sort of wreck The Ploughman today?'

Corin laughed. 'Oh, Barrat'll have it fixed by tomorrow, I'm sure. He knows I'm good for it and won't hold a grudge.'

'You do that sort of thing often, then?'

'Often enough that Rafi has set up a permanent repair fund and a list of tradesmen in every city.' He grinned. 'I'll take you to your room in a moment. First, I have something to show you.'

Alere followed him down the stairs towards the back of the castle, through the kitchens and into the cellar's dark recesses. He passed the last racks of wine and continued walking. The lights dimmed overhead. The temperature dropped. Alere slid the dagger from her boot, into her belt.

'Never fear,' Corin said. 'I've not lured you here to murder you. This is where the tour starts.' He produced an iron key, opened several cumbersome iron locks and shoved open a thick timber door. The click of a switch flooded the chamber beyond with soft yellow light.

Alere entered and paused, astonished. 'It's beautiful.'

The room appeared to be hewn out of the rock itself, the walls made of glittering, multifaceted crystalline shards. Where had she seen something like that before? Oh, yes, the walls of the hidden valley near Gaton. How odd. Pickmarks had obscured or shattered most of the crystal faces, but the structures were unmistakably similar.

Corin waved her on and strolled deeper into the chamber. The rock changed; the pick-marked walls arching overhead became dusty red. Red stone pillars held up a low ceiling of the same red rock. Corin stopped when the floor ended in a maw of cavernous, echoing blackness that sucked light into the bowels of the mountain.

He flipped another switch. An eye-aching spotlight banished night. Below, a vertical shaft plunged into the earth. Alere peered over the edge. A rush of warm, damp air lifted her hair and carried an odd, yet familiar, metallic tang that caught in the back of her nose. Bamboo scaffolding lined the pit walls, forming platforms, ladders, and a complicated system of ropes, pulleys and buckets. The steady drip of water echoed in the cool space. Occasional streaks of glistening water changed the walls to blood.

Blood, yes, that was the taste in the air.

Alere studied the rock underfoot. She ran a finger across the stone. A reddish powder covered her fingertip and dusted her sleeve where she'd brushed up against the wall.

'What is it?' She touched a damp part of the wall and rubbed her fingers together. The wet powder smeared into smooth carmine streaks.

No. Surely, it wasn't possible. Was it?

She showed Corin the stain. 'You're not saying…?'

'Rust,' he said, and opened his arms wide. '*This* is the iron deposit. One, very large, very solid lump of meteoric iron. The whole valley was created by this meteor. Mining the iron would not only destroy the castle, but also produce enough iron weapons to arm thousands of junren. The Zah-Hill family could even bring guns to Kalima.'

'Guns!' Alere stared at the red powder and the bloody walls. The implications were frightening, but why did the mention of guns also tease her with an elusive memory?

Corin's laugh was bitter. 'Ironic, isn't it? Our ancestors left Earth in hopes of finding peace. They deliberately left behind industry, and wars over resources and religion. Now it seems stupidity and greed have finally overcome idealism.'

Only half-listening, Alere stared into the darkness at her feet.

'Alere?'

'Shut up a minute,' she said. 'Let me think.' What was it? Something she'd seen or heard recently, connected to guns. But the only time she'd discussed the subject was with Kett. What had they been doing? Oh yes, the Weishi House library. Kett made her study the history of guns, gun-making and...

'That's what it was!' She sprinted towards the exit.

'What *what* was?' Corin caught up and grabbed her arm. 'What are you talking about?'

'Let go,' she twisted free. 'I must speak to Rafi. Find him. If I'm right, there's worse to worry about than the possibility of Ven arming his men with guns.'

'Worse? What the—'

She glared. He growled in frustration and waved her out of the room. As they passed through the kitchen, Corin collared a servant and demanded the Jun's whereabouts. The servant muttered something about the Blue Parlour and hurried away.

Corin swore. 'Yasmin's room. Can it wait?'

'Believe me, this *cannot* wait. I'm sorry if my existence upsets Yasmin. Better that than losing Shanzhai.'

'Right,' Corin said, with a frown.

They reached the Blue Parlour on the second floor.

'Let me go in first.' Corin held her back when she raised a hand to knock. 'I'd rather you didn't give the poor woman a heart attack.'

He left Alere outside and she hastily tucked her dagger into her shirt. Corin returned a moment later and invited her into the room. His eyes were dark with worry.

Rafi and a dark-haired woman stood near the far wall. The woman turned, her hands twisting a kerchief. Her face was a thinner, wearier version of Sura's. She gasped, hope and grief warring in her brown eyes. Her dark green, silk robe whispered as she ran to Alere.

Alere waited, uncomfortable in the emotion-laden atmosphere. Yasmin's steps slowed and her shoulders slumped.

'I'm sorry I'm not Lianna, shunu,' Alere blurted, unable to stand the misery and silence. 'I'm so sorry.'

Tears spilled down Yasmin's cheeks. She opened her arms. 'It's not your fault, my dear girl. You look so like her. For a moment...' she sighed. 'Never mind. Come, please.'

Alere embraced Yasmin, ill-at-ease in her aunt's tight grip. But Yasmin wore the same calla-flower perfume as Elmira and the scent filled Alere with a sense of familiarity and security.

Yasmin released her and gave a weak, watery chuckle. 'I'm sorry to cry all over you. Sit, please. Tell me all about yourself and my dearest Sura. We thought her dead these twenty years. I've missed her so much.' Yasmin seated Alere on a low couch opposite Corin.

'Ma'am, I promise we'll speak of these things, but right now I must talk with Rafi.' Alere clasped Yasmin's fingers in her own. 'When there's time, we'll drink a glass of wine and I'll tell you everything. Is that all right?'

Yasmin nodded, her eyes wide. Rafi drew up a chair.

'Corin showed me the iron beneath the castle.' Alere's tongue stumbled over the words. 'He mentioned the possibility of guns, which reminded me of something. In Madina—'

'Slow down,' Rafi said, holding up a hand. 'Are you saying you've seen a gun? How's that possible? No-one else has enough iron to create such weapons.'

'No.' Alere clenched her teeth, trying to control the words spilling free, wishing she was wrong. She pictured the rain, the secret door, the workshops in the alley. 'When I was escaping from the Alcazar, men were moving barrels out of the rain. I thought it strange because it was night, but I had other things on my mind. The smells, though – they were unforgettable: urine from the stables, sulphur, wood-smoke. And something else; something acrid and harsh.'

'What?' Rafi frowned.

'If I'm right,' Alere said, holding her father's doubtful gaze, 'Ven's not here simply to invade Shanzhai, he's here to obliterate the city.'

CHAPTER TWENTY-SEVEN

'You're making no sense.' Rafi rose, dismissive. 'Ven has no weapons capable of destroying Shanzhai.'

'Hear me out,' Alere snapped. 'Those smells – the people at the Alcazar workshops were making gunpowder. There were dozens of barrels, full of gunpowder.'

A silence followed. Corin eyed her askance.

'How can you be sure?' Rafi sank back into his seat and frowned. 'There can't be more than a half-dozen people in the whole jundom who know how to make gunpowder. Miner House and fireworks makers guard the secret closely.'

'The Weishi House library contains a lot of information about weapons. I've read most of it.' She jabbed a finger into her chest, willing him to believe. '*I* could make gunpowder. What I saw and smelled outside the Alcazar matches all the descriptions. I'm sure I'm right.' She looked to Corin. 'Those weishi we captured today. Did you notice the smell and the black dust on their clothes?'

'Yes, now you mention it. I did,' Corin mused. 'You think that dust was gunpowder? We still have their clothes. We can check.'

'Do it,' she said. 'But quickly. They must have been in contact with it recently, which means Ven has gunpowder *here*.' She spread her arms. 'With his honour guard. And with those men we caught today.'

'But without guns, what use is it?' Yasmin asked. 'I mean, what else can you do with it?'

'Khara!' Corin sprang up, his eyes wide, staring at the floor in horror. 'The sewers. She's right. They could plant those barrels in the sewers and raze Shanzhai to the ground in one day.'

CORIN

'Fifty.' Corin rolled out a map of the city on the zitan-wood table.

Along with Rafi and Yasmin, ten other people sat around the meeting room table: Alere, Gavon; Farah, the castle Shangwei; Maha, her second in command; and five trusted weishi. In an attempt to keep the threat secret, and Ven ignorant, Rafi had opted to keep to a minimum the number of people aware of the gunpowder. So only ten would participate in this madness. Yasmin and Rafi protested at Alere's inclusion, but Alere refused to be left out. Corin was tempted to knock her unconscious, but she'd earned a place. He grinned wryly. Knocking her out would prove difficult, anyway.

Corin studied the assembled team. Could this even be achieved with so few? There were fifty red circles marked on the street map in front of them. He grimaced .They had no choice but to try.

'Ven's men will need to keep the barrels dry. And stored in an easily-accessed place so the fuses can be lit at the right time.' Corin pointed to the red marks. 'These are the fifty most likely spots.'

'Do we know how many and if they'll be guarded?' Maha indicated four marks nearest the castle. He was a strict disciplinarian of the castle weishi, loyal to his profession and the Koh-Lins. His priority would be to protect the castle.

'Impossible to know,' Corin replied. 'Our two weishi guests have been...stubborn. We don't have time for a drawn-out interrogation.'

'It's not feasible to keep men in the sewers for long.' Farah raised a hand. 'My brother, Dameer, is a sewer worker. He says the toxic fumes are lethal. Ten minutes is about the maximum exposure.'

'Can we get your brother here to assist?' Rafi asked. 'His insight could be useful.'

'Bai, shenshi. I'll send a runner for him.' Farah left the room.

'So.' Corin took back control of the conversation. Every moment was vital. 'That means any guards will be on the surface, nearby. We need to find and eliminate them before we go into the manholes. If we miss even one guard, the whole operation could fail.

He caught each person's eye, confirming their commitment and understanding. 'It'll be dark in a little over two hours. Remove the barrels if you have time. If not, empty their contents into the water.' He pushed the map into the centre of the table. 'A small huoche, ropes and dark-lanterns are waiting for each team. We'll go in pairs, ten sites each to clear tonight.'

Corin rubbed the back of his neck, trying to ease the fatigue of the previous days' hard riding. 'It's going to be a long night so if you're not up to it, now's the time to say so.' He eyed Alere pointedly.

She raised a scornful brow but said nothing, although dark circles beneath her eyes revealed her exhaustion.

'Very well. Alek, you're with me,' Corin said. 'Everyone else pair off. Make sure one person carries a bow or throwing knives. Gather whatever supplies, food and water you might need. Maha, send someone to Miner House for breathing masks and goggles. We'll meet back in the great hall just before dusk. It's vital you understand the need for stealth and discretion.'

The weishi dispersed leaving only Alere, Corin, Rafi and Yasmin in the room.

'Are you sure?' Yasmin laid a hand on Alere's arm, her eyes dark with worry.

'I'm sure.' Alere smiled. 'The fewer people who know the better. Besides, you've no idea how much trouble Corin gets into without someone to keep him in line.'

Rafi laughed. 'Oh yes, I do, believe me. Very well. But be careful. Keep me appraised. I'll assist Farah and Maha with the organisation.'

'I still think you should evacuate to your western estates, shenshi,' Corin said, though they'd already had this argument twice. Rafi sent him a weary, tolerant look and led Yasmin from the room.

Alere examined the map and Corin took the opportunity to watch her. She was again the intense young boy he'd taken a liking to three weeks before – dressed in weishi black and with her ridiculous moustache back in place. Yet so much had changed. Corin cleared his throat and grinned at the quixotic taste that, after all these years of guarding his heart, made him care for the one girl he could never have.

She looked up, night-velvet eyes questioning.

Corin shoved his hands into his pockets to prevent himself reaching for her. 'I received a bird from Jacksa. It also carried a message from Ahkma.'

'Did you get news of Kett and Mina?' She smiled so ingenuously he moved away. It was either that or kiss her, which would be enjoyable, but unwise.

'Yes, shunu.' Calling Alere 'shunu' reminded him of her position.

Alere lit up. Who in that party was so important to her? Her sister or perhaps this weishi, Kett?

'Your friends,' Corin continued, 'left Ahkma's caravan over a week and a half ago. Trying to get here faster. Jacksa passed them on the road, half a day after we parted company. Jacksa didn't know who they were until Ahkma's bird arrived. Kett evidently asked Hellor after you. Hellor told them why you'd ridden ahead.'

'Oh,' she said, the smile falling away. 'They wouldn't have received my message. If they ride hard they might arrive tonight or tomorrow. Jiche!' She smoothed a curl behind her ear. 'I hope they don't get caught in this mess.' She raised frightened eyes. 'Does Ven have junren marching on the city from the southeast as well? It's the easiest place to cross the river.'

Corin shook his head. 'Rafi sent out scouts after you met with him. They rode twenty gongli in each direction and sent back flitters. All clear.'

'But there's no way to reach Kett before he arrives. Hopefully he'll get my message at Healer House. It'll be good to see...them again.' Her cheeks flushed.

A servant delivered a steaming platter of yum-cha. When they were alone again, Corin eyed Alere thoughtfully. 'Why, if I may ask, did you choose to travel under the name Johnston?' He pulled two chairs up to the table.

'It was just a name of an extinct family line Rohne saw...in a history book.' Alere frowned into the distance then shrugged and chose a steamed pork bun. 'Why?'

Corin undid his swordbelt and laid it on the table. He removed the plain leather wrap and revealed a scabbard decorated with intricate geometric designs in bronze. He unwound a second wrap and exposed a large, milky gemstone set in the sword's pommel. Hiding the scabbard and stone allowed Corin to travel without being targeted by thieves. He angled the scabbard towards Alere.

'See the crest?'

She inspected the design and her widened eyes flew to his. What an interesting reaction. Corin ran a finger over the spur-and-buckle motif and continued,

'The Johnston family crest. I introduced myself as Mal-kin, but that's my travelling name. I'm the last of the Johnstons. Proud owner of an old and distinguished name. No money or lands to accompany it, though.'

'Oh.' Alere smoothed a hand down her stomach but snatched it away when she caught him watching. 'What an odd coincidence.'

Corin put his feet up on a chair and studied her from beneath drooping eyelids. What was she hiding?

'Yes, isn't it? In fact, Shanzhai was originally settled by the Johnston family. This castle was built by them.' He indicated the dark timber and stone walls. 'A warlike bunch, evidently.'

Alere studied the map, fingertips fiddling with her shirt-front. 'So,' she said, her tone disinterested, 'how did Shanzhai pass into Koh-Lin hands?'

'Nothing spectacular.' He flicked a hand. 'The last of the direct line married a Koh-Lin. But they had no children, not even kin. The estate passed to his wife's nephew. The only other Johnstons lived far to the north, and didn't know the estate had been lost.' Corin spread his arms to encompass the castle. 'By the time my branch of the family found out, the Koh-Lins were well-established and powerful.' He dropped his feet to the floor and sat up. 'However, the family legend about ownership and the iron deposit persisted. I came here in search of truths ten years ago, when I was sixteen.'

'And did you find them?' Wariness collided with curiosity in her eyes.

Corin laughed, disinclined to answer a question too close to the bone for a casual conversation. 'Not sure. Still looking, I think. What

I did find was a man I could respect and a cause I could throw my heart into: protecting this land and these people.'

Alere ran a hand down her shirt front again, frowning. 'I can relate to that.' There followed a long pause and Corin watched her, waiting for more. She nibbled on a fingertip and eyed him intently, then sighed.

'Oh, jiche. I'm a shazi and I'll probably regret this.' She reached into her shirt and withdrew a sheathed dagger and thrust it towards him. 'Here. Take it before I change my mind.' She pointed an accusatory finger at him. 'But I want a replacement and fast. That dagger saved my life and I feel naked without it.'

'Now that's an interesting thought.' Corin unsheathed and inspected the weapon. He ran a thumb over the steel blade and milk-translucent stone set into the pommel. Disbelieving suspicion crept over him.

'Is this what I think it is?' He turned the dagger over twice, his heart pounding. It couldn't be, could it?

'I don't know,' she growled. 'What do you think it is?'

'This weapon,' Corin said, picking at the hilt-binding, 'matches the descriptions of the Johnston family dirk – the pair to my sword. But the dirk's been missing for over two hundred years – since one of my ancestors made an abortive attempt to dethrone the Jun First.'

'Finish unwrapping it.'

Corin pulled off the last of the binding and revealed his family's distinctive crest on the tang. For a long time he was unable to do more than stare. His throat swelled with a feeling of belonging and connection he'd thought impossible to find again after his parents' death.

'You've had this the whole time?' He held the dagger reverently and, with great care, rewound the binding. 'Where did you find it?'

Alere scrubbed her palms together and bowed her head. 'Radan gave it to me. He said it was taken from a rebel two hundred years ago in the anti-slavery attacks on the Alcazar. He said it was appropriate I have a rebel's weapon.' Her voice cracked and Corin suspected she was crying.

He said nothing, giving her time to regain her composure.

She sent him a tight smile. 'It's also the dagger he used...to end everything.'

'Khara!' Corin laid the dagger down and frowned.

Alere flinched, her hands sweeping restlessly over the table. 'What's the stone? I thought it was a yanstone, but it lacks the fire.' Her fingers brushed the stone's surface. 'Although – how odd.' Deep in the stone, a faint silver-gilt fire jumped with her touch.

Corin tilted the knife. The glimmer vanished.

'It *is* a yanstone and matches the stone on my sword.' He stroked the pommel. 'But legend says the fire in both was extinguished – an implausible story for a later time.' His tongue was clumsy. 'I don't know how to thank you. You've given me a gift I can never repay – a connection to family. Thank you.'

'You're welcome.' She touched the blade once more then gave a regretful sigh. 'Don't forget, I need a replacement.'

'Agreed.' He rose and settled the weapons on his hips. The weight balanced perfectly. 'I'll have the smith make one, but in the meantime, take mine.' With a deep bow, Corin passed Alere his plain, but serviceable ceramic dagger.

'Thank you.' She tapped the map with the blade tip. 'The smith might have to wait a day. We have work to do.'

Corin studied the vulnerable sites marked on the map. There was no way of knowing if the number of barrels or their marked locations were correct. If Rafi's men missed even a third of the barrels, the result would be disastrous.

'There's no getting around it, Cor.' Alere spread her hand flat on the map. 'We need more information.'

'I know, but the weishi we have in custody are trained to resist torture. We don't have time to break them.'

She folded her arms and lifted her chin. 'Then let me try.'

Corin laughed then sobered before of her frown. 'You can't be serious.' He waved a hand in the direction of the zinzana downstairs. 'If I let you into the cell, they'll take you hostage.'

'Now *that* was an insult.' She gripped his wrist. 'Trust me, Corin. I've had the same training as a weishi. I can get the information quickly. Let me try. Please?'

He fought the urge to kiss her, afraid of what might happen if she got her way – or if she didn't. He needed that information.

'Alright! But ten minutes, no more.' He wagged a finger then groaned. 'I sound like my mother. What do you need?'

She drummed her nails on the table. 'My bag, a waterskin, a sealed wine bottle and a couple of things from Healer House. We'll need to be quick, though.'

Twenty minutes later, Corin regretted his decision and battled a strong desire to steal her from the castle and keep her safe. Gaisi! He was a zift.

Dressed in a clinging red-robe and veil, Alere was unrecognisable. Gone was the masculine stride with swinging arms and out-thrust chest; gone the arrogant lift of chin, and defiant spark that had defined Alek. Instead, the woman who glided through the castle's lower tunnels was the epitome of a jiaoji: confident, sensual, and alluring; her lips painted red to match the fluttering robe; eyes luminous behind the veil.

Outside the cell's thick timber door, Corin murmured. 'Ten minutes, remember?'

'Don't come in unless you hear *me* yell for help.' Alere kissed his cheek and took the sack he carried. Her sultry smile made his pulse race.

Hoping Rafi would *never* find out, Corin unlocked the door and let her into the cell. He eased into the empty cell next door, climbed onto a bunk and peered through the ventilation hole connecting the rooms. He had a view of everything but a small area closest to the wall beneath him. The prisoners' cell was barely big enough for a bunk bed and space for two men to stand up.

The two weishi leapt from their beds. Alere's scarlet softness threw into harsh relief the bleak surroundings and the weishi's brown woollen prison garb. She seemed delicate and frightened, holding the sack protectively as she backed away from the prisoners. Corin laughed silently at the image. He'd met few people less frail and helpless.

'Who are you? What are you doing here, jiaoji?' Prato spat the last word and advanced on Alere.

Corin clenched his fists.

'If you're here to make us talk, forget it.' Prato raised a belligerent chin. 'We are *gangzhi.*'

Corin started. Where had he heard that word? The weishi looked Alere over, his lip curling to a sneer. Corin itched to leap to her rescue.

'Don't you recognise me, Prato?' Alere's voice quavered. She shrank away and clutched the bag. 'Didn't Shenshi Ven send you?'

'Why would we recognise you, girl?' Prato's eyes narrowed. 'Raise the veil.'

Alere gasped and held the scrap of cloth in place. Corin grinned. She was masterful. For a jiaoji to unveil in front of a man not in her contract was unthinkable.

'You must know me.' She stumbled away until her back pressed against the door. 'I'm Shenshi Radan's last jiaoji. We met at the Alcazar not two months ago. Don't you remember? You bumped into me in the hall and helped me pick up the sheets I'd dropped.' A demure little smile played at her lips. 'I thought…'

'You!' Prato stepped forward then stopped. 'But…' He lifted a tentative hand and Alere touched his fingertips.

Corin smiled. She almost had them.

'Prato?' Kal, the junior of the pair, tugged at his superior's arm.

'No.' Prato withdrew from Alere, glowering. 'What are you doing here? How did you get in? Are you working for the Koh-Lins?' He grabbed Alere's shoulders and shook her.

Alere let out a choked sob. 'You're hurting me. I'm here to help you.'

'You killed Jun Radan.' Prato's nails pressed deep into her skin.

Corin gripped the bed frame to stop himself shouting.

'No, no.' A tear trickled down her cheek. 'You know he was sick before I even came to the Alcazar. Please, let me explain. I bribed the weishi outside, so I have only a few minutes. Look, here's food and drink. I'm here to help.'

Prato snatched the bag from her and threw it to Kal.

'Just bread, cheese, wine and water,' Kal reported. 'No weapons.'

Scowling, Prato released Alere. Corin relaxed; he was a zift to think she needed protection.

'Don't drink the water, Kal,' Prato said. 'The wine's sealed so it'll be safe. Give it here.' Taking a long drink from the wine sack, Prato jerked his chin at Alere. 'So talk.' He bit into a chunk of bread and cheese, glowering at her.

Alere wrung her hands. 'Shunu Hanna and Mistress Celia asked me to help. They wanted a spy inside the Koh-Lin house, but every weishi they sent was discovered.'

Prato drank and passed the wine to Kal.

'Go on.' Prato's suspicious glare softened.

She was getting to him. Corin grinned. It was true that Rafi had found four infiltrators in the last eight months. But Alere had heard the information from Corin only twenty minutes before.

'When Shenshi Radan died,' she continued, 'Shunu Hanna asked me to be a scapegoat. I told the Koh-Lins I was being blamed for the Jun First's murder. I said I was loyal to Shenshi Radan and afraid of Shunu Hanna.' She tilted her head to the side and sniffed disdainfully. 'Rafi believed me. Now I can spy on the Koh-Lins. We can be ready when Shenshi Ven comes to take possession of the city.'

Her fingers curled into claws. 'I could kill Rafi tonight, when he comes to my bed, but I have no orders.'

Hesitantly, her breath fluttering the red silk, Alere paid Prato the ultimate compliment: she raised the veil. She swayed close, hands on his chest, lower lip pouting. Even Corin was mesmerised by the trusting plea in those bottomless eyes.

'Please, Prato, I'm afraid,' she murmured, her gaze flicking to his mouth. 'Tell me what I should do.'

Prato's head dipped towards hers, his breath quickening, eyes fixed on her lips. Kal cleared his throat and Prato started.

'You leave the killing to us, little one,' he muttered, drawing a thick knuckle down Alere's cheek. 'Just make sure you're clear of the city before dawn.'

She touched his lower lip. 'But why? I can't leave you now.'

Prato chuckled low in his throat. 'Just before dawn, the Koh-Lins won't know what hit them. There's thirty bombs planted beneath this city. Four right here under the castle walls. All set to explode at once. The city will be ours.' His eyes glittered with a fanatical light. 'Flames of justice and the steel blades of the righteous will prevail, for we are *gangzhi*. The House will survive.'

Alere pressed against him, trembling. She slid her arms around his neck and gazed, wide-eyed up at him. 'But what about you? Come with me. But how can I get you out? There are too many weishi.'

'Never mind me.' Prato's voice was rough. 'We're all prepared to die for our cause. We *will* die to ensure victory. But make sure you get clear. I'll die happier knowing you're safe.' His hands stole around her waist and stroked her back. 'I'd die even happier if...' He murmured something into her ear. Alere gasped when his lips brushed her neck and he dragged her robe off one shoulder.

Corin leapt off the bunk and hammered on their cell door. Enough was enough.

'Time's up, jiaoji. Stand back.' Rattling the lock, he opened the door – and laughed in relief.

Alere, with a sickened look, stood over the two unconscious weishi. Corin opened his mouth but she silenced him with a finger to her lips. She crouched and whispered into the prisoners' ears, then grabbed Prato's ankles.

'Help me get him into the bunk.' They swung the dead weight into the lower bunk. 'Lucky for him the istilqa in the wine took effect. I was going to break something if he tried to kiss me again. Corin, look.' She pointed to the soles of Prato's bare feet, which were covered in faded burn scars.

Corin shrugged but deep in his stomach, unease knotted. 'Means he was a slave in Melcor. Unusual to find that mark in Madina's weishi ranks, though. Slaves are rarely freed and even more rarely escape.' He rolled up the man's sleeve, revealing a blurred, blue N tattooed on the pale upper arm.

'What's the tattoo stand for?' Alere asked.

'Nasim. Hallon Nasim, a Slavemaster in Melcor,' Corin said shortly.

This was news for Rafi's ears. Alere flashed Corin a questioning look but said nothing as they heaved Kal into the top bunk. Corin collected the bottles and food, followed Alere from the cell and locked the door.

Once back in the castle proper, Alere leaned against a wall and yanked the veil off her head. She wrapped her arms around herself, breathing hard.

'Hey.' Corin dropped the bag and gripped her shoulder.

She shoved his hand away.

'Don't. Give me a minute, would you?' She tugged the robe close about her body. 'I feel dirty. I'd make a terrible unveiled jiaoji. I've never been very good at compartmentalising with people I dislike.' She balled the veil in her hand. 'The sewers will be better than dealing with that scum.'

'You say that now,' Corin said lightly. 'Wait until the smell hits you. Pity Prato didn't stay awake long enough to say where the bombs are planted.'

Alere tossed her head and sniffed disdainfully. 'Istilqa injected into a sealed wine bottle; oldest jiaoji trick there is. Honestly. How did he graduate Weishi House?'

'Probably didn't,' Corin said. 'It's not hard to fake the Weishi House tattoo, after all. If he's not a real weishi that could explain the scars.'

'Pretending to be weishi? That's…that's unthinkable.'

'You have led a sheltered life, haven't you?' he said, chuckling. 'He may be a spy in Ven's ranks, working for Slavemaster Hallon Nasim. This gets more complex at every turn.'

'Oh good,' she shot back, 'because it was so simple before. What does *gangzhi* mean? And what was all that about protecting a House if he's a spy for a slaver? How could Ven's men, or a spy, be ready to die for a House? Which House? It makes no sense.'

Corin shrugged. 'Men have been known to work for more than one master. But you're right, there's more going on than a war over the iron. Right now, though, the gunpowder takes priority.'

'Yes.' She glanced dubiously towards the prison.

'What suggestion did you plant?' Corin wasn't surprised Alere was aware of the little-known side effect of istilqa: hypnotic suggestion. Healers had strict regulations about the drug's use. Jiaoji, however, had no such qualms and used it regularly, if in secret. A strong, trained mind could overcome an istilqa suggestion, but Corin doubted the two low-life hundan in the cell were either strong or trained.

'I suggested they forget I'd been there,' she replied. 'And to trust me if we met again.' She walked faster. 'Let's go. We need to warn Farah and Maha. We might have to change plans.'

Corin hurried to keep up with her hasty stride. 'Not a great deal. There's four barrels under the castle, so we need to narrow down which buildings are targeted with the other twenty-six barrels.'

'No, there's more to it.' Alere stopped. 'Didn't you hear him? He said all the barrels will explode together. So, either each barrel must have a clock, set to go off at the same time—'

'Or they're wired to a single trigger to set them all off?' Corin shook his head. 'No, I've seen old illustrations of remote timing devices. Kalima doesn't have the technology to produce anything that complex. It should be easy enough to disconnect the wires. I don't see the problem.'

'It's not the triggers I'm worried about,' Alere said, raising fear-filled eyes. 'Prato didn't say "we *would* die for the cause", he said "we *all will*". We only have ten people. Ven must have thirty or maybe sixty fanatics prepared to die protecting those barrels.'

CHAPTER TWENTY-EIGHT

ALERE

'Clear.' Alere crouched in the shadows, her breath clouding in the crisp night air. She watched the street as, behind her, Corin and Dameer struggled with a manhole cover. Luna-Er, encircled in a faint rainbow, glowed through a thin layer of ice-cloud and washed the cold night death-pale. Two of Ven's weishi lay crumpled on blood-slicked cobblestones, while occupants of nearby houses slept on unaware.

After six gruelling hours, twenty-seven of the thirty barrels had been found and disarmed, with the loss of only two castle weishi. No Alcazar weishi survived. Rafi had ordered no prisoners, deeming time and discretion more important.

Farah's brother, Dameer, insisted on joining Alere's team. Alere suspected Corin had engineered the choice, but she didn't object. Dameer's assistance proved vital. His updated sewer map showed recent blockages and collapses which ruled out several possible barrel sites. He also equipped the teams with masks, goggles, firedamp-safe oil lanterns and a small grey bird in a bamboo cage. The bird was trained to sing when exposed to toxic levels of methane gas or ammonia.

With Dameer along, Alere's job became that of lookout and xiongshou. Her fractured ribs made helping Corin heft manhole covers and barrels impossible, anyway. And she was glad to avoid the task of sliding into the fetid tunnels. The smells wafting from the open manholes caused her to retch. Corin and Dameer bore a miasma even soap might not remove.

But acting as Corin's guardian against the Alcazar weishi came at a cost, and exhaustion made Alere careless. She'd taken a hit from a bo-staff to her cracked ribs. She tested the soft spot on her chest. At least the pain countered sleep's drag on her eyelids. A twinge shot through her shoulder – strained when an Alcazar weishi caught her unawares and almost slit her throat. The fleshy sounds of his death threatened her hard-won calm. She thrust the memory aside.

This evening needed to be put into a section of her mind separate from reality. What she did tonight, who she was tonight, was not the real Alere. It was the person she had to be at this moment, and this moment only. Bu was there a danger the detachment Gavon taught, and which grew with each passing of a human life by her hand, would become part of her real self? If it did, if she saw people as disposable liabilities, she risked becoming something less than human.

Wood scraped on stone and she started, angry with herself. She had lost focus again, endangering her companions.

Behind, Corin and Dameer hauled free the fifth of their allotted six barrels. Cut copper wires dangled from the barrel lid. A primitive timing device, strapped to each barrel, was connected to a spark-striking mechanism under the lid. Prato's boast that the barrels would explode simultaneously was an exaggeration. The devices weren't synchronised, though most would have exploded within an hour of the first.

A soft thumping of rag-wrapped hooves signalled the approach of the small huoche assigned to their team. Corin and Dameer hefted the dead weishi and the disarmed barrel into the huoche, and covered both with dark rugs. A plain-clothes runner-girl, assigned to shadow the team and report back to Rafi, appeared from nowhere. She leapt into the passenger seat next to the taciturn driver and tipped her hat to Corin as the vehicle rattled around the corner.

Corin's stench reached Alere before he did and she backed away from his extended hand.

'Don't put that on me,' she muttered, coughing and covering her nose. Only his teeth flashed white in the moonlight. The rest of him was spattered in dark muck.

'We're almost done,' he whispered, glancing up the quiet, tree-lined street, 'and so are you. Why don't you head back? Dameer and I can handle the last barrel.'

'I'll see it out, Cor, and sleep better tomorrow for knowing we got them all. This is *my* family they've threatened,' she added fiercely. Even in the short time she'd known them, Rafi and Yasmin felt more like family than anyone but Kett and Elmira ever had.

'I'll sleep better for having a hot bath with a bucket load of soap.' Corin chuckled. 'I can't wait to see Ven's face when he enters the city tomorrow and finds it intact.'

'We're not done yet.' Alere inspected the empty street. A unease frissoned along her spine. 'Don't get too cocky.'

'Me?' Corin swept a graceful bow, at odds with his disgusting appearance. 'Never. C'mon. Last barrel's a few blocks away – next to The Ploughman. Should be easy, given Prato and his partner were the weishi assigned to guard it.'

'Again with the overconfidence. Do you find that bites you?'

'On occasion. Can't say life's dull, though.' Corin slipped from the shadows into the moonlit street. Alere followed, holding her side and gritting her teeth, each step a stab into her chest. Dameer's footsteps squelched close behind.

After a block, Alere stopped and rested against a wall to catch her breath.

'Alright?' Corin asked.

'Yes.' She panted. 'Hurts to breathe.'

'Lean on me.'

She screwed up her nose. 'No, thanks. I'll be fine.'

'Liar.' Corin eyed the moon. 'We're ahead of schedule. Walk for a while but let's keep moving.'

Alere bit her lip in an effort to distract herself, galled that her pride and stupidity slowed their pace. By the time Corin dodged into an alley across from The Ploughman, her cheeks were wet with tears. She wiped them away before Corin checked on her again.

The Ploughman was still open for business, though the night was now well into early morning. Light, laughter and music spilled from the inn's repaired windows. Inside, drunken men, women and unveiled jiaoji ate, sang and danced. Barmaids balanced trays of ale and purple wine high over their heads and shuffled between tight-packed tables. The scent of roasted meats, stale beer and wine drifted on the cold air when the door opened.

'Told you he fixes things fast,' Corin murmured in Alere's ear.

'Clearly he's used to your patronage.'

Around the corner, Messenger House also blazed with light. Runners in orange came and went, although far fewer than during daylight. A rider emerged from the stable yard and galloped away, his horse's hooves clattering on the cobbles. Two flitter-birds darted into the air, silhouetted against the moon.

Corin watched the birds vanish into the night sky. 'Who'd send a flitter to the southeast at this time of night?'

'Could be anything. A message to Jidad.' Alere ignored the birds and watched the street.

'No,' Corin said. 'The Jidad flitters are long-flight animals that relay through a station directly south, in the mountains. Those were short-flight birds. They only have the stamina for about fifty or sixty gongli.'

She waved a hand in front of his face. 'Let's keep our minds on our job. The manhole cover's in the middle of the street, in full view of the tavern and Messenger House.'

'Ah.' Corin raised a finger. 'Therein lies the genius. Look behind us.'

Alere turned around. A large, midnight-blue huoche approached, driven by their runner-girl. The huoche was the sort used to transport a body to a death-rite; a solid timber box with curtained windows, and wheels hidden by a skirt of funereal, dark-blue cloth.

Alere sent Corin an incredulous look. 'That's a prophetic sort of ruse.'

'You know me: I like to live dangerously.' He chuckled.

'It's not the living I have an issue with,' she muttered and climbed into the dark space inside the huoche. Dameer and Corin joined her. Alere gagged and held her breath.

'Sorry,' Dameer said. 'My wife says you never get used to it. I lost my sense of smell a long time ago. Probably lucky.'

'Definitely.' Alere peered through the curtains as the huoche rumbled forward. In a corner, the sewer-bird chirruped from its cage.

The vehicle rumbled into the main street. Corin lifted a trapdoor in the floor and watched the ground below. When the manhole's edge came into view, he knocked on the huoche's front wall. The vehicle lurched to a stop. The runner-girl climbed down and fussed with a wheel. Corin and Dameer dropped into the sewer while Alere kept watch. Tavern patrons ignored the huoche and passing runners gave it a wide berth. Maybe a hearse was not such a bad cover after all.

Several tense minutes passed before Corin heaved himself out of the manhole, his breath harsh through the mask. He handed Alere the birdcage. The reptile cocked an eye and twittered before flipping back its furry wings and settling. Corin hauled on a net and pulled the last barrel into the hearse while Dameer replaced the manhole cover.

'If that's it, shenshi, I'll be off.' Dameer lowered his mask and squinted up through the trapdoor. 'I've men working their way through the tunnels, in case we missed something. I want to get their reports. I'll send a runner if we find anything.'

Corin passed him the birdcage and gripped his forearm. 'Shenshi Rafi is grateful for your help, Dameer. I know we can trust you to keep this night's work quiet.'

Dameer saluted and, after a quick look from beneath the vehicle's skirts, vanished into the night.

Corin patted the barrel. 'Time to go home and have that bath, I think.'

He knocked three times on the hearse's roof and sighed, his shoulders drooping. It was the first time Alere had seen him look tired. She shut her eyes ang gave way to the fatigue seeping into her limbs.

A thump on the huoche's side and the runner girl's terrified scream jolted Alere awake. A sword-blade speared through the hearse's timber side, tearing Alere's sleeve. She wrenched free and reached for her sword. Corin swore and kicked the back door open.

ROHNE

Rohne stretched his back, relieved to be off his horse and glad the trip was over. He downed the last mouthful of rich, dark ale and signalled to The Ploughman's overworked barmaid. Another drink might help get rid of the niggling headache which, over the past few weeks, had grown into a constant low-key pain. The girl thumped a tankard in front of him and left with a saucy wink and a flip of her skirt. He was tempted. Almost three weeks of Mina fussing over Kett was enough to drive any man insane.

Jahim! Kett was so cool Rohne couldn't even tell if the man had feelings at all, let alone for Mina. It was painfully clear she'd fallen in love with the weishi. Even after Kett'd healed enough to travel, she still waited on him, despite his gentle discouragement.

Kett slid into the seat opposite and accepted the tankard Rohne had ordered for him.

'Mina alright?' Rohne asked.

'We rode hard to get here this fast. She's exhausted. I made her eat. She'll be asleep in two minutes, even with this noise.' Kett nodded at the taproom.

The room reverberated with raucous laugher and song. Smoke curled from the fireplace up to the timber ceiling and hung there in a blue haze. Drinkers beat pewter tankards on wooden tables as the musicians struck up a dance tune. Those few souls still steady on their feet braved the dance floor in a stomping, bawdy romp. A brown-clad tradesman slipped his arm around the waist of an unveiled jiaoji and dragged her away from her dance partner. Her partner took umbrage, swung a wild punch and missed. Laughter ensued as other dancers dragged the combatants apart and the music volume increased.

Rohne sniggered into his tankard. A bar fight would almost make up for the lack of raiders on the journey. The trip from Newmec had been disappointing in that aspect. He'd been looking forward to spilling a few raider brains. But when they'd reached Paradise, rumour said the previous caravan – Alere's – had all but wiped the raiders out.

'Mina still wanted to find Alere.' Kett frowned.

Rohne laughed. 'It's the middle of the night. And that runner you hired brought us the message Alere left with Healer House, so we know she's alright. She'll find us.'

'But since Paradise, when you had that Seeing of Alere injured in an alley, Mina's been convinced Alere will die without our help.'

'I knew I should've kept my mouth shut.'

'Mina wouldn't be impressed if you'd told her about the Seeing *after* Alere was injured.' Kett held Rohne's gaze. 'Me either, for that matter.'

Rohne flushed, annoyed Kett's disapproval bothered him. Rohne was torn between disliking Kett for Mina's obsession and liking the man for his shrewd insight and open-mindedness. Everyone else in the caravan had been dull and uneducated. Kett was the only one with more than half a brain. Over the past few days, Rohne found it increasingly difficult to keep secret his deeper thoughts and plans. But Kett was, essentially, of Xintou House and therefore a potential enemy.

Rohne swigged his drink. The second ale hadn't killed the headache, but did numb the unrest and dissatisfaction seething in his guts. He drank quickly, ordering a third before the tankard was empty. Across the table, Kett merely raised a brow at him, then scanned the room.

He gripped Rohne's arm. 'Do you see that hearse outside?'

Rohne spotted it through the grimy window, half-lit in the flickering light of the street torches. Ordinary, if a little oddly timed. But no-one liked to be reminded of death, so perhaps it was policy to transport dead people late at night.

'It's been there for almost half an hour,' Kett added, 'and the driver's been pretending to fix a perfectly sound wheel.'

Rohne shrugged. 'So? Maybe she doesn't want to be working at this hour. Who would?'

Kett rose from the table. 'Someone came out from under it. Someone alive, that is. Carrying a birdcage. Definitely not normal for a hearse.'

'Zhenshide!' Rohne slammed the empty tankard onto the table. 'So you're going to *look* for trouble now? It's nothing to do with us.'

'I thought trouble's what *you* were looking for. You complained there were no raiders to fight. Here's your chance.'

Rohne laughed. 'Well, when you put it like that…'

They wove through the room, skirting tables and stepping over outstretched legs, food scraps and spilled ale. Rohne neared the door and lost sight of the huoche. Kett's hand gripped the doorknob when the sharp *ching* of metal on ceramic cut through the laughter and music. Rohne reached for his sword but Kett held up a warning hand.

'Don't draw in here. That came from outside,' Kett said. 'Wait 'til we know who's fighting before you take sides.'

Rohne reluctantly released the hilt. Once out of the tavern, Kett faded into the shadows, invisible. Rohne stayed close to a window where the light would distract attention from his pale shirt.

In the middle of the street, ten men had a slight, black-clad weishi and a blond man backed up against the hearse. The body of the driver, a child, lay limp on the cobbles. Rohne studied the scene. The ten men wore matching dark uniforms; probably the city guard apprehending criminals. Disappointing, but they hardly needed assistance. Rohne shifted, ready to return to the inn's warmth. Kett remained, unmoving.

'Wait.' Kett's deep voice emerged from the darkness. 'They're not in House or Family colours. Why attack another weishi and a yongbing? And no true weishi would strike an unarmed girl-child.'

Rohne looked closer. The blond defender moved so fast his silver-metal sword flickered like lightning. His white teeth gleamed as he ran an attacker through. His partner, the small weishi, moved awkwardly, favouring his left leg. Blood glistened on his dark trous. He feinted. His sword deflected a blade and stabbed beneath it in a perfect time-thrust. The tip sank deep into his opponent's chest. The small weishi followed through with an elbow-strike to the next attacker's throat, then spun and slit the jugular of another.

Kett uttered an oath and leapt from the shadows. 'That's Alere!'

'What?' Rohne followed, unsure who to help. 'How do you know?'

'I know how she fights. I taught her that move.'

Kett's sword slickered free of its scabbard. He sprinted into the street with Rohne close behind. They waded in to the fray, blades swinging.

For the first time, Rohne saw Kett in action against an enemy. The man was extraordinary. In four precise moves, Kett took out three of Alere's attackers. He wasn't even breathing hard when he engaged a fourth. Rohne, head spinning with alcohol, deflected a ceramic sword. He drove a knee into an attacker's stomach, then jammed his dagger into the man's chest. By the time he drew the blade free, nine weishi lay bleeding on the ground.

Alere's blond companion lifted his sword, ready to strike at Rohne.

Rohne raised his blade.

A rattling noise echoed off the surrounding buildings. The hearse rolled along the street. The blond man glanced around and swore.

'Corin,' Alere yelled. 'The barrel – there's another man.'

The hearse gathered momentum and the blond man glanced back and forth between Rohne and the huoche.

'I'm on Alere's side, friend.' Rohne pointed his dagger at Alere, who limped after the huoche.

The man she'd called Corin sent Rohne a puzzled frown, backed out of striking distance then turned and dashed after Alere. Rohne raised his brows and flicked blood from his sword. What was so important about a hearse? The huoche veered across the street towards Messenger House, brightly lit and buzzing with activity. An orange light glimmered through the hearse's curtains. The orange of House uniforms? No. Flame licked through a window and smoke spiralled into the night sky. Why on Kalima would someone set the thing alight?

Rohne looked to Kett, who frowned.

Corin caught up with Alere and grabbed her arm. She pulled against his grip, pointing at the huoche.

They exchanged words Rohne couldn't hear over the rattling of wheels. Corin shook his head and half-dragged and half-carried Alere towards a nearby alley.

Sword in hand, Kett ran in Alere's direction. Rohne called after him.

The huoche exploded into brilliance. Too bright, too hot, too loud. A tongue of fire licked at the moon. Smoke ate the stars and swallowed the sky. Something roared and kicked Rohne in the chest. He slammed into the ground and curled up, protecting his head as the sky vomited dirt, glass, stone and timber.

Fingers touched his neck. Rohne groaned but heard no sound, only felt a rumbling in his chest. He rolled onto his back and pain speared through his hip and ribs. Dust caked his eyelashes. His arms were too heavy to lift. Someone sponged his eyes clean and the world swam into focus.

Mina leaned over him, frowning in concentration, gently probing for injuries. Her mouth moved, but no sound penetrated the dull thump of his heartbeat in his ears.

'Can't hear you,' he said, unsure if any sound emerged. Mina shook her head and pointed to her mouth then to his ears. Did that mean she couldn't hear him, either? Jahim. Lip-reading could only get so much across.

Apart from a few cuts and bruises, and a lump on the back of his head, Rohne found no serious injuries. Grit dug into his palms as he pushed up to his knees. He stood, swaying, and Mina steadied him.

Flames danced up the walls of Messenger House and leapt into the sky. Dazed, half-dressed runners flooded into the street. Flitterbirds circled overhead, their white breasts pink in the fire's glow. Horses and che-ma pranced and tugged against their halters as riders dragged them from the stables into the street. Without the crackle of fire or the screams of human pain to make it real, Rohne viewed the scene with detachment, as if through a thick window.

People hurried from surrounding buildings, clutching each other in horror and confusion. A bucket brigade fought to stop the flames spreading. Six che-ma arrived, towing a huge bronze water tank that rumbled to a halt before Messenger House. Men leapt from the huoche and pumped water onto the flames. A second firewatch huoche arrived and the firefighters soon had the blaze under control. Smoke billowed high into the darkness. Ash settled on Rohne's hair and shoulders.

Rohne fought the fog and ache in his head. He peered at the chaos and ruined buildings. The front of Messenger House was a gaping hole. Timber and stone fragments littered the street. Windows in nearby buildings had imploded. The scent of smoke, dust and another, acrid, but not unpleasant, smell hung in the air. Rohne coughed and blinked away the sting of smoke.

Not far away, Mina crouched over a prone form – one of the weishi killed in the attack on Alere. Where was Alere? And Kett? Or the other man, Corin?

He drove his thoughts into Mina's distracted Outers.

You alright? Where's Kett?

She started. Rohne usually warned her before inserting his thoughts. He tapped his ears.

Can't hear you, so this is best.

She nodded, wiping bloody hands on her robe.

I'm fine. The explosion woke me. Your hearing should come back in a day or so. Kett's alright as well, although his hearing's partly affected, too. He went that way. She pointed to the alley where Corin and Alere had taken refuge. *He asked me to help anyone in need. He said Alere was here. Have you seen her? He didn't say where. Is she alright?*

Rohne peered down the street. Chunks of timber and masonry half-blocked the alley. If Corin and Alere were trapped in the rubble, Kett would need help.

Alere was closer to the explosion. Kett's looking for her. I'll go help.

A female runner grabbed at Mina's arm and tugged her to where a body lay sprawled in the street. Mina hesitated, tucking the healer bag she'd bought in Newmec under her arm but looking towards the alley.

Rohne waved her ahead. *Go help. I'll call the second we find Alere, I promise.*

He staggered along the street on unsteady legs and paused at the alley's entrance – the alley he'd Seen in his precog about Alere. If his vision was right, she was unconscious and injured.

'Kett?' Rohne yelled. The word sounded muffled and distant. 'If you can hear me, let me into your Outer. I can't hear.'

He reached for Kett's mind and found him not far away, past the blockage. The man was intent on something, but partially dropped his shallowest Outer ward to allow Rohne access.

Did you find Alere?

Yes. I've just about got them free. Get Mina. Alli's injured.

Rohne acknowledged and called Mina. *Alere's injured. Kett's bringing her out.*

Mina gathered her skirts and bag and ran to the alley. Kett clambered over the rubble, bearing a limp, black-clad body in his arms. Corin staggered clear of the debris, collapsed onto a stone block, and held his head in his hands. Blood streaked scarlet through the grey dust that shrouded his skin and clothing.

Rohne cleared a space and Kett laid Alere on the road. Mina ripped open Alere's shirt and gently prodded the purpling skin over her ribs, then checked her head. She used Rohne's dagger to cut away Alere's bloodied trous, exposing a deep slice on her thigh. Mina's frown deepened. She bandaged the oozing wound and gestured to Kett, who gathered Alere in his arms. Then Mina turned to Corin, but he batted away her hands. She backed off, her nose wrinkling. Rohne caught a whiff of raw sewage and coughed.

Mina gestured to Rohne and tapped her temple, raising her little finger. He reached for her Outers. She pointed at Corin.

I need more information and to get somewhere I can work on Alere's injuries. She's badly hurt. Quickly. Talk to this man. Find out where Healer House is. He can't hear me.

Rohne grimaced. This was not going to be that simple. Mina and Kett stared at him expectantly.

Mina gripped his arm, her eyes wide and frightened. *Hurry, Rohne.* She glanced at Alere's limp form. *I can't tell if she has internal injuries but she's very pale and her pulse is weak. She could die.*

He crouched in front of Corin. If the man was trained to ward as well as Kett, this would be over before it started. Tentatively, Rohne reached out. Corin had solid foundations for warding, but his mind was scattered and unfocussed; his wards fractured by memories of the explosion and fear for Alere. Rohne slid in through a crack.

Corin, don't panic. My name's Rohne. I'm a friend of Alere's. I'm here with Mina and Kett to help.

Corin reeled back as if punched, his green eyes wide and vivid against the grey dust. His wards slammed up. Rohne jerked, stunned. Corin leapt to his feet, dagger drawn, poised to attack.

Rohne held both hands up and mouthed, 'Let me help.' He tapped his temple and pointed to Alere's limp body in Kett's arms. The gesture seemed to stir Corin into decision and his Outer wards came partway down. Head aching, Rohne tried again.

We need to get Alere somewhere safe. She's badly hurt. Where's Healer House?

Corin started towards Kett, but paused with a filthy hand half-raised. *How bad is she?* His rich mental voice was underlain with layers of intelligence, fear, and hidden pain.

Mina is worried she may have internal injuries. Could be bad. Possibly fatal if she's not seen to soon.

Corin swore aloud and swiped a hand over his head, raising a cloud of dust. *We can't take her to Healer House. She would be recog—* He stared at Mina, his eyes widening. *We have to go to the castle. Rafi's expecting us. All of us.* He pointed up the hill at the castle, a black bulk against the starry sky. His gaze returned to Mina. *Tell her to do everything she can. Alere* must *survive. The Jundom depends on it.*

Rohne hesitated then passed the information to Mina and added to her: *I'll get our gear and the horses. You and Kett take Alere and follow Corin. Make sure the gate weishi know I'm coming.*

Mina nodded and Rohne repeated the message to Kett and Corin.

Then Mina and the two men vanished carried Alere into the darkness. Rohne, left in roaring silence, studied the looming, dark-stone edifice on the hill.

The jundom depended on Alere's survival? And what if she didn't survive? Was the Jun Second's private residence a smart place for a male xintou involved in her death to be? Getting in should be easy. Getting out might be another matter if Rafi was as prejudiced against male xintou as most of the populace. What was so important about Alere? She was only kin-child, not Jun-Heir.

Rohne grimaced. What the jahim was he doing and where would this take him?

PART III

CHAPTER TWENTY-NINE

ALERE

Alere fought against sleep; struggled out of nightmares. A frightening lethargy pinned her limbs to a too-soft bed that smelled earthy; of fennaro leaves. She lay still, listening, slowing her panting breaths. A scraping noise broke the silence. A door opening? She felt for her dagger. Soft footsteps neared. She scrabbled under the pillow. Where was her dagger? Her ribs twinged as she pushed onto one elbow. The green velvet bed-curtains parted. Alere raised an arm and squinted at the figure silhouetted against the brilliant afternoon sunshine.

'What are you doing awake?' A female voice chided. 'I gave you enough istilqa to put you out for a few more hours yet.'

'Mina?' Alere groaned and collapsed onto the pillows.

Mina lifted the white healer veil onto her forehead and laid a cool hand on Alere's cheek. 'Of course it's me. Do you know anyone else who looks exactly like you?'

'What are you doing here?' Alere studied her sister's shadowed face, half-inclined to think her an istilqa-induced hallucination.

'Either you've got amnesia or you're still half-asleep,' Mina said. 'I've ridden across most of the Jundom to meet you, remember? Keep talking like that and I'll think you aren't glad to see me.'

Alere chuckled and gripped Mina's fingers. 'Sorry. I am glad. I wasn't expecting you to be here.'

Mina sighed. 'No, I'm sorry I snapped. It's been a long night.'

'The explosion!' Alere tried to sit up, only to fall back with a gasp. 'What happened? Is Corin all right?' She kicked irritably at the quilt that lay heavily on her legs. 'Where am I?'

Mina flung open the bed curtains. A vaulted timber ceiling disappeared behind a green velvet bed canopy. The room's simple, timber furnishings were upholstered in green, matching the delicate flowers embroidered on the quilt.

'Corin's fine. We're in the castle. Don't try to get up,' her sister admonished. 'You should still be sleeping. Is something troubling you? Are you in pain?'

Fighting lassitude, Alere moved her limbs beneath the stifling covers. Her left leg and shoulder were stiff.

'No,' she said, 'but I probably will be when the istilqa wears off. You sure Corin's all right? Where's Kett?'

Mina fussed with the blankets then sighed and sank onto the bed. Dark circles shadowed her eyes and exhaustion cloaked her shoulders.

'You look like diyu, Mina. What happened?'

Mina hesitated, then gave what Alere suspected was the short version of her hurried ride to Shanzhai and last night's events. Alere listened in silence.

Mina stopped at last, peering at Alere, her lips pursed. 'Now it's your turn. How did you come here? What was last night about? No one will tell me anything. Two castle weishi are dead and two more are seriously injured – plus you, Corin, and the runner-girl. And

Messenger House is in ruins.' She folded her arms. 'You owe me an explanation.'

Alere plucked at quilt. 'You're right, but we need to see Rafi and Corin first. It's not my secret to share. Oh! Did we find all the barrels?'

'Barrels?'

'Long story. Help me up and I'll tell you.'

'You really should stay in bed,' Mina said, frowning. 'You lost a lot of blood, and your ribs are fractured. Corin tells me they were just healing, too. You're just lucky you didn't have internal injuries.'

'I won't sleep until I know what happened. But I'd rather not have everyone in here while I'm lying naked in bed.'

Mina giggled. 'Yes, that might be a little embarrassing. Fine. But this is against my better judgement. Hold out your arm.' She took an alzin needle and small, glass phial from her healer bag. She swabbed Alere's inner elbow with a bamboo cloth that reeked of pure alcohol and injected a clear fluid into the vein. 'This is maqa. It will counteract the istilqa and still dull the pain. But if you need to talk, do it fast. You'll crash in about an hour.'

She helped Alere use the bathroom and dress in a Koh-Lin green house-robe. Then Mina tugged a bell-rope and sent a servant for Corin and Rafi. She propped Alere on the chaise-lounge.

'At least you look alive, not half-dead like last night. You scared me.' She stroked Alere's hair 'I've been so worried about you these last two weeks. When I saw you injured last night—'

'Don't fuss, Mina.' Alere pushed Mina's hand gently away. Would she ever get used to having a sister who cared so much?

Mina flushed and turned away.

'I'm sorry, Mina.' Alere sighed. 'I'm just not used to...' She waved a hand vaguely in her sister's direction.

Mina raised haunted eyes and touched Alere's arm. 'I understand. Kett told me a bit about Xintou House and how they isolated you girls. It must have been difficult.'

Alere stared resolutely out at the winter-green sky, hurt that Kett had talked behind her back. What else had he told? How close were he and Mina? 'Yes,' she said. 'But I'd rather not talk about it.'

Her sister rose, brushing at her robe. 'I have to check on the weishi. Don't start explaining what's happening until I get back.' With a worried look over her shoulder, she left the room.

Alere closed her eyes and tried to ignore her throbbing ribs and thigh.

After several minutes, the door opened. Corin leant against the door frame, his hands thrust deep in his pockets. He wore a nobleman's rich clothing: a pale-grey silk shirt, with deep green trous and vest that matched his eyes. He bowed deeply, the wide sweep of his arms swirling a storm-grey cloak edged with glass-rabbit fur.

'Do you approve?' His grin broadened and he brushed two fingers along his jaw. Gone was the two-day growth he maintained on the road. His hair was clean and smoothed back. He sat on the couch with his legs stretched under the table. On his hip rested the ornate scabbard he usually hid, but the Johnston dagger was still plain-sheathed.

'I definitely approve,' Alere replied. 'And you certainly smell better than last night. I had no idea you could clean up so nicely.' She touched her forehead. His handsome face was marred by a neat bandage over his left eyebrow. 'Nothing serious?'

'No. A few bruises. Couldn't hear for a while but that's improved. You?' he asked, raking her with a narrow look. 'Mina said there was nothing life-threatening, but she's so gaisi cool I wasn't sure she was telling the truth.'

'To be honest, she's got me so full of painkillers I can't tell. I'll be fine in a couple of days, I'm sure. Thank you for shielding me from the explosion.' She stretched a hand towards him. 'Sure you're alright?'

Corin raised her palm to his lips.

Alere sucked a quick breath and snatched her hand back.

His eyes softened. 'I'm sure.'

The door handle rattled. He chuckled wryly, shook his head and strolled to the window.

Kett and Rohne entered and greeted Corin, who nodded amicably. Kett knelt and drew Alere into a gentle hug. Conscious of Corin's scrutiny, Alere suppressed an urge to dissolve into relieved tears on Kett's shoulder. She managed a smile when Kett studied her.

'I did say I expected to find you in one piece,' he said.

'I am.' She shrugged at his skeptical look. 'Well, sort of. I'll be all right, I promise.'

Apparently satisfied, Kett relaxed into the couch vacated by Corin, watching her from beneath half-closed lids.

'You two arrived at the right time last night,' Alere said. 'You must've ridden hard to get here so fast.'

'Mina's been anxious about you for the last two weeks.' Kett inclined his head at Rohne. 'Then Rohne Saw parts of last night so we thought it best to get here quickly.'

Unease crawled across Alere's skin. Rohne had precognitive abilities?

The door opened to admit Mina. She eyed each of them narrowly. 'Corin, is that cut infected?'

'No, shunu,' he replied, grinning. 'I promise I washed, just like you told me to.'

Mina ignored his levity and addressed Rohne. 'What about your hearing? And that bruise on the back on your head? No headaches?' She reached towards his head.

'It's fine, Mina. We're all fine,' he said, shoving her hand aside. She pursed her lips and dropped onto the couch next to Kett. Rohne scowled.

'Are the injured recovering?' Kett asked Mina.

'Yes, Healer House here is amazing.' Her face lit up. 'I'd love to study with them.'

'You look tired. Make sure you take care of yourself.' Kett squeezed her hand and she smiled gratefully.

'I'll make sure the servants look after her.' Rohne spoke too loudly in the small room. Mina flushed and pulled her hand free of Kett's.

Unperturbed, Kett directed his attention to Alere. 'Perhaps you can tell us what's going on – before Rafi arrives.'

Alere checked with Corin. He nodded. She twisted a lock of hair around one finger and tried to organise her thoughts. What could she say to convince all of them to stay and help? Rohne, especially, could be invaluable in the upcoming confrontation – if he was willing and if Corin and Rafi didn't overreact when faced with a male xintou.

'I need to tell you all something important, then I'm hoping you'll help me,' she said.

'Of course,' Mina grasped her sister's arm. 'If we can.'

'Thanks, Mina. Now please let me get this out before I panic and change my mind.' Alere sneaked a guilty look at Kett.

Kett scrubbed a hand over his face. 'All right. Out with it, Alli.'

Corin strode from his place at the window and stood behind her. His hands fell, warm and reassuring, onto her shoulders. Kett sent him a sharp glance, then his expression blanked again.

Alere launched into an explanation of her last few days. Even leaving out the iron ore the tale was enough to make Rohne and Mina gasp. Kett seemed intent on his hands, which hung, clasped and white-knuckled, between his knees. The small muscles in his jaw worked.

'Poisoned with manxing!' Mina cried. 'How *could* they? That poor girl – and Jun Radan, too.'

Rohne frowned and stared at the floor.

'You'll become Jun-Heir,' Kett said, his voice low and strained. He leaned forward, elbows on his knees.

Alere nodded and pressed her lips together to prevent herself babbling the tangle of defensive reasons swirling in her head. A big part of her wanted his approval; his advice; his support. But she wasn't going to beg him to stay. It had to be his choice.

'To what end? What do you want, Alli?' he asked.

She smoothed a strand of hair behind her ear. 'Not the position and wealth, if that's what you mean. And certainly not the responsibility. I've enjoyed being free.'

'No, that's not what I meant.' Kett searched her face. 'What do *you* want? Not what's best for the Koh-Lins or the Jundom or even us. This is your life, Alli. Are you willing to sacrifice it and live someone else's? You've spent your youth under other people's rules, and hated it. Do this and you'll be bound again – and vulnerable if Ven and Hanna learn the truth. Never safe, Alli.'

Alere suppressed a flutter of unease. 'You know me, Kett. When did I ever choose the safe option? I can't live that way. I know I'll be restricted, but they need me here. In Xintou House I was an unwanted extra. But here I'm worth something, even if it's just as a substitute for Lianna.'

'Who are you trying to convince, Alli?' Kett frowned 'I admit the cause is just. I'm as angry as you are at Hanna and Ven. But what happens afterward? These people will just use you for their own ends. You're so much more than a poor copy of Lianna. You deserve better.'

'Rafi's not...' Her certainty withered under Kett's cool cynicism. She glanced involuntarily at Corin, seeking support. Kett's mouth thinned. He rose and took a step towards the musician.

Alere grabbed Kett's arm. 'Don't.'

'Acquit me, my friend.' Corin raised his hands. 'I hold nothing over her. And none of us consider her a poor copy of Lianna. But this is her choice alone.' He cocked his head and smiled at Alere. 'I don't rate my charms so highly that she'd succumb to my influence.'

Blood rose to Alere's cheeks. 'This is my choice, Kett. I care about Rafi and Yasmin. I want to help. I can't let Ven, Hanna and Celia do this. I promised Radan.'

Kett shook free of her grip and turned away, his expression grim. 'Very well, if that's your decision then you know I'll support you. Mina? Rohne? It's a secret that can only be kept by agreement of all.'

'I'll stay for a while if you need me, though I'm not sure why you would,' Mina said. Her glance flicked to Kett, and Alere caught a puzzling hint of longing in her sister's expression. Were they arguing?

Rohne watched Mina and Kett, his amber eyes scornful beneath half-closed lids.

'In honest truth,' he drawled, setting his feet on the table and interlacing his fingers behind his head, 'it means little to me who sits on the Koh-Lin throne. I promised the girls would arrive safely. Beyond that, if they choose to stay, there's nothing keeping me here. But I'll stay until Mina decides whether she needs an escort home or not.' He shrugged. 'And if Alere really does look like Lianna, then no-one would believe the Jun-Heir was a fake, even if I told them.'

Relief leapt into Alere's heart. The affection between Kett and Mina must be torture for Rohne yet he was still willing to help if it meant protecting his childhood friend.

'Thank you, Rohne, Mina. You don't know what that means to me,' she said. 'I—'

'But there's something else, isn't there?' Rohne sat forward and pointed at Alere. 'You're not telling us something. So, my only proviso is this: if your plans are likely to endanger Mina or even Nasra, then tell me now.'

'Understood,' Alere replied stiffly. 'You're right: there is more. But we need to wait for Rafi before I tell you the rest.'

Rohne leaned back again in his chair, a hint of satisfaction hovering about his mouth.

A knock fell on the door. Rafi and Yasmin, elegant and regal, swept into the room.

'Shenshi, shunu,' said Corin, bowing, 'may I introduce Rohne Marin-kin, Mina Sura-kin – or rather Koh-Lin – and Kett Peter-kin.'

Alere watched anxiously as her new parents exchanged polite greetings with her friends. Yasmin rushed to greet Mina. Rafi bowed to Rohne before turning to Kett. Rafi's eyes widened and faint worry lines creased his brow. He hesitated before stiffly inclining his head. Kett bowed then retreated to a corner, silent and watchful. Rafi, his expression still uneasy, addressed Alere.

'You're well?' He regarded her.

Alere nodded.

'Look Rafi.' Yasmin brushed tears from her cheeks. 'Now we have two daughters.' She hugged Mina close.

'Oh, shunu.' Mina's eyes brimmed and she returned the embrace. 'Alere told us. We can't replace Lianna. I'm so sorry.'

'We know. But Sura and Yasmin are identical twins, so you are – in a way – Yasmin's daughters, too,' Rafi replied gravely. 'We don't want Alere to be Lianna, except in name. We're simply grateful to have you both here. All of you. Thank you. Please, sit.'

Yasmin and Mina sat on Alere's couch while Kett continued to stand. He ignored Alere's gesture to join them. She frowned but there was no point in forcing him to sit if he was uncomfortable in the Jun's presence.

Rafi gathered everyone's attention. 'I'm sure Alere has told you some of our story. Let me fill in the blanks. But what's said here must not go beyond this room, is that understood? Should you betray Alere's trust or ours, there will be consequences. Do I make myself clear?' He pinned first Rohne then Kett with a narrow stare. Both men nodded; Kett's expression thoughtful, Rohne's cool.

Rafi placed an irregular block of silvery metal, the size of a fist, on the table. A collective sigh swept the room at the sight of the iron. Sharp, crystalline striations patterned the flattest surfaces and lifted it into the realm of beauty – like Alere's bracelet.

'This is the reason for last night's explosion and why Lianna was killed.' Rafi touched the ingot. 'For this Hanna, Ven and Celia murdered an innocent girl, along with a man I was glad to call friend, and many more. Radan wasn't strong, but he didn't deserve to die; any more than Lianna or the others. Radan sent Alere to warn me that Hanna intends to find and exploit the iron deposit on my lands. Hanna plans to destroy Xintou House and make war on Melcor.'

Mina gasped and clutched at Alere's hand.

'Hanna wants to destroy Xintou House?' Rohne rubbed at his mouth.

Alere looked at him sharply. Was that gleam in his eye concern or excitement? After all, he had the most to gain if Xintou fell.

'In the seven centuries we've been on this planet,' Rafi said, 'we've never had a major war. But we seem to court conflict and it was only a matter of time before someone flexed their muscles. I'd rather not go down in the history of Kalima as the first, though.' He hefted the chunk of metal in his hands. 'And I'd rather the iron from my land wasn't responsible for the deaths of thousands.'

'But how,' Rohne asked, 'could Ven take the city, or the iron? Corin says Ven has only five thousand men.'

'We're not sure yet,' Rafi said. 'Ven failed in negotiating a marriage treaty for Lianna. She swore to me she wouldn't be sold in marriage to a man she detested. If you've met Ven, you'll understand what she meant.'

Alere needed no reminders after Ven's attack on Nahlia. She shivered, remembering the way he stared through people – as though they weren't human, but merely an inconvenience or resource.

'Ven is also my second cousin. Lianna's death would open the way for him to take over if I died without an heir,' Rafi continued, his voice flat. 'But now I have an heir again and I don't intend to die soon, unless Hanna finds a way to poison me as well.' He smiled sourly.

'Rafi!' Yasmin cried. Corin's brows twitched into a frown.

'Never fear,' Rafi said. 'I've increased security around our kitchens. Our food will be bland for a while. But I'm more concerned about Hanna's immediate plans. After the failure of last night's attack, I believe her next move will be to march on Shanzhai *en force*.' He held up a hand when Yasmin uttered a faint protest. 'News has already arrived. While Ven's here with his five thousand "honour guard", Hanna marches from Madina to Shanzhai with an equal number of junren. And, if my information is correct, five thousand more will join her from the Zah-Hill estates in Asalam.'

Alere looked for Corin's reaction, but he showed none. Had he known even before she'd agreed to play Lianna's part? Why had he said nothing?

'According to my source,' Rafi said, 'Hanna began marching this morning. She must've heard of last night's failed attack and decided not to wait any longer. She will take two to three weeks to get here. Also, a runner from Ven arrived a few moments ago.'

Rafi unrolled a tiny sheet of paper and read aloud. 'Jun First, Ven Zah-Hill, is distressed to hear of the disaster that occurred last night. He trusts it will in no way impinge on Shunu Lianna's eighteenth nameday celebrations. Given the circumstances, his formal visit will be postponed for two days to allow the citizens of Shanzhai to deal with this difficulty.

'So: Ven buys us time for Alere to recover.' Rafi crushed the message and tossed it onto the table. 'And also buys himself time to make new plans to invade under the guise of a friendly visit. I am forced to open the gates to him or be deemed a traitor and thus justify his attack.'

A shocked silence followed his calm words. Alere instinctively sought Kett, but his gaze remained fixed on the floor. Even Corin was unusually grave, the sparkle gone from his eyes.

'May I ask, shenshi,' Rohne said, his eyes darting from person to person. 'Where's your Xintou in this? Surely she and your Shangwei should be included in this discussion?'

Alere started. Rohne was right. She'd seen no hint of the iconic gold veil, nor heard mention of a Bonded Xintou. Rafi lowered his head. When he looked up, the answer lay in the shadows that darkened his eyes.

'No,' she whispered.

'At the time, I thought only of the loss of a dear and trusted friend.' Rafi drove his fingers through his hair. 'Now I see her death may not have been an accident. Letta was with our family for almost fifteen years. About three months ago she visited Jun Fifth Zhou-

Issa. He has no Xintou at present and Letta offered to help him settle a dispute. Five of my weishi accompanied her.'

'What happened?' Alere asked.

'She fell from her horse and struck her head.' His voice cracked. 'We blamed the stable lads for not maintaining her tack. The girth-strap was worn. Now...'

'Why hasn't Mistress Li sent a gene-daughter replacement?' Kett's deep voice cut through the silence. 'Why didn't we hear of it at the House?'

'Did Mistress Li not make it public?' Rafi frowned. 'Perhaps Mistress Li was trying to minimise unease by keeping silence. Letta's oldest daughter's not yet of age. We must wait a year.'

'We don't have that long,' Alere said. 'If Hanna's coming then Celia will be too, if she's not here already, with Ven. You have too many secrets to be left unprotected. Without a Xintou, you won't be able to ward against Celia. There must be another way.' She lifted a brow at Rohne, who stilled.

His amber eyes hardened and swept the room, lingering on each person in turn. He folded his arms across his chest and gave Alere a slow nod. She swallowed fluttering uncertainty.

'Rafi.' Alere gripped her father's arm. 'Desperate times call for desperate measures. I have a suggestion. But please keep an open mind and don't make a snap judgement. Can you do that?'

Rafi eyed Corin, who shrugged.

'Very well,' the Jun Second said. 'What?'

'Rohne can help.' Hopefully she wasn't making a major mistake in her assessment of Rafi's character. 'He's a xintou.'

Rafi stiffened and his hand dropped to his hip, though he wore no weapon. Kett copied the gesture, his eyes fixed on Rafi.

Rohne laughed; a harsh, bitter sound that made Yasmin flinch and Rafi purse his lips.

'How can this be?' Rafi threw the question to Alere, but his gaze shifted back to Rohne. 'It's forbidden. How did Mistress Li allow it?'

Responding to a steady look from Rohne, Alere shook her head. 'As far as I know, she's not aware of his existence. As to how it happened, that's Rohne's story to tell, if he will. All I ask, shenshi, is that you suspend judgement. Xintou or not, Rohne's been a true friend to Mina – and to me these past few weeks. He has nothing to gain and much to lose by revealing his skills. It's up to you, of course, but I don't know that you're in a position to turn him down. Don't let your pride put your people at risk.'

Rafi's jaw clenched and his eyes glittered. He studied her, Mina, Rohne and lastly, Kett. Alere frowned. What did her father see in Kett to keep his attention for so long? Kett's calm expression revealed nothing, as usual.

Finally, Rafi inclined his head with distant politeness. 'Very well. We appreciate your offer. How can you assist?'

Rohne sat forward, intense and eager. 'Well, not being Bonded to your family does limit my usefulness. But there are certain things I can do that others can't. With people I've met, I can Read and Send Outers up to thirty gongli.'

Rafi's eyes blazed. 'That's further than any xintou I've ever heard of.' He leaned back and steepled his fingers. 'So, once you've met Hanna, Celia and Ven you could Read them in places they believe themselves safe. Yes, that is helpful. Anything else? It will help to plan a strategy if I understand your strengths.'

With a smug smile, Rohne pointed to the table. The iron rock rose into the air and slapped in his open palm. He twirled the metal in his fingertips like a toy. Then he flipped it into the air where it wafted, featherlike, back to the table.

Silence prevailed for several thick moment, until Rohne shifted and his chair creaked.

'Wasai!' Alere breathed.

CHAPTER THIRTY

Corin uttered a crack of laughter, breaking the tension. '*That's* the understatement of the year.'

Alere sent him a grateful smile. Introducing Rohne's abilities was a risk and she hadn't been certain how her father would handle the situation. The revelation of his teleketic gift frightened her more than she wanted to admit. What else was he hiding?

Someone knocked at the door. A servant edged into the room and whispered a message to Rafi. Rohne's dark brows snapped together in a swift frown. The Jun Second rose and squared his shoulders.

'Thank you for your offer, son,' he said, bowing to Rohne. 'Let me consider how your unique skills may be best utilised. Kett, Rohne. If you will?' Rafi indicated the servant. 'Danno will show you to your rooms. I know you slept where you could after last night's chaos. You must be tired and I'd like a word with Mina, Alere and Yasmin. Corin, you stay.'

Dismissed, Rohne scowled. Kett's annoyance was visible in the stiffness of his bow and the stony look in his eyes as he left. Why had Rafi been so abrupt?

Rafi sank into a chair and scrubbed at his face.

'What on Kalima was that about?' Alere demanded. 'Why send Rohne and Kett away like that? It was rude. Rohne has amazing gifts and I'd trust Kett with my life.'

'Rohne's now in the room we reserve for visiting xintou,' Rafi said. 'The walls are painted in a bismuth compound and shield us from his ability to Read. Mina, can you ward well enough to keep him from Reading, later, what we speak of here?'

Mina nodded, her eyes huge. 'I think so. Why? I trust him. What's he done wrong?'

'Nothing, my dear. I just prefer to keep our conversation private for it concerns only you two. We have little time and I need to investigate all options that might help us against Ven. Rohne is one.' Rafi withdrew a cloth from his pocket. 'This is another.' He unwrapped the steel-yanstone bracelet Alere had brought to him and laid it on the table. The bracelet flicked with gold-fire caught from the chandelier overhead.

'There's more to this than you know, Alere,' Rafi said. 'Radan was right when he said I didn't know what I'd created. I didn't – when I made them. Afterwards I did, but it was too late. I'd already sent this away with Sura and couldn't risk exposing her to get it back.'

The afternoon sun streamed through the window and stroked fingers of blood across Rafi's cheek. Alere shuddered, uneasy for no clear reason.

'Yasmin?' Rafi touched his wife's hand.

'Are you sure?' Yasmin fiddled with the matching bracelet shimmering on her wrist.

'We must,' he said. 'Ven's left us no choice. We don't know if they'll feel it.'

With trembling fingers, Yasmin unclasped her bracelet and laid it on the table.

Side by side, the strings of jewels seemed to feed off each other, their inner fire growing, until they glittered with blinding intensity. Alere squinted against the light. The bracelets' hypnotic fire both drew and repelled her. Something in her wanted to touch; urged her to gather the fire close. Frightened by the strength of that desire, she resisted. When Mina stretched out a hand, Alere stifled a warning shout. What was there to be afraid of in jewelry? Yet the inexplicable fear remained.

'They're beautiful,' Mina whispered. The stone-fire played across her fascinated expression.

Mina touched a stone and Alere's unease vanished; replaced by a muted excitement and anticipation that felt alien, almost external. The craving to pick up the bracelet seeped into every cell and muscle until Alere was helpless to resist. She clipped the strand about her wrist, half expecting it to burn. Instead, it was cold, almost icy.

Mina fixed on the other bracelet and stroked it, studying the dancing fires. Alere turned her wrist, drawn into the swirling, silver-gilt lights. The stones' shifting glimmer was hypnotic; warm. The faintest taste of iron and woodsmoke teased her tongue.

I wish I could tell him.

'What?' Alere blinked at Mina. 'What did you say?'

Mina shook her head. 'Nothing.' *I just want to go home.*

'But you said—' Silver-gilt flames surged from darkness and swept the words from Alere's tongue. Joyously welcoming, they connected her to the stones. Lights danced in her vision, but vanished when she tried to bring them into focus. They swirled through her thoughts and prised open her Inner wards like a curious, living being – investigating her blackest thoughts, laying her bare, judging.

A dam burst. A hubbub of voices surged into her head, rising tide of meaningless sound – a thousand strangers' emotions eddying through her mind. Their worries, decisions, fears, joy, love, anger flooded in. Alere screamed a denial and spat the taste of iron and smoke from her mouth. She retreated to the darkest corner of her self, drowning. She covered her ears in a vain attempt to block the ocean of insanity.

'Alere!' Corin yanked her hands away. Concern in his Outers added to the onslaught. 'What's wrong?'

'Get it off her!' Rafi ordered.

Fingers scrabbled at Alere's wrist and the bracelet's weight vanished. The voices evaporated, the taste diminished, leaving her shaky, but alone again in the desert of her own fears.

Slowly she raised her head. Corin touched her face. She pressed her cheek into his palm, trying to settle her racing heart and gather her thoughts.

'Do try not to do that again,' he murmured. 'That was quite alarming to watch.'

'What happened?' Mina stroked Alere's shoulder. 'You frightened us.'

'I...I don't know,' Alere said. 'There were so many voices. Jiche!' The bracelet glittered on the table. 'It's the bracelet. Corin took it off me and the voices stopped.'

'Yes,' Rafi said, 'it's the bracelets. Both of them.'

'Why the diyu didn't you warn me?' Alere glared at her father.

He raised his chin, eyes cool. 'We didn't know if the bracelets would work on you. Or what the result would be. Everyone else we've tried felt nothing.'

'Except Sura and I,' Yasmin said. 'And it didn't bother me that much. I'm so sorry. We didn't want to influence your reaction. I didn't expect your connection to be so strong.'

'What *was* it?' Alere said. 'I don't understand.'

'It's what being a xintou is like,' Yasmin replied, quiet pride in her words.

'But I'm not...' Alere stared at the glittering gems. Xintou. The idea seduced her. After all these years. Could she finally be xintou? She reached for the bracelet.

'You must ward against thoughts coming *in,*' Yasmin said. 'Not just your own Outers being Read. You know how. Better than I did when I experienced the bracelet's power. Think about your training.'

Yasmin was right. Alere dredged up half-ignored lessons from Xintou House. She closed her eyes and painstakingly constructed the additional Outer wards. Before she could change her mind, she slipped on the bracelet, tensing in anticipation. The ward held. The silver-gilt lights were a glimmer in the distance; the voices a background susurration of waves washing to shore; the smoky taste of iron just a hint.

'Tell me…' Her voice cracked. 'Tell me how it works.'

'Twenty years ago,' Rafi said, clearing his throat, 'when Sura was first pregnant, I made the bracelets as gifts for her and Yasmin.' He squeezed his wife's hand and she smiled lovingly back. 'Unfortunately, the day I presented my gifts was also the day runners brought word of Hanna's kin-child laws. All we could do was bundle Sura up with what she could carry and get her away as fast as possible. It wasn't until after Sura left that Yasmin realised she heard her sister's thoughts. But their connection weakened, and broke a few weeks later.'

'We thought Sura was dead,' Yasmin added, 'or out of range. Now I realise she must have taken the bracelet off when she arrived in Gaton.'

'That's a *huge* distance.' Alere stared at Yasmin. 'But why isn't Mina affected? Why can't she hear everyone else?'

'We don't know.' Yasmin said. 'It was similar to Sura and me. I could hear others, though not clearly and not all the time. Sura seemed oblivious to thoughts. But I think she may have developed precognition. I didn't believe she needed to leave so quickly after the runner brought the news. Sura insisted. She was certain someone from the Alcazar was coming for her. A day after she left, Hanna's men arrived with orders to kill Rafi's kin-children.'

The bracelets glimmered on Alere and Mina's arms, the lights shifting in time with their heartbeats.

'Twins,' Yasmin continued, 'are rare and we had no further opportunity to try the bracelets with another set – until now.'

'You've tried this with others? Not only twins?' Mina chewed her lip.

'Yes.' Rafi held up his wrist. On it glowed a circlet of ten small yanstones. 'I made a bracelet for myself, but Yasmin and I felt no connection. I couldn't, obviously, try with too many people, but those who wore the stones had no reaction.'

'The bracelets awaken xintou skills, but only in twins?' Mina lifted her wrist and inspected the bracelet. 'But yanstones have no known power to release psychic abilities.'

'Not on their own, no,' Rafi said.

'Sura and I once wore matching gold and yanstone necklaces,' Yasmin put in. 'Nothing like this happened.'

'I think combining the stones with meteoric iron is the key,' Rafi added. 'But I don't understand how it works.'

'You need two pairs of genes to be a true xintou,' Mina said quietly. 'Both pairs on the X chromosomes. One pair carries the psychic gifts. They're not uncommon. Less common is the second pair, which unlocks and controls the gifts at puberty. That's why male xintou are only ever born from female xintou. And why they can be...unstable – because they have the gene that unlocks the gifts, but not the matching one that allows their control.' She traced her finger over the bracelet. 'Maybe the yanstones and iron together act like the second pair, allowing unlocking and control the first. How fascinating.' She held the bracelet up towards Rafi. 'What do you plan to do with the bracelets? Why give them to us now?'

Alere reached out tentatively, testing her ability to Read her sister's Outers. Mina's Healer's ethics were foremost. She was also reluctant to be thrust into the middle of an aggressive meeting with Ven and his junren. And she was angry on Alere's behalf; dwelling on the increasingly violent path her sister followed. Unable to resist, Alere dug deeper, sliding through Mina's Outers, seeking intimate information about Mina's relationship with Kett. Were they a couple?

No! Alere groaned and withdrew. What was she thinking? That way led to madness or mental Fusion. Had she forgotten Xintou House's basic ethics so soon? She wasn't worthy.

She undid the bracelet, placed it on the table and pushed the glittering gems away. The searing babble of external thoughts eased. The silver-gilt flames in her mind subsided and died. She massaged her temples.

'I gave the bracelets to you,' Rafi said, 'in the hopes we can use them in this crisis.'

Alere tried to think through the flowering of pain as the medication began to wear off.

'But this thing with Mina and I, and the bracelets – it makes no sense,' she said. 'Radan knew the bracelets were the key to something. But how? He's not a twin.'

'I don't know,' Rafi replied. 'That's something to find out later. We have only two days before Ven walks in. Two weeks before his reinforcements arrive. We need every advantage. It's worth exploring the stones' potential. Even if all the bracelets give us is better communication in battle, they'll be useful.'

Mina turned her bracelet around her wrist. 'Why send Rohne away? He knows more about how to use xintou skills than we do.'

'I understand,' Alere said, quietly, her heart heavy. 'Rafi wants this kept quiet. Twins are rare. Imagine if this knowledge got out.

Imagine if Hanna recruited twins untrained in Xintou House techniques and ethics? Even limited to twin-bonds, the implications are frightening.'

She sat up, her ribs protesting. 'Communications in battle, and across the Jundom, is just the start. Hanna could have her own, independent spy network; invisible without the gold veil.' Alere refused to even consider the potential danger to her sisters in Xintou House.

'The House has strict rules about how a xintou uses her powers,' she continued, watching Rafi. 'Bonding enhances powers but also limits a Xintou's ability to betray her Bonded family.'

'Yes,' Rafi said, 'And I think even Celia will be constrained by those parameters.'

'But,' Alere said, staring at her bracelet in fascinated horror, 'if you take away those restrictions and give power to untrained girls, the world's a different place. A place where it's not safe even to *think* traitorous thoughts.' Alere shook her head. 'Hanna wouldn't be able to control such women for long. The Jundom would end with an unrestrained xintou on the throne.'

'A possibility,' Rafi admitted. 'Which is why we have to keep this secret.'

Alere touched the yanstones. Welcoming warmth sparked up her arm and she snatched her hand away.

'But,' she whispered, 'you're asking us to be exactly those unrestrained xintou for you. How does that make you any better than Hanna?' Was Kett right? Did Rafi just want to use her? Did her father care for her at all? She wrapped her arms around her stomach and absorbed the hurt.

Rafi laughed bitterly and flung his arms wide. 'Questions I've already asked myself, my dear. I have no good answer. I wasn't even sure the bracelets would work until you put them on. Now I'm presented with new ethical dilemmas and no time to consider their implications.' Weariness edged his voice. 'I don't think I'm cut from the same cloth as Hanna. Fortunately, I'm surrounded by people willing to stand up to me. I trust you'll continue to do so; especially should I show signs of becoming a megalomaniac with plans to rule the whole of Kalima.'

The tension eased in the room. Alere sat back, leaving the bracelet on the table, half-afraid to wear the stones again. They represented everything she'd wanted as a child – and everything she hated. To have the telepathic gifts, she must tie herself irrevocably to Mina. She must give up freedom and choice and shoulder an even heavier responsibility than that of pretend Jun-Heir.

She buried her head in her hands. Impossible. Every decision took her further into a maze from which she could see no escape. But her father, her sister, the people of Mamlakah, of this Jundom, of this castle...they deserved her help and her protection. So why did her heart ache?

'What do we do?' Mina asked.

'Corin will, discreetly, alert our junren,' Rafi replied.

Alere lifted her head, frowning at him. 'You have junren?'

'Yes.' He grimaced. 'I've known for several years that Hanna and Ven were raising an army and may pose a threat. We have around eighteen thousand trained and armed junren – ready when Ven's honour guard turns out to be less than honourable.'

He grasped Alere's and Mina's hands. 'In whatever time you find before Ven's arrival, you should test the limits of your abilities. Mina will stay as your personal healer.' He addressed Mina. 'You must keep wearing the veil, to hide your face, if that's acceptable?'

Mina nodded, her smile wan and forced.

'And Kett?' Alere glanced at her sister.

What would he choose to do? Had he fallen in love with Mina? She was certainly infatuated with him. As painful as it was, Alere needed to release him from any obligation to herself. He should be free to walk away with Mina.

But the thought of his absence hurt.

'Kett is...difficult,' Rafi said. 'How well do you know him? What's your relationship?'

Alere bridled and tugged her hand free of his grip. 'I already told you. I've known him for ten years. He's my shifu, weishi and friend. I trust him above anyone else.'

'But where do his loyalties lie?' Rafi's eyes narrowed. 'With you, Xintou House, or elsewhere? If Mistress Li calls on him to counter our plans, will he betray us?'

Heat rushed to Alere's cheeks and she clenched her fists. She ground her teeth, unable to speak for Kett and too angry to respond calmly. She struggled to her feet.

'Since you don't believe me, I'll ask him. Tomorrow.' She ignored Mina's protest and clutched at the lounge to hold herself upright. 'Now, if you don't mind, I need to rest.'

Rafi hesitated then rose, his expression cool. Yasmin drew him from the room, murmuring into his ear.

As the door closed, Alere vaguely heard Mina's urgent call to Corin. The room faded to grey. Corin scooped her up and Alere rested her head gratefully on his shoulder. He carried her to the bed.

'Zift,' he said, with a smile.

The world stopped spinning and Alere relaxed into the soft mattress. 'Don't start, Corin.'

'Did I say anything?' He tucked a strand of hair behind her ear and smiled, cocking his head.

Alere's anger drained away and she heaved a sigh.

'How do you do that?' she grumbled. 'I can't stay angry with you when you look at me like that.'

Corin laughed. 'Can't give away my trade secrets. Besides, you weren't angry with me, just off-balance after wearing the bracelet. You don't like to feel out of control any more than you like taking orders.'

Mina shut the curtains and blocked the blinding afternoon light.

'Sleep,' Corin said, 'and then tomorrow find Kett. He's two doors away. Clearly you two have things to sort out, but you need to recover first.'

Alere slanted a look up at him, fighting to keep her eyes open. 'And will you be there to keep tabs on what I say to him?'

'No need.' He quirked a twisted smile. 'You'll do the right thing and so will he.'

'How can you be sure? You've only known me three weeks, and Kett half a day.'

'Half a day; a three-week; it makes little difference.' He kissed her forehead. 'Because I know what I'd choose were I in his position. Sleep, woman. As they say: morning will bring light into darkness.' He left, but his usual lazy saunter was a jarring stride and he slammed the door.

Mina felt Alere's pulse, then tucked in the thick bamboo-cloth sheets and quilt. 'You sleep yourself out, you hear? You need rest. Ven and Rafi's little war won't start without you.'

Alere chuckled sleepily. Mina closed the last bed-curtain. Unable to fight the maqa any longer, Alere sank into blackness.

CHAPTER THIRTY-ONE

Alere awoke to a disorientating half-darkness cut into slices by thin blades of dusty light. Soft warmth cocooned her lax body. Where was she? Ah, her bed. Yes. But how long had she slept?

Apprehension seized her. She flipped the covers and bedcurtains aside, grabbed the bedpost for support, and dragged herself upright. Her left side blossomed into agony. She groaned and assessed the damage. The long slice on her thigh was neatly stitched and healing, but there would be a scar. Her ribs were blue and purple, slathered in a sticky yellow cream smelling of comfrey and herbs. Her shoulder only ached, so the muscles probably weren't torn.

But she could barely stand up and breathing hurt. She shuffled towards the bathroom. Tears clouded her vision and she bit back another groan. She'd been stupid and lucky not to be worse off.

Pink dawn-light seeped in around the closed window drapes. She'd slept most of a day and all night. It must be what, Arba'a? Only today and half of tomorrow before Ven arrived for Lianna's nameday on Khamsa the eleventh. Whatever his plan, the failure of the gunpowder bombs had to put him on the back foot. How could Rafi take advantage of that?

First things first. Alere made her way to the bathroom. Half an hour later, she emerged clean, clear-headed and deeply appreciative of whatever past Koh-Lin had installed hot water and showering amenities in the castle. She ignored a green house-robe laid out on a chair and wore, instead, her cleaned and mended weishi outfit. Until she was officially presented as Lianna she intended to enjoy the liberty of not being Jun-Heir.

Light-headed, she steadied herself against the wall and sought out Kett's room.

Outside his door, she hesitated. Would he be alone? The thought he might not be hurt almost as much as her ribs. Alone or not the uncomfortable distance between them needed to be resolved and Rafi's doubts about Kett's loyalty, answered. She knocked.

The door swung open. Kett looked at her, tension in the set of his broad shoulders and sharp jaw. After a thorough inspection of her face, he opened the door further and gestured to a low table in the centre of the room. The table was set for two, with breakfast laid out. For Mina? The smell of eggs turned Alere's stomach.

Standing awkwardly just inside the door, she checked the room for a second occupant. Kett's room was furnished much like Alere's: a timber four-post bed on a raised dais, a few pieces of sturdy, timber furniture, a blanket box and a window-seat. The red velvet bed curtains were the only difference. She was ashamed of the relief that came with not finding her sister there.

Unable to delay any longer, Alere raised her eyes and studied Kett's familiar features. She saw him now as Gavon would have her see people: clearly. Under the visible signs of exhaustion, Kett carried himself with tense reserve; guarded and wary. She had never before wondered why he was always so cautious; so withdrawn – not just on her behalf, either. What did he hide?

Was he...afraid? No. Not possible.

Then he smiled and the sense of strangeness dissipated, leaving only her dear friend.

'So...' She limped to the table, fiddled with a spoon, annoyed at the flutter in her stomach. What cause had she to be nervous around Kett? This wasn't the training mat and she'd done nothing wrong.

'Where's Mina?' She felt like a shazi for blurting out the question.

Kett raised his brows. 'At the infirmary. One of the castle weishi took a turn for the worse. Do you need her?'

'No…I just…it doesn't matter.' It was barely past dawn. Mina must have been here for Kett to know where she was at this hour. The breakfast was Mina's, after all. Alere put the spoon aside, swallowing down the ache in her throat.

'You're markedly improved,' Kett said. 'I was hoping you'd stop by. Or did Rafi send you?'

'I'm fine and no one sent me.' She held out her hands to him and forced a brighter smile. 'I missed you. Are you recovered?'

He watched her expressionlessly for a moment, then took her hands. 'I missed you too, Alli, and yes, I'm fine.' He flexed his shoulders and grimaced. 'Well, still a few twinges, but only when I breathe.'

'I'm sorry,' Alere said. 'I should have been able to stop—'

'Shazi. As I said: you take ownership of something that was not yours to own,' he said, smiling. 'Let it go. Tell me what's been happening. What's this I hear about you falling off a roof? And taking a bo-staff in the ribs? Did I teach you nothing?' He led her to the window-seat.

'How…?' She gaped. 'Corin. That saafil hundan.'

Kett chuckled. 'Evidently. And I see you've learned some new words as well. Tell me about the trip.'

He raised a brow and left a silence that she felt obliged to fill. She revealed everything, even things she meant to keep secret like her attraction to Corin. She described the trip to Shanzhai and meeting with Rafi; the effects of the yanstones; even Rafi's questioning of Kett's loyalty. Words spilled like beads from a broken necklace: scattering, jumping about, and finally dribbling to a halt. As the last ones fell from her lips, the weight of secrecy and responsibility around her neck lifted.

Kett rose and leaned an elbow on the wall, resting his head on his forearm as he gazed out the window. Alere joined him. To the east, the Aswad Ranges were swathed in white as winter bled up from the south, piled snow in the passes and dusted the fields around Shanzhai with the season's first light falls. Alere waited with the forced serenity of experience. There was no point in nagging Kett for his thoughts until he was ready.

At last, Kett straightened and ran a hand over his face then looked at her. 'If I asked, would you put this behind us and let me take you and Mina to safety in Jadid?' The question was so out of character, Alere found no words with which to reply. Part of her was tempted, but Kett knew she'd given her word to Rafi, so why ask? Kett was no coward, and his expression was serious, so his worry must be for Mina.

'Kett...' She fought for the strength to do the right thing. 'Don't feel bound to me. Take Mina to safety if you wish. You've already given up your life in Madina and done more than anyone could ask. Go, if you need to, but I can't go with you.'

'I thought not.' He grimaced. 'Very well. Thank you for offering to release me but, since we have no contract, it's not in your power to do so. My loyalty, however, *is* with you.'

'Why?' she asked. 'This isn't your fight, it's mine. I've pledged to protect Rafi and his people. My people. Go. Take...the opportunity. Be happy. Make a new life.'

'You're wrong, Alli, this is my fight as well. More than you know.' He hesitated, such pain in his eyes that she was taken aback. 'In truth, it's probably past time I held my ground, anyway. One can only hide from the past for so long. Since you've chosen this path, I'll fight by your side. Make no mistake, though, it will lead to war.'

'Not so much chosen,' she said, 'as been forced onto this path. If I could, I'd go, believe me.'

Kett smiled wryly. 'Your instincts have always been to protect people weaker than yourself. We both know you wouldn't leave Rafi and his people in such dire straits. Nor would I.'

'But you—'

He held up a hand. 'There are two conditions to my staying. One: I won't help put Rafi on the Jun First Throne, no matter how justified it seems. Stop a war, yes. Revolution, no. The Jundom works partly because the First's power is limited by the Seconds. Put two thirds of the power in one man's control and you have a tyranny in the making.'

'He wouldn't.' Alere's certainty faltered under Kett's bleak cynicism.

'Don't be naïve,' he said. 'Rafi was raised to be a ruler. He's most qualified to take Ven's place. But after that? Petar and Leah Ma-Safra have no heir. Would Rafi take that Jundom, too?'

'Who else is there? Hassan's not someone you want in charge of the First's Jundom.'

'That's not my place to say.' Kett swiped a hand over his mouth. 'But I'm sure Radan had kin-children as yet unaccounted for. Plant the seed in Rafi's mind now and see what he does. That may tell you what sort of man he is.'

Alere limped a few steps away then returned. His words made sense. 'Agreed. And your second condition?'

'I won't stand by quietly and let you put Mina in danger.' He laid his hands on her shoulders, his grey eyes searching her face for something. 'You can handle yourself. I couldn't stop you anyway. But Mina has neither the skill nor the temperament for battle. So, if your plans involve Mina, give her the choice. Let her part be passive. Away from the front line. Agreed?'

Alere turned her back so he wouldn't see the unexpected tears stinging her eyelids.

'Yes,' she managed. 'I'm glad you care for her.'

'Of course I do,' Kett said, sounding surprised. 'And so do you, though I know you find it hard to show. She's your family and she's special; one of the kindest, gentlest people I've ever met. I don't want her hurt.'

'No. You're right,' Alere managed, though her throat was almost closed.

Outside, a distant bell chimed the hour.

'I have to go. I promised to meet with Rafi this morning.'

'Alli?' Kett touched her wrist, but she jerked away.

She limped to the door and escaped, ignoring his repeated call after her. Clearly Kett and Mina had formed a strong attachment. Alere needed to let him go, for the sake of his happiness. It just wasn't as easy as she'd expected.

She wandered through endless empty halls and corridors, trying to find the stables. It was all happening far too fast. Her world had flipped upside down; her foundations gone and her feet not yet on new solid ground. She needed time and space to think. Difficult work lay ahead and the tumult of emotions clouded her ability to make decisions.

In the stables behind the castle, Rumi greeted Alere with a snorting head toss and a foot stamp. Alere threw her arm over the mare's neck and quashed an impulse to fly; to find solace in the wild freedom of riding. She no longer had that luxury and wasn't strong enough, anyway.

'You're up early. Thinking of running away?'

Alere turned slowly, dizzy and weak, not wanting to get into a witty back-and-forth with Corin.

'Don't. Please?' she said. 'I...just leave me alone for a while. I can take care of myself.'

Corin's smile dropped away. He pulled her close and gently stroked her back.

'Hey.' He tugged Alere's cap off her head and tossed it aside, lifting her chin with one thumb. 'What happened? I'm guessing you saw Kett. What did he say?'

Instead of answering, Alere stopped resisting. She kissed him, needing something more than friendship, no matter how unwise. Corin's arm tightened around her waist, his mouth softened, his lips warm and strong. His heart raced as she slid her hands up his chest and twined her fingers in his hair. Alere pressed against him, drowning loss in desire. He groaned deep in his throat and broke the kiss.

'Ah, khara,' he growled, regret and longing in his eyes. 'I'll kick myself later for a zift, but don't, Alli. You're not well. You're afraid and looking for something you can be in control of. You'd hate me and I really...' He stroked her cheek and kissed her again; a mere brush of the lips. 'Really don't want you to hate me.'

Alere sighed and rested her head on his shoulder. He was right. She'd turned to him because she felt rejected, afraid and alone.

'I hate it when you're right, Cor.' She listened to his heart slow, feeling secure in his arms.

A laugh rumbled through his chest. 'You must find me incredibly annoying then, given how often it happens.'

She chuckled, appreciating his light-hearted friendship and restraint. She steeled herself and broke away.

'I feel like a bit of a shazi now,' she said. 'Should I thank you for your chivalry, or be annoyed you were able to resist me.'

'Call it turnabout's fair play,' he said lightly. 'After all, you resisted me on Eagle pass that night. Was that because of Kett?'

'No.' She glowered at him. 'We're not…It was because I thought you were…'

He raised one brow, smiling. 'Go on.'

'Given your reputation, I mean. You believed I was jiaoji. I thought…' Flushing, she focussed on stroking Rumi's nose.

'I'm a spy, Alli. My reputation is a useful cover, nothing more. The women, they're…' Amusement fell away and he leaned against the stall, looking into nothing. 'I was betrothed once, ten years ago, just before I came here.'

Alere held back the questions on her tongue.

'Shasa and I were very young – sixteen. She was sweet and shy. Our parents were making us wait until our eighteenth namedays before holding the hunli ceremony.' He fell silent, his hands fisted by his sides.

Alere, unable to stand the pain in his eyes, lifted a hand and cupped his cheek. He kissed her palm.

'What happened?' she asked.

'Hanna,' he said, bitterly. 'Shasa was a kin-child of our Jun Fourth, Meron Gray-Saud. Hanna's spies found out. Alcazar junren murdered Shasa. And my parents, who were visiting Shasa and her mother at the time. I was away in Asalam. I came back to find both our homes burnt to the ground.' He paused, his eyes haunted. 'That is, I have to assume Shasa was killed. There were only three bodies. We never knew if the third body was Shasa or her mother.'

'Oh, Corin,' Alere murmured. 'What did you do?'

'What could I do against Hanna?' He gave a short, regretful laugh. 'I came here, searching for…who knows what. A connection to family, maybe. I kept looking for Shasa for years, though. When Rafi sent me out on missions, I discovered the unveiled jiaoji girls are a valuable source of information.' His smile gentled. 'They appreciate someone who pays them, treats them with respect and wants nothing but information in return.'

He waved dismissively. 'Of course there have been women. I'm human. But, until now, I've never met anyone I wanted to spend time with out of bed, as well as in.'

'I'm sorry,' she said thickly and hugged him hard, ignoring the protest from her ribs.

He buried his face in her neck and held her close, then eased away, holding her off when she would have kissed him again to ease the pain.

'That's not why I told you, Alli. I don't need pity. If there is anything real here, then you have to want *me*, not a substitute for Kett or as an object of sympathy.'

Alere wanted to give him the answer he needed; tried to find it as truth in her own heart, but couldn't. There were too many factors influencing her at the moment. Her feelings could well be just sexual attraction. She hesitated. Disappointment flickered through his eyes and was quickly hidden behind his lightning smile. He kissed her swiftly then strode from stall.

'Corin?' She clutched at the stall door. 'Ah...jiche.' Her legs gave way and she collapsed into the straw at Rumi's feet. Blood roared in her ears and the world receded into sepia and silence.

Corin swore and picked her up. She curled into his chest as he carried her into the castle.

'Sorry to spoil your exit,' she murmured.

He laughed. 'Serves me right for being melodramatic.'

'Told you,' she replied, yawning, 'you should have worn the purple hat. What's wrong with me? I'm so tired.'

'When was the last time you ate?' He frowned at her then shouted orders at the astonished kitchen staff.

'No idea.' Exhaustion blurred the words on her tongue.

'That's what I thought. Here.' He sat her down and she clung to the scarred timber tabletop. A cup of warm lancha tea appeared, its rich blue diluted pale with milk. She gagged on the tea's sickly-sweetness, but Corin insisted she drink.

'You're low on blood sugar, woman,' he grumbled. 'I don't think I've ever met anyone who drives themselves as hard as you do. Why do you do it?'

'I guess I need to prove that I'm good enough,' she blurted. The truth of that statement closed her throat and drove bitter tears into her eyes.

Corin scrutinised her. 'Good enough for what? For who?'

'I think,' she said, though her tongue needed to be forced, 'Elmira to start with. Because I wasn't xintou-Gifted. Then Mistress Li and Kett. Now you, Rafi, Yasmin, the whole gouri jundom apparently. I don't know if I can do this.'

Alere covered her face with her hands. What had she got herself into? How could she pretend to be Lianna and confront a man who was more monster than human? Looks weren't enough. What about Lianna's friends, the household staff, and the routines and traditions that should be second nature?

'Hey.' Corin hugged her. 'You're scared, but I'll be with you the whole time. I won't let you slip up. You don't have to prove anything to me, I promise.'

'But you didn't know Lianna that well, did you? I mean you've spent a lot of time away. You don't know her friends, her quirks, her habits. How can I learn all that before tomorrow night?'

He stroked a thumb across her cheek. 'All good points. Yasmin will help. As will Lianna's old nurse, her tutor and even the housekeeper. They know about Lia and are loyal to the family.' He reached into his pocket and produced her yanstone bracelet. 'Use these, too. Mina asked me to hold onto yours when you collapsed last night. You can use them to Read people you're speaking with. Enough to find out what they expect of Lianna.'

'But what am I supposed to *do?*' She groaned. 'I don't know what a Jun-Heir does.'

'Lianna was only seventeen and her official duties weren't to start until after her Threshold nameday, tomorrow.' Corin shrugged. 'Anyway, it sounds like Mistress Li knew what she was doing. You learnt politics and economics from her, weapons and warcraft from Kett, and about people from your jiaoji training. If anything, you're overqualified for the job.' He kissed her lightly. 'It isn't like you to be so negative. You're tired, hungry and overwhelmed. You can do this.'

He was right. Again.

'Thanks,' she said, meaning it. A plate of honey-slathered bread, fried rong, and scrambled eggs appeared. The salt-sweet smells made her mouth water and she picked up the bronze fork.

'You're most welcome, shunu.' He inclined his head formally. 'Now hurry up and eat so I don't get in trouble with Mina.'

'Oh yes,' she mumbled, mouth half full, 'she's terrifying.'

He laughed. 'It's the quiet ones you have to watch. Speaking of which, what can you tell me about Rohne?'

'Not much more than you already know,' she said. 'He's the kin-child of Jada Marin-kin and Nasra Connor. She was the Xintou Bonded to Jun Second Petar Ma-Safra before Elmira came of age and took her place. I don't know what he can do, beyond what he showed us yesterday. Oh, and precognition, apparently. But he does seem stronger than the female xintou I've met, except maybe Mistress Li.'

'Interesting.' Corin stole a slice of rong off her plate, grinning when she protested. 'He tried to intrude on my wards yesterday evening at dinner. I had to bury my dagger in the table in front of him before he'd stop. If he's powerful, he's not terribly skilled.'

'That's not possible.' Alere stared at him in astonishment. 'A non-xintou isn't supposed to be able to tell when their wards are breached. But now that you mention it…I felt when he tried mine, back in Gaton. I wonder if it's just because he's a male xintou?'

Corin licked his fingers. 'No idea. Question for Mistress Li. But why, if he's so powerful, has he wasted his life in a backwater like Gaton?' He rolled his eyes. 'And please don't give me any feihua about fear of being found out. I've never met anyone less afraid of other people, or less interested in what they think.'

'Really?' Alere sipped a mouthful of tepid tea. Her thinking was clearer now. 'I don't know then, although Nasra kept him tied to her apron strings. Maybe we were just an excuse for him to leave her? Honestly, though, Kett owes his life to Rohne. Besides, Rhone's staying to help now when he has nothing to gain.'

'Really?' Corin mimicked. 'Nothing to gain? The respect and gratitude of the second most powerful Jun is nothing? Switch on your political brain, Alere. You can't afford to take people on face value any more. What's his endgame?'

'I can't have friends?' She put her fork down with a snap, trying to keep a lid on her reactions.

'Look,' Corin said, tugging restlessly on his mawei, 'part of my job for Rafi is keeping his feet on the ground. Yours too, now. It's not easy, believe me. Holding an opposing view to someone who can have you executed is an adrenalin rush. It's probably part of the reason I stay, if I'm honest.' He chuckled. 'The point is: friends are easy to find when you're Jun-Heir. Trusted, honest advisors and supporters are harder. Ask yourself: do you trust Rohne? Or even Kett or Mina for that matter.'

'Of course I—'

'Just think about it.' He held up a hand and rose from the table. 'I'll make that exit. When you're ready, ask someone to bring you to the conference room. We're short on time, ideas and information. We need to find out what Ven's up to and come up with a solution fast.'

She watched his retreating back. Corin was wrong about Rohne, but right about one thing: finding out Ven's plans was the priority. She hadn't come all this way, hoping to prevent a war, to fail now.

Alere worked through two serves of breakfast and considered possible ways to get the intelligence they needed. But each idea had a fatal flaw and, eventually, she was left with one. Not one she liked and not one guaranteed to succeed, but one that would be least likely to harm anyone she cared about. Any other option put too many people in danger. This plan wouldn't, however, meet with everyone's approval. Strike that. It wouldn't meet with *anyone's* approval.

CHAPTER THIRTY-TWO

Alere pocketed the bracelet, rose from the kitchen table and sought out the castle housekeeper. The woman proved intensely loyal to Lianna Koh-Lin and eager to help. Runners, sworn to secrecy and bearing lists in Alere's best imitation of Lianna's hand, went to Healer House and Jiaoji House.

Alere made her way to the conference room and paused to consider her options one more time. Was she risking everything, and everyone, on a moment of madness? No, this was the best way to protect everyone in the castle. Though the chances of her returning were small, the risk was worth it. With a rueful shrug, she knocked on the door. Better to seek forgiveness than permission.

Inside, Rafi had gathered those he trusted: Kett, Rohne, Corin, Yasmin and Mina, plus Farah, Maha and Gavon. Alere brushed off Mina's fussing and took a place at the table. After a sideways glance at Rohne, she shored up her wards.

Most of the morning she spent listening to dozens of possible scenarios Ven might launch, and plans for counter-attack, escape, even evacuation. Rafi and Kett were frequently at loggerheads: Rafi advocating confrontation, Kett favouring negotiation and stalling tactics over war. Rohne suggested hiring xiongshou, which shocked everyone into silence. No Jun First had ever been assassinated – except Radan, and only a few knew of that. Alere wavered, wanting a quick resolution, but reluctant to go into battle, risk the lives of her friends, or submit to Ven's demands. He was not someone who would negotiate with any care for the humanity of his opponents.

But none of the ideas solved the basic problem: lack of information about Ven's plans. Alere's heart sank and she stared at the map, daunted now by thought of what lay ahead.

'We are, at least, agreed,' Rafi said, waving to silence an argument between Corin and Farah, 'that we must act before the rest of Ven's troops arrive with Hanna.' He pointed to a map on the table. 'Ven's camped across the river. To take the city he'd have to bring his troops across. If he uses coming to Lianna's Nameday celebration as an excuse to bring his troops over, then his forces will be split when Hanna arrives. If he waits the two weeks until she arrives then he'll still have to bring fifteen thousand junren across the two bridges and the Kuaisu Ford.'

He swept a shrewd look around the table. 'It would be prudent to use some of his own gunpowder to blow the bridges, as soon as we know his mind.'

There was a general murmur of consensus.

'Farah,' Rafi continued, 'you and Gavon take four of the men who helped recover the gunpowder and supervise laying the barrels. Maha, you get word – discreetly – to the junren to be armed and on standby. Dismissed.'

Mina stood and tugged her veil down. 'I'd like to go into Healer House, if I may, and replenish supplies. Shouldn't we warn the House Mistress of the possibility of casualties if this does come to war?'

'Wise thought.' Rafi inclined his head. 'Take Rohne as an escort. Yasmin, will you go too?'

His wife nodded. 'I know the Mistress well. She'll keep silent if I ask. We don't want word to spread and panic the city.'

As they left, Alere caught first Corin's eye then Kett's and Rafi's.

Rafi waited for the door to close before speaking 'What is it?'

'Have you thought at all about who would succeed Ven if something happens to him in the next few days?' she asked bluntly.

Rafi stilled. 'Yes, I've considered it. Why?'

'For yourself?'

'Yes.' Rafi raised his chin. 'How could I not? My people are content. Why shouldn't I help Ven's people the same way?'

'Because,' Alere said, folding her arms, 'as someone pointed out to me, the Jundom works because there are three Jun powers in balance. To put two seats into the hands of one is to create a tyrant.'

Cold anger froze Rafi's face. Corin sucked a quick breath and muttered her name in a warning tone.

Alere hurried on. 'Maybe not you, or me, but what about our descendants? Are you willing to risk that? I'm not. I don't even want responsibility for two Jundoms. Surely Radan or his father had kin-children that are still out there.'

Rafi paced the room, head bent and forehead furrowed. 'I can see the sense in what you say, hard as it is to admit.' He glanced narrowly at Kett. 'I see the benefits of the three-way balance. Combined with Xintou House's influence, it does mean no one Jun can become a tyrant.'

A kernel of tension in Alere's gut, relaxed. Part of her had doubted Rafi would make the right choice.

'You're right, too,' Rafi said, sitting, 'in thinking Radan had several kin-children who escaped Hanna's wrath. Two are here in Shanzhai. Their mothers sought my protection twenty years ago. I gave it, thinking this day might come. My personal choice would be the elder, Jarran Dan-kin. He's twenty-five, two years a widower, with two daughters. He's steady, intelligent and a skilled fighter. He owns four successful bakeries, one not far from the castle.' Rafi smiled. 'Makes an extremely good song cake.

'Dirat, however,' he continued, 'is a bit of a hmar, if you'll forgive the crudity. He's twenty-one and I wouldn't trust him to babysit my xiao-kitten, let alone an entire jundom. Not particularly bright, either.'

'Wouldn't it make sense, then,' Alere said 'to bring both of them into the castle? To protect Jarran and prime him. And to prevent anyone else using Dirat as a puppet to control the Jundom.'

Rafi's eyes gleamed with respect. 'Indeed it would. Jarran and his family will be brought here today. Dirat is, unfortunately, in Madina visiting family.'

'Madina? Is he mad?' Alere exclaimed.

He shrugged. 'I can hardly imprison the man. If he wishes to risk his life in the heart of his enemy's city well... that reveals his intelligence level.' He inclined his head. 'Now, if there's nothing else?'

His ironic tone made her flush but she lifted her chin. Corin was right: someone had to stand up to the Jun and it may as well be her.

'There is one other thing, shenshi.' She inspected the map. 'The rivers on either side of Shanzhai to the northeast and northwest. The gorges are deep, aren't they?'

Rafi traced the Kabir River, from Madina in the north, upriver to where it split into the two rivers protecting Shanzhai.

'Yes, the Kuaisu and the Seryeh are deep and fast. There are only the two bridges over the Kuaisu. Ven can't attack the city easily from where he's camped.'

'Which is here.' She indicated a spot northeast of the city, close to the main overland route from Madina to Shanzhai and near one of the two bridges. 'So if he brings troops over the river tomorrow, he'll have either ask you to board his men in the city, or camp somewhere. Are they boarding?'

Rafi shook his head.

'Then they'd have to camp here.' She pointed to a narrow strip of land between the city walls and the river's sheer, rocky cliffs. 'But that would be madness. It's a kill-zone. No one's insane enough to put their army in such a vulnerable position.'

'True,' Rafi said. 'But he must have thought the city would be in chaos from the gunpowder bombs.'

'You're right, shenshi.' Kett tapped the site of Ven's current camp. 'But even if the gunpowder had worked Ven would still be waiting two weeks for Hanna to arrive with supporting troops.'

'What are you saying?' Rafi scowled at the map.

'I don't know,' Alere admitted. 'I just have a feeling…'

'You're right, Alli,' Kett said. 'We're missing something important. We need to know what Ven's planning.'

'Yes.' Rafi spread his hands wide, palms up. 'But until Rohne meets Ven and Reads him I don't see what we can do.'

'But if we wait,' she said, 'and he brings the junren across the river tomorrow, we lose our chance to destroy the bridges. We need to know his intentions now. Before he comes to the castle tomorrow night.'

Rafi stroked his chin and scrutinised the map.

'She has a point.' Corin grimaced. 'I'm willing to try and get into Ven's camp tonight, but I doubt even I'm good enough to get close to Ven. And the chances of hearing something vital are slim.'

'I agree and I wouldn't ask it of anyone,' Rafi said. 'No, the only way to safely discover Ven's plans is for Rohne to meet him. I could send an envoy and include Rohne as one of the escort party.'

'Won't work,' Alere replied. 'Rohne needs to see Ven to be able to Read him over the distance between the castle and the camp. If Rohne's an escort he'd wait outside Ven's tent. We'd be relying on luck to bring Ven out.'

'He could *be* the envoy, then,' Corin suggested.

'No,' she said. 'If Celia's there she'd know his true nature the second she laid eyes on him. Too risky.'

Kett, who'd been watching her silently, said, 'Don't even say it, Alere. You can *not* go yourself.'

She laughed away Rafi and Corin's chorus of protests. 'Don't be a shazi, Kett. Of course I can't. I was going to suggest we use the two weishi prisoners. If we connect Rohne to one and let them escape, we'll at least find out if Celia's there. Rohne can Read them as they report to Ven.'

Kett's eyes narrowed.

'That could work,' Rafi said. 'But how do we release them without suspicion?'

'I know how. Leave it to me and Corin,' Alere said.

Corin groaned and backed away from Kett and Rafi.

Twenty minutes later, wearing fitted, flesh-coloured leggings and shirt under the red-robe, Alere opened her door to admit Corin and Kett and waved them in.

'I see Kett hasn't killed you yet for letting me do this?' She laughed at Corin.

'There's still time.' He cast her a hang-dog expression.

Kett dropped onto a couch and watched her move about the room.

She placed her dagger on the bedside table. 'Just to be clear: all I'm doing is setting the weishi free. You two ensure they escape with just enough of a fight to allay suspicion. And make sure they leave me behind.'

Corin picked a black jilla-fruit from a bowl and took a bite. 'Already arranged.' Green juice dribbled down his chin.

The lunch she'd ordered for all three of them lay on the small table and she waved the men to it. 'Oh, go ahead and eat. I already did. I'll finish getting ready, if you'll excuse me. Is Rohne on his way?'

'He's just meeting the weishi. He'll be here shortly.' Corin poured wine for Kett and himself. He stabbed a slice of roast lu-deer with a fork and sank onto the couch with his feet up on the table.

Alere ducked into the bath room. She kept the leggings and shirt on, reluctant to wear only the flimsy red-robe out in the winter chill. A hollow needle-blade and two small waterproof sacs of liquid nestled in the lining of her breast-binder. She pinned the red veil to her hair with two new, bejewelled blades serving as hairpins. The housekeeper and runners had outdone themselves fulfilling her requests.

Now for the final touch. Alere had already made sure Mina wore the yanstone bracelet. Mentally girding herself, Alere clasped the matching bracelet to her ankle. It was a tight fit, but if she was searched it would be considered decorative, and it was key to the success of her task. The sense of connection to the stones flared and wrapped her in a reassuring warmth. External voices were whispers beyond her Outers. Alere tightened her wards to prevent her sister Reading her intentions.

She slid her feet into soft house slippers. Boots would signal her intentions. One last check in the mirror, a mouthful of willowbark medicine to dull the ache in her ribs and leg, and she was as ready as she could be. She smoothed her robe and re-entered the bedroom.

Kett and Corin lay sprawled on the lounges, asleep; glasses spilled, wine staining the rug. Alere breathed a sigh. They'd drunk the wine. She'd set the stage by leaving her own half-empty wineglass and lunch remnants, then acting blasé in the hopes Kett wouldn't read her purpose. Surprisingly, it worked.

Now they would be safe.

She kissed both men and murmured instructions into their ears. Before she could change her mind, she threw on a plain black cloak and left.

The escape went almost to her plan. Corin couldn't have known Alere had countermanded his orders for the Koh-Lin weishi to capture her. She did regret that Prato had seized a weapon and, as a result, two of Rafi's weishi were injured. However, it was done and there were more important issues to deal with.

As they galloped to Ven's campsite, the two Alcazar weishi boasted about their escape and discussed what to say to Penon. Up in the saddle before Prato, Alere listened in absent contempt as their bravery grew more remarkable with each recounting.

At the same time, she rehearsed what to say to Ven. She would, undoubtedly, be brought before the Jun. That part was easy. The rest of her sketchy plan relied on Ven being alone. Her chances of deceiving Ven vanished if Celia was present.

Whatever happened, the risks of discovery and death were higher than she liked. Now was the time to check her escape options. If she'd calculated the istilqa dose correctly Kett should be awake. She opened her mind to the yanstones and lowered one of her Outer wards. The taste of iron and woodsmoke danced on her tongue. Silver-gilt warmth and lights beckoned from the depths of her Inners. She ignored them, intent on listening for Rohne.

Alere?

Rohne. Drawing on her House training, she kept strict ward over her Inners and let him into her shallowest Outers, only far enough to communicate.

Alere? Where the jahim are you? Kett just came to me and said to find you. What's going on?

I'm fine. Shut up and listen. She sent pictures of the camp, as far as she could see it from horseback. *I'll keep sending as long as I can. Don't let Rafi send anyone after me. I'll be back soon.*

After brief hesitation, Rohne gave a short acknowledgement and a visual of Rafi's horror. Alere grimaced and sent an apology for putting Rohne in a difficult position. Rohne's response was tinged with amusement, scorn and a hint of envy.

How are Kett & Corin?

Philosophical. Rohne flashed images of their worried, angry expressions. His amusement at their reactions lay unshielded and he invited her to share in it.

She pulled back and refocussed on her wards. She felt more confident using the xintou skills now, but the danger of Fusion remained real. There was an almost irresistible temptation to burrow deep into someone's head in an attempt to truly understand them. A skilled xintou knew how much blending was enough. Alere lacked that experience and it frightened her. Horror stories of Fusion abounded in the House: both people died as two minds fought for control of one body and failed.

What are you going to do? Rohne's query appeared in her mind as she was about to close their connection.

Alere didn't reply. Truth was, she wasn't yet sure. What she needed from Ven he wouldn't give willingly. She'd have to get into his head. The trick would be getting out again.

Prato and Kal swaggered through both checkpoints and junren directed the weishi to Ven's tent to find Penon and the Jun First. As they approached the tent, Alere's hands shook and her breath came quick and fast. No, she could do this. She held a deep breath, slowed her heart and relaxed every muscle. All she had to do was find out what Ven planned.

The escaped weishi slowed as they approached Ven's striking black and silver pavilion. Pennants atop the tent fluttered and the canvas walls bulged and flapped in the storm-driven wind. Alere quashed the tempest of doubt that threatened to uproot her artificial serenity. She could do this.

Prato helped Alere from the horse, led her to Ven's pavilion, and demanded to see the Shangwei. Penon appeared in the door. Tall and arrogant, his black hair touched with grey at the temples, he inspected Prato and Kal with cold distaste.

'Report.'

Prato stumbled through an explanation of their capture and escape. At the mention of Alere's part, Penon shoved Prato to one side and prowled around her. She forced herself to stay still, fighting the ancient urge of the prey to run and hide. No. *He* was the prey, she the predator.

'Take these two shazis. Give them forty lashes each for stupidity and failure,' Penon snapped to nearby guards. 'In front of the junren so they'll know what becomes of hmari who allow themselves to be captured.' He regarded Alere.

'You are another matter. Ven will see to you. Inside. Now.'

She followed, head bowed, fingers twitching for want of a weapon.

Inside, the pavilion was austere to the point of barrenness. A dozen mel-oil lanterns banished shadows. A black and silver rug covered the floor, its geometric pattern ruthlessly simple. A black curtain divided the interior space in half.

Seated before the curtain, Ven waited, straight-backed and brooding. Across his lap lay a slim, steel sword. He wore black, relieved only by the steel circlet on his forehead and the desert sand of his eyes.

In this bleak colour scheme, Alere's red-robe was as blood on an obsidian knife: vivid and portentous. Her heart thundered. Ven's sense of the dramatic suddenly struck her as funny. She dropped to her knees with bent head to hide a smile. The urge to giggle was just a reaction to fear. Fear was normal; laughing was insanity.

Instead, she stretched forth with a thought and touched Ven's Outers. His wards were intact and rock solid. He was well-trained and she was unskilled. She needed more time to get him to relax so she could drive a wedge into his wards. She knew the technique, in theory. But how long would it take her to master?

'Give me a good reason not to kill you, jiaoji.' Ven's voice was eerily flat.

Alere played her first card: naivete. She lifted her veil and, with widened eyes, allowed her lips to fall open, mimicking shock. There was a risk he could recognise her face as Lianna's, but Yasmin said both she and Lianna had always worn the veil at court, so it was unlikely.

'Kill me? Shensi Ven, I don't understand.' She touched her lips then throat with light fingertips, subtly drawing attention to the erogenous areas. 'I've done as Mistress Celia asked haven't I?'

Ven's eyes narrowed in doubt, then sharpened on her. She'd never before raised the veil for him. Doing so played on his social conditioning around jiaoji and ought to encourage trust.

'Explain yourself.' He displayed less interest than he might in a bug crawling on his sleeve. But he relaxed his grip on the sword.

The pounding of her heart against her ribcage eased. Alere chewed her bottom lip and tilted her head. 'Well, shenshi, I'm not sure...perhaps we should wait for Mistress Celia? She took my oath of silence and can confirm my words.' It was an untruth easily exposed if Celia was present.

This was the moment that could end everything. Alere held her breath and kept her calm.

Ven's eyes flicked to Penon, then back to Alere. His lips pressed thin and he lifted his chin.

'Celia's with my mother, in Madina. Your loyalty is to me, not her. Tell me.'

Alere hid exultation and bowed her head in agreement. His body language betrayed him: he disliked Celia. That could be useful.

'Well...' She spread her hands, showing the palms, then rushed into breathless speech. 'Mistress Celia asked me to win Jun Radan's trust and discover the whereabouts of an iron deposit. Of course, I understood how important that could be to your rule. Celia said to do whatever he asked. I tried—'

'And what about my father? Do you deny you killed him?' Ven's cold question cut through her earnestness.

'I don't understand, shenshi.' Alere widened her eyes. 'When I left the room he was still alive. He was so sick, though, I thought—'

'My father was stabbed.' Ven's lips thinned.

Alere gasped. 'Stabbed! You don't think I...? Oh!' She curled her hands into fists and narrowed her eyes in simulated anger. 'Shenshi, I didn't think she would go so far. I thought the murder charges were just...Celia said she'd make sure I had a good reason to need Jun Second Koh-Lin's protection...' She lilted the last word and let him fill in the blank with his own paranoia.

'Celia?' He half-rose from the throne, twisting his black robe in white fingers. 'Are you saying she murdered my father?'

'I...I don't know, shenshi,' she whispered, lowering her eyes.

'It's not possible. She's Bonded to us. She cannot betray us.' Filaments of doubt twined through his statement. He stalked several steps towards the door, scowling.

'No, shenshi,' Alere said meekly. 'I'm sure a Xintou could never betray her Bonded family, or her House. It's unthinkable.'

Ven froze and stared at her; through her. Then he glanced at the door again.

Alere watched him from beneath lowered lids, her face carefully neutral. She'd seeded doubt. Now she needed to redirect his thoughts. If he sent a message to Celia, demanding an explanation, it could undo everything.

'Rafi has taken me in, shenshi,' she said, raising her voice. 'I can help you take Shanzhai.'

He paused, returned and sank back onto his seat. 'Explain.'

'The plan worked.' She let disdain colour her tone. 'Rafi trusts me and the deposit is in his lands, somewhere. I just need a little more time to find it.'

'Really?' Ven's lip curled. 'But haven't you betrayed that trust by helping those hmari of mine escape? What use are you now, pray?'

Alere shared a secret, wicked smile. 'That's the best part, shenshi. Rafi thinks I'm here on his behalf, to spy on you. I'll need to go back soon, though, to allay suspicion. Then I can feed him whatever false information you see fit.'

'I see.'

He stepped from the dais and idly swung the sword, each swish bringing the steel edge closer. In keeping with her character, Alere gasped and flinched away. Ven leaned in until his wine-scented breath brushed her cheek. Tempting though it was to drive a hairpin into his heart, his wards still held. She would die under Penon's blade and Hanna would still live to wreak vengeance.

'And *are* you here to spy on me?' Ven's cold gaze drilled into her.

'Of course not, shenshi,' she said simply, countering his suspicion with openness and a touch of worship. 'My contract is with you. Give me leave and I'll kill Rafi tonight, if you wish.'

There followed a long, heavy silence in which his unblinking distrust held her motionless. Keeping her expression open, Alere attempted again to pierce his ward, but her lack of skill told. He held firm. Jiche! There was nothing else for it. She would have to use her role as jiaoji and trust that, in the distraction of the moment, his wards would crack.

Ven touched the sword's cold tip beneath her chin and raised her face. She parted her lips and increased her rate of breathing.

'Please, shenshi?' she begged. Beneath the pretence, cold anger froze out fear.

A faint flush rose in his sallow cheeks. His breath quickened and his pupils dilated. Was it the thought of having her or killing her that aroused him? His gaze flicked to her cleavage. Now she had him. He sheathed his sword and caught her chin with his fingertips.

'Very well,' he purred. 'We have time. Tell me what you know of Lianna Koh-Lin and the iron.' He stripped off his cloak and handed it to his Shangwei. 'Penon, I am not to be disturbed while I...speak with my jiaoji. Go.'

'Shenshi, remember, in an hour we have a meeting with the senior junren about moving across the river tomorrow,' Penon replied.

Ven scowled. 'I know that, you shazi. You don't need me for something that simple. Prepare the men. You'll begin the move as soon as the nameday festivities start tomorrow evening, as we discussed. Now *go*.'

Penon bowed, strode from the tent. Ven held out a hand. Alere allowed him to help her rise and lead her through the black curtain to the back of the tent. Rohne's Outers were still linked with hers so she passed along Ven's intent to move his troops. Now she had an hour to find out the rest of his plan. Little enough time, yet more than she wanted to spend in Ven's company.

The curtain fell closed behind her. Before her waited a vast bed of blackened timber and black-and-silver linen.

'Now.' Ven's fingers brushed her collar, slipped across her skin and tightened around her throat. His eyes gleamed. 'Now you'll truly belong to me.'

CHAPTER THIRTY-THREE

CORIN

The bedroom door closed and Alere's footsteps faded down the hall. Corin waited a minute before sitting up.

'Gaisi, Kett.' Corin resisted the urge to lick spilled wine off his fingers. 'Playing along with Alere's little game did no good at all. We still have no idea what she's doing.'

'No.' Kett rose and headed for the ensuite. 'And I'd like to know why she Suggested that I connect Rohne to her.' His voice echoed in the bathroom.

'And why drug us?' Corin asked. 'Why not just tell us and get us to help? We should have just asked her, as I suggested. Lucky the housekeeper warned me Alere was up to something, otherwise...'

'Asking Alli wouldn't have done any good.' Kett sounded amused. 'She'd have lied. She's clearly doing something I'll disapprove of.'

'Well, I don't need your gouri approval,' Corin snapped. 'I'm going to stop her.'

'Ah-hah.' Kett emerged from the bathroom carrying three small, glass bottles: one red, one green and one an exquisitely-tiny black bottle.

Corin hesitated on his way to the door.

'Istilqa, mayao and watu.' Kett turned the black bottle, distaste flickering across his face. 'One-dose bottle. A favourite of the xiongshou. Quick and difficult to cure. Empty.'

'Xiongshou use that in blowdarts.' Corin plucked the bottle from Kett's fingers and brandished it at the weishi. 'Where the jahim did she *get* this?

'She often carries a single dose.' Kett gave a short, derisive laugh. 'Something Jiaoji House taught her, in case she was ever in a position where she...needed it.'

'That doesn't even bear considering. But what's she planning to do with anaesthetic, painkiller, and poison?' Corin asked.

'I have an idea. Did her Suggestion to you have any relevance?'

'No. Just an instruction to come get her if she wasn't back by sunset. But from where?' Corin left out her request to make sure Mina kept her bracelet on. Although he was reasonably certain Alere had told Kett about the bracelets, keeping secrets was Corin's business and he wasn't going to risk revealing their existence if she hadn't.

'She won't get past Ven's guards carrying a dartpipe,' Kett muttered. 'And she didn't take her dagger.'

'You think she's headed to Ven's camp?' Corin threw up his hands. 'How? She can't sneak in wearing that jiaoji red robe.'

'Best guess,' Kett replied, 'she intends to go with the escaping weishi.'

'Khara! Did she consider what'll happen if she's caught with poison?'

'Possibly.' Kett tilted his head and shrugged one shoulder. 'Possibly not. Alere tends to be...determined. Especially if she's certain of her plans and wants to protect people she cares about. However, she will listen if someone points out a flaw, I'll give her that. But you're asking the wrong questions.'

'We should go after her.' Corin flexed a hand around his dagger.

'No, there's no point bringing her back. She'll find another way, believe me. I spent ten years unsuccessfully trying to keep her in Xintou House,' Kett replied. 'Once, Mistress Li bolted Alere's door. Alli climbed out by cutting a hole in the ceiling and removing the roof tiles. She was twelve. And if we hadn't played along with her little ruse today, she'd have found another way to escape, or incapacitate us. But we wouldn't have seen it coming.'

'Gah!' Corin hurled the watu bottle at Kett.

Kett caught it easily and set it on the table. He lifted the red istilqa phial up to the light. 'This is a four-dose bottle. None left. Two doses, I assume, for the weishi she interrogated. A half-dose each for us, because she obviously expected us to wake quickly. And the other, I suspect, is for Ven.' He inspected the green bottle. 'And the mayao is empty. Is that to numb her current injuries or for something else?' Kett placed the green bottle next to the others and moved around the room, methodically studying the effects Alere had left behind.

'Istilqa for Ven? What good will that do?' Corin snarled. 'She can't mean to spy on Ven, herself, can she? No, it's not possible. She must intend to kill him.' He rubbed at the back of his neck. 'But she's in no fit state… They'll kill her. Even if she gets through, how will it look if Ven dies with a watu dart in his neck? On Koh-Lin land.'

'She wouldn't be clumsy enough to use a dart. You forget the breadth of her education.' Kett's reply was low and hard. 'Jiaoji training teaches poison delivery in many ways. Wine is only one. And, if she does poison Ven, the symptoms of watu are almost identical to the bite of a gu-spider. She could've used xi-sing or dusu. Both are faster but have more obvious symptoms of poisoning. But I doubt she'll use the watu unless absolutely necessary.'

'If she's not going to poison him, she must intend to get information out of him. But how?' Corin picked up the red bottle. 'Istilqa's not much use as a truth drug, even with Suggestions. It's hard to get someone to talk when they're asleep.'

'Yes,' Kett said. 'How she intends to get Ven to talk is exactly what's worrying me.'

'She's dressed as jiaoji.'

'I know,' Kett said, grimly.

'We have to stop her. Ven's tastes are—'

'No.' Kett stared out the window. 'I'm inclined to let her go.'

'Are you mad?' Corin grabbed Kett by the shirtfront. 'I don't want her near Ven.'

Kett didn't flinch.

'I thought you cared about her.' Corin sneered and shoved Kett away. 'But if you did, you'd go after her. Stay if you want. I'm going.'

Corin's back hit the wall, with Kett's forearm pressed against his jaw. Kett's face was inches away, his eyes as cold as the snow-laden clouds hanging heavy over the city.

'I care more about that girl than you could imagine,' Kett growled. 'I've protected her since she was a terrified child, desperate to prove herself in a world she couldn't master.' Kett ground his teeth. 'She was the only one I *could* protect.'

Corin opened his mouth to ask what Kett meant, but the weishi's eyes held such implacable wrath, Corin was silenced.

'I also know, better than you,' Kett continued, 'the nature of the man she's going to see. Alere understands what's important here. She's trying to protect us. Out of all of us, she has the best chance of finding out Ven's plans.' His anger slid away. 'And I don't think she'll be best served by us gutting each other, do you?' He relaxed his arm and withdrew the knife he held against Corin's stomach.

Corin pulled his own dagger away from Kett's heart. His palms were slick with sweat and he couldn't shake the feeling he'd just escaped death by a hairsbreadth.

He worked his jaw and cleared his throat. 'So, how's she planning to get in, get information and get back?'

Kett picked up his wineglass and held the dregs of purple liquid up to the light. 'Now you're asking the right question.'

'And I suppose you have the answer?' Corin glared at Kett, still shaken by the weishi's unexpected ferocity.

'Not at all.' Kett headed for the door. 'I doubt Alere knows the answers, either. She tends to make things up as she goes. She has taken the yanstone bracelet, though. We need to be patient and await her signal. You may not trust her ability to take care of herself, but I do. The only question we can answer is: how are we going to get into Ven's camp to extract her, should she need us?'

He strode into the hall.

'I'm beginning to see why she hates it when you tell her to be patient,' Corin muttered, and hurried to catch up.

Kett response was a steady, ironic look.

Corin pictured Ven's camp as last reported by spies and runners: encircled by two rows of watchmen spaced at close, regular intervals. It was hard to imagine how anyone could slip past unseen.

Something in his own thinking tweaked a memory. Corin stopped in mid-stride. What was it? Something Alere had said...

'Orange.' He snapped his fingers. 'That's our ticket in. Let's go. We need to find Rohne and whoever's in charge of Messenger House, just in case we need uniforms in a hurry.'

As they entered the great hall, shouts arose outside, followed by the distinctive clash of weapons and the tattoo of hoofbeats. Corin and Kett reached the front door in time to see two brown-clad prisoners ahorseback. One held Alere before him on the saddle. Her red-robe fluttered like a flag as the horses vanished beneath the slowly-lowering portcullis.

Corin started forward but Kett threw an arm out and stopped him. Corin glared and watched helplessly as Alere and the escaped prisoners disappeared towards the northeast gate. Two injured weishi lay on the ground. Corin shoved aside Kett's arm as Farah rounded the corner.

'Get these men moved to the infirmary,' Corin ordered the Shangwei. 'And get a healer.'

Mina arrived with Rohne. She carried her healer bag and the yanstone bracelet glittered on her wrist. Corin pulled her aside after checking to see Kett had Rohne engaged in conversation.

'Can you come to the conference room as soon as you're free?' Corin tapped the bracelet. 'Alere needs our help and I think you're part of her plan. Don't ask me how. Keep the bracelet on and ward well.'

Mina pursed her lips, but nodded. Corin watched her attend to the injured men. How long would it be before Mina refused to help in this war against Ven Zah-Hill? She clearly disliked the tumult Alere generated. It was only a matter of time before Mina dug her heels in or walked away. If needed, he'd appeal to her sense of family and duty to Alere. Preventing Ven from taking Shanzhai was more important than Mina's personal ethics.

Corin hailed a passing servant. 'I must speak to Rafi urgently – in the conference room. And get a runner to Master Lan at Messenger House, as well.'

'She's done *what?*' Rafi slammed his hands onto the table. 'How dare you flout my authority and put my heir in such danger? Corin, I expected better of you.' Stone-faced, he jabbed a finger in Kett's direction. 'And you! I should have known better than to let you stay.

Your vision must be clouded by emotion and ambition or you would never have let her go.'

A long silence followed, in which Kett returned Rafi's glare coolly. The two men sized each other up like the prelude to a xiao-catfight.

Ambition? Corin studied the weishi in bemusement. Kett, ambitious? Did Rafi know something about the weishi? Rohne, catching Corin's eye, shrugged and sipped at a glass of wine.

Kett stood opposite Rafi and, with deliberate care, placed his palms on the table.

'I'm no danger to you, Rafi,' Kett said, his voice low. 'Now or ever. Unless you endanger Alere or Mina. My sole reason for still existing is to keep them, and others like them, safe.' He leaned forward, eyes glittering. 'If I had ambitions, there would be little *you* could do about it and things would be very different right now.'

Rafi eyes narrowed. 'Is that a threat?'

'Not at all.' Kett straightened, a smile tugging at the corner of his mouth. 'Simply a truth. Now if you'll put aside your ego and hear us out, we can explain.'

Rafi stood rigidly upright, his face pale and set. Corin frowned. Who was Kett to unsettle a Jun Second so badly?

When Rafi spoke again, it was in a calmer tone, though steel underpinned his words. 'If you're here to keep her safe, why is she riding into Ven's camp as we speak?'

Kett poured two glasses of wine and offered one to the older man. 'Sit, please, shenshi. I'll explain.'

'So,' Kett said, finishing his tale and placing his empty glass on the table, 'that's our best guess at Alere's intentions. I wanted her to go as little as you and Corin. But she *is* our best chance of finding out

Ven's plans. No man could get close enough. Alere understood the risks. She knows what Ven's like.'

Rafi nodded and revulsion glinted in his eyes.

Corin shuddered. Kett was right. Ven had a disconcerting way of looking through people, dismissing their humanity. The thought of Alere in the power of someone like that made Corin's fists itch.

'Ven's weakness,' Kett continued, 'is that he sees women as...tools if you like. To be used for one purpose. He fails to recognise their intelligence and that's Alere's advantage over us. He won't see her as a threat. Even when she's sliding the istilqa needle into his vein.'

'How do you know him so well?' Corin asked. 'Alere said you didn't go with her into the Alcazar.'

'Oh, I know him,' Kett replied dryly. 'Too well. And he, me. Another reason I couldn't take her place today.' He addressed Rohne. 'This would be about the right time for Corin and I to wake from the istilqa dose. Can you reach her?'

Rohne, who had his eyes closed and one thumb pressed to his temple, put his wineglass down.

'Make sure she's...' Kett grimaced. '...knows we'll come for her.'

A smile twitched at Rohne's mouth. His face twitched with a montage of expressions, reflecting an inner conversation. He opened his eyes, picked up his glass and took a long drink. Corin suppressed a flare of impatience.

'She's fine at the moment,' Rohne said. 'About to see Ven. Nothing useful yet except to confirm that Ven's sending his junren across the bridge tomorrow. I'll stay connected.'

A servant knocked and beckoned to Corin, who excused himself. Corin found the head of Messenger House outside and made arrangements for uniforms and the password into Ven's camp.

Mina arrived and Corin brought her up to date.

'She went on her own? That's crazy.' Mina wiped her palms on her thighs. 'Why does she do these things? Why won't she let me – or anyone – help instead of taking such risks?'

'I know,' Corin said soothingly. 'But Kett's certain she'll be alright. We might need your help, though.'

'Me? What can I do?'

'Keep the bracelet on and listen for her. She'll call you if she needs us.'

'But if I sit around waiting I'll worry,' Mina said. 'If I'm working, I have something else to think about. Tell Rohne to call for me if you need me. I'll be in the infirmary.' She spun on a heel and marched away, her jarring strides unlike her normal, swaying walk. Had he pushed her too far?

CHAPTER THIRTY-FOUR

ALERE

'Wine, shenshi.' Alere made the words a statement. When Ven hesitated, she sipped from the quarter-full glass, smiled and handed it to him. Then she drank deeply from her own glass, hoping to still the flutters of fear in her stomach. There were so many ways this could go wrong.

Ven watched her narrowly for a moment, then threw back his drink and set the glass on a black timber side table.

She kept her relief hidden.

He smiled thinly and drew forth a riding crop from behind the table. 'Now,' he murmured, 'if you make a sound...any sound...it will add one to the total. Understood?' He slapped the crop against his palm.

Alere nodded. Her mouth dried to salt and her skin prickled in anticipation. She clenched her teeth, disrobed and lay face down on the enormous midnight bed, as he instructed.

Ven chuckled, low in his throat. Alere fisted the sheets and poured all her concentration into the silver-gilt fire of the yanstones. Iron and woodsmoke filled her mouth. The yanstones' exultation flared from deep within her Inners, threatening to derail her focus. She just needed a few minutes to work through his Outer wards.

'One.' Ven's breathy count echoed his action.

Crack.

She jumped and bit back a cry as pain sliced through. Not enough mayao, clearly. Jiche! As if this wasn't difficult enough. She needed to work fast. Drawing on the yanstones' power, she sharpened her thoughts into a spearpoint and drove them at Ven's wards.

'Two.'

Crack.

She closed her eyes, using weishi techniques to sideline the pain. But that took precious time. Tears stung and dripped onto the silk. Her thoughts battered against Ven's wards. There only needed to be a crack; the tiniest flaw and she could prise his wards open. Somewhere. No-one's wards were perfect. Just a crack.

'Three.'

A tiny gasp escaped her lips and he laughed in triumph.

'One more, for that. Four.'

Alere dropped her head onto her fists. She could do this.

There.

Triumph surged. A hairline fracture. Swiftly, she drove the spear into the seam and wrenched his Outer wards open. Ven's thoughts were a swirling mess of conflicting emotions and desires; the mind of a thwarted child desperately seeking approval. Control. Power. Lust. No sign of his plans for Shanzhai. His self-hatred dragged her deeper. She struggled to make sense of him. Caught in a maelstrom of his pain, she lost sight of herself.

Panicked, she fought against his madness. His anger captured and bound her, sucked her towards his Inners. No! There they would Fuse and she would be trapped. Her body would be his to abuse. Her mind imprisoned, powerless, deep within his psychotic Inners.

'Five.'

The pain served as an anchor, flaring along the connection between them. She clung to the silver-gilt thread. But the sinking-sand of his mind wrenched at her and she couldn't break away.

'Six.'

There! Ven's thoughts on revenge against Rafi leapt to the fore. Plans flashed through his Outers, triumphant, certain, terrifying. She had to warn Rafi or the city would fall. Alere withdrew.

But Ven's darkness engulfed her and dragged her down. She screamed into the black and it laughed back at her. Her struggles were in vain; his grip on her mind too strong. Panic rose, suffocating rational thought. The silver-gilt thread tying Alere to her body attenuated to a hairsbreadth. She cried out in desperation to Mina but met only smothering blankness.

She had failed. She was worthless. Everyone she cared about would die. She would be imprisoned in Ven's mind.

The sharp chaos of his thoughts softened, thoughts blurring. His wards relaxed. The whirlpool of his conscious settled into a roiling subconscious tarpit.

And released her from its deadly suction.

Something heavy fell across her legs. Alere hauled on the silver-gilt thread, wrenched free of his mind and retreated to the safety of her own. Before she extricated herself, she left false memories to lull any suspicions he may have when he awoke.

She lay still for a while, panting, sobbing in relief and pain. Then she kicked at Ven's limp body until her legs were clear, sat up and stared at his istilqua-drugged body with loathing. Her hand crept to the dagger-pin in her hair, but she hesitated. She still had to walk back to the castle. Once she left, Penon was sure to check on his master.

So she kicked Ven once more, in the ribs, for good measure then dragged him onto the bed and drew the covers up, as she had once for his father. In sleep the lines of dissipation and cynicism faded and Ven looked like nothing more than a child – lips softly opened, eyes fluttering in dreams.

Pain flared across Alere's shoulders as she straightened and she shoved aside the moment of empathy. He had none and deserved none. She bundled her shirt and breastbinder under one arm then drew her leggings and robe on, sucking a sharp breath as the cloth stuck to her back. Pity she'd missed the istilqa time-window. A Suggestion to commit suicide would have ended him and his ambitions neatly.

Alere draped the cloak over her shoulders and pinned the veil back in place. She avoided Penon's sneering gaze as she emerged from the pavilion. 'Shenshi Ven is sending me back now. He's sleeping.' She walked out of camp with her head high, expecting hoofbeats and a sword at any second.

The pale wintersun rode low on the horizon by the time Alere stumbled into view of the city gates. Willowbark and mayao had long since worn off. Fire clawed across her back and the old injuries to her thigh and ribs throbbed. Sharp stones jabbed through her thin house-slippers.

She clung to the sandstone balustrade of the bridge over the Kuaisu. Snow-laden wind whipped hair into her eyes and stole moisture from her lips. In the chasm below, the green-white river waters roiled, deep in afternoon shadow. She tore the red-robe from her body and hurled it into the abyss. Tears froze on her cheeks. She scrubbed at them, refastened the cloak around her bare shoulders and staggered on.

The wind swept her around the corner of the northeast gatehouse and she stumbled into the arms of the weishi guarding the river gate.

'Gates are closed for the day. You'll need the night-entry password.' His grip dug into her upper arms as she swayed. 'You alright?'

'Leave her, weishi. I'll take over.' Corin's arm slid under hers.

She leaned into Corin's strength and opened her mouth to thank him.

'Don't say anything until we get back to the castle,' he growled. 'I want the privilege of shouting at you in private. Can you mount?'

Numbly, she nodded and concentrated on putting one foot into the stirrup. She didn't have the energy to object, and he had every right to shout at her. She'd been foolhardy and suffered for it now. Corin swung up behind her, pulling her close. She whimpered as the horse jumped into a slow canter.

Kett waited inside the castle gates, his expression grim. She half-fell from the saddle and groaned as her bruised feet hit the cobbles. Kett steadied her.

'Alli…' His voice cracked and he swiped a hand over his mouth. 'Jiangui! I shouldn't have—'

'We need to get her out of this cold, and out of sight,' Corin said.

Kett nodded. He and Corin half-carried her up the stairs. Their arms pressed against Alere's back and pain sliced through her flesh. She clenched her teeth to prevent a cry.

'To her room.' Kett's deep voice rumbled over her head.

Alere clutched at his arm. 'No. I have to see Rafi. There's things he must set in motion before Ven arrives. Just get me some willowbark.'

Kett exchanged a doubtful look with Corin but helped her to a chair in Rafi's meeting room. Rohne arrived, studied her face narrowly then poured a glass of wine, watered and laced with willowbark.

'What happened?' Kett asked. 'Rohne stopped receiving from you. We were about to mount a rescue when you sent word you were leaving the camp.'

Alere gathered her scattered thoughts and held the cloak close. Rohne watched her with horrified fascination. She didn't need his pity and let him Read a warning to keep silent, then shored up her wards. She considered what to say about her time with Ven. Rohne was not aware of her new-found xintou skills brought on by the bracelet. She needed to speak circumspectly.

'I was having trouble…concentrating on what I was sending to Rohne, and also on doing what was necessary,' she admitted. 'I had to cut the connection while I worked on Ven. Sorry.'

The door opened and Rafi came in, his expression troubled. Corin moved aside so Rafi could sit next to her. She flinched as he laid a fatherly arm across her shoulders. He snatched his arm away with an apology and a thunderous scowl at Corin and Kett.

'I…I'm fine.' Alere straightened.

'You're lying,' Rafi said harshly. 'But at least you're safe. We'll speak of this later, in private. What did you find out?'

'Ven will attend the ball tomorrow night,' she said. 'With his Jun Third, Fourths and a few retainers and court officials – witnesses to prove Lianna's gone. He intends to force you to admit she's dead, then establish a blood claim through his paternal grandmother, a Koh-Lin. The rest of his men will, supposedly, stay in camp.' Alere took a deep breath, feeling skin tear afresh. 'In reality, Penon will bring the men across the Kuaisu, under cover of darkness, while everyone's at the ball. They plan to take the gate and hide in the city.'

'Yes,' Rafi said. 'You sent that much to Rohne, and I already suspected Ven's claim to my seat. Was there anything else?'

'Yes. Ven's men are a distraction.' She twitched the map closer. 'You've been misled. The Asalam forces joined Hanna's men before her army even left Madina. Ten thousand junren began marching down the eastern side of the Aswad Ranges over three weeks ago.' She pointed at Eagle's Pass. 'That's why Penon bribed the raiders – to let the Alcazar troops through unchallenged, and to act as spies. Hanna and Celia are already on the Aswads' western side. Heading for Shanzhai.' She traced the route on the map. 'They must have circled south, behind the foothills. Otherwise Corin and I would've seen them when we left the caravan.'

Horrified understanding bloomed in Rafi.

Alere hurried on. 'Ven's men will attack from inside the city while Hanna attacks your weaker southern side.'

'Gaisi!' Rafi traced along the line of the city wall. 'We've long outgrown the city's original walls. We can't fight along the length of the city limits with just eighteen thousand men.'

'You'll have to get everyone inside the old-wall tonight.' Kett leant forward to inspect the map. 'Under cover of darkness in case Ven has spies in the city.'

'And you must stop his men crossing the river,' Alere added. 'If you don't, Hanna will march right into the city and you'll be helpless to stop her.'

Rafi paced the room before stopping in front of Alere. 'And does Ven suspect you? Could he be misleading *you*?'

'No. He believes me. And he believes he got what he wanted from me. But mostly it's false memories.'

'Mostly?' Corin pounced on the word. 'What—'

'Leave her,' Kett ordered. She caught his eye. Kett's gaze held understanding paired with what looked like self-loathing – but that was ridiculous.

'Is that all of it?' he asked, gently.

'Yes.' Alere shifted beneath her father's narrow gaze. Cloth stuck and ripped at her skin. She dug her nails into her palms. Now was not the time to break down. Rafi must see her strength and believe. None of them needed to know how close she'd come to failure; to irreversible Fusion. How lacking her xintou skills really were.

'Enough. We need to get you to your room.' Kett helped her stand and supported her as she swayed. He waved Corin away. 'You have preparations to make. Rohne, would you please find Mina?'

Dazed, Alere went without protest. How had Kett come to command such authority in Rafi's presence? Something had changed in her absence, but what?

Kett guided her to her room and into the bathroom.

'I wish,' he said, his voice breaking, 'for your sake, you hadn't done this, Alli. This whole gouri Jundom is not worth you suffering this sort of pain.'

'It was the only way to find out and protect them. You know it was or you would have come after me.' Alere lifted his hand to her cheek. 'I knew what might happen, Kett. The jiaoji in the Alcazar told me what he was like.'

He cupped her jaw in both hands, a hint of wonder in his gaze. 'I suspected as much when I saw the bottle of mayao empty. You don't need much to numb for an istilqa injection, but you need a lot for what Ven considers pleasurable. Mina will be here in a moment to help.'

'No!' Alere grabbed at his wrists. Mina would sense how close Alere had come to failure. 'Please. I don't want anyone to know. Please, give me a little time to get clean.' She managed a smile. 'Then help me with whatever treatment Mina recommends, but don't let her see me like this.'

Kett nodded. 'Call me if you need help.' He closed the bathroom door and swore, his voice muffled through the timber. Something hit the wall.

Alere eased the cloak from her shoulders and fumbled with the water pump controls. She stood under the water. Each drop flayed her back anew. She leant against the wall, gasping and crying, until the ringing in her ears subsided and the nausea passed enough that she could wash.

Even after she was clean, she stood numbly beneath the water, staring blankly at the yanstones still glittering around her ankle. They were a symbol of everything she'd ever wanted; and everything she wasn't. She wasn't xintou. Even with the stone, with all her training, she wasn't capable of preventing Fusion with just an ordinary human. Yet Rafi needed her to be xintou; needed her help to prevent this war.

But, if she faced Celia… The Xintou was so much stronger; so much more skilful. There was no hope.

Tears mingled with the water and only pain prevented Alere from curling into a ball on the floor.

A knock fell on the door.

'Alli?'

She cleared her throat and straightened. 'Coming.'

When she emerged, Alere found the bedroom lit by only a small night-lamp. Kett inspected her face and, apparently satisfied, patted the bed. Self-conscious, she eased onto the mattress and lay face down, dragging the sheet across her hips.

'Ah…jiangui,' Kett growled. 'I shouldn't have let you go.'

She sighed. 'To give your own words back: you take ownership of something not yours to own. You couldn't have stopped me.'

With a feather-light touch, Kett smeared ointment across her back. She jumped and clutched the pillow.

'Hold still. It's mayao to numb and luhui to heal,' he murmured. The pain soon eased and she relaxed.

'Riding whip?' Kett sounded detached, clinical.

'Yes.'

'Six,' he noted, smearing on more cream. 'Why so many?'

Kett was trying to help her deal with the situation analytically, to detach from the emotion. Standard weishi debriefing techniques. She was grateful.

'The first cut was a shock, even with the mayao.' She tried to keep her voice steady, but a quaver betrayed her. She coughed and continued, dispassionate. 'Then it took me awhile to get through his wards and control him without killing him or Fusing. I was tempted to kill him, believe me.'

'I'm impressed by your restraint. Acquit me of the need to exercise the same when I meet him.' The repressed anger in Kett's tone made her look up.

'How did you know?' she asked. 'And if you knew what he might do, why did you let me go?'

Kett put the cream aside. He crouched beside the bed and smoothed her wet hair back.

'One day I'll tell you, Alli. I promise. But not now.' His twisted smile made her heart skip. 'And I let you go because I trusted your judgement. You're a woman grown. You don't need me to tell you what you can and can't handle. I still say this whole gouri Jundom is not worth a drop of your blood. But it's your choice and I'll support you.'

He handed her a glass. She drank the willowbark and grimaced at it's strength.

Then Alere twined her fingers in his and dropped her head back to the pillow as the mayao took effect. The willowbark loosened her tongue.

'I almost didn't get out, Kett,' she whispered.

'What do you mean?' He leaned closer, frowning.

'It was so dark.' She sighed, her eyes heavy. 'I couldn't reach Mina. And he…his mind…we almost Fused…I wasn't strong enough…I'll never be good enough…' Her eyelids drifted closed, bringing blackness.

Kett's fingers shifted and fear leapt to the fore. She clutched at his hand.

'Don't go, please. I don't want to be alone.'

'I won't. Not ever.' He stroked her hair. 'Sleep. Morning will bring light into darkness and, I think, revenge. For this and more.'

CHAPTER THIRTY-FIVE

Morning did bring light, and clarity, and focus. Alere awoke more clear-headed than she'd felt since arriving in Shanzhai. She ignored the doubts that niggled in the back of her mind and smiled at Kett where he lay, still clothed, beside her on the bed. Dark shadows smudged the skin beneath his eyes.

'You had nightmares.' His thumb stroked the back of her hand.

'Hardly surprising. I don't remember them,' she lied. Memories of oblivion and imprisonment shook her false serenity and she had to force another smile. 'Sorry if I kept you awake.'

'Stay where you are.' He swung out of bed, reapplied the cream and added light bandages to her back. After that, she shooed him from the room.

'Go help Rafi and Corin. I'll be fine.'

He hesitated, inclined his head and strode out.

Left alone, Alere drew a deep breath and slid from under the covers. Everything hurt. She limped to the bathroom and cursed her haggard reflection in the mirror. Kett had left a glass of willowbark infusion on the sink. She downed it, gagging at the bitterness.

She dressed in an emerald house-robe and loose black silk trous. A servant brought breakfast. After eating she felt human enough to face her father again.

Alere arrived in the conference room to find the core team already there. Silence fell as she entered. They rose to their feet, their expressions varying from respect to worry. Clearly the knowledge she was injured was no secret. She eased herself into a seat.

'Sit.' She laughed, trying to sound natural. 'You look ridiculous. I'm not going to break.'

'Are you well?' Yasmin took Alere's hand and peered anxiously at her.

Alere forced a smile. 'It's been a long couple of weeks. Things caught up to me, that's all.' She stared down Corin's sceptical look. 'What's the plan?'

Clearing his throat, Rafi outlined the bones of the defence plan, devised while she slept. He intended to bring the citizens inside the city walls, forbid entrance to Ven's men, and ready the junren against Hanna's troops. Rafi had received confirmation overnight: Hanna's army waited less than a day's ride away, to the southeast; and ready to move at a moment's notice. It would only take a flitter from Ven to set Hanna in motion.

Alere listened and, when the last comment left a silence, she pinned Rafi with a straight stare.

'These are plans for a long siege. Is that what you really want?'

Rafi shrugged. 'I'd rather not pit my men against Hanna's in outright war. With winter upon us, our best option is the siege. She won't last long once the worst storms hit. Especially if we can cut her supply lines.'

'You're right,' Alere said, 'but there might be an alternative. One that could end this almost without bloodshed.'

'I'm listening,' Rafi said warily.

'We need the Jundom to know what sort of man Ven is,' she said, 'and reveal his true intentions. And the true state of his mind.' She thrust aside darkness.

'How?' Rafi frowned.

'We show them,' Alere said, lifting her chin. 'We break him. Get him to confess. In front of hundreds of guests. Tonight. But to make it work I'll need everyone's help. And one of Lianna's dresses to wear. One recognisably hers, but not too fitted.'

Several hours later, Alere found herself alone for he first time since her return. She suspected a roster had been arranged so someone was always with her. Determined to find a few solitary moments, she ducked into the library, a massive room on the third floor, lined from floor to ceiling with leather-bound books, and rarely used.

Rather than reading, she perched on the edge of a couch, breathing in the scent of leather and dust, treasuring the thick silence. With a sigh, she dropped her head into her hands. As always, when she stopped being busy, whispering voices impinged on her wards, distracting and irritating. She fingered the bracelet on her wrist and licked the taste of iron off her lips.

Foreknowledge made her glance at the door a few seconds before it opened to admit Mina. Her sister closed the door and looked around the room in awe.

'Rohne would love this,' Mina said.

Alere cocked her head. 'Your turn to babysit?'

Mina trailed her fingers along the books on the nearest shelf, twisting her head to read the titles. 'Corin's worried you'll do something stupid.'

'You forgot the "again".'

A smile tugged at Mina's lips. 'He didn't. I left it off.' She dusted her fingertips on her healer's robe and perched on the couch. 'You look pale.'

'It's been a tough couple of days,' Alere said lightly. She shrugged and a reminder of yesterday flared across her shoulders.

Mina stayed silent, watching. Alere fiddled with the bracelet, unsure what to say.

'Want to tell me what happened?' Mina's gentle words cut to the bone and Alere's eyes filled with tears.

'Jiche.' Alere wiped them away and sniffed. 'No, thank you though. Maybe after this is all over.' She touched her sister's arm, trying to soften the rejection. 'Right now I need to hold it together. I'll dissolve into a useless mess if I talk now.'

Mina pressed her lips together. 'It's not all about being useful. It's all right to look after yourself, too.'

'Don't.' Alere's voice caught. 'Please?'

'Alli.' Mina dropped to her knees and took Alere's hands. 'You can't keep pushing people away like this. We're here to help. You don't need to do everything yourself.'

Suppressing her xintou-trained urge to pull free, Alere willed the tightness in her throat away and forced herself to relax.

'I know, Mina. You think I don't care about people but that's not true. I just...' She shrugged. 'I don't want to endanger anyone. I couldn't bear to lose any of you.'

'You can't protect everyone.' Mina searched Alere's face. 'And what if we lost you? How would we feel? Have you thought of that? Rafi, Yasmin, Corin, me...Kett.'

Alere's fingers twitched involuntarily.

'We all love you,' Mina continued. 'We're your family and nothing's more important.'

'Don't...' Alere yanked her hands free. All her life she'd felt unwanted and unworthy. Elmira had been busy; Kett restrained and respectful; Mistress Li distant. Now she had a family and, although she would gladly give her life to protect them, it was harder than she expected to accept and return their love.

'I'm sorry,' she said, seeing the hurt in Mina. 'I'm just not very good at...' She couldn't put her feelings into words. 'Can we talk about something else?'

'Very well.' Mina sat on the couch, smoothing her skirt. 'Can we talk about me, then?'

'Of course. What can I do for you?' The ache in Alere's chest eased.

'It's not about what you can do, Alli. It's about us and this.' Mina indicated the opulent room. 'You were born to do this. You thrive on it. It doesn't even occur to you to doubt that you can do this whole Jun-Heir thing.'

Alere laughed bitterly. 'If only that were true.'

'You know what I mean,' Mina said. 'You were never meant to live an ordinary life in a small town. I am. I can't stay here. As soon as this war is over, I need to go back to Gaton. To Mother.'

'I do understand, Mina,' Alere said, her heart heavy. 'I know I ride roughshod over people sometimes. I'm sorry if I've done that to you. Don't go because of me and what I've dragged you into, please. Rafi and Yasmin would love to have you here and so would I. I'm only just getting to know you.' She struggled to verbalise her feelings, for Mina's sake. 'I feel...without you I don't feel complete. I can't explain it.'

Mina smiled gently. 'It's not you that makes me want to leave. I feel the same – like I'm whole now I've found you. Strange, isn't it?' She cocked her head. 'But I need... stability. You need adventure. Once things are settled, Rohne's offered to escort me home. I'll return to Gaton to be a healer and look after Mother. You'll be Jun-Heir. Both where we belong.'

'What about Kett?' Alere gripped her sister's slender hands.

'He spent the night in your room. I thought...' Mina flushed.

'He was looking after me, nothing more.' Alere forced herself to sound easy and dismissive. 'Haven't you two come to an understanding?'

Hope sparked in Mina's eyes. 'I haven't asked him for anything permanent and he's said nothing to me. Do you think he cares enough for me to come to Gaton?'

'I honestly don't know, Mina. Can I make a suggestion, though?' Alere rose from the couch and gasped as pain flared across her back.

Mina shot to her feet, lending Alere an arm to lean on.

'Thank you.' Alere regarded Mina's hopeful expression and swallowed emptiness. 'My advice is to be straightforward. He's not the sort to play games, but Kett holds his emotions close so you'll never know what he's feeling if you don't ask.'

Mina nodded. 'That makes sense, much as it scares me to take such a risk.'

'The risk isn't in asking and being rejected. It's in not asking and spending the rest of your life regretting and wondering. Be brave.'

'I will,' Mina said. 'Thank you.'

Alere managed a smile. 'Shall we go get ready for tonight?'

'Tonight. I wanted to talk to you about that.' Mina scrubbed her hands down her thighs. 'I'm not sure about this plan to expose Ven. If something goes wrong, I don't want either of us to have his death on our conscience. Even if things run smoothly, what you want to do goes against everything I've been trained for. I don't think I can do this to another human.'

Alere considered how to persuade her sister to help. Mina's role in the plan was essential, but her healer's reservations were valid. The only way was to show exactly how inhuman Ven was. Alere undid the buttons on her robe and showed her back to Mina.

'Look under the bandages.' Alere gritted her teeth as the bandages came away. Cool air brushed the exposed wounds and she shuddered.

Mina gasped. 'Oh, Alli. I had no idea it was so bad.' She gently pressed the bandages back in place and lifted the robe onto Alere's shoulders.

Refastening the buttons gave Alere a chance to compose herself. 'This is nothing to what he's done to some of the Alcazar jiaoji, Mina. And even worse to slaves he's had secretly sent up from Melcor. Just imagine what he'll do to Shanzhai, for their loyalty to Rafi.'

'I see.' Mina wrapped her arms around herself, her brow furrowed in thought. At last she sighed and nodded. 'Very well. I'll help. But I'm still scared – for your sake as well as my own. I have an awful feeling... Don't be alone with him again. Don't even let him touch you. Promise?'

Alere kissed her cheek. 'I'm scared too. I don't want to be alone with him, believe me. But right now I need your help for something else.'

Mina's brows rose.

'The ball tonight.' Alere grinned, trying to lighten the mood. 'I hate getting ready for these sorts of functions. I need someone to keep Yasmin from seeing my injuries and she's insisting on helping me dress. And there'll be unending discussions over hair and makeup. I need you to stop me from stabbing someone with a hairpin.'

Mina laughed, her giggle so infectious that Alere joined in as they linked arms and headed for Alere's room.

Once there, Alere unbuttoned her robe again. 'Help me get dressed before Yasmin arrives.'

'Let me check your injuries first.' Mina's touch was gentle and steady. She inspected the leg wound, ribs and, lastly, peeled the dressings off Alere's back.

'How could he do this?' Mina murmured.

Alere gave a bitter crack of laughter. 'Easily, believe me. I expected worse, though I may have killed him for it.'

'As much as it goes against my oath, I do understand,' Mina said, her voice shaking. Tears shimmered on her lower lids. 'I felt this happen, you know. Not as you did, of course. Only the faintest sting. Enough to know what was happening.'

'What?' Alere slewed around. 'You couldn't. I was warding tightly so it wouldn't get through to Rohne.'

'Nevertheless,' Mina said. She frowned. 'I felt it. Until you were gone and there was nothing but blackness. That frightened me even more.'

Alere shook her head, shivering. How close she had come to Fusing with him. If he hadn't fallen unconscious, she might have been lost. Whatever it took, she needed to avoid a confrontation with Celia. There was no way to win against her.

'You don't believe me?' Mina asked. She lowered the healer robe and revealed her back.

Alere could only stare. There, on her sister's back, were six faint, red stripes. Mere ghosts of the real thing. She touched Mina's skin.

'I don't understand. Why didn't you tell me? Why did you make me show you, before?'

'I don't either.' Mina tied her robe closed. 'It obviously has something to do with the bracelets and our twin-bond.' She kissed Alere's cheek. 'Now you see why I can't do this much longer? I can't bear to see you – to feel you – go through this, and I can't stop you.'

'I'm so sorry, Mina. I had no idea.'

'I know.' She picked up the mayao cream again. 'I'm glad you showed me, Alli. I know you wanted to convince me about Ven, but it meant a lot that you trusted me. You felt vulnerable but you to let me be part of that. I'm your sister. Now turn around. I'll re-dress those injuries.'

Alere gripped Mina's wrist. 'No. Wash them and put on a little cream. No dressings.'

'But—'

'After this evening, I promise.' Alere kissed her sister's hand. 'Thankyou,' she added, and meant it.

Alere winced as the warm water and cream stung the welts. Mina finished and draped the house-robe over Alere's shoulders. A knock fell on the door and Yasmin peeked in. She carried two dresses of such loveliness that even Alere gasped.

Alere lifted a deep green-and-silver silk creation delicately, afraid to mark it. 'It's beautiful, Yasmin. Thank you. You know it's likely to get ruined, though?'

Yasmin swung the fabric so it drifted through the air and settled over the couch back. She stroked the material. 'If it helps us destroy my daughter's murderer, then it's a small sacrifice.'

She sent the girls a cool smile and Alere knew shame. She had been so centred on her own physical pain that she'd almost forgotten how many others Ven and Hanna had hurt.

'And Ven will know this dress?'

Yasmin nodded grimly. 'Oh yes. Lia wore it – along with the veil, of course – when she was presented at court in Madina on her sixteenth nameday.'

After a long silence, Yasmin sighed and held the dress up to Alere's shoulders. 'You're a little thinner and taller than Lia. I had my ladies let the hem out so it should fit, even if the stitches are rushed. Put it on? Mina, yours is barely tacked together, so be careful. We had no time to do more.'

Mina helped Alere into the dress. Yasmin exclaimed at the leg-wound and purple bruising on Alere's ribs, but Mina kept her from seeing Alere's back and Yasmin eventually stopped fussing. Alere sat on a stool as Yasmin applied kohl to Alere's eyes and Mina did up the dress fasteners. The back of the dress was quite low and didn't touch the broken skin.

'Thank you, Mina. Yasmin, I'll need a wrap and the veil.'

Yasmin exchanged surprised looks with Mina. 'Koh-Lin women haven't worn the veil at home for years. In the Alcazar, always, but here?'

'Trust me, Yasmin,' Alere said. 'If Ven is to suffer, let me do this my way. I guarantee he will.'

She re-clasped the yanstone bracelet around her wrist and suppressed a shudder of fear as the ghost of their near-Fusion rose like smoke in her mind.

CHAPTER THIRTY-SIX

CORIN

The great hall was ablaze with light. From the top of the stairs, Corin scanned the room and grinned in anticipation. For two years, the Koh-Lins had no cause for celebration so tonight the staff had outdone themselves. Fresh everblue branches twined up every pillar and post, filling the room with a sharp, clean scent. Hundreds of white snowflowers, braided into the everblue, sparkled and glittered in the light. Overhead, lengths of silver silk hung like a tent from the ceiling, reflecting light from the chandelier. In the western wall, a fire crackled in the enormous hearth, warming the huge hall against the winter chill.

Three long tables were set in a u-shape at the hall's eastern end. The head table was raised on a dais against the east wall. Corin inspected the table, which was covered by a pale green tablecloth, edged with silver lace. Set evenly along the table, six silver candelabra held shimmering electric bulbs, cleverly designed to look like candles. Branches of everblue, tied with more silver lace and snowflowers, framed the table and the glittering array of silver plate at each place setting. Corin eyed the carafes of blood-purple wine that stood next to fine green-glass goblets. Maybe later.

Behind the head table stood the Jun-Second's throne crafted in rich, red zitan wood. The throne's back was decorated with the Koh-Lin coat of arms – a green jade dragon holding a silver sun in its claws. Two smaller, equally ornate, chairs stood on either side of the

Jun-Second's seat. Those were for Yasmin and Alere. Corin chuckled at the sight of the final chair: Ven's, a plain, yar-pine seat, such as might be owned by any ordinary citizen. Even better, it was set to Alere's left, putting the Jun First below the Jun-Heir in position at the table.

As a coup de grace, Lianna's portrait hung on the wall behind the table. The picture was hidden by dark green drapes, which would be opened at the appropriate time. Corin rubbed his hands together in anticipation. This was going to be fun.

He hummed a tune and skipped down the plant-bedecked stairs to the centre of the hall. Off to one side, a quartet of musicians tuned their instruments. Nearby, the buffet tables creaked as servants delivered platter after platter of food. A whole roast lu-deer, three types of miso soup, salt-and-vinegar chicken legs, a pile of dumplings, rich blue salads tossed with yar-nuts and glass-rabbit meat. The scent of roast meats filled the room, making Corin's mouth water and his stomach rumble. Lunch had been a sketchy affair in between briefing junren commanders and arranging weapons distributions.

He should sneak a plateful now, before things started. It was unlikely he'd be able to stay for the dinner, if it eventuated. He had things to supervise and observe, but they shouldn't take long. Maybe the revelry would still be going when he returned. Who knew, there might even be dancing.

It had been a long time since he'd danced with the court ladies. Perhaps someone could divert his attention from Alere. Her interest in him was probably a first-love infatuation that wouldn't last past her father's objections. Besides, he couldn't risk rupturing the tentative relationship between father and daughter, which was destined to be a rough ride, since they were so similar in temperament.

The doorman announced the first guests and Corin looked up. The Master of Messenger House, resplendent in burnt orange and black, arrived arm in arm with his much younger, simpering wife. As though the couple had opened floodgates, the finely-dressed elite of Shanzhai poured in and filled the ballroom.

As the volume of chatter swelled, Corin knew a moment of trepidation. The plan for this evening centred on Alere. Timing was paramount and much could go awry. Most of the guests knew Lianna Koh-Lin, to some degree. Alere must have every advantage and no obstacles to make it safely through the evening. Corin needed to check everything, and everyone, was in place before she arrived.

He spotted Kett, in formal Koh-Lin weishi black and green, lurking in a corner, surveying the room. Corin sauntered over.

'Couldn't stay away, huh?' He leant against a pillar with his back to Kett. 'Aren't you worried Ven might recognise you?'

'No.'

'Why not? How well does he know you?' Corin asked.

'Can we concentrate on keeping Alere safe?' Kett said, coolly.

Irritated, Corin eyed the room, picking out the castle weishi, some uniformed and others disguised as guests. Gavon tugged at the high collar of his blue silk suit and Corin grinned mockingly. Gavon glared back and edged into a corner, a wineglass held awkwardly in his thick fingertips. He studied, with deep suspicion, every passing guest. Rohne, relaxed in flamboyant, gold-trimmed burgundy, peered from the mezzanine overhead. His eyes were half-closed as he assessed each person's Outers.

More guests filtered into the castle. Corin nodded to a few acquaintances, but avoided conversations that might distract his focus from the shifting patterns of people. There was a danger Ven might slip a few spies or xiongshou into the crowd and tip the balance of the evening to his favour.

'Corin,' Kett called softly. 'The man in dark blue, across the room.'

Corin swept the throng with a casual look. He spotted a short, dark-haired man, well-dressed and chatting with the florid and loud Master of the Shanzhai Merchant House.

'Xiongshou?' Corin hazarded.

There was something about the way the man held himself and sized up each person who walked past. He kept his back to the wall and assessed newcomers as they entered. He had to be one of the Weishi House's elite assassins.

'Yes,' Kett said. 'His partner's the woman in green to his left. They're armed, which should give Maha an excuse to detain them. The man has knives in his boot, left sleeve and middle of his back. See how he touches them to make sure they haven't shifted. Bad habit. The woman has two in her hair and one on each arm. Under the long sleeves.'

'Right.'

Corin wandered over to the buffet and picked up a roast fowl leg. Under cover of nibbling at the tender meat, he caught Rohne's eye and let the xintou see the question in his Outers. Rohne focussed on the two guests and nodded. Corin flicked five small hand gestures at Maha, using a communication code devised by Farah years before. Maha signalled his undercover weishi, who eased through the crowd and closed on each threat. Surrounded by eight armed weishi, the male xiongshou wisely offered no resistance. The woman raised her voice in haughty anger, but stopped when Gavon appeared at her side and whispered in her ear. She paled and quietly followed her companion. Corin strolled around the room and returned to his position near Kett.

Thrice more, before Rafi and Yasmin made their entrance, Kett and Rohne picked out potential threats. On Corin's hand signals, the castle weishi removed the suspects. Kett's observational skills and Rohne's analysis were faultless. Eight xiongshou now languished, naked and shaved bald, in the zinzana downstairs. As expected, they refused to name who'd hired them, or who they'd been contracted to kill. Interrogating xiongshou, who were famously reticent under torture, was pointless. But had every threat been accounted for?

A servant announced Rafi and Yasmin. The room hushed and Corin studied the couple as they descended the stairs. Rafi's severely cut dark green and silver suit contrasted deliberately with what his wife and daughter wore. Corin chuckled and silently applauded Yasmin's dress. She'd added another twist to the vice being applied to Ven's mind tonight. The colour of her gown, while not true jiaoji red, was close enough to cause a flurry of whispered comments. And Yasmin's resemblance to Alere was striking.

Corin grinned. Let the games begin.

The doorman announced Jun First, Ven Zah-Hill. A corridor opened between the door and stairs. Corin edged to the front of the crowd to see Ven.

Ven cut a startling figure among the multi-hued dresses and robes of the local nobility. He paused in the doorway, dead eyes scanning the crowd with indifference. He wore a tunic and trous of unrelieved, matt black. Only the steel circlet around his head and two rings on his fingers gleamed silvery in the dancing lights. Corin struggled against the urge to laugh aloud. Alere was right about Ven's flair for the dramatic.

Behind Ven, his Jun Third and one of his Jun Fourths also wore their family colours of black or grey, with accents of gold or copper. But Jun Fourth Bren Gray-Saud was missing. Was he with Hanna?

Ven and Rafi strode towards each other, eyes locked, footsteps echoing on the flagstones. Both ignored the wave of bows to either side as they moved between the lines of guests. Silence gripped the room. Even the musicians paused as everyone sensed an impending moment of significance.

With impeccable timing, Rafi stopped the instant Ven did. The two men stood three paces apart. Ven's eyes flickered to Yasmin and widened. The glittering smile Yasmin bestowed on Ven was diamond-hard and sugar-crystal brittle. The men exchanged bows, but Ven's eyes kept returning to Yasmin.

Corin was too far away to hear the brief exchange of words.

The upper servant rapped his staff on the floor and called out in sonorous tones:

'Ladies and Gentlemen, having reached her Threshold today, I bid you acknowledge the Jun-Heir to Shenshi Rafi Koh-Lin. And, according to tradition, she has chosen her adult name.' The servant waved a hand to the stairs. 'May I present Shunu Lia Koh-Lin.'

Ven stiffened and looked up.

Alere appeared at the top of the stairs and wild applause erupted from the crowd. Relief tinged the excited, admiring whispers that reached Corin's ears.

Alere glided down the steps, head high, one hand lifting the hem of her skirt. The green dress floated around her slender form, highlighting her curves with its soft drape and flow; silver embroidery accentuating the lines of her body. For jewelry she wore the yanstone bracelet, a delicate filigree-steel necklace lying across her breast, and an emerald-studded steel hairpin to hold the silvery veil in place. Below the veil, her scarlet lips parted and trembled into a small smile. Around her shoulders and back, a silver wrap lent the final touch of elegance.

Corin held his breath, struck anew by her grace. He elbowed through the crowd, wanting to be close enough to hear her greeting to Ven. She reached her parents and bowed before the Jun First.

'I'm so pleased to see you're well, Shunu Lia.' Ven inclined his head. 'We heard of your illness. We'd almost given up hope of your recovery. Rumours had you on death's door.' His forced laugh dwindled as Rafi and Yasmin's cool expressions remained unchanged.

Voices and chatter swelled as the crowd broke apart and picked up lost conversations. The musicians launched into a lively tune. Corin edged closer, straining to hear Alere's reply. He and Yasmin had coached her as best they could on Lianna's personality and conversation style. The yanstones would help her Read others' expectations. The name "Lia" most closely resembled Alere's own name, so she should answer to it automatically. But could she keep up the pretense?

Alere averted her face as though shy. 'Thank you, shenshi. I was very ill but, as you can see…' She smiled sweetly and extended a hand to him. 'Thank you so much for coming to my Threshold ceremony.'

She was uncannily like her half-sister. Corin glanced at Yasmin, relieved to see her calm.

'Of course.' Ven kissed Alere's hand, turning it from side to side. 'What a lovely bracelet. It looks familiar.'

Alere plucked her fingers free and raised her wrist so the yanstones caught the light and flared into stone-fire. 'My father made it. Steel and yanstones. Very rare.'

'Indeed. And he made it?' Ven asked.

Corin caught Ven's eagerness and a hint of uncertainty.

'He found some old iron somewhere.' Alere shrugged. 'Pretty, isn't it? Sometimes I wear it on my ankle.'

Shock flashed across Ven's face. His jaw clenched.

Alere prattled on. 'And Mother made me wear the veil tonight. So old-fashioned. No-one else is wearing one.'

Ven seemed to collect himself. 'Why must you, then?'

'It's a surprise for—' She took a quick breath. 'Oh, forgive me, shenshi. I'm not supposed to say.'

'Then I shall not press you, shunu.' Ven bowed, but his eyes narrowed.

Alere touched Ven's arm. 'But you must tell me how my dearest Farima is. It's been so long since I've seen her or had a letter.'

Ven's face blanked.

'Your cousin, Farima Han-Asad?' Alere clasped her hands over her breasts and heaved a sigh. 'She's my best friend and I miss her. She often sends me sugarfires from Asadia. Just before I turned sixteen, she sent a packet so large I was almost sick because I ate too many. I honestly thought I was going to die, I felt so bad.'

Ven stiffened. His hand half-reached towards Alere's veil before dropping back to his side. Corin strained to hear Alere's next words.

'Do you have anything like that, shenshi? Her lilted question was a perfection of innocence. 'You know? Something you love but you're not supposed to do. And part of the fun is the chance you might get caught? I swear,' she added, rueful, 'my parents would probably whip me if they knew I'd eaten the whole bag of sugarfires. I've been such a trial to them. Oh. Please excuse me.' Alere waved at someone across the room. 'I've seen a dear friend I must speak to.'

She hurried through the crowd, leaving Ven pale and scowling. Ven motioned to his Jun Fourth, Yan Qin-Turner. Corin kept his back turned and listened.

'Yan, send a message to Penon. Get the junren over the bridge and into the city, now.' As the Jun Fourth moved away, Ven grabbed his arm. 'And get the Shunu Lia back. Something's going on here. The jiaoji told me she was close to death.'

Corin pointed at the door in a prearranged signal to the upstairs servant.

The servant struck the floor with his staff and waited until the hubbub died away. 'Please direct your attention outside. There will be a tao drumming display with fireworks, then dinner will be served.'

Chatter and laughter rose as guests jostled into the courtyard. After first ensuring Alere was under Rafi's protection, Corin wormed his way through the crowd and sprinted out a back door onto the castle wall overlooking the river. He snatched up a torch and waved it four times. Far below a glimmer of torchlight responded.

Luna-Er rode low in the sky, half-hidden by clouds, shedding an uncertain light. Corin produced his scope and, by the moon's fitful glow, made out the lines of tents and glowing orange fires in Ven's campsite across the river. A shadowy mass of junren, headed for Shanzhai, marched along the pale road that cut between dark fields.

The thunder of ceremonial drums pounded through Corin's chest and fireworks exploded overhead. In the gorge below, beyond the castle's outer wall, fire blossomed in two white-hot flowers. Perfectly timed, another spray of colour burst in the sky, followed by the boom and crackle of fireworks. The northeastern bridge collapsed into the black abyss and fell unheard to the riverbed. Corin kissed his fingertips to Farah and her men. Upriver, the eastern bridge exploded, timed to a spectacular shower of silver fireworks. Delighted, Corin swung the scope on Ven's army, which marched on, unaware.

He snapped the scope shut and slid it into a pocket. With any luck, Penon would fall into the river before he realised the bridge was gone. Laughing, Corin ran back inside, impatient to see stage two unfold.

p458 *Aiki Flinthart*

CHAPTER THIRTY-SEVEN

The firework displays fizzed to a close and the crowd streamed back inside; a kaleidoscope of colour and glittering jewelry. In the brilliant movement, Ven's sombre, black stillness stood out. A nondescript man, dressed as a servant, wove through the crowd, heading for Ven. Corin flicked a hand signal to Maha. The weishi intercepted and quietly removed the messenger. Now was not yet the right time for Ven to know about the bridges' destruction.

Corin caught Rafi's attention and pointed at Ven. The Jun First strode towards Alere, who stood only ten paces away. She seemed to be holding her own, chatting animatedly with a handsome young nobleman Corin recognised as a friend of Lianna's. Alere seemed to be comfortable, so Corin refrained from stepping in and edged his way towards Rafi instead.

Rafi caught Ven's elbow, talking earnestly. Corin arrived in time to hear the last few words.

'...right shenshi, of course,' Rafi said. 'She was very, very ill. But...' He eyed the chattering crowd. 'Perhaps this is not the time and place, but I would appreciate your counsel on an urgent matter regarding Lia. In here perhaps?' He gestured to a door, in the eastern wall, which led to a room set aside for this evening's events.

Ven glanced at Alere.

Corin gestured to the servant waiting beside the curtained portrait of Lianna. The servant tugged a silver rope and drew the curtains aside. Soft lights picked out the newly-cleaned gilding on the frame. Sixteen-year-old Lianna, in an indigo ball gown, no veil, and with Alere's face, watched over the room. An engraved silver plaque bore Lianna's name in clear letters.

Alere's jaw hardened as she saw the painting. Ven was still watching her. She caught his eye, gave a sultry smile that was pure jiaoji, then blew him a kiss.

Rafi called Ven's name. The Jun First hesitated then turned. He froze, staring at the painting of Lianna; of Alere. Corin grinned. Ven paled and the vein in his neck pulsed. One more lash of the whip; one more nail in the coffin.

'Shenshi?' Rafi waved the Jun First towards the open door. With several backward looks at the painting, Ven followed.

Corin laughed softly and nodded to Alere. Her eyes became abstracted. Presumably she spoke with Mina, warning her. Corin tugged at his mawei and frowned.

The next step was the trickiest as it depended on Mina. She'd sought out Corin, before the banquet, wanting assurance that Ven would be brought to justice. Corin was happy to oblige, although Mina probably had little comprehension of what justice meant in this instance. Alere and Mina believed they were only exposing Ven as a madman. But there were six people in the great hall tonight who were unlikely to let the Jun leave should anything happen to Alere. Corin refrained from enlightening Mina. She was a healer, after all, and he didn't want her ethics disrupting the plan.

Corin headed around to a second entrance and let himself into the eastern room. He edged in behind a privacy screen, sat on a leather stool, and waited for Rafi and Ven. In front of the screen stood a table covered by a midnight-blue cloth. Otherwise, the room was bare of furnishings. The door opened and Corin shifted so he could see the two men through the screen's pierced-wood pattern.

'Are you alright, shenshi?' Rafi closed the door and hovered solicitously over Ven, whose cheek was still pale.

'Yes.' Ven glowered down his nose at Rafi. 'Get on with it. What about Lia?'

Rafi bowed. 'Shenshi I'm entrusting you with a secret that cannot be shared. Have I your promise?'

'Of course.' Ven waved a dismissive hand.

'Shenshi,' Rafi said, 'you were right to question me about our daughter. She was extremely ill. So unwell that, in fact...' He cleared his throat. 'She died very recently; this morning, in fact.' Tears glistened in his eyes.

'What?' Ven staggered backward. 'Then who...who's that girl outside?'

'She's a jiaoji. She looks identical to Lianna. When I saw her...' Rafi's voice cracked as he continued. 'I knew she could be the solution.'

'A jiaoji?' Ven's eyes flicked around the room to the door, then came sharply back to the table. Ven's scowl deepened. Corin checked the blue silk tablecloth still covered and clung to what lay on the table. Doubt flickered across the Jun's face.

Corin picked up a slender item he'd placed behind the screen in preparation for this moment.

Rohne slipped into the room and silently joined Corin.

'Yes, a jiaoji. I know,' Rafi said, shaking his head. 'Now you see why I needed to speak with you. I've done the right thing, haven't I? We cannot have my seat in doubt. The jundom's too unsettled. People need surety and stability.'

'You...she...' Ven's eyes returned to the table. He scowled at Rafi. 'No. You can't pass some jiaoji whore off as your daughter.'

'The jiaoji profession is highly respected.' Rafi straightened. 'She's intelligent and learns fast. No one will know. But perhaps the best way to convince the world of her right to be Jun-Heir is for us to resume marriage negotiations.'

Ven recoiled. 'Me, bound in the hunli to a *jiaoji?* You've taken leave of your senses. I'll do no such thing.' He elbowed Rafi aside and strode towards the door.

'Where are you going, shenshi?' Rafi's question was sharp.

'To tell the world the truth. Your daughter is dead and you're attempting to pass off a jiaoji in her place.' Ven raked Rafi with a scornful glare. 'You're unfit to be Jun.' He reached for the door handle.

The sound of a whip cracked through the silence.

'What was that noise?' Ven spun and glared at the cloth-covered table.

'I heard nothing,' Rafi said stiffly.

Corin gripped the riding crop and slashed it across the leather stool again. Ven started. Corin nodded to Rohne, who pointed at the ceiling. The small chandelier dimmed to feeble orange before brightening once more.

'What's wrong with the lights?'

'Nothing,' Rafi said. 'They're perfectly fine. We were discussing Lia. My daughter is dead and you are—'

'Watch your tongue,' Ven snarled. 'Her death is none of my doing.' His gaze slid to the shape on the table. The blue fabric fluttered and Ven's eyes widened.

The lights guttered again. Corin cracked the whip a third time. A moan, throbbing with pain, drifted through the room.

'It wasn't my doing.' Ven's throat worked. He backed towards the door, hands out defensively.

Rohne pointed at the table; his eyes narrowed. The fabric shimmered, rippling like water.

The whip cracked, followed by a sobbing cry.

'But she didn't cry out when I...' Ven pointed, his hand trembling. 'What's that?'

'What shenshi? It's just a table,' Rafi replied.

The fabric shifted. An arm appeared from beneath it, fingers white and lax. A scarlet drop of liquid dripped off a fingertip and splashed onto the polished timber floor. Ven's face turned grey.

'No! *On* the table.' Hysteria tinged his voice. Ghost-pale, he edged closer to the table and stretched out one shaking hand. 'What's under that cloth?'

Rafi followed. 'The table's empty, Ven. It's a tablecloth, nothing else.'

'You're lying!'

Crack! Corin laid the whip across the seat. Ven clamped his hands over his ears.

'That noise. Make it stop.'

'What noise? There is none,' Rafi insisted. 'You're not well. Come, let me take you to our healer.'

Corin indicated the table. Rohne raised a hand and the cloth swirled into the air. The silk twisted into balletic shapes, but never rose high enough to reveal what lay beneath. Ven watched, wide-eyed and sweating.

The whip cracked. Corin smiled thinly.

Ven cried out; his knees sagged. Rafi caught him up, all mock concern.

'Sit for a moment. Let me get you a glass of wine.' Rafi tried to move away but Ven clutched at the Jun Second's arm. Ven's nails dug deep into Rafi's skin and drew blood.

Rohne moved his fingers. The cloth floated to the floor and settled in a shining heap. Ven pointed wordlessly at the table, face stark with horror.

Mina lay on the yar-pine table. Her eyes were closed, her lips parted; makeup tinted her skin pale and bloodless. On her forehead, lips and eyelids were five dark-blue dots of paint – the traditional death-mask adornment for women.

'No, it's not possible. Who *is* she?' Ven whispered.

She wore a short, black wig and a copy of Alere's green dress. In one open hand, she held five sugarfire sweets. The cinnamon scent drifted through the room. In her other hand lay a riding crop.

'Who?' Rafi grabbed Ven by the shoulders and turned him from the table. 'There's no one there.'

Ven fought and twisted to look back at Mina.

Rafi sighed and walked to the table and laid his palm on Mina's stomach. 'See? Nothing. Just a table.' He coolly picked a sweet from Mina's hand and thrust it into his mouth.

'What are you doing?' Ven cried. He pointed at Rafi. 'You ate one. You...' His expression became crafty. 'No, that's good. Go ahead. Eat them all.'

'What are you talking about, man?' Rafi took another sugarfire. 'I ate nothing. There's nothing here.'

'No!'

Darkness consumed the room. Ven let out a strangled cry. Someone laughed softly.

'The lights! Turn them back on.'

'They are on.' Rafi's reply was tinged with concern. 'I can see you perfectly. Are you quite well? You look pale.'

The lights snapped on again. The table lay empty.

'But I saw her.' Ven blinked.

'Who?' Rafi gripped Ven's arm.

Ven snarled, pushed his Jun Second away and fled. He came face to face with Mina, who blocked the exit.

She opened accusing dark eyes. 'You murdered me, shenshi,' she said and turned away, giving Ven a clear view of her back. Angry red stripes glistened, vivid against the green fabric and the gold of her skin. Corin gritted his teeth. The marks were painted versions of those on Alere's back but they looked real enough.

'Gah! No. I didn't.' Ven threw his arms up and backed away.

Mina glided towards him, flexing the whip. 'You murdered me.' She offered Ven the sugarfires.

Ven stumbled backwards. 'No. Stop saying that.'

'You murdered me.'

Rafi ignored Mina and hauled Ven to the door. 'Ven, enough. Get a grip. There's nothing there!'

'No, no, no, no.' Ven shut his eyes and hunched his shoulders.

Mina joined Corin and Rohne behind the screen. Rohne kissed her cheek. Her eyes were troubled. Rohne focussed his attention on the cloth and waved his hand.

'Control yourself. There's nothing there. Look.' Rafi spun Ven to face the table.

It was empty, the midnight silk smooth across its surface; the drop of blood gone from the floor.

'But I saw…' Ven wiped sweat from his forehead and plunged from the room.

Corin wrapped Mina in a cloak and pointed her to the servants exit. Then he hurried back into the great hall. Rohne split off and resumed his position on the mezzanine.

Corin arrived in time to see Ven jostle an elderly merchant master aside. Ven leapt onto the dais and inspected the painting behind the Jun throne. His white-knuckled fingers gripped the back of a chair. He scanned the room and spotted Alere surrounded by a bevy of admiring young men. Ven raced to the edge of the dais, his gaze intent on her.

Kett, now dressed in a finely embroidered grey tunic, appeared before the dais and stared, unspeaking. The Jun First hesitated, his jaw dropping. One hand fell to his hip, but he carried no weapon.

Corin raised his brows. This hadn't been part of the plan. What was Kett up to?

'Tekettan? But…you're dead.' Ven reached for him, but Kett stood out of range. Ven's eyes narrowed. 'You're not real.'

Kett smiled enigmatically.

Ven's certainty faded. 'You're dead. It's mine. Mother said. Get away!'

Kett remained a moment longer, then moved into the crowd. Ven glanced at Alere, then at Kett. He took a step in Kett's direction. Corin snatched a drink from a tray and collided with the Jun First, spilling the wine.

'So sorry.' Corin grabbed a napkin and dabbed at Ven's shirt. 'I'm so clumsy. Let me—'

'Get away from me, you shazi.' Ven craned over Corin's his head and swore.

Corin risked a quick look. Kett was gone. What had that been about?

'Shenshi!' Jun Third, Kennor Han-Asad caught Ven's arm and murmured into the Jun First's ear.

'The bridges? How did they…?' Ven snarled and shook off his Third. '*She* did this.' He stalked towards Alere.

Alere's clear laugh pealed over the babble of talk. Ven's eyes were wild as he shouldered through a throng of her admirers. A pool of silence rippled through the crowd. People backed away.

'You!' Ven stripped the silver veil from Alere's face. He balled the cloth in his fist and shook it at her. 'You did this.'

A shocked murmur passed through the onlookers.

Alere gasped, eyes wide. 'Shenshi! I gave you no permission to remove my veil. You insult me in my father's house.'

Men looked askance at each other. She had a right to call on someone to avenge the insult, but none seemed willing to lay hands on the Jun First. Corin smiled bleakly and hung back, watching, ready to intervene.

He checked with Rohne. The xintou shook his head. Gaisi! Ven's wards were still in place and Rohne was not yet able to breach them. With an effort, Corin held himself still. Alere was safe enough for now.

'Your father?' Ven sneered, circling her like a roc-eagle inspecting its quivering prey. He jabbed a finger at her. 'You're not a Koh-Lin. You're nothing but a common jiaoji. *My* jiaoji, to do with as I please.'

'No!' Alere cringed, tears gathering.

'Don't deny it. You're mine.' Ven laughed harshly. 'My mark is still on you. You can't deny that.' He ripped the silver wrap from her shoulders, grabbed her arms and spun Alere so bystanders could see the raw, red weals on her back.

'Shenshi!' Rafi's voice cracked the shocked silence like a whip. He thrust the crowd aside. 'What are you saying? Explain this.'

Corin held his breath. This was the moment that could make or break their gambit.

CHAPTER THIRTY-EIGHT

ALERE

Alere checked the crowd. Their expressions ranged from horrified, to doubtful, to puzzled, but none were outright hostile as they looked at her – even those of Ven's party. But it was up to her to sway them, now.

'Father, please?' She ran to Rafi and clutched at his arm. 'I was afraid to tell you. Yesterday, those two weishi who escaped.' She allowed tears to spill. 'You were away in the city. They…they took me hostage.' Cool air stung the exposed welts on her back and she cringed at the awareness that hundreds of people saw the injuries. Would they think her…Lianna…weak?

'What?' Rafi thundered. 'Why wasn't I told?'

'I begged the staff not to, Father. I was too humiliated and ashamed.' She spoke between breathy sobs, trying to tread the line between drama and believability. 'The weishi took me to Shenshi Ven's camp. He…' She buried her head in Rafi's shoulder. 'B-beat me. Threatened to kill you and mother unless I p-promised to marry him. He returned me to the castle. He's here to announce our betrothal. But I can't Father, please?'

Ven's mouth dropped open. 'Ha! What feihua. How can you believe such deceit? This jiaoji came to me yesterday, with a mouth full of lies. She said she was spying on you, for me. She belongs to me. Only two months ago she lived in the Alcazar as one of my father's jiaoji.'

'Lia hasn't been to Madina in two years.' Rafi said. 'This innocent child you kidnapped, beat and threatened, is my daughter. How *dare* you insult my family so?'

'You lie.' Ven pointed at Rafi. 'Not ten minutes ago you told me your daughter is dead.'

'Are you mad? She's right here.' Rafi scanned the crowd and called out, 'I need people who can identify my daughter. Come forward. Tell Shenshi Ven how you know this girl.'

The first man stepped forward, twisting a purple hat in his hands. He gulped and cast a quick, scared look at Ven. 'I'm Halmat, shenshi, artist. Two years ago I painted the portrait you see hanging in this very room. This is the girl I painted. It is her image, I swear.'

Alere smiled tremulously at him, sniffed and dried her tears.

One by one, three more respected city members swore Alere to be Lianna Koh-Lin. Most damning, Jun Third Kennor Han-Asad, Zah-Hill's own vassal, stepped reluctantly forward.

'This is Lianna – my daughter's close friend of many years. Lia's stayed with us several times. Tonight we spoke and she knew things about my family only Lia would know. I'm sorry Shenshi Ven.' He bowed and scurried from the hall. Maha sent men after him.

White spittle formed at the corners of Ven's mouth. 'No. You're all lying. Lianna's dead. I've seen her shade myself.' He pointed to the mezzanine floor. 'Look, there! Lianna's ghost walks there. See? She was poisoned. The Koh-Lin Jundom falls to me as heir.'

Heads turned but the mezzanine was empty. Whispers rushed through the crowd.

Alere risked a glance at Rohne, standing on the opposite end of the balcony. The xintou's eyes were half-closed, a scornful smirk on his mouth. He'd broken through Ven's wards at last and now played with the man's mind. His grin widened. He cocked his head and made a small, twisting motion with his hand.

Ven's eyes widened. 'No!' He threw up his arms and ducked. 'Don't come near me. Keep her away from me.'

The spectators muttered and tension swelled into anger. A dozen people closest to the Jun laid hands on hips, as though searching for the weapons they'd left at the door. One of Lia's friends grabbed Alere's elbow and tried to drag her away from the Jun. Alere twisted free.

'Arrest him!' someone cried from the crowd. 'Call for the Xintou House Law Mistress.'

Alere suspected the voice was Gavon's.

Ven lowered his arms and blinked. On the mezzanine, Rohne scowled and shook his head. Ven must have strengthened his wards enough to keep Rohne out again.

Jiche! Now what did she do? He hadn't confessed to killing Lianna, yet. There must be some way—

With a cry of fury, Ven snatched Alere's arm. She screamed and tugged at his grip – not so hard as to actually break free.

'You warned them,' he snarled at her, his face contorted into monstrosity by rage. 'You warned them my men were marching to take the city. The bridges have been destroyed. The city should be mine by now. Rafi dead. You…you ruined it. I didn't beat you hard enough yesterday.'

'Shenshi! You're hurting me.' Where were Kett and Corin? She couldn't release herself without betraying skills Lianna Koh-Lin didn't have. But she didn't want Kett and Corin interfering before Ven had confessed to Lianna's murder.

'Ven! Release her,' Rafi yelled. Three of Ven's weishi held Rafi immobile. Maha was working his way through the crowd with four weishi close behind.

Around them, the crowd shuffled and shoved, glancing at each other in fearful indecision.

Ven yanked Alere close and wrapped long fingers around her neck. 'Well, if you're already dead, perhaps I'll make sure you stay that way.'

Alere let out a little scream and clawed at his arms. 'Shenshi!'

His grip tightened.

She coughed. Her nails tore his sleeve and left scarlet gouges in his skin. The room darkened. She had to break his hold and risk revealing her weishi training or she would die.

Ven smiled in satisfaction. 'I'll kill you properly, this time. With my own hands. Poisoning you was no fun, anyway.'

There. No-one could fault her action, now.

Corin was less than three steps from her side. He reached for a sword he wasn't carrying. Kett shoved through the crowd opposite, sword drawn. Both were too late. This was her moment.

But did she kill him or just injure and let him stand trial?

His fingers dug deep into her neck and he laughed.

The yanstones on Alere's wrist flared into eye-aching brilliance. Fear vanished and she stilled beneath Ven's grip. Her path was clear, now. He could not be allowed to live. He was a danger to Jundom and everyone she cared for.

She tugged the emerald-studded dagger-pin from her hair. Her breath caught and the room faded as he squeezed harder. Eye or heart? Which would be faster? Heart, of course. She plunged the blade into Ven's heart and twisted. Rib bones cracked. The yanstones on her wrist flashed fire. Blood glistened on Ven's shirt, warmed her icy fingers and and stained her hand scarlet.

The room held its breath. Ven swayed on his feet, madness fading into confusion. He coughed and blood painted his lips jiaoji-red. His hands relaxed, fingers stroking Alere's neck like a lover's caress. Eyes glazing, he slumped to the floor.

CORIN

Corin caught Alere as she sagged, coughing and gasping. Her eyes closed and he scooped her into his arms. The emerald dagger-pin clattered to the floor in a pool of Ven's blood. Was she alive? She sighed into unconsciousness, but her heart still fluttered against his chest. Corin held back a cry of relief.

A babble of shocked speculation erupted. The crowd pressed in, craning and jostling to see the events. Gavon and Kett shouldered through and cleared a path to the stairs for Corin.

'Gavon, Kett, help Maha.' Rafi's commands cut through the hubbub. 'Detain Ven's party for questioning. Everyone else, clear the room. Go home and stay there. The city is closed to traffic. No riders or flitters to leave, either.'

Inside Alere's room, Corin found Mina pacing and wringing her hands. She cried out in horror as Corin entered and laid her sister on the bed.

'No, not on her back. I need to dress the cuts. Oh, her throat.' Mina touched the darkening bruises on Alere's neck and felt her pulse. 'She's just unconscious. Help me roll her.'

Mina cut the dress from Alere's body. Faced with the true extent of Alere's injuries, Corin turned away, fists clenched with the desire to hit a man already dead.

'Is she alright?' He struggled to keep his voice calm.

'Her back's bleeding again and her throat's bruised, but she'll live.' Mina's voice was strained. 'He's dead, isn't he?'

'She did it herself.'

'And that makes it better?' Mina snapped. 'You lied to me. You said she wouldn't have to kill him.'

Corin turned to find Mina standing close, her hands fisted, her whole body shaking.

'She didn't have to, Mina,' he said coolly. 'She *chose* to. None of us knew she was carrying a weapon. Kett was only a step away. So was I.'

The door opened. Kett, Rafi, Rohne, and Yasmin hurried into the room, demanding, questioning.

Mina rounded on them, tears marking her cheeks. 'Physically, she'll survive this, yes. But how could you? She was a lonely, scared little girl and you...' She raked Kett, Rafi and Corin with a scornful look. 'All of you, have made her into a murderer.'

She brandished the yanstone bracelet on her left arm. 'I heard everything she was thinking. She didn't care about the beating, or the bruises. Even with his hands on her throat all she cared about was protecting us. Fulfilling her duty to you and *your* people, Rafi. Proving she was worth something to us. We're all responsible. We did this to her.' She sank onto the bed, covered her face and cried.

Yasmin sat next to her, but Mina pushed her aunt away.

'Just leave us alone. All of you.' No-one moved, and Mina shouted, 'Get. Out!'

Yasmin herded the others from the room. Rohne glanced over his shoulder, his expression one of speculative interest. Corin checked the room. What was Rohne looking at?

ALERE

Alere woke to darkness and confusion. The soft bed gave beneath her stomach and blankets weighed on her legs. A click broke the silence and a dim, orange light filled the room. Her room. She pushed up on her elbows, wincing.

'Who's there?' Her voice emerged as a croak.

Mina knelt at her side, her eyes shadowed. She stroked Alere's hair.

'It's just me. Go back to sleep. Everything's all right.'

'Oh.' Alere lay down and smiled sleepily at her sister. 'We're together…no, not quite. I'll be alright, when we are.' She drifted back to sleep. Why on Kalima had she said such an odd thing?

The next time Alere woke pink dawnlight bathed the room. Mina rose from a chair and lay a hand on Alere's forehead. Apparently satisfied, she helped Alere rise and shower. Mina spoke little. She ignored Alere's swearing, treated her injuries, then helped her dress. Her hands were gentle, but her eyes held pain and deep melancholy.

A servant brought breakfast but every painful swallow recalled the image that haunted Alere's sleep: Ven's fingers around her neck; the sadistic gleam in his eyes. She set the plate aside, the thought of food nauseating.

'You must eat,' Mina said. 'You've hardly had anything for two days. You can't heal if you don't eat. Sit.' She picked at her own food, her expression troubled.

Having forced herself to eat a bowl of miso soup, Alere rose to seek out Rafi.

'Do you have to do this, Alli?' Mina asked. 'I know what you're planning. Your Outer wards don't work against me anymore. I hear everything you're thinking. You're still angry at Hanna and Celia, but isn't Ven's death enough? Without him, Hanna has nothing. The Jun Seconds will choose another First. It's over.'

Alere caught her sister close, trying to hide the unease Mina's words caused. That Mina could Read all that so easily was discomfiting.

'Here.' Alere unclasped her own bracelet and laid it on the table, relieved to have an excuse to break the connection with Mina. With Rohne by Rafi's side today, there would be no need for the bracelet and its powers, anyway. 'Don't mistake determination for anger. Of course I was angry and hurt. But I'm not now, I promise. Hanna won't relinquish the throne without a fight, you know that. I'm sorry this has affected you so much.'

When Mina didn't move, Alere gently removed her sister's bracelet. 'We don't need to wear them. With Ven dead, I don't think we'll even have to fight Hanna's junren. It was unfair to involve you yesterday. I didn't intend to kill Ven. It just...happened. Thank you for taking care of me and thank you for worrying, but I have to finish this.' She kissed Mina on the cheek.

'I won't do it again, Alli.' Mina said, tears shimmering on her lower lids. 'I'm a healer and I helped you murder a human being. I'll have that on my conscience forever. And I can't stay and watch you become this person.'

'What are you talking about? I'm still me.' Alere gave a half-laugh.

'When we first met,' Mina said, 'you were just as scared as me. You put a better face on it, that's all. And when you killed that weishi in Pelon, your hands shook and you almost threw up. I saw.'

Alere sobered. 'I remember.'

'But last night...' Mina scrubbed her hands down her thighs. 'I heard your thoughts when Ven was.... You were scared. But then there was a kind of...brightness in your mind. Then you decided he needed to die to protect all of us. After that you were so clinical it terrified me. You thought about where to drive the blade into his chest. Or whether his eye would be better.' She pressed two fingers to her lips. 'It was like he wasn't even a person…just…a thing…an inconvenience to be rid of.'

Horrified by her sister's insight, Alere stayed silent. It was true. She remembered the yanstones flaring in the light before she chose the best way to kill the Jun. Then it had all seemed clear and easy. She frowned. Ven had thought like that: he saw people as things; an obstacle or a resource. What was she becoming?

'I'm sorry,' Alere said. 'I…I still have to finish this. You know I do.' Unable to speak further and overwhelmed with self-loathing, she hugged Mina and left the room. Mina's soft sobs followed Alere along the hall.

Alere was pacing the mezzanine balcony when Corin found her. The black look marring his handsome face softened. Drawing her into an empty room, he inspected her face and neck.

'I'll only ask once, so tell me the truth.' He caressed her cheek.

Her heart warmed under his loving touch. 'I'll be fine.'

'Physically, yes, but how about mentally?' He cocked his head, frowning again.

Alere forced a laugh. 'You sound like Mina. I promise I'll be fine. Tell me what's happening?'

'Ah…gaisi.' He snatched her close and kissed her. She melted against him, seeking reassurance, needing his strength. His fingers brushed her back. She gasped and cried out.

'Khara!' He snatched his hand away. 'I'm sorry.'

Alere laughed again, this time with regret, and rested her head on his shoulder. He gingerly wrapped his arms low around her body.

'No,' she said, 'don't be sorry. I'm not.'

'What's that mean?' Hope blossomed in his eyes.

Alere disengaged from his embrace and his face fell.

'I don't...' She sighed. 'We have terrible timing, Cor. There's too much happening. Too much for me to deal with right now. Don't tie up your hopes in me.' She kissed him, hating the flare of pain in his eyes. 'I'm still not sure who I am. I don't want to hurt you with my uncertainty. Give me some time, if you can.'

'Agreed.' He gave a rueful chuckle. 'Though I may need to go away a lot to avoid putting undue pressure on you.'

'Now *that* is unfair,' she said. 'I'd want to go with you and I can't now. I miss being on the road with you.'

Corin laughed, offering an elbow as they left the room. 'What, the bad food or Gavon pounding you into the ground every day?'

'Both, strangely enough. Now tell me what's happened.'

'The bridges over the Kuaisu are destroyed. The ford is being watched. Hanna's marching to the ford and Penon's rushing south with Ven's men to join her.'

'Do they know about Ven?' Alere touched her neck.

'I don't think so. Hanna's moving at a slow march,' Corin said. 'Rafi locked the city down last night. We expect Hanna will cross the river in about five hours. Rafi needs to get his men in place on the high ground before then.'

Alere halted outside the conference room. 'We must stop things becoming a bloodbath, Cor. Hanna and Celia are at fault, not the men they lead.'

Corin ran a hand over the back of his neck. 'I agree, but I'm not sure Rafi's open to suggestion. He was rather...upset when he saw your injuries. We all were. I should have stopped you going to Ven's camp.'

'Kett must've told you how useless any attempt would've been. Let it go. I don't need your protection, Corin.' She kissed his cheek. 'We've rid the Jundom of a madman. Now we need to stop a war.'

The meeting room was full. Alere's core team were present, plus the six lesser Juns – Third through to Sixths – who owed allegiance to the Koh-Lins. Behind each Jun stood their shangwei. Rafi denied access to the Xintou, though, for there was no way of knowing who might report to Celia. The only person missing was Mina.

Alere listened to the Juns argue for close to half an hour before her patience snapped.

'Shenshis and shunus.' She rose and waited for the babble of argument to die away. Now she had their attention, her palms slicked with sweat. They all knew Lianna as a headstrong, fun-loving child. She needed to show them a different side and win them over, or war would come to Shanzhai today.

'Shenshis and shunus,' she repeated, lowering her voice. She caught the eye of each Jun and their Shangwei. Wearing the yanstones and Reading people's Outers would have made things easier. Now she had to rely on their faces. Their expressions ranged from sympathy, to tolerance, to irritation. This would not be simple.

'Most of you knew me before I went away. But you knew me as a child so I beg your indulgence for a few minutes.' She leaned on the table. 'In the time I was away from Shanzhai I learned a great deal and suffered a great deal. Probably more than many of you would believe.' Their sceptical smiles softened to thoughtfulness.

Alere continued. 'As part of my…recovery…I trained in combat and studied warfare so please, believe me: we have little time to make the right choices. Nor do we have the luxury of debating whether or not to go into the field today. The choice has been taken from us by Hanna and Ven. Our only decision now is: what we do once we're there.' She straightened and spread her hands, palms up. 'I believe, if given the chance, we can negotiate a peace with Hanna. Please, let me try.'

Rafi shot to his feet. 'No. I forbid you!' His tone gentled and he laid a hand on her wrist. 'You've done enough. Leave this to us.'

'You know I can't, Father,' Alere said calmly. 'This started with me and I'll finish it. Nothing you can say will stop me. We have a duty to prevent unnecessary deaths.' She indicated the map showing the escarpment overlooking a swathe of open ground between the river and Shanzhai. 'Deploy your army here. Hanna will see you have superior numbers. But set a pavilion here.' She pointed to a spot in the middle of the level ground. 'With the green truce flag flying. Let's see if we can end this before it begins.'

CHAPTER THIRTY-NINE

'A…Lia!' Corin's call brought Alere up short as she headed for the stable to prepare Rumi.

'Not you, too?' She groaned. 'I'm not staying here and we don't have time to argue. Rafi's men are already moving. I need to get geared up and out there.'

She'd already changed into travel clothes and borrowed alzin armour from one of the junior weishi. The welts on her back meant she couldn't wear a quiver so, instead, she tucked five throwing knives into the back of her belt. It was time to go.

He laughed and held up his hands in surrender. 'I know trying to stop you is pointless. I have two gifts for you. Come with me.' He led her into the great hall. On a long dining table lay a bulky parcel wrapped in silver silk. Next to it was the steel cage from Lia's room. Inside, the jin-bird, Reya, fluttered restlessly.

'Rafi thought you might like her. Lia and that zift bird were inseparable.'

Alere considered the little reptile. Its golden fur glittered in the light and the silvery eye held surprising intelligence. Reya chirruped. Alere glanced around at the great hall's iron-bound splendour and power. She flipped open the cage and held out a hand. Reya inspected Alere's fingers, then hopped onto one. The little reptile rubbed its furry head on Alere's arm and tickled her skin with a scarlet forked tongue.

'Go, little one.' She flicked her arm. Reya squawked and flapped her wings. She took off, circled Alere's head twice then vanished out the front door into the leaden sky. Alere's heart sank. She'd half-hoped the animal would stay.

Corin raised a brow at her.

She shrugged. 'I'm not Lianna. I chose this. Reya should get to choose, too.'

'Perhaps this will serve you better.' With a formal bow, he handed over the other parcel. 'For you, as promised.'

Alere laid it on the table and unwrapped the shimmering cloth. She gasped. Steel gleamed in the afternoon light. Not just the dagger he'd promised, but a matching sword, too. They were so beautifully crafted, lustrous and sharp, she was afraid to touch them and mar the smooth finish. The grips were bound in green leather. On each weapon, eight small yanstones glittered in a ring around the pommel, with a larger stone set in the pommel's end. The stones refracted golden light from the chandelier in a hypnotic play that held her entranced.

'It's alright to touch them.' Corin grasped her hand and laid it on the sword's hilt.

She wrapped her fingers lovingly around the leather and slid the weapon free of the silk. It was perfectly weighted and moulded to her palm like an extension of her arm. She swung the blade, watching it slice through the air.

'You've given me an heirloom,' she said simply. 'Thank you. I don't have the words to tell you how much I love these. They're perfect.'

'I can't take all the credit,' Corin said. 'I designed and ordered them, but the castle smith hasn't slept for two days.' He removed his old dagger from the sheath at her hip and slid the new blade into place. 'Rafi paid. I couldn't afford these stones. The iron is from here.' He pointed to the floor.

Alere kissed his cheek and sheathed the sword, leaving her ceramic weapon on the table. 'I'll thank you properly later, Cor. Let's go.'

At the stable, Kett waited with their horses saddled and ready. Gavon was mounted on a dancing, impatient Iblis. Alere patted Rumi.

'Where's Rohne?' she asked. 'It seems unlike him to avoid a battle. He knows Rafi will need him.'

Kett gathered his reins. 'I don't know. Perhaps with Rafi already.'

'Maybe he's with Mina.' Alere shot Kett a narrow look. 'She's upset after last night. Have you spoken with her?'

'I have.' He swung into the saddle and kicked Bol into a trot. Baffled, Alere followed.

By the time they reached the outskirts of Shanzhai, the winter sun struggled to its zenith in the teal sky. A sharp southern breeze tossed the hood from Alere's face and she shivered. Stormclouds gathered on the southern horizon, promising more cold weather. Last night's snow was no more than muddied meltwater on a road filthied by the hurried passage of many feet.

Inside the city walls a press of people watched her party pass; the adults with fear, children with excited non-comprehension. Outside the walls, abandoned houses with vacant-window eyes lined the streets. Only the occasional slam of an unsecured door, or bark of a scavenging feral dog, broke the silence.

Passing the last straggling houses, Alere's party arrived at the edge of the great plateau upon which Shanzhai was built. The escarpment swept in a long curve south and west, the land falling gently to a wide floodplain. The Kuaisu, cold and ice-green with meltwater from the southern glaciers, snaked through the plain; a bright, braided ribbon against the broad riverbed of silvery rocks.

Rafi's eighteen thousand green-clad junren ranged in nervous silence along the escarpment, archers kneeling before the riders, foot junren behind. On the plain below, Hanna's men faced them. Her archers stood in front, with bows at the ready. Black and silver pennants snapped in the wind; horses stamped and whickered in the cold.

Equidistant between the two forces, a grey pavilion shuddered as the wind rose. A green and white truce flag fluttered from its peak.

A drumbeat of hooves brought Rafi and his Jun Third, Dal Lee-Hay, cantering to join Alere's party. Rafi turned his horse and headed for the pavilion. Dal fell in behind, sending Alere and her companions a look of open curiosity. Dal, Rafi's staunchest supporter, was a xiao-bear of a man with a thick black beard and hands that made his double-headed axe look small. Alere nudged Rumi forward. Corin, Kett and Gavon followed. From enemy lines, twenty-four horses cantered forth.

Rafi sent Dal ahead and slowed to the horses to a walk as they neared the tent.

'All of you: keep quiet,' Rafi instructed, flicking a stern look at Corin and Alere. 'And Kett, stay out of Hanna's sight. We do not need accusations of revolution before I even open my mouth.'

Alere gaped in astonishment. What on Kalima did Kett have to do with anything? Kett merely nodded.

Rafi twisted in the saddle, frowning at his escort. 'Where's Rohne?'

'We don't know,' Corin admitted.

Rafi swore. 'Then hold your wards well, all of you. Celia will do all she can to break us. She is Xintou to the First. If she finds out what happened last night, her word will be considered truth. Lia?' Rafi waved her forward.

Alere rode up beside him.

He glanced narrowly at her. 'What are Celia's strengths as a xintou?'

'Telepathy – both Reading and Sending. She has Empathy, as well. If she breaks through your Inner wards she can impose emotions and thoughts on you.' Alere grimaced and drew a shaky breath. 'But she risks Fusion if she tries and your mind proves the stronger.' She shivered.

'Jiche!' he growled. 'And we have no xintou to strengthen our wards. Where the diyu is Rohne? What about your bracelet?' He raised his arm. His yanstone bracelet glittered in the weak afternoon light.

Alere lifted her bare wrist. 'Mina was upset so we both took them off. I'm sorry.' Her stomach sank. Without either Rohne or Alere acting as Xintou, Rafi was unprotected and there was no way of knowing if Celia breached anyone's wards.

Rafi growled. 'Well, at least we only have to contend with Celia.'

She studied the opposing army line, frowning. Neither army contained the gold-robes. 'Where are all the other Xintou, Bonded to Hanna's Juns? And yours? I know they don't usually go to public celebrations, like last night, but I thought they'd be here today.'

'Dal says the Xintou all received word from the House that if they couldn't stop this war they must absent themselves.' Rafi sent Alere a wry grimace. 'Mistress Li's way of slapping our wrists. I suspect there will be worse to come from the House if we survive this.'

Alere dropped behind Rafi and exchanged a worried look with Corin.

They reached the pavilion a few seconds before Hanna's party and dismounted, looping reins over a hitching post. The pavilion was open on two sides, with only a few fluttering wall panels to break the knife-edged wind. Beneath the shelter stood a small table, flanked by two chairs.

Alere flicked up her hood and palmed one of her throwing knives. Kett beckoned. His jaw hardened as the Zah-Hill party approached. He led Alere out of sight behind one of the silk panels.

'Alere,' he said, 'are you prepared to do what it takes to end this?'

'What do you mean?' She shrank from the harshness of his tone.

'Celia's your House sister. You've been brought up to be loyal to Xintou House and to the Jun First. You killed Ven, but the personal element made that easier, didn't it?'

He waited for her reluctant agreement. 'When you confront Celia it will be different. If she breaks your wards, she'll twist your loyalty to the House against you. She'll find out who you are and everyone here will die.'

'I know.' Alere glanced uneasily towards the approaching Xintou. 'I understand what you're saying: I may need to kill her. Mina would counsel otherwise and even Mistress Li wouldn't approve...' She wrapped her arms around herself. 'I think I can but, like you say, I won't know until the point comes.'

Kett backed away, his eyes harder than the bluestone underfoot. 'If you can't, I will. Those women cannot walk out of here.'

He turned his back, leaving her dumbfounded and shaken.

Corin called her name and she hurried inside the pavilion. She ranged herself with the others behind Rafi as Hanna entered. Hanna paused, regal and supercilious. Her black cloak was lined with silvery spice-otter fur, her blonde hair pinned beneath a steel crown and scraped into a smooth chignon. Under the cloak, she wore alzin over sensible travel clothing. Perhaps this pared down, no-frills

Hanna was the real woman. The ice of Hanna's white face and chill in her pale eyes lent weight to that idea.

Penon, Celia and Jun Fourth Bren Gray-Saud took their places behind her. Hanna's choice of Bren as support surprised Alere. In court he had openly questioned some of Hanna's decisions in the past. Of course, he was the most senior Jun in Hanna's army, with Han-Asad still imprisoned in the castle. Bren eyed Rafi and his attendants with shrewd interest, his attention resting longest on Alere. She inclined her head. His mouth twitched into the smallest of smiles before he looked away.

Celia stood behind Hanna and inspected each of Rafi's companions. She wore a heavy gold robe, black cloak and the gold veil. Her attire meant she intended to play the Xintou role to the hilt; to engender fear which might cause cracks in Rafi's wards, or those of his people.

Outside the tent, Penon's twenty weishi stood silent, watchful, their hands already resting on swords and daggers.

Rafi bowed deeply to Hanna, who barely nodded. Rafi's fingers whitened on his sword hilt, but his expression remained unchanged. He sank onto a seat, still holding Hanna's gaze. She followed suit.

Alere watched Celia. The Xintou made no move to step forward. Normally a Xintou would use physical contact to strengthen wards. Rafi had no gold in his entourage so Celia probably felt confident. Jiche! Where was Rohne?

Rafi relaxed and waited. Kett had coached him on the technique only that morning in council. The person who spoke first subtly lost power in this mind game. Hanna remained calm and aloof for several long minutes before she frowned and shifted in her seat.

Alere caught Celia's eye, sheathed the throwing knife and laid her hands on the pommels of her new weapons as an understated threat. The Xintou stiffened.

The yanstones on Alere's weapons felt warm and smooth. A silvery, welcoming flare and a whispering of mental voices danced through her mind. Her palms itched with a strange tingle that slipped beneath the skin, into flesh and spread through her body like a slow, golden syrup. Muscles, skin and bone gathered the energy. Pain, Alere's constant companion for many days, dissolved.

She sucked a quick, surprised breath and lifted her hands. The warmth stopped. Pain oozed back into her body. Alere gripped the yanstones and allowed the energy to fill her. The fatigue and fear of the last few days vanished. Her body and mind thrummed with clarity and strength. The faintest taste of woodsmoke and iron teased her tongue.

A scratch on Alere's Outer ward begged her notice. Celia.

Hanna lifted her chin. 'Where is my son?'

Rafi let the silence extend a fraction longer than was comfortable. He sat up swiftly and Hanna jerked back. Behind her, twenty hands yanked at twenty swords, but stopped as Penon held a palm up. Bren folded his arms across his chest.

Rafi raised a brow. 'Your weishi are jumpy. Do they suspect me of treachery? You're the one on my doorstep with an army, Hanna. Why?'

'You know well, why.' Hanna shot back. 'My son has been taken captive.'

'When? To reach Shanzhai today, you must have left Madina three weeks ago.' Rafi didn't bother to mask the sarcasm. 'Come, Hanna. Let's not hide our teeth. Why are you here?'

The scratch on Alere's wards became a knife-point as Celia tried to break through. Alere reached through her own wards, touched lightly on Celia's probe, and followed it back to its source. She stroked a thought across Celia's wards. Celia's concentration was divided. The Xintou attempted to pierce Rafi, Corin, Dal, and

Alere's wards all at once. Sloppy and overconfident. But Gavon, nondescript in his scruffy yongbing clothing, Celia ignored.

Alere withdrew from Celia and directed her thoughts to Gavon. He had no wards, but was thinking hard about how to keep Rafi and Alere safe. She slipped into his Outers, pleased his reaction was no more than a slight stiffening. Swiftly, Alere and Gavon planned Rafi's defence, should things go wrong.

In the distance, a lone horseman galloped across the Zah-Hill lines, heading for the cluster of Jun Fifths and Sixths in the army's front line. By the gold lining of his flapping black cloak, it was Jun Third, Kennor Han-Asad. Rafi must have released Kennor to tell Hanna's Juns of Ven's madness. Had Rafi seen Kennor's arrival? Corin must have, for he signalled to the Koh-Lin junren on the hill to keep their position.

Rafi related the tale of Ven's actions at the ball, his attention focussed on Hanna.

Hanna slammed a hand on the table, interrupting Rafi's soft, steady words. Rafi showed nothing but mild interest.

'My son would never kidnap and beat an innocent girl. Certainly not your daughter!' She was vehement, but doubt lurked behind her certainty. Bren's eyes narrowed and Celia pursed her lips.

'Your son,' Rafi said, steel in his tone, 'inherited your father's insanity, Hanna. You know it. And your scheming to make sure Ven was Jun-Heir pandered to his arrogance and sense of entitlement. He could no longer see the line between right and wrong, or the value of human life. You raised a monster who respected no-one, Hanna. Ven—'

'Do not speak of my son in such a way!' Hanna snapped. 'This isn't about Ven. It's about your lies and treachery. The girl Ven beat wasn't your daughter. Penon witnessed their meeting in Ven's pavilion. The girl is a jiaoji that *we* own.' She sneered. 'I have it on good authority that your daughter is dead. Your Jundom has no heir.'

A gust of icy wind swept through the pavilion, fluttering cloaks and bringing with it the clean scent of snow. Rafi's jaw muscles jumped and his fingers curled into a fist. Then he relaxed and laid his palm up on the table.

'You're wrong, Hanna.' Rafi beckoned and Alere stepped forward. 'My daughter, and heir, is right by my side. Lia.'

Alere flipped back her hood and raised her chin rather than bowing. She had no intention of taking her eyes off Celia or Hanna, even for a moment.

'You've met Yasmin in Madina, when she unveiled in the women's quarters. You can see the likeness, I'm sure,' he added.

Hanna paled, glanced at Celia, and put a hand to her breast. 'That...it's not possible. She should be...I was told she was...'

'Dead? Of poison, perhaps? That's what Ven thought, too,' Rafi said. 'Isn't life funny? Maybe the poisoned sugarfires you sent didn't work? Did your niece, Farima, even know you were using her to assassinate my daughter?' He ignored Hanna's betraying gasp.

Bren frowned. Tension in the small space twisted tighter. Penon and his men shifted uneasily.

'Or,' Rafi continued, 'maybe things I thought were lost forever came back to me.'

'No.' Celia stepped forward, haughty, certain. 'This is not your daughter. I know this mind. This is the jiaoji. This is Alere Connor.'

Rafi surged to his feet. 'Prove it,' he snarled. 'Bring your healers and nai-xintou.' He flung out a hand at Alere. 'Have them check her face, her blood, her genes against mine and against Yasmin's. They'll find a match. This girl *is* my daughter and heir.'

Celia's mind sharpened to a point and drove like a spear into Alere's wards.

Alere deflected the attack with ease. How had she used the *chuizi* technique to knock out Rohne in Gaton? If only she could remember.

'It's not possible!' Hanna cried, looking to Celia again.

'Yes, it is.' Rafi placed both palms on the table and leaned towards Hanna. 'Now take your army and leave my land. This will end today.'

'I demand to see my son!' Hanna shot to her feet, glaring at Rafi.

'You have two choices, Hanna.' Rafi straightened and raised his voice. 'You will either leave, without what you came for – and I do know what you really came for – or you will die. As your son did last night: in a fit of insanity, with a blade through his gouri heart when he tried to strangle my Jun-Heir in front of two hundred witnesses.'

Rafi's flat words slapped his listeners like an open palm. The world held its breath: the wind dropped, clouds covered the sun and the temperature plummeted.

Hanna screamed; a banshee wail that scraped from the heights of her angry disbelief to the rawest depths of despair. Grief and anger twisted her face. She launched herself across the table, scrabbling at Rafi. Penon grabbed his mistress by the waist and hauled her back.

'Kill them!' Hanna shrieked at her guards. 'Kill them all. They murdered the Jun First. My son.' She dissolved into tears and incomprehensible curses.

After a moment's hesitation, Penon nodded. Twenty weishi drew their weapons and advanced on Rafi's little group. Bren, after a quick look at Hanna struggling in Penon's grip, let go of his weapons. He held up an open hand in an unmistakable stop signal towards Hanna's waiting army and backed away from the pavilion.

'Hold.' Rafi's low-voiced instruction stayed his own people. 'They must be seen to strike first.'

'I get the impression they might be scared to, shenshi,' Corin murmured.

'We should be so lucky,' Rafi replied. 'Signal our men on the hill to stay. We may yet prevail without a war.'

Corin waved twice at Rafi's army then his sword slithered free of its sheath.

Hanna screamed, 'Now! I *command* you.'

Five weishi attacked Rafi, swords swinging in full view of both armies. Gavon stepped in front of his shenshi and flipped the table up. The yongbing stabbed through the thin wood, using the table to push the weishi back. Dal flung a chair at the others and waded forward, axe swinging dangerously close to friend and foe alike. Blood sprayed as he cleaved an Alcazar weishi almost in two. Kett stepped into the pavilion, hauled Rafi back and took up a protective stance before the Jun.

'Get out of my way,' Rafi snapped.

Kett ignored him.

Alere snatched out a throwing-knife and flicked it. The blade lodged in the throat of the female weishi guarding Celia. The Xintou gasped and threw her mind against Alere's wards. A touch on the yanstones kept her at bay. Alere drew her sword and dagger, feeling the silver-gilt energy fade as she gripped the leather instead of the stones. She could still sense if Celia tried to trespass, but little more than that. How could she fight and protect her mind at the same time?

A sword sliced at Alere's head. She had no time to think. Her first block chipped the ceramic blade. A pommel-strike stunned the man. She sank her dagger into his neck, shoved him aside, and turned to the next. Kett's sword appeared and blocked a strike aimed at her head. Kett drove his dagger into the attacker's armpit and took up a stance at Alere's back.

A few paces away, Gavon fought like a demon, two men already at his feet. Corin had Gavon's back, steel sword and dagger gleaming in the cold air as he dueled with two weishi. Penon still held Hanna, who writhed in his arms. Rafi, where was he? Alere's father knelt on the ground behind her, sword lost, hands clasped to his head. His face was a rictus of agony.

Celia! The Xintou had retreated behind two weishi, her triumphant gaze fixed on Rafi.

'Corin. Kett!' Alere yelled and dropped to her knees. 'Protect Rafi. I need to help him.'

She placed her hands on the yanstones. The full strength of the gems washed through her, bringing calm and certainty, detaching her from fear. Full of silver-gilt power, tasting iron and smoke, she stretched out with her mind.

There. Celia had broken Rafi's Outer wards. Her vengeful self poured against his Inners. If she broke those, all his secrets would be hers. But, by holding nothing back, she risked Fusion.

Alere had to sever their connection, but how? She had no training for this. Didn't even know if it was possible.

A blow struck her back. She cried out as the alzin buckled and sliced her skin. Kett swore and a body fell to the mud behind her. Kett withdrew his sword from the man's throat. Thrust forward by the hit to her back, Alere braced her dagger-hand against Rafi's leg and tried to straighten. Fire spread across her back as bent alzin dug into her skin. Drawing shallow, quick breaths, she tried to focus, but couldn't ignore the fresh pain.

Rafi groaned and slumped forward, one hand plunging into the muddy grass. Something on his wrist glittered in the light. His yanstone bracelet. Perhaps he could help himself. Alere forced the pommel of her dagger into his palm. His body relaxed; his eyes emptied of pain. He shook his head as if to clear it then nodded.

'Thank you. Go.' He kept her dagger, snatched up his sword and leapt to his feet. He rounded on Celia. Before Rafi could strike, a weishi leapt at him. Rafi raised his sword, forced back by the attack's ferocity. Alere stood alone.

Only two weishi now protected Celia.

Alere swapped the sword to her left hand. She threw her four small blades in quick succession. One took a weishi in the throat. He coughed and slid to the ground, a confused look on his face. Blood stained the blue grass purple. The second and third knives missed. Both vanished into the ground as a female weishi shoved Celia aside. The fourth flew true and embedded in the weishi's eye. She fell at Celia's feet. Blood splashed scarlet on the gold silk robe.

Alere had no knives left. She kept a grip on the sword's yanstones. Their energy wasn't strong enough without the dagger; a mere taste. She barely felt Celia's desperate probing at her wards.

'It won't work, Celia,' she grated, stalking close enough to the Xintou to be heard. 'I can feel you. Stop. I don't want to have to kill you. We're of the same House. We should be working together for the Jundom.'

'But...how?' Celia stammered, her face white and strained. 'It's not possible. You're not a xintou. You have no Gift! You're not a true sister of the House.'

Alere sneered to hide the hurt. 'That makes us even. You have the Gift, but you're no true Xintou. You've betrayed everything the House stands for. You've brought the Jundom to the brink of war when you're meant to keep the peace.'

Celia speared a thought into Alere's wards.

'I said, stop.' Alere gritted her teeth and held hard against the assault.

Celia stepped closer, wielding a little bronze knife. Her mouth smiled, but her eyes were those of a hunted, frightened animal. Overhead, clouds darkened the sky. Celia's thoughts pressed, stabbing, searching for a way in.

'You haven't the skill or strength to stand against me.' She attacked again, repeatedly slamming her mind against Alere's wards.

Alere gasped. Even gripping the yanstones with her whole hand wasn't enough. Cracks fractured her wards. The Outer wards shattered. Alere cried out. Celia's mouth stretched into a triumphant grin. She surged in, pouring every ounce of strength against Alere's Inner wards. If she broke through, Alere would be helpless to resist Celia's control.

CHAPTER FORTY

The onslaught forced Alere back physically and mentally. She looked for Rafi and her knife. He was too far away and too occupied to see her need.

'You're not meant to be alive at all. You're kin-child.' Celia panted, success twisting her face into arrogance. 'You shazi. You think you're saving Mamlakah from me? I assure you, it's the opposite. The House has outlived its usefulness. The world needs to change. Mistress Li refuses to see what's coming. You're just another of Li's puppets. A sacrifice to her fear of change. So suffer the consequence of your choice and die.'

Battered by the attack, Alere dropped to her knees. Celia found a break in her Inner Ward and prised it open. Pain lanced through Alere's head. Celia's triumph rang in Alere's mind.

Could Celia be right? Mistress Li kept many secrets and controlled many people. What if Alere had chosen to fight for the wrong side? Perhaps Nasra was right. What if Alere's efforts to protect those she loved took the Jundom down a worse path? How could she know what was best?

The Xintou slid into the deepest recesses and dragged out Alere's worst fears. Alere faced her truest self.

Unworthy; unlovable; imperfect. Murderer. Unwanted by her mother. Rejected by her father before she was even born. An inconvenience in Elmira's life. A burden and constant trial to Kett. Alere's life was nothing. She was nothing. Her arrogance and focus on duty had even driven her own sister away. How had she ever believed she could do anything worthwhile, or choose her own way? Radan must have been desperate to entrust such an important mission to someone like her.

To Mistress Li she was a disposable, flawed liability to throw away in a vain attempt to stop the inevitable. Even when Alere was gifted xintou powers, she had no control, no skill. She was unworthy of them. All her loved ones would be murdered because of her inability to protect them.

And Rafi chose Alere for heir, but only because he had no choice. He thought her rash and uncontrolled. Unreliable. Nothing but a puppet, to be used by everyone for their own ends. She had betrayed her House sister. Murdered two Juns. Her life was without value. Unloved. Unworthy. Trapped in a pointless existence, controlled by others, deluding herself that she had choices. Suited for nothing but meaningless exploitation. Never to taste freedom. Dutybound for life.

Paralysed, Alere retreated.

She stood in darkness. No sight, no sound, no sense of touch, oblivion; emptiness neither physical nor mental, but something else entirely. She cried out, but couldn't hear her voice, or feel her body, or even the ground underfoot. Was this Fusion? Had she failed again?

No, she was alone, not enmeshed with another mind. She'd been forced behind her innermost ward, deep into her own mind. How ironic. After fighting so hard against Xintou House's restrictions. Now the core of her self was imprisoned by a Xintou.

Celia's attack bludgeoned at her mind. Bit by bit, Alere's resistance drained away. She hadn't the strength to prevent Celia's control. In a few moments the spark that was Alere would be subsumed into Fusion with Celia, extinguished by the Xintou's stronger mind.

Perhaps that was not such a bad thing. Her life was nothing if she existed only to fulfil a duty, to fill a space left by Lianna. An object to be revered and manipulated, but not loved or respected.

In the corner of her eye, a flicker of silver-gilt light appeared then vanished. It appeared again, bigger, only to vanish once more. Again, but now the light was a fire and a song of welcome. Without heat or sensation, the fire embraced her; reassuring.

Fear, hate and self-doubt vanished, leaving only cool intellect. Separated from the roiling emotions, the illogic of the insecurities Celia had dredged became clear. Alere understood. Celia's own doubts bled through as the imminent Fusion of two minds fed back through the connection. In a few seconds, Celia would have control of Alere and one, or both women would die.

There were two paths to take. Fusion or death. Both could lead to great pain and suffering for the people Alere cared most about. Only death led to the ultimate peace and freedom for herself. Was her life worthwhile? She'd lost the freedom she craved; bound now in an iron cage as Jun-Heir under someone else's name. Responsible for so many lives. Loved. Was that enough?

As Celia's triumph chipped at the final walls of her resistance, Alere found the truth.

A third path.

Freedom was a state of mind. Alere's life was, and always had been, her choice. She had chosen to take every step of this journey in search of freedom, and it led her to the family she'd always craved. Yes, they came with ties and responsibilities, but being loved was a kind of freedom in itself. The people here – Kett, Mina, Rafi, Corin, Gavon, Yasmin…even Rohne – they lent her the strength to find out who she was.

They were what she wanted.

They were worth fighting for.

The silver-gilt fires exploded from her Inners, displacing the darkness. Alere pushed with them and forced Celia back, fighting against the onslaught of the Xintou's hatred. Reality reappeared and Alere returned to her body and mind; both damaged, in pain and under attack, yet somehow stronger. She knew what she wanted. That lent her the strength to do what was needed.

Alere flung Celia's mind away, as she once had Rohne's, and re-established her wards. She glanced down. Both the yanstone-set weapons lay in her hands; the dagger in her right. Rafi and Kett fought close by, guarding her back. Shakily, she climbed to her feet.

Celia gasped, a hand to her head. Fear and pain glazed her face.

'What are you? How did you do that?' She shook her head. 'No. It doesn't matter. You're a threat to our plans. The knowledge of what you've become will die with you.'

'Celia.' Alere tried for reason, the whisper of Mina's distress in her memory. 'Don't do this. Don't make me kill you, too. We're of the same House. We can talk to Mistress Li together. There'll be a new Jun and we can help Mamlakah to a better future.'

Celia's mouth twisted into a snarl. She clutched her little dagger. 'No. The only way to a better future is to be rid of the House. It's held Kalima back for five hundred years. If it weren't for Mistress Li and her kind, we'd long ago have regained the technology of our forefathers. The iron hidden here is the key. You stand in the way of all we can achieve with it.' She sneered. 'You can't be allowed this power, or the Jun Second's throne. You're too dangerous.'

'I could say the same thing of you,' Alere said coldly.

This woman was prepared to plunge Mamlakah into chaos and war for her own ambition. Whether she was right about the House, or not, was irrelevant. Change did not have to come through war. There must be other paths to progress for the Jundom.

Alere drove her dagger through gold silk and flesh, between bone and into Celia's heart.

The Xintou gasped and clutched at Alere's arms. Celia's blade snapped off in Alere's armour, too small to penetrate.

'You stupid little shazi,' Celia gasped. 'You have no idea, do you? You haven't saved the Jundom from me or Ven. You've opened it up for those I was trying to stop.' She sagged in Alere's arms and dragged her the muddy, cold ground.

Alere frowned at her. 'What do you mean? Who were you trying to stop?'

Celia's mouth twitched into a grimace. 'Someone far stronger than me and far worse than Ven. I Saw...but Mistress Li wouldn't listen. She thinks she can control...but she can't...I tried...' Her eyes closed and a last breath bubbled red from her lips.

'Celia!' Alere felt for a pulse; nothing. She stared at the body in confusion. Someone stronger than Celia and worse than Ven? What did that mean? Who had Celia Seen? What did Mistress Li think she could control? Apprehension fluttered low in Alere's stomach. She lay Celia on the grass and straightened the gold robe.

Alere looked up to find Rafi and the others standing over her, bloodied, filthy but alive. Blood seeped from a wound on Gavon's left arm and another on his scalp. Corin sported a new cut over one eye, scarlet staining his cheek and shirt. At the pavilion's edge, Penon still held a sobbing Hanna, his face a study of conflicting emotions.

Bodies of dead weishi littered the muddy battlefield. To the north and south, the armies of Koh-Lin and Zah-Hill held their ground and awaited news of a victor. Dal ripped a strip of cloth from his shirt and tied it around a slash on his thigh. He picked up a fallen Koh-Lin pennant and limped out, waving it. A cheer went up on the escarpment. Juns from both sides trotted forward.

Kett crouched beside Alere and hauled her upright. He was spattered with gore, not his own though. Alere sheathed her weapons and stared at Celia's limp form. Regret twisted through her stomach. Perhaps she could have tried harder to get through to Celia. If the Xintou was right, and something worse was coming, Alere might have just killed the one person who could prevent disaster.

'I'm not sure I did the right thing,' Alere said, drawn back Celia's peaceful face.

'You did,' Kett said. 'But we're not done yet.'

'But she said—'

'No, Alli.' His fingers locked around her wrist. 'Don't second-guess yourself. She would have killed you and all of us. She was an accessory to murdering Radan and Lianna. You made the right choice.'

Alere said nothing. Guilt washed through her. The blood on her hands was cold and sticky. First Radan's blood, then Ven's, now Celia's. When would it end? Her gaze returned to Celia.

The soft patter of rain on the pavilion broke the silence.

'You're injured,' Kett said, inspecting Alere's back.

'I'll be fine.'

Rafi cleared his throat. 'We need to decide what happens next, while Hanna's here. We need paper and a pen.'

Corin produced both from inside his vest, although the paper was creased and damp. Gavon righted the table and chairs. Rafi gestured to Penon. The shangwei half-dragged Hanna back to the table and sat her in a chair. Hanna covered her eyes, tears flowing unrestrained. Her hair escaped the chignon and flew loose around her ravaged face. Bereft of son and victory, she collapsed in on herself.

Rafi took his seat and wrote, his hand swift and clear. He finished the short document as the lesser Juns arrived. He passed the paper to Corin, who read and returned it with a nod. Rafi stood and addressed the assembled men and women, calm and authoritative.

'Today we've come to a point I hoped we'd never reach. Two Juns were ready to do battle in a scale unseen on Kalima. Thank you all for your restraint.'

Hands dropped away from swords as he spoke.

He read the paper aloud. The document contained an agreement by Hanna to withdraw her troops, and an apology for Ven's attack on Rafi's heir. Alere fought to stay impassive as the opposing Juns stared at her. The earthy smell of churned mud failed to disguise the sickening scent of death. Celia's blank eyes stared accusingly from the muddy ground.

Alere focussed on Rafi as he rattled off a rescindment of the kin-child laws; and the appointment of Jarran Radan-kin as nominated heir-elect to the Jun First throne. Rafi finished with several other, minor conditions, the whole penned in flowery, diplomatic language designed to show goodwill.

He called on the Juns to witness the document. Corin had been rapidly writing two extra copies and now handed them to Rafi. The Jun Second placed the three copies, and the pen, before Hanna. Bren, after a quick look at the Zah-Hill vassals, murmured into her ear. She hesitated for a tense moment before signing each paper with a quick, angry flourish.

'And what happens to me?' Hanna yanked the steel circlet from her head and placed it atop the papers.

'Go home to your parents' estates, in Asadia.' Rafi folded his arms. 'Live quietly in retirement.' He indicated Kennor Han-Asad. 'I'm sure your brother will escort you home and help you settle. You've given much to the Jundom, Hanna. Rest now.'

She rose and curled a lip. 'You'll regret putting a kin-child on the Jun First throne. Mark my words. We were your only hope of preventing…' She gathered her cloak close. 'Well, I just hope you're prepared for the consequences of your stupidity.'

Rafi bowed and pointed at the exit.

Hanna caught sight of Kett. She paled and clutched at her chest. 'You? But you're dead! I ordered your death myself.'

Kett's face blanked.

Hanna pointed accusingly. 'You're the real cause of all this. You're the reason for Ven's madness, not me or my father. You always hated Ven. *You* made him what he was.'

Her hand flashed out. The slap to Kett's cheek echoed sharply in the cold silence. Penon and Bren leapt to restrain her. She snatched a knife from Penon's belt but Bren wrenched the blade from her hand. She screamed, baring her teeth.

Kett gripped his weapons. Soul-deep loathing turned his eyes to ice. Corin grabbed one of Kett's wrists and Alere the other. Kett twisted free. He drew his blades and shortened his arm for the thrust, his sword-tip aimed at Hanna's heart.

'Kett! No.' Alere yelled.

He looked at her.

'No,' Alere said. 'You're better than that. She's unarmed. She can't hurt any of us, now.'

He hesitated, his face white and set, then re-sheathed his weapons and backed away.

'Remember this, Hanna,' Kett said. 'You owe Lia your life. Now you have to live with the knowledge that your ambitions, not mine, killed your son.'

Hanna stopped struggling, sobbing once more.

'Go, Hanna,' Rafi said. 'You've done enough damage.'

Bren and Penon released her. She straightened her clothing and, with cold deliberation, spat at Rafi's feet. Without waiting for an escort, she strode to her horse, mounted and galloped away.

Rafi called the remaining Juns forward. One by one, shuffling their feet and exchanging confused looks, they signed the documents then quit the field. Corin signalled the Koh-Lin troops and, slowly, both armies marched away. Bren was the last to leave.

He signed the documents and looked at Alere with narrowed eyes. 'I'm not sure what happened here, but you did the right thing.' He nodded at Celia's body, limp in the arms of one of his weishi. 'What do you want me to tell Mistress Li when we return her body to the House?'

'Tell her...' She looked at the yanstones on her daggers. 'Tell her she has no claim on me and never did. She'll know what I mean.'

Bren frowned and bowed himself out.

CHAPTER FORTY-ONE

Alere and her companions returned to the castle in silence. In the forecourt, Kett helped her dismount. She refused to be carried, reluctant to appear weak before what were now her people. Kett and Corin flanked her as she walked stiffly to her room.

'I need help to get this armour off,' she said, groaning as the armour dug into her back. 'And send for Mina, please. Why's it always me that gets hurt?'

'My training's at fault,' Kett said. 'Clearly I didn't emphasise the importance of self-preservation over martyrdom.'

Alere rolled her eyes and tugged at the lacing on the alzin vest. She took the armour off carefully and tossed it, dented and slashed, to the floor. Kett and Corin refused to leave until Mina came, so Alere turned her back and pulled off her shirt, relieved it didn't stick to her injuries.

'Khara!' Corin exclaimed.

'What?' Alere pressed the shirt against her breasts, alarmed.

'Your back.' Corin peeled off the ruined bandages.

Kett gripped her shoulders, angling her into the pale grey light from the window. Alere craned her neck, attempting to see her own back.

'What's wrong? It doesn't feel too bad.'

'Nothing's wrong,' Kett said. 'That's why we're surprised. The whip-marks are healed. There's only old scars, and a few scratches from the bent armour. Interesting.'

'Interesting?' Corin laughed. 'That's all you can say? What about miraculous?'

Kett shrugged. 'Miracles belong to religions we left behind on old Earth. There must be an explanation. Just what, I'm not yet sure.'

Alere, used to his calm logic, laughed at Corin's bemusement. She touched the weapons on her hips. Could the yanstones, somehow, be responsible? What other explanation could there be?

She put on a clean shirt, relieved at the absence of pain for the first time in weeks. Even the slice on her thigh was only a thin scar.

'We shouldn't keep Rafi waiting,' she said. 'We all have questions.'

'Indeed.' Kett opened the door.

The conference room was empty save for Rafi and Yasmin. Alere was thankful. Her part of the day's happenings should not be spread any further. Decisions needed to be made and she feared what that might entail.

Rafi waited only to hear she was well, and for everyone to be seated, before he spoke. 'What happened out there?'

'You'll need to be more specific,' Alere said with a half-smile.

'Prevarication. I get enough of that from Corin,' Rafi snapped. 'You know what I mean. Show me your blades.'

She laid them, unsheathed, on the table. Celia's blood stained the dagger. Alere shuddered. The yanstones glowed and flickered under the lights.

'It's the stones,' she admitted. 'Mina and I took the bracelets off. She was upset because she could hear my thoughts. Then Corin gave me these.' She fingered the blades. 'When I touched the stones, it was as though I wore the bracelet again, only stronger and…I don't know… different. It gave me xintou Gifts. Temporary, but unmistakable.'

'When you gave me the dagger,' Rafi said, 'I was able to resist Celia.'

'I don't think the bracelets work just because of the twin-bond,' Alere said. She stroked the dagger pommel and warmth oozed up her arm. The stone-lights flared as though recognising her and she knew an urge to caress them like pets. Ridiculous.

'I think,' she continued, 'the latent gene is triggered by the iron and the quantity of stones. That's why Radan knew what the bracelet did. Who else would have enough yanstones and iron to reach the tipping point? And that's why you could resist Celia. You wore your bracelet while holding my dagger. It explains how, in Gaton, I heard Nasra. And repulsed Rohne. I was touching the bracelet and Corin's dagger both times.'

Alere looked up at her father. 'This is what Radan feared. If you put enough iron and stones together, then anyone with the right gene is xintou.'

Rafi sat down hard and dropped his head into his hands. Along the table, Kett drew the blades close. Rafi's head snapped up.

'Don't—' he began, but Kett had already grasped the pommels of both weapons.

Alere laid her hands on the blades, ready to pull them back.

Kett ran his thumbs over the largest stones and Alere stifled a gasp. Even though he sat out of reach, he stroked her skin, sensuous. Kett looked steadily at Alere and warmth rushed to her cheeks. He shook his head and opened his hands. Alere jerked in reaction, stunned by the withdrawal of their connection. Did he have the gene or was it her own powers that felt his touch?

'It would appear you're safe from me.' Kett smiled at Rafi's half-frightened expression.

Corin handed his own weapons along the table to Alere.

'But mine are without the fire, so how did the dagger work for you in Gaton?'

The sword's stone was plain, milky-white. But the dagger's stone glinted with a seed of light that grew into a hypnotic fire, though faint and pale compared to Alere's stones.

'Didn't you say there was some sort of improbable story?' Alere asked.

Corin gave an uneasy laugh. 'I always thought it was, but now I'm not sure. The blades are Earth-steel. The yanstones and pommel-steel were added by the wife of an ancestor. Part of her hunli ceremony gift. A few years later, my ancestor caught her in an affair and used these weapons to kill the lovers. The husband then killed himself. According to the legend, the fire in the stones died with him.'

'That's so sad.' Alere drew his dagger and sword closer. 'The dagger-stone *was* blank when I first found it. I noticed the little light on our journey to Gaton. Maybe, because it was close to the bracelet?' She gripped the pommels of her own blades then stretched out two fingers to touch the large gems embedded in Corin's weapons.

'Alli!' Kett's warning came too late.

Hot lightning arced through her hands into Corin's yanstones and flared, brighter than the sun, behind her eyes.

Stunned, Alere snatched her hands back. They were unmarked. Her sword and dagger unaffected. The stones in Corin's weapons, however, had changed. Silver-gilt stone-fire flared in the depths of both jewels, growing stronger each second.

'What...?' Corin yanked back the blades and inspected the stones in disbelief. Tentatively, he wrapped his hands around the gems.

Alere touched her weapons and reached for Corin's mind. He connected with the stones, caught her eye, and dropped his Outer wards. She Read there, as he meant her to, the depth of his regard. She released the yanstones, her cheeks burning.

'And it appears I don't have the gene, either,' Corin lied. He offered the weapons to Rafi, who waved them away.

'I think we've already established it works for me,' the Jun said. 'But no more impulsiveness. No more recklessness. From either of you.' He pointed at Alere and Corin. 'We need to consult with someone about what these mean.' He touched the tip of one blade. 'And how to manage them. I'm…not sure how to proceed. The intelligent thing to do would be as Radan advised and destroy them.'

'Shensi!' Alere snatched her weapons into her lap. Something in her recoiled at being separated from the yanstones and she would resist strenuously should anyone try.

'No, you're right,' Rafi said. 'We need to study the stones. Destroying the iron deposit is impossible and luckily yanstones are rare.' He indicated the swords and his bracelet. 'Apart from a necklace I gave Yasmin years ago, and the bracelets, this collection represents the entire Koh-Lin inheritance.'

He rubbed wearily at his eyes. 'Another secret to keep. If knowledge of the yanstones became public… The situation was bad enough when limited to twins. We should consult Rohne and consider speaking with Mistress Li. Where is Rohne?'

'I've asked Maha to perform a discreet search of the city,' Corin said. 'So far no word. They can't have gone far.'

'They?' Alere caught the word. 'You think Mina and Rohne left Shanzhai? Together? Why, and where would they go? Mina was upset with me, but surely she wouldn't leave without saying anything. Kett?'

'Mina and I spoke before the battle, but she said nothing about leaving.' Kett folded his arms, his expression stoic.

Alere didn't press. His conversation with Mina must have been of a personal nature.

Rafi glowered at Kett. 'Mina's my daughter; my kin-child. Her resemblance to Alere, and to Yasmin, is too marked to go unnoticed in Shanzhai. We must find her before one of Hanna's spies does.'

'We'll make sure the new laws are spread quickly, shenshi,' Corin said. 'That will protect her life if she is recognised.'

Alere stifled a gasp of fear. She hadn't considered Mina might be in danger.

'I'm sorry.' Rafi gripped Alere's arm, concern in his eyes. 'Corin's right. She'll be fine. Rohne will protect her. We'll cry the new kin-child laws all over the Jundom by tomorrow. We'll find her.'

His words held little comfort. Had Mina left because she'd grown tired of being kept at arms length by her own sister? Unable to dismiss a growing sense of unease, Alere groaned and covered her eyes. Mina had repeatedly tried to close the gap between them, but Alere, afraid of being hurt, shut her out. Was Mina now at risk because of that fear? Was she safe with Rohne? There must be some way of finding out.

The yanstones, perhaps? Could she use them to reach Mina, even if her sister wasn't wearing a bracelet? Light flared off the stones on Rafi's wrist; echoed by those in Corin's weapons lying on the table.

'The bracelets,' Alere groaned again. 'Oh, gouri…'

'What?' Rafi inspected his bracelet.

'I left them on the table in my room.'

'And?' Corin prompted.

'They were gone, just now, when we came back.'

A knock on the door interrupted. A servant entered and beckoned to Corin, who hurried out and came back a few seconds later.

'Maha spoke with the cargo-master at the Seryeh River docks. Shenshi,' Corin addressed Rafi, 'you sent the new Jun First, Jarran, and his family downriver to Madina on Master Yun's chuan, didn't you?'

'Just a short while ago.' Rafi frowned. 'I gave him a copy of the peace treaty signed by Hanna and a note to the Council. I wanted him to be seen arriving in Madina as his own man, not with me at his side as kingmaker. He has ten weishi as escort. Why?'

Corin rubbed the back of his neck. 'The cargo master reported the chuan took on two passengers fitting the descriptions of Rohne and Mina. Rohne carried his companion on board. She was unconscious. Afraid of the whitewater. Asked to be sedated.'

'That's possible,' Kett said. 'She can't swim and is terrified of drowning.'

'Mina must have the bracelets,' Alere said. 'But why take them? She hated what they did.'

'No,' Corin said. 'I think Rohne took them. When I carried you to your room last night, Mina mentioned how the bracelets gave her the ability to hear your Outers. I saw a strange look on Rohne's face at the time, but gave it little thought. Now, I understand.' He brushed the yanstones in his dagger. 'Rohne doesn't know the twin-limitation of a single bracelet, but it won't matter. If Mina has both bracelets she'll have enough stones to be xintou.'

'Jiche.' Alere rubbed at her forehead. 'When she was dying, Celia said we'd opened the way for someone more powerful and worse than Ven. She was trying to prevent that.' She looked around at the others and fear awakened in them.

'What happens,' she said, 'if a xintou – a *male* xintou – gets hold of enough iron and yanstones? What does he become?'

Rafi leaned back in his chair, exhaustion aging him.

'I don't think anyone even understands why male xintou are forbidden,' he said. 'Whatever the original reason, it's long lost. Has Mistress Li ever explained it?'

Alere shook her head. 'There's few sayings called the Teachings of Lei. They supposedly come from a lost journal written by one of the co-founders of Xintou House five hundred years ago. But no details to tell why they're banned. And Mistress Li just drilled into us that twins and male xintou were forbidden. It couldn't be anything to do with yanstones, though. No-one knew pairing them with meteoric iron would have this effect.'

'That we know of,' Kett said quietly. 'As you said, the journal containing the original reason is long gone. I think we need to go after Rohne, just in case. Mina is my responsibility. She was under my protection.'

Corin frowned. 'How do you figure that? She's known Rohne since childhood. I've seen the way he hovers over her. What makes her your responsibility?'

Kett dropped his head into his hands and speared his fingers into his hair. 'She's kin-child. I took an oath, twenty years ago, to protect those I could.'

'Why? You would have only been a boy twenty years ago.' Corin glanced back and forth between Kett and Rafi. 'Rafi? What's this about?'

Alere said nothing. Kett had always been passionate about the kin-child murders; his anger slow and deep-buried. But his focus on Mina was more than that, she knew.

The Jun Second pressed his lips together and heaved a sigh. 'Tekettan, perhaps it's time.'

'Wait.' Corin pointed at Kett. 'Ven called you "Tekettan", too. Why did Hanna blame the kin-child laws and Ven's madness on you? Who are you?'

Kett lifted his head, his eyes clouded with pain.

'I'm sorry,' Corin said. 'You don't have to say.'

'No, you have a right to know. If it weren't for me none of this would have ever happened.' Kett leaned back, raising his eyes to the ceiling. 'My child-name was Tekettan Zah-Hill. I'm oldest kin-child to Jun First Radan Zah-Hill and Ji Ma-Safra, Jun Second Petar's older sister.'

'Oldest kin-child? Older sister!' Alere looked at her father for confirmation. The set expression on Rafi's face said he already knew. 'But...'

'Yes,' Kett said bitterly. 'My mother's affair with Radan started years before I was born. It only ended with her death, two years after Radan and Hanna were bound in the hunli. Ji's pregnancy was accidental. She knew the danger of putting two Jun seats into one person's control. She gave up her Jun Second inheritance rights when I was born.'

'But the Jun First inheritance? That makes you heir, not Ven or Jarran.' Shock paralysed Alere's thinking. All the years they'd known each other he'd never said, never even hinted. How could he have withheld such a thing?

'I don't want the gouri Jundom, Alli.' Kett shoved up from the table. 'All I ever wanted was to have my father back, and not be to blame for this gouri...' He laid a palm on the wall as though holding himself up, his back to the table.

Alere gripped the table edge as the truth hit home. Guilt was a knife in her stomach. She'd murdered Kett's father. How could she ever tell Kett the truth, now?

Rafi took up the tale, watching Kett. 'Hanna's marriage to Radan was political. Hanna was deeply jealous of Ji. When Ji died, a year after her child's birth, Radan brought Tekettan to the Alcazar to be raised as heir. Shortly after, Ven was born. Hanna became obsessed with the idea that Tekettan stood in the way of her son's inheritance. The fact that Ven was…unwell, didn't seem to matter.'

Kett held up a hand and Rafi bit off his next words. Kett put his back against the wall, folded his arms and stared at the floor. When he spoke, his deep voice was full of regret.

'As a child I didn't understand what was wrong with Ven. Even as a toddler he was…cruel, manipulative and unrepentant. Hanna overlooked and hid his viciousness; fostered his belief that he was untouchable and should be Jun-Heir.' Kett's mouth twisted into bitterness. 'But he was my brother and for a long time I protected him. I took the blame for things he did. Hid the evidence of his cruelty. Until he did something so unthinkable I could no longer remain silent. I brought it to Radan's attention. He confronted Hanna.' He fell into brooding silence, his gaze fixed on his feet.

'And?' Corin prompted.

'Because I'd taken the blame before, she turned it back on me. Said I was lying. That I was unstable and unfit to be Jun-Heir.' Kett's face was bleak with memory. 'That was when Hanna created the kin-child laws. She looked me in the eye and ordered my execution. Radan was always the weaker minded of the two, but from that day he was broken.'

There was a long silence, heavy with shock.

'Radan's Shangwei at that time was a good man,' Kett continued. 'When Hanna ordered him to kill me, he smuggled me into Weishi House instead. Begged the House Master to hide me. Probably under Radan's orders. I was seven.' Kett's mouth stretched into a grimace of pain and the faint sheen of unshed tears glimmered in his eyes.

'Jiangui!' His fist thumped the wall, rattling a dreary landscape painting.

Alere rose and gripped his fingers, holding on when he tried to break free.

He avoided her eyes. 'I'm the cause of all of this. Everything.'

'No, Kett.'

'Yes.' He twisted loose. 'I'm the reason you were separated from your family. Why countless families lost innocent children. Since I was old enough to understand what had happened, I've had to live with that knowledge. If Hanna hadn't been so afraid of me she wouldn't have created those gouri laws.'

'Stop it, Kett.' Alere grabbed his arms. 'Stop. As you so often tell me: you take ownership of that which is not yours to own. The choices Hanna made are not the fault of a seven-year-old child. They are her choices, stemming from her fears and ambitions. As a boy you couldn't have stopped her, any more you could stop Luna-Er rising.'

She smiled through tears. 'As an adult you have beaten Hanna. You and I, and these people who've befriended and accepted us. You've redeemed whatever imaginary fault you took to heart, Kett. Let it go, now. Please. It's time we all began living anew.'

Kett cradled her face in his hands and, after a quick look at Corin, kissed her forehead.

'It's a nice sentiment, Alli,' he said softly, 'but I can't let twenty years of killing in my name go just for the wanting of it. Too much blood's been shed and it's not over yet.' He looked at Rafi. 'Word of the rescindment will take time to disseminate. There'll be unrest when the manner of Ven's death is known. Those benefitting from the kin-child law have a lot to lose if it's overturned and any living kin-siblings take issue. I won't let Mina become another victim of the laws or their backlash.'

He stalked from the room. Corin rose but Alere waved him back.

'I'll go.' She followed, calling Kett's name.

He paused at the head of the stairs, eyes lined with old pain.

'Where are you going?' she asked.

Kett glanced towards the open front door. Flurries of snow drifted onto the basalt floor. Outside, raised voices, a glimpse of orange in the doorway, and the clatter of hooves on cobbles said the Messengers responsible for delivering the new edicts were about to depart.

'I have to go after her, Alli. Whether Rohne is rogue or not is irrelevant. He's not skilled enough to protect her if she's recognised.'

Alere reached for him, but he moved away and drew himself upright, impassive.

'You stay.' His smile was bleak. 'You don't need me anymore. She does.'

Alere's throat tightened. For a moment she wished they were back in the House; just her and Kett, friends and comrades. Now there was an awkward distance between them she didn't know how to bridge. An aching hole in her chest.

Nasra had warned Alere she might not like the outcome of what occurred in Shanzhai. While there was much Alere didn't regret, there was also much that would haunt her sleep. Her dream of freedom was lost, but she'd gained a family who loved her and a firmer foundation for her own self-belief. But by far the worst, was the suffering she'd caused Kett and Mina – the two people who deserved it least.

'We'll go after her, Kett,' she said. 'Together.'

'Your place is here.' Kett shook his head and stared out the open door. 'Mine's out there.'

Alere followed his gaze. A flash of gold in the brilliance outside caught her eye. She squinted against light, then smiled. With a fluttering of damp wings, Reya swooped into the great hall, circled once and landed on the railing beside Alere. The little reptile squawked, scuttled over and huddled against her hip.

'Whose is that?' Kett asked.

Alere stroked the furry head. 'She used to be Lia's. I let her go, but it looks like she's decided to stay. I won't cage her again. She can come and go as she likes.'

With his eyes on the jin-bird, Kett spoke again. 'You're not free to leave whenever you want.'

She lifted her chin. 'I remember you saying I could choose to be free; that freedom was a state of mind.'

He nodded, frowning. 'That's different. You accepted the responsibility of Jun-Heir.'

'Yes. But I can still forge my own path,' she said softly. 'Mina's my sister and you're my sword brother. We're family, Kett. You've protected me for ten years. Let me help you for a change. I'm coming with you.'

The hint of a smile tugged at his mouth. 'I know that look. I have no hope of convincing you to stay, do I?'

'None at all.' She leaned against his shoulder and he drew her close.

'Very well,' he murmured. 'Thank you.'

THE END

If you enjoyed this novel, *please* go and leave a review.
Reviews help other people find great books.
Share the love!

Connect with me on Facebook
Twitter: @aikiflinthart
Instagram: Aikiflinthart
Website: www.aikiflinthart.com

Other books by Aiki Flinthart

Discover other titles by Aiki Flinthart at: **www.aikiflinthart.com**

The 80AD series (YA Adventure/Fantasy)
80AD Book 1: *The Jewel of Asgard*
80AD Book 2: *The Hammer of Thor*
80AD Book 3: *The Tekhen of Anuket*
80AD Book 4: *The Sudarshana*
80AD Book 5: *The Yu Dragon*

The Ruadhan Sidhe novels (YA Urban fantasy)
Shadows Wake (Bk1)
Shadows Bane (Bk2)
Shadows Fate (Bk 3)

The Kalima Chronicles (YA Adventure/Fantasy)
IRON – Book One
FIRE – Book Two
STEEL – Book Three (due July 2019)

Other Novels
Sold! (Contemporary Romance/Adventure)

Short Story Anthologies
Return
Like a Woman

APPENDIX

Story facts and background

Kalima means 'World' in Arabic. The planet was settled by idealists from Earth seeking a world without conflict. The planet's sun is a K-type orange star in the Gliese 167 system. Rayleigh scattering of light combined with atmospheric dust high in copper oxide, gives Kalima a pale teal-green sky. This combination of filtered orange light resulted in dark blue and black-leafed plantlife.

Kalima is third planet from this sun. Gliese 167 is a cooler sun than Sol, but Kalima is closer to their sun than Earth is to Sol. Kalima's 14 month year and its axial tilt and elliptical orbit means the southern hemisphere (the location of the colony cities) has a long spring-summer-autumn cycle and a short, 2-month winter. The northern hemisphere has larger extremes of weather and is, as yet, uninhabited.

Kalima has a 6-day week and a 5-week month. 30 days per month. 14 months in a year and 422 days in a year – two days at the end of the year are not part of any month and are called Yirun and Er'run.

Kalima has an active geologic past, which formed continents, volcanoes, oceans and rivers. But, until the terraforming teams arrived, Kalima was bare of life. The rocks created by the presence of life on Earth—such as marble, oils, methane, coal, chalk, limestone, or banded ironstone—do not exist on Kalima. The few iron deposits in existence are iron-sand beaches created by volcanic activity, and meteoric iron. The planet has high levels of copper and a vast desert of copper-rich soil on one of the other continents has contributed to the levels of copper oxide dust in the atmosphere, which causes the green sky.

The colonists chose a lifeless planet and paid to have it Terraformed and seeded with life and complex ecological webs.

Initial terraform teams were sent to Kalima on faster-than-light flip-ships, while colonists took slower sleep-ships to allow the teams sufficient time to complete the infrastructure. A hundred years after departing Earth, the first of three ships arrived, carrying twenty thousand carefully selected colonists.

Mainly of Chinese, Arabic and European descent, colonists were chosen and screened for their desire to live a peaceful, agrarian existence. Kalima's twenty-one Jun families descend from the original twenty-one Funding families who financed the expedition.

Two hundred years after settlement, supply ships from old Earth ceased and colonists were obliged to be self-sufficient. Lack of iron prevented the colonists from creating a high-tech society, forcing them to live in semi-medieval conditions, although many old ideas and skills have been retained.

Electricity generation through wind or water power exists in limited form. The ability to make telescopes, lenses and microscopes has not been lost and, although medical understanding of surgery, physiology and healing exists, it is limited by the lack of modern technology. Many books on old technologies have been preserved and some colonists retained information regarding warfare and weaponry—the basis of knowledge in the Weishi House.

Kalima society is substantially feudal, the Jundom of Mamlakah being ruled by 21 Juns, under the leadership of the Jun First and two Jun Seconds. Melcor, to the north, and Jadid, to the south, are also feudal societies but Melcor's society and economy is built on slavery. Shemal, northwest of Melcor, is a democracy.

Languages are mixed. A version of English, borrowing many words from Arabic and Mandrin, is the dominant language in Mamlakah, the first colony site. Similarly, cultural crossovers are normal. Women and men wear robes or high-collared shirts and trous (loose trousers tied at the waist). Robes are worn indoors or while employed in non-active trades and management positions. Otherwise it is common for trous and shirts with jackets or cloaks to be worn.

Women wear their hair long and loose or, if of a higher caste, long and up in elaborate hairstyles. Men in Mamlakah wear their hair long and tied back in a mawei (low ponytail or plait). Although now less fashionable, women may wear a transparent veil that covers the eyes and nose only. The veil is symbolic of mystery and high ranking rather than an indication of women's inferiority.

In Mamlakahn society, women are, basically, equal in standing to men. They may be Juns or Trade Masters in any House and are free to undertake any training and job. In any colony, however, women are more valuable than men. Women are the bearers of the next generation and the survival of a colony depends on how quickly women can give birth and outstrip death rates.

Built into the psyche of the colony is the need to protect women that has continued into today's thinking. Weishi House came into being primarily as protection for women of childbearing age from natural hazards, though its scope expanded as the colony grew.

The need for high birth rates, and genetic diversity, led to the practice of kin-children. In the early days of the colony, a couple unable to have children was a wasted pairing. Women needed to have children by several fathers in order to keep the gene-pool as diverse as possible. After seven hundred years, the population is approximately half a million.

People/Places/Things

Ahmar – Red (Ahmar Mountains run down the Eastern boundary of the Mamlakah Jundom)

Alzin – an aluminium-zinc alloy.

Asalam – northerly seat of the Zah-Hill family.

Aswad – Black (Aswad ranges run down the centre of the Mamlakah Jundum)

Ceramic swords are made of zirconium dioxide

Days of the week are: Ahad (one), Ithnan (two), Thalatha (three), Arba'a (four), Khamsa (five), Sitta (six)

Ghadeb – 'angry' (Ghadeb sea to the northeast)

Gharb – west (Gharb ranges run down the Western boundary of the jundom)

Gunpowder = saltpetre + sulphur + charcoal

Jiali – 'home' – Capital city of the Ma-Safra family lands

Jadid – New – the Jadid Jundom lies south of Mamlakah.

Kabir – big (the Kabir river runs through the middle of the kingdom and empties into Melcor's port 700 gongli away to the east)

Kalima – World. Earth-sized planet.

Kuaisu River – 'fast/rapid' river (wraps around the eastern side of Shanzhai)

Luna-Yi – red moon

Luna-Er – blue-white moon

Madina – capital city of Mamlakah. Palace - The Alkazar.

Melcor – second kingdom to be settled – to the northeast of Madina and on the Ghadeb sea. Reached by trade on the Kabir river.

Metsa – the river running through the western section of the Ma-Safra Jundom, near Newmec. It eventually joins with the Kabir just north of Madina

Mianshou – end of year 2 day celebration during Yirun & Er-run.

Plants are dark blue and black-leafed (absorbing different, greater range of the red spectra and reflecting less green)

Seryeh River – 'quick' river (wraps around the western side of Shanzhai). The two rivers join and become the Kabir, just north of madina

Shanzhai – seat of Jun Second Rafi Koh-Lin.

Sulcrete – concrete where the binding agent is sulphur rather than lime (limestone does not exist on a planet without an organic geologic history)

Yan – 'flame' = yanstones

Yirun & Er'run – extra two days at the end of the year. Mianshou = End of year celebrations last for these two days and anything done on these days (apart from violence) is unpunishable.

Zalam – slums within Madina

…..

Trade Houses

Artist House (purple veil/purple hat)

Healer House (white veil/hat, grey robe)

Jiaoji (Courtesan) House (red veil)

Merchant House (green veil/green hat)

Messenger House (orange)

Miner House (grey hat)

Trades House (brown hat/veil)

Weishi House (black veil/black hat)

Xintou House (gold veil, gold robe) Mistress Li

…..

Jun Families

Jun First Radan Zah-Hill (Wife Hanna; Son Ven) – Silver and Black.

Jun Second Petar Ma-Safra (wife Leah) - silver and purple. No children.

Jun Second Rafi Koh-Lin (wife Yasmin;) - silver and green.

Jun third Kennor Han-Asad (daughter Farima) - gold and black (controls Madina city guards. Vassal to Zah-Hill)

Jun Third Dal Lee-Hay - gold and green (vassal to Koh-Lin)

Jun Third Yu-Smith - gold and purple (vassal to Ma-Safra)

Jun Fourth Hassan Wen-Gates - copper and purple.

(Kin-brother to Jun First.) (vassal to Ma-Safra)

Jun Fourth Bren Gray-Saud - copper and black (vassal to Zah-Hill)

Jun Fourth Qin-Turner - copper and grey (vassal to Zah-Hill)

Jun Fourth Knight-Hun - copper and green (vassal to Koh-Lin)

Jun Fifth Jaber-Lun - red and purple (vassal to Ma-Safra)

Jun Fifth Seif-Li - red and green (vassal to Koh-Lin)

Jun Fifth Zhou-Issa - red and teal (vassal to Koh-Lin)

Jun Fifth Easton-Green - red and black (vassal to Zah-Hill)

Jun Fifth Amoudi-Mann - red and grey (vassal to Zah-Hill)

Jun Sixth Ortega-Miller - blue and black (Zah-Hill)

Jun Sixth Quing-Mai - blue and grey (Zah-Hill)

Jun Sixth Price-Khan - blue and green (Koh-Lin)

Jun Sixth Yasif-Do - blue and teal (Koh-Lin)

Jun Sixth Khoury-Ban - blue and purple (Ma-Safra)

Jun Sixth Blake-Swift - blue and indigo (Ma-Safra)

Johnston house - blue & green tartan

.....

Mandrin

Numbers and distances and times

Yi – one (Luna-Yi = first moon – reddish)

Er – two (Luna-Er = second moon – silver)

San - three

Si - four

wu - five

Liu - six

Qi - seven

Ba - eight

…..

Chi – approx 33.33cm

Zhang – approx 3.33m

Gongli – kilometre

…..

Months:

Yiyue – first month of the lunar year (1st month of spring)

Eryue – second (spring 2)

Sanyue – 3rd (spring 3)

Siyue – 4th (summer 1)

Wuyue – 5th (summer 2)

Liuyue – 6th (summer 3

Qiyue – 7th (summer 4)

Bayue – 8th (summer 5)

Jiuyue – 9th (summer 6)

Shiyue – 10th (autumn)

Shiyiyue – 11th (autumn)

Shi'eryue – 12th (autumn)

Shisanyue – 13th (winter1)

Shisiyue – 14th (winter2)

…..

Words:

ading – antiseptic/disinfectant

Bai - to pay respect / worship / visit / salute

Bei – flower bud

Bi – coin

Che-ma – cart horse

Chuizi – a hammer-strike

Erheyi – two-in-one

Feihua – nonsense, rubbish.

Gangzhi – made of steel

Gongren - worker

Gu – archaic - legendary venomous insect / to poison / to bewitch / to drive to insanity / to harm by witchcraft / intestinal parasite

Hepan – river plains

hunli - wedding

Huoche – wagon/truck/van

Jiali - Home (name of Ma-Safra city)

Nari – double-edged sword

Jiaoji – courtesan

Jin - gold

Jinbi – gold coin

jiu – rice wine/liquor/alcohol

Jun - monarch/lord/gentleman/ruler

Junren – soldier/serviceman/military personnel

Kuaisu – fast/rapid

Kui - Chief/head/outstanding/stalwart/exceptional

Lanse – blue (lancha tea)

Lanhua - orchid

Lu – deer

Luotuo – camel

Manxing – slow poison

Mawei – ponytail

mayao – anaesthetic

Mianshou - to avoid suffering / to prevent / to protect against (damage) / immunity (from prosecution) / freedom (from pain, damage etc) / exempt from punishment

Molian – to temper oneself/ to steel oneself/ self-discipline/ endurance

Nai – mother

Quan - dog

Rong – salamander

Runiu – dairy cattle

Shangwei – captain (military rank)

Shanzhai – fortified hill village/mountain stronghold

Shenshi – my lord

Shi - is / are / am / yes / to be

Shifu – teacher

Shunu – my lady

Song – sponge (cake)

Tiebi – iron coin

Tongbi – copper coin

Watu – poison frog toxin

Weishi - guardian/defender

xiao – similar to/resembling (ie: xiao-cat)

Xintou – thoughts/heart/mind

Xiongshou – assassin

Xue – blood

xun – herb

ya-zheng - correct (literary) / upright / (hon.) Please point out my shortcomings. / I await your esteemed corrections.

Yan – flame

Yinbi – silver coin

Yongbing – mercenary/hired gun

Zhi – to stop/prohibit

Zitan – red sandalwood

Zuoce – left side

.....

Insults/swearing

Chouhuo - bitch

diyu – hell/underworld

Feihua – nonsense / rubbish / superfluous words / You don't say! / No kidding!

gaisi – damn it!

gouri - lit. fucked or spawned by a dog / contemptible / lousy, fucking

hundan – scoundrel/bastard/hoodlum/wretch

huo-zui – living hell/suffering/hardship

jian-gui – curse it/to hell with it

Jiba – penis (vulgar)

Jiche – pain in the ass/damn!/crap!

qusi – go to hell/drop dead

salai – make a scene/raise hell

shazi – idiot/fool

Wasai – exclamation to express amazement/wow!

zhen-shide - Really! (interj. of annoyance or frustration)

.....

Rabic

.....

Days: Ahad (one), Ithnan (two), Thalatha (three), Arba'a (four), Khamsa (five), Sitta (six)

Ahad (one), Ithnan (two), thalatha (three), Arba'a (four), Khamsa (five), Sitta (six)

Ahmar – Red (Ahmar Mountains run down the Eastern boundary of the kingdom)

Al Mamlakah – the kingdom

Alcazar – from Al-qasr – fort, castle, palace

alem'erekh – fight

Aswad – Black (Aswad ranges run down the centre of the kingdom)

Badiya – desert

Dafdae - frog

Gharb – west (Gharb ranges run down the Western boundary of the jundom)

Herq – burn

Heryeq - fire

Iblis - Devil

Istilqa – sleep

Jabal – Mountain

Jadid – New (name for the southern jundom)

Jiyl – generation.

Kabir – big (the Kabir river runs through the middle of the kingdom and empties into Melcor's port 700 gongli away to the northeast)

Kalima – World

Khiba – tent

Madina – City

Malik – King

Mamlakah – the kingdom

Menzel - home

Mhareb – warrior/fighter

Mumit - deadly

Selb – Steel, betterment, loin, crucifixion

sery'eh – Quick (Seryeh River to northwest of Shanzhai)

Tabib – doctor

Zalam - Darkness

Zinzana – cell/prison

…..

Insults/swearing

Hamagi (hamag = plural) – uncivilised, barbaric

Haraami – thief

Hmar – jackass

Jahim - hell

Kaddaab – liar

Kalb – dog

Kalet – filthy street bastard

Khara – shit! (frustration)

Saafil – base;loathsome

Waa faqri – damn!

Wisix – dirty/filthy (morally)

Zift – Idiot

FIRE

CHAPTER ONE

Freedom was a state of mind, as much as a state of being.

Alere leaned on the *Kuailong*'s gunwale and raised her face to the star-spattered sky, welcoming the night's ice-sharp emptiness; revelling in a moment of respite after the last week of war and destruction.

The calm solitude wouldn't last. The liberty she had hoped for when she left Madina had been a rebellious child's dream. She was bound, now, by the iron chains of privilege to an inescapable path.

She smiled wryly and straightened. Only a shazi would complain about choosing to live a life of luxury as Jun-Heir to the second most powerful man in Mamlakah. Alere glanced south, towards Shanzhai city, but there was little to be seen. Around the anchored chuan, the deep river gorge lay shadowed and silent, hoary with frost.

Overhead, Luna-Yi's red crescent washed watered-blood light over pale pockets of snow that clung to rocks and branches. Bare twigs of winter-stripped trees scratched at the sky's black-sapphire expanse. Night-shadows slipped across the deck, dancing to the wind's whistling and the chuan's gentle creaking.

This... Alere sucked a deep breath. The clean scent of snow and ice cleared her nose and honed her wits. Her eyes watered in the thin air. She sighed and her breath billowed, cloaking the world in the fog of her resignation.

The adventure, the freedom...this she would miss.

The future branched out from her choices. And she might be chained by iron now, but those ties were her choice as well.

Most of them. Alere stared down at the Kabir River's black-silk waters and ran her thumb over the faintly-glimmering yanstone embedded in her steel dagger's pommel. As always, the silver-gilt lure of her twin sister's mind pulled at her. Mina had left Shanzhai because of Alere's choices.

She shook her head and pushed uncertainty aside. She had done the right thing. The important thing. Her conscience should be clear. When this was all over, she would find a way to live her own life. Come to terms with the deaths she'd caused.

No, the murders.

But, for now, it was more important to focus on catching up with Mina – and Rohne Marin-Kin.

Regret was the killer of confidence and imagining what-might-have-been was time wasted.

The danger to Mina was real; here and now.

She smoothed her thumb over the yanstones again. Warm reassurance oozed into her body, easing the tension that was her constant companion since Mina had left Shanzhai city four days before. There was nothing she could do to find her twin right now. In the east, the weak orange winter-sun was merely a glow behind the Aswad Ranges' sharp teeth. Perhaps, as the old saying went, morning would bring light into darkness.

Dawn wasn't far off and they would get underway soon. The chuanzhu, Dalor Khan, had ordered the *Kuailong* tied for the night, close to shore, in a quiet section of the Kabir River. Even by day, the tumbling white-jade waters were winter-shallow and treacherous with exposed rocks. Night travel was impossible, which meant frustrating delays in catching up with the chuan carrying Mina and Rohne.

If Mina was caught and recognised before the new rulings legalising kin-children were made public, she would be executed. Or held hostage as proof that Alere was not who she pretended to be. That her Jun Second father, Rafi Koh-Lin, had lied to the twenty other Juns who ruled Mamlakah. And that could plunge Mamlakah into the very war Alere had fought so hard to prevent.

So why had Rohne taken Mina away from Shanzhai? He must have understood the danger.

There were too many unanswered questions.

They kept Alere awake at night. Those and the nightmares. Even the rhythmic sloshing of water against the chuan's magnal alloy hull wasn't enough to dampen the dreams of fire and death.

Had she freed the whole Jundom of Mamlakah only to imprison herself in regrets? And a life of servitude as Jun-Heir to her Jun Second father, Rafi? Was that the result Mistress Li had intended when she advised choosing the important over personal desires? She had set Alere's feet on the path to prevent war. But had she truly wanted Alere to kill Ven Zah-Hill – Jun First of Mamlakah – and his Bonded Xintou-telepath?

With a growl, Alere sheathed the yanstone-and-steel dagger. Who knew what Mistress Li thought or intended? She had been leader of Xintou House and the power behind the Jun First throne forever, espousing stability at all costs.

At any cost, apparently.

Only time would dull the memory of Jun First Ven Zah-Hill's death at Alere's hand; by her blade. Until then, she'd have to bear with the nightmares – like those that had driven her from her warm bed tonight.

Cold prickled across her skin. She was a shazi for leaving her cloak and boots in her cabin. She shoved unruly dark hair back from her face and rubbed briskly at her arms.

She touched the yanstones again. Warmth slipped under skin, through muscles, and she relaxed. But a familiar compulsion to find Mina surged immediately after, stronger than before, leaving the taste of iron and smoke on her tongue. Alere paced the small upper deck. She tried to reach Mina's thoughts, but her twin sister was too far away, and too deeply asleep.

A buzz of insect wings made her duck and cover her ears. Nightwings. Three, each with a wingspan as wide as her arms, circling the chuan in an intricate tri-gender mating dance. It wasn't yet egg-laying season, but they were still capable of delivering a nasty sting. They buzzed past again, only visible by the faint silver luminescence streaking their undersides. She watched warily, dagger drawn.

They darted downstream, chasing each other in a dizzying display of aerobatics.

Past another chuan.

Alere straightened, squinting in the half-light, trying to make out any identifying marks. What was another chuan doing on this part of the river? It lay, dark and silent, only a hundred or so paces downriver. Was it a wreck? Should she rouse the crew to give aid?

Rafi had spent two days and a staggering number of iron coins convincing Chuanzhu Dalor Khan to risk his new vessel, the *Kuailong,* on the Kabir in winter. With the low water levels, floating ice and winter storms, Dalor's shallow-drafted chuan with its tough, light magnal hull was the only one left in Shanzhai that could make the trip to Madina.

Could the vessel ahead be Rohne and Mina's? No. They'd left four days before on a chuan marked with Shanzhai's green dragon. The same one that carried Jarran Zah-Hill, the new Jun First, to Madina. This one seemed to have a salamander emblem. The symbol for the Jundom of Melcor, to the north. The name was difficult to make out in the gloom. The *Nasir*. A type of scavenger bird. What was a Melcori vessel doing so far upriver? A few portaged overland from Madina to Shanzhai each year and sailed back to Melcor with trade goods, but Dalor said they'd all left two weeks before.

Alere frowned. Where was Dalor's watchman? He should have sounded the alert with a vessel that close. It must have been there a while, so perhaps he hadn't seen it in the dark. She checked the lower deck and swore softly.

A body lay crumpled on the pale bamboo surface. Eight figures prowled the lower deck. They moved with smooth stealth and carried long, sinuous daggers that gleamed in the half-light. Headed for the door leading to the sleeping quarters. Too many to take on by herself. Her fingers and bare toes were numb with cold. Her limbs stiff. And she had stupidly left her alzin armour stored under the bunk in her cabin, along with her bow and throwing knives.

'Jiche!' Alere crouched out of sight. She laid her hands on the yanstones in her weapons. The stones' silver-gilt warmth engulfed her mind. The taste of iron and smoke filled her mouth. She stretched her thoughts out, seeking her companions belowdecks.

Kett slept. Trained in Weishi House and in Xintou House, her former weishi-bodyguard's mind was too well-warded to breach. Rafi, and Corin Johnston, were the same. Hardly surprising as her father and her father's spymaster had also been trained by xintou-telepaths to ward their thoughts.

Only Gavon Abdul-kin, yongbing-mercenary, was unwarded.

She swore again. He would hate the intrusion but there was no helping it.

Gavon! Wake up. We're boarded.

He snapped awake like the experienced warrior he was. She repeated the warning. Without wasting time on questions, he roused the others.

Corin was then simple to find: an intensity of energy, intelligence, and life-joy. He was still drowsy, his waking-wards not yet complete.

Cor?

His Outer wards slammed into place, shielding his mind and sending her reeling. She blinked and tried again. He relaxed and let her in.

Alere? Gaisi! You scared me, woman. Voices in your head is a sign of insanity.

Then keep your wards up. She was acerbic, shaken by the force of his rejection. *I'm on the upper deck. There's a chuan downstream. Melcori markings. There are eight men on the lower deck. Not sure how many more. Take Gavon through the access hatch in the cabin, down to crewquarters. Wake them. Send Kett and Rafi to Dalor's cabin. They can climb out through his windows and stand with me. Tell Kett to bring my bow.*

Done. His reply was unhesitating. *Stay hidden until we get there.*

She basked in the mental equivalent of a blown kiss as they parted.

There was nowhere to hide, though. Any moment the dawnlight would be bright enough to reveal her position. She was better off taking a stand at the top of the stairs. Hopefully they didn't have bows.

Holding the sword sheath so it wouldn't clatter against the deck, she half-crawled alongside the gunwale and put her back against the solid railing close to the stairs.

The first head appeared. She waited until his foot was on the deck.

She rose, drew her steel and drove it to the hilt through his alzin vest. A scream burst from his lips. She swore and thrust him ungracefully backward, into his companions. His shout echoed off the river gorge's high, black-rock walls and spawned copies from the mouths of the other boarders.

Trapdoors flew open on the lower deck. Corin, Gavon, and Dalor's crew spilled from every possible opening at once. The clash of steel, ceramic, and bronze ricocheted. A clamour of voices rose, filling the narrow valley with unintelligible sound. An arrow arced over from the Melcori chuan. It scythed through the brightening sky to land less than a pace from Corin's feet, where he fought on the lower deck.

Another landed in the timber at Alere's feet. More. Each one closer as the archers found their range. A shaft brushed her shoulder. They were good. She skipped backward and four men swarmed up the stairs. They advanced on her in a semi-circle.

Jiche! Where was Kett?

A ceramic blade swept in from her left. She stepped back. The tip skimmed her throat. She moved in and sliced low. Her edge bit through a leather leg guard, into flesh. Not deeply, but enough to make the man pause. She wrenched the blade free and struck aside his half-raised sword. Her dagger sliced backhand across his exposed throat.

'Take 'em alive!' A huge body slammed into her. And a second. She staggered, driven back against the railing. Her attacker's rank breath gusted from a mouth full of blackened, broken teeth. Alere jabbed the sword-pommel at his jaw. He struck the inside of her wrist, numbing her hand. The sword clattered to the deck. She drove a knee into his groin. He grunted and fell back a step. The other boarder grabbed her dagger-hand. She twisted free and plunged the blade into his neck. Blood spurted, making the hilt slippery.

The first recovered and smashed her dagger-hand into the railing, jarring the blade loose. The fourth man leapt in.

Alere kicked at his knee and it crunched beneath her heel. He screamed and collapsed. Only one holding her now. The biggest. Twice her weight, and all muscle. His thick hand still held her wrist. She jabbed with stiffened fingers at his throat. He blocked and his fist struck her temple. Light burst behind her eyes, blinding. Darkness roared. Pressed against the railing, she couldn't make space to recover. Huge hands shoved at her chest. She toppled backwards, scrabbling at the gunwale as she went over.

'Alli!'

Something latched onto her wrist and she jerked to a halt, wrenching her shoulder. A large body flew past and splashed into the water. Her heels hit the side of the chuan, jarring pain through her legs. She squinted up. Kett half-lay over the gunwale, one hand wrapped around her wrist, the other gripping the railing.

Icy water splashed Alere's feet and she glanced down. The river's cold, black depth swirled and rippled just a bodylength below. Her heart thudded blood in her ears.

'Alli, I can't...pull you up.' Kett bared his teeth in a grimace. His arms and shoulders shook.

Alere looked up at him, then back down at the river; at its seductive, dark draw. The water held a kind of peace in the midst of the chaos.

'Alli?' Kett's call held urgency, fear. The chuan rocked as a surge of water eddied against it. Kett's grip on her arm slipped and he swore. 'Alli!' His grey eyes caught hers. 'I can't...you have to help. You have to climb. If you don't, you'll die. The river's too cold and deep here. And there are shaytan-salamanders.'

She glanced once more at the blackness below.

Something, deep in her mind, urged her to let go.

'Alli...please?'

End of Chapter 1

FIRE will be released early 2019

www.aikiflinthart.com

www.ingramcontent.com/pod-product-compliance
Lightning Source LLC
Chambersburg PA
CBHW020645110726
47901CB00001B/52